THE WIELDER'S SACRIFICE

Editing by Kelly Hammond, Pickles Editing & Erin Larson-Burnett, EKB Book Services

Book Cover by Maria Spada

Map by Saga Mackenzie

1st edition, 2025

ISBN: E-Book 979-8-9905423-3-4

ISBN: Paperback 979-8-9905423-2-7

Library of Congress Control Number: 2025916855

To Chris, my #1, forever and always.

Better than any book boyfriend any author could ever write.

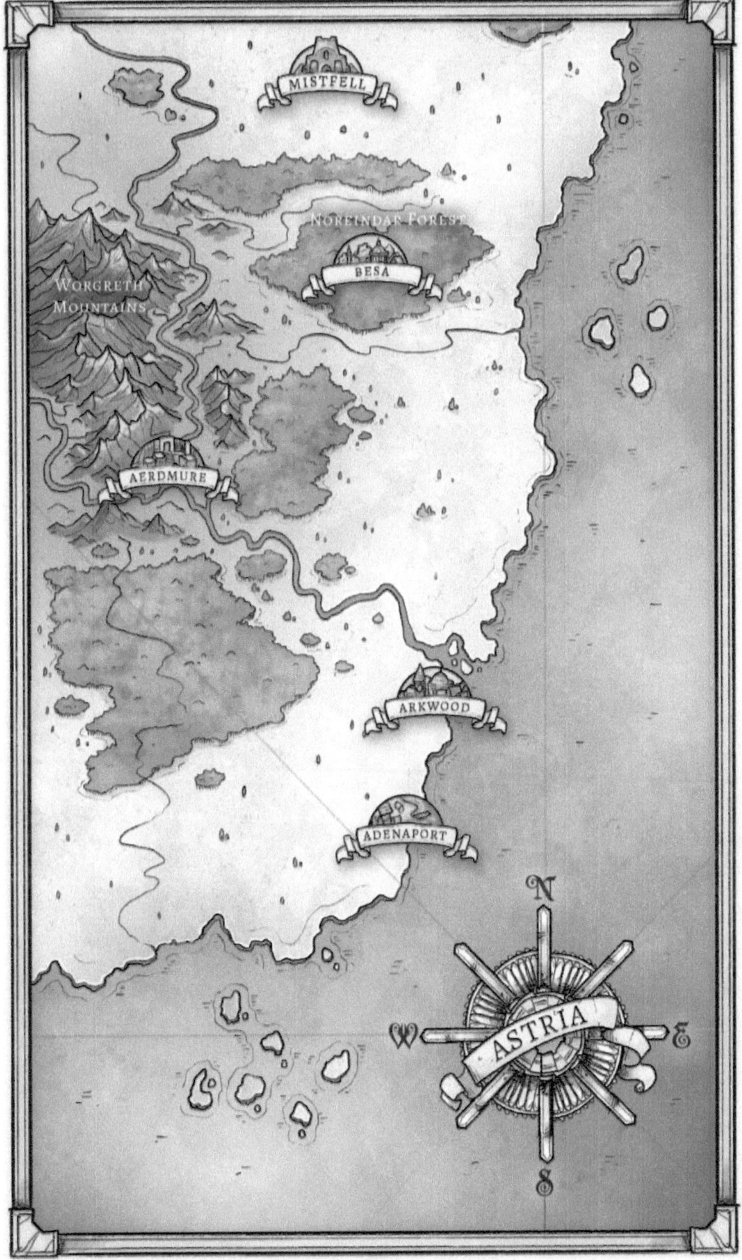

MISTFELL
NOREINDAR FOREST
BESA
WORGRETH MOUNTAINS
AERDMURE
ARKWOOD
ADENAPORT
ASTRIA
N
S
E
W

PROLOGUE

THE BABY IN RAELLA Astor's arms was screaming. Again.

Any other mother would probably have been beyond frustrated that she couldn't get her baby to settle. That a tiny being who had only existed for one week could cause so much turmoil and upheaval in one's life had *certainly* driven other women into despair.

But not Raella.

She'd been waiting for this moment for years. Her whole life, really. All she had ever wanted was to be a mother. And now that she finally held her baby girl in her arms...there was no comparison to this feeling.

She'd take the sleep deprivation, the swollen breasts, the raging hormones, if the reward was a baby of her own. The rest would pass, but this baby—her Raelyn—was forever.

Raella bounced the baby as she walked around the penthouse apartment. "Shhhhh, little one, it's ok. Mother's here."

There was no telling what had set Raelyn off this time. Raella had fed her not even half an hour ago, so there was no way she was hungry. Maybe she was tired? But no, she'd fallen asleep at the breast and slept until she started crying again. *Must be gas*, Raella thought, moving toward the sofa.

She sat, laying the baby down next to her and rubbing Raelyn's belly in light circles, the way Wynna had shown her.

"This works wonders on babies. Allie loved it," Wynna had said.

Raella's heart lurched at the thought of her best friend, the healer who had not only helped Raella get pregnant, but who had attended her entire pregnancy and stood by her throughout the ordeal of labor. What an excruciating experience that had been. The lingering soreness was a reminder that her body was still healing and would be healing for weeks if Wynna was correct.

And she usually *was* correct.

Except in her decision to pursue the research she and her husband, Kael, had been working on. When Luc had told Raella last night that Wynna and Kael had been implicated in illegal research and would be arrested today to face charges, Raella had nearly collapsed, a response she couldn't entirely blame on the hormones. She wasn't proud of how she'd reacted, and Luc certainly hadn't appreciated it either, but Wynna was her best friend. She couldn't believe the accusations leveled against the witch she'd known for years. The witch who had been by her side through good times and bad.

Raelyn continued to fuss despite the soothing circles Raella was administering on her belly. Raella scooped her up, cradling her neck carefully, and tucked her up on her shoulder, patting her back. "Do you need to burp, love?"

After a moment or two, Raelyn did indeed release the much-needed burp, then nestled her face into Raella's shoulder. Raella smiled, pressing her lips to the baby's head, the soft wisps of Raelyn's curls tickling her cheeks.

Goddess, Raelyn smelled heavenly. Was there anything quite like the scent of a newborn, especially your own?

She leaned back on the sofa, still holding her daughter close. Raelyn's eyes drifted shut, evidently soothed by the relief of the belch and now ready to return to her nap.

Raella could sit like this all day.

Her thoughts wandered back to her friend. Luc had said that both Wynna and Kael would be arrested, so where would that leave baby Allie? The little wielder Raella had hoped would be Raelyn's best friend, the two as close as their mothers were.

When Raella had asked Luc as much, he'd snarled. "She's a wielder, too, Rae. She'll probably end up just like her parents. I should throw her into Mistfell with them."

But the thought of sending a baby, not yet one year old, to Mistfell was an unspeakable and ridiculous thought. Public opinion would turn against Luc so fast that he'd be out of office before he even realized what had happened.

It was bad enough that his radical views on wielders were already turning heads. Honestly, she wasn't sure where his fear stemmed from, but it had come on so quickly after he'd been elected governor that it had surprised even her. In the past, they'd spoken about everything: their deepest desires, darkest fears, and wildest dreams. But evidently, Luc had been holding back.

That was the first red flag she should've heeded.

She sighed. Surely this research business was all a misunderstanding. Wynna and Kael were good people. They were all friends, for Canta's sake! Although how friendly could Luc really be toward Kael, if he truly believed that wielders were dangerous?

The sun was setting outside, the penthouse descending into darkness. Raella would need to stand to light the lamps soon, but that might disturb Raelyn. Sitting in darkness was a small price to pay for a few more moments of peace, breathing in this marvelous newborn scent. These days with her tiny baby were numbered, after all.

The front door to the penthouse flew open, jolting Raella upright. Her heart thundered. Raelyn stirred but miraculously stayed asleep. "Who's there?"

"It's me, Rae."

Luc! He was home.

Raella stood and padded over to the small bassinet they had placed in the living room. A place to put the baby when Raella needed to give her arms a break. She'd rarely used it, unwilling to let Raelyn out of her sight for more than a few moments, but something in the tone of Luc's voice told her now was a good time to test it out. He needed her full attention.

Raelyn stirred as she was laid in the bassinet, but, after a firm pat on her belly, she fell silent and still.

Really, this mothering thing was so easy!

Raella turned back to face the entryway, where Luc's shadowed figure sauntered into the living room.

"How did it go?" she asked, keeping her voice low, desperate not to wake Raelyn.

"It was a success. Only one complication." Luc took a step forward, coming into full view. Raella bent over to turn on a lamp and nearly startled at the look on his face.

His dark eyes were glassy and crazed, almost like there wasn't anything living behind them. And his skin was as pale as the white wall behind him. His hands clenched into fists.

"Complication?" Raella stepped closer, reaching for his hand, but he pulled his arm away.

"Well, yes, you see—they're dead. They're all dead."

The room began to spin. He didn't mean...all of them? Wynna? *Allie?* She put a hand on the wall for support.

"Dead? Who?" She wasn't sure how she found the words, how her brain was still functioning.

"Everyone except Kael. The guards executed the plan flawlessly, killing the partners and bringing Kael in to take the fall for it all."

What the hell was he talking about? Killing them was the plan? No, that wasn't right. There was to be a trial, wasn't there? Raella really needed to sit down...

"But I couldn't get your voice out of my head, Raella, telling me last night not to hurt Allie. It...complicated things." He stepped to the side, revealing a tiny figure standing just behind him, wide green eyes taking in the space around her and wispy black hair falling onto her face.

Allie!

Raella ran to the toddler, who recognized her and allowed herself to be scooped up. The dizziness that had enveloped Raella a moment ago evaporated, replaced with nothing but steadfast love and relief that this little one was still alive.

"So, I brought her home. For you." His upper lip curled. He walked over to the mini bar across the room and poured himself a whiskey. "You can keep her, if you want, or I can have her killed, and no one will be any the wiser."

"*What?*" He was crazy. He was speaking absolute nonsense.

"You heard me. Keep her, raise her with Raelyn. We'll pass her off as our own, keep her magic restrained, and she can be a reminder to both of us about the power of wielders left unchecked. Fuel for us to continue our mission."

What was this "us" he was talking about? Raella's heart thundered again as she clutched Wynna's daughter to her chest. Allie's little fists clenched into the fabric of Raella's tunic.

"Or," he sipped his whiskey, "we kill her. One less wielder in this world and Astria better for it."

He stared at her with those glassy eyes, a darkness in them she'd never seen before. Who was this man, and what had he done with her husband? Had she ever really known Luc Astor? Had she married and started a family with a monster?

Her eyes darted over to Raelyn, so tiny, so defenseless. And the child in her arms, the last remaining legacy of her best friend. It would ache to watch her grow up looking so much like her mother, but what other choice did she have?

The cogs in her brain spun quickly, forming a plan for what she needed to do. How she needed to respond. How she could play this game to protect her own daughter, her friend's daughter, and even herself.

This wouldn't be easy. And it would be a long game. But she could do it. She could do it for the girls. *Her* girls.

Raella straightened and looked back at Luc, who was watching her, tapping his finger on his glass. She cleared her throat. "We'll keep her. We can change her name, announce her and Raelyn together. We'll have to figure out what to do about her magic, but the rest can be sorted..."

The vicious, evil grin that spread across Luc's face was the second red flag. But this time, she recognized it, acknowledged it.

And knew it was all on her to protect her daughters from it.

1

FYNN

FYNN VOSS WAS CLOSE. He could feel it. *Smell* it.

His father's scent used to remind him of growing up: sparring together, swimming together, listening to Persy tell him and Aury stories of elven lore, of Astrian history.

But somewhere along the way, over the years, that sentiment of nostalgia had vanished. He no longer associated Persy Voss with anything that could resemble happiness or familial ties. Sometime around when his mother and Lena had been killed, the part of Fynn that thought of his father fondly burned to ash.

Maybe it was the fact that he'd never forgiven Persy for his mother's death. Like he believed Persy could have done more to prevent it. And then, so shortly afterward, Lena had been killed. Fynn's heart had hardened.

Until he met Nova Astor.

Goddess-damn, he missed her already. It had only been a matter of minutes—*minutes*—but already he felt the tug in his heart willing him to turn around, to return to her side. He'd been unable to protect his mother or Lena, but he could still protect Nova. Why the hell was he running away from that now?

Because he had to protect himself from the ramifications of his actions in the lab.

Nova was no longer in danger, of that much he was certain. Kael Blackmore was not the threat they initially perceived—the real threat had been extinguished by his own blade. But if word got out about that, if his father told anyone he suspected Fynn killed Luc Astor...

His time with Nova would be over.

To be with her, to protect her, he needed to do this first. He had to ensure no one revealed what had been done before they had the chance to unveil the truth about Luc and Kael.

He sprinted off in the direction of his father's scent; the tracks Persy had tried to conceal were no match for Fynn. He knew every one of his father's secrets, including how to be stealthy. Hell, Fynn had learned most of what he knew on that subject from him.

The soft crack of a branch up ahead caught Fynn's attention. He grinned. *Gotcha.*

He slowed to a normal run, keeping his own steps light on the ground. As he rounded a large boulder, he found Persy a few yards ahead, sprinting frantically toward Arkwood.

In one swift motion, Fynn lunged for his father, throwing his arms around his waist and tackling him to the ground. The two tumbled together through the dirt, twigs, and leaves lining the forest floor. Persy let out a yelp, birds flying out of the tree canopy in response.

But Fynn was larger and stronger than Persy. He pinned his father down as they rolled to a stop. His left forearm pressed against Persy's throat while his right hand reached for a dagger, which he suspended over his father's face.

"Fynn," Persy said between breaths. He might have been a few decades older than Fynn, but he'd never been one to let age define his abilities. He should've been more winded after a sprint like that, and Fynn couldn't help but momentarily admire his father's physical strength.

If only his emotional strength had been as hardy.

"Father," Fynn responded, narrowing his eyes on the older elf. "Where are you going in such a hurry?"

Persy's eyes darted from right to left—searching for who the hell knew what—but there was no one else around. "Arkwood. I need to speak with Fox."

Of all the things he could have said, that sure wasn't what Fynn expected. The dagger in his hand nearly slipped, but he caught it before it could prick Persy's cheek. "Why do you want to see Lena's brother?"

Fynn hadn't spoken to Fox since the funeral. He hadn't been able to stomach it. Fox blamed Fynn for Lena's death in the same way Fynn blamed Persy for his mother's death. If Lena hadn't been with Fynn, if they hadn't loved each other, she would still be alive.

So why in Dalia's name did Persy want to speak to Fox?

"Let go of me, and I'll tell you." Persy gritted his teeth as his face flushed from the lack of air.

But Fynn didn't let up. "And have you run off again before I get answers? You know too much about what went down back there, and I don't trust you."

"We don't have time for this. Do you know what's going on at this very moment? What chain reaction you and your hot-headed friends have set into motion?"

Fynn dug his forearm down harder and leaned in so his nose nearly touched Persy's. "I know we've discovered a truth about Luc Astor that could spell trouble for you if it gets out. There are many who would think you were complicit in his crimes, given how close you've been the last few years."

Persy's eyes widened. "You've got it all wrong." He moved his left arm so fast, Fynn didn't have time to react as his dagger was flung from his grip. Persy dug his knees into Fynn's abdomen, causing Fynn to double over and release his arm from Persy's throat. Fynn rolled off and jumped to his feet, Persy doing the same and reaching for the hilt of the longsword at his side, but he didn't remove it.

In a swift movement, Fynn unsheathed his own sword, the blade still bearing sanguine stains from its last use not an hour ago.

"Fynn—son—let me explain. We're on the same side." Persy's voice was still ragged, his neck red from where Fynn's arm had just been.

"Like hell we are," Fynn said through clenched teeth. "You've been working for Astor for years. How could you not have known what he was doing? How could you not have sensed he was a wielder? That he'd overtaken every single governor?"

They moved in a circle, facing each other, blades at the ready. Fynn's chest heaved with each breath. He didn't recognize the man across from him. How could his own father, who had instilled such a sense of Astrian pride and patriotism in him, have sat by and watched as one man toppled the entire system?

Persy held up his hands in defeat. "You have me there. I admit that I did not realize he'd overtaken the elven governors. We believed they were still themselves."

We?

Fynn's blood ran cold, and he stopped moving. His arms dropped slightly. "What the fuck are you talking about?"

Persy dropped his hands, reaching one out toward Fynn. "Son, it's time I told you something I should've told you long ago. Come with me to find Fox, and not only will I answer all your questions, but I swear to you that I will do whatever it takes to ensure you live a long and happy life with Nova."

Fynn's head hurt from lack of sleep and utter confusion. But a voice in his head that sounded an awful lot like Nova urged him to listen to Persy. To mend this broken relationship. The past few weeks were proof enough that no one could guess what the goddesses had woven into their fates. Better to keep family close, at least while they were still needed.

He narrowed his eyes at Persy, slowly lowering his sword and sheathing it. "Fine. We'll do this your way."

Persy smiled, the first genuine smile Fynn could remember seeing from him in years.

"Fynn, it's high time I told you about the Defiance."

2

❧

NOVA

THE HEAT WAS BECOMING unbearable.

Sweat trickled down Nova Astor's neck onto her back and pooled at the waist of her leggings. Though the canopy of the trees kept out most of the sun's direct heat, the leaves acted like a dome, holding in the humidity, preventing a breeze from cooling her off.

While she had traversed the same terrain with Fynn on their way to Aerdmure only a few weeks ago, the weather had already shifted dramatically. Summer had just started to awaken then, and though it had been hot, it had been nothing compared to the oppressive heat that surrounded her now as the season waned.

"Can we take another quick break?" her sister, Raelyn, asked. She had stopped walking, hands pressed to her thighs, bending at the waist. Her face was flushed, her short curls pulled back into a haphazard ponytail.

Esta turned and approached Raelyn, offering her water skin. "Drink. It will do no good for you to be dehydrated."

Raelyn drank greedily, and Nova used the opportunity to drink from her own. She tilted the canister to her lips, but only a trickle came out. Her mouth seemed to dry out even more in response.

"We need to find a water source," she said to the group. Her eyes met Jax's, who stood at the front of the group. He groaned and rolled his eyes, but before he could say anything, she held up a hand. "In fact, why don't we take a longer break? There's no use in continuing during the hottest part of the day."

Jax shook his head. "We aren't far enough away from the lab yet, Nova. We could still be easily found—"

"I'll ward us," she interrupted. "You and...Blackmore can rest up better if we stay in the shade without moving. Then you two can head off to Aerdmure to get Mehta."

"She's right," Esta said, crossing her arms. "We don't have the right supplies to continue in this heat right now."

Jax's eyes flicked toward Kael Blackmore, who was standing closest to Nova.

Blackmore held his hands up in defeat, clearly trying not to get involved. "I'm not going to turn down the opportunity to sit and rest. It will help me get my powers back so I can jump us back to Aerdmure quicker."

Jax ran a hand through his short hair. "Fine. I'll do a short scout. Nova, wards, *now*."

Without another word, he was gone.

"Is he always that snippy?" Blackmore asked, turning to Nova.

She forced a weak grin. "Unfortunately, yes."

She, Blackmore, Esta, and Raelyn selected the shadiest area they could find to sit and rest. Esta collected all their water skins—most of which Jax and Blackmore had conjured—and headed off for the stream, which was close enough for her to hear, though none of the witches could.

Raelyn curled up on the ground and closed her eyes, while Nova set to work on building the wards around them. She raised her arms in front of her, wincing at the dead weights they had become from the lack of sleep over the last two days. But the spell had become second nature and came easily to her despite the exhaustion.

A sigh escaped her lips when her arms fell to her sides.

"That's some beautiful spell work, Nova," Blackmore said as she finished.

She looked over at him, having forgotten momentarily that he was sitting right next to her—this man, her real father, unknown to her until just a few weeks ago. And even when she had become aware he existed, she thought he was chasing after her powers to run magical experiments on her after having killed his family and coworkers almost twenty-five years ago. It had only been mere hours since the truth had been revealed, and though she believed him, her heart had some catching up to do with her brain.

Still, a compliment was a compliment, and her heart swelled nonetheless.

"Thank you." She leaned against the tree behind her but kept her gaze on him. "Did you...who did you learn wielding from?"

"My parents. Your grandparents, I suppose. They passed before you were born, but they were both wielders. They enjoyed certain freedoms with their powers that I understand wielders have not been able to in recent years."

She raised an eyebrow. "You mean Luc's restrictions?"

"In part." Blackmore picked at the grass near his feet. "But he didn't start it. He merely picked up where other governors had left off, then took it a step further."

"What were...your parents able to do that we can't now?" She couldn't bring herself to call them her grandparents yet. Her grandparents, or at least the ones she'd grown up believing were hers, had also all passed in recent years, but they'd never treated her any differently from Raelyn. Not in the same ways that Raella and Luc had.

"Well, for starters, there were no restrictions on the types of jobs they could hold. If they wanted to work in government, they could. If they wanted to run their own businesses, they could."

"Wielders can't own their own businesses?" Though Nova had known that wielders were banned from government positions—the theory was that it put them too close to power—she had been unaware that other lines of work were closed to them.

Blackmore nodded. "Nor can they own property inside of Arkwood. It's why so many of them moved outside the city or fled to Aerdmure."

She pulled her knees into her chest and wrapped her arms around her shins. "It's all propaganda, isn't it? That wielders are power-hungry monsters and need to be controlled."

"You're one of *them* now," Blackmore replied. "You tell me."

His tone was soft, kind, but there was a challenge hidden in his words.

She tucked a loose strand of hair behind her ear and rested her forehead on her knees. This was the life she would be leading now. Maybe she'd felt inferior before because her magic hadn't been powerful enough, but now she was *too* powerful. Inferior for another reason entirely. Still tabooed, still on the fringe of society.

"I mentioned that this is the beginning."

She looked back over at Blackmore, who was still watching her with eyes that were like looking in a mirror. As green as the canopy above them, the grass and moss below them.

"You did."

His gaze shifted to Raelyn, whose steady breath confirmed she had fallen asleep, then back to Nova.

"I think we can change it together." Blackmore drew in a deep breath before continuing. "We can set Astria back on the path of equal treatment of all races, of all types of witches. Eliminate those laws holding us back."

"No offense," Nova held up her hands in front of her chest, palms facing Blackmore, "but you tried the equality thing once already and look how that went."

Blackmore chuckled. "Point made. This time, though, it's just about repealing laws that never should have been made. Righting wrongs that have been done."

"Instead of upending our entire magic system and sending the country into a free-for-all."

"Precisely."

Twigs crunched behind them, followed by Esta reappearing with five filled water skins. "Drink up," the female elf said as she passed them around.

Nova gulped half of hers in one go, then replaced the cap and turned back to Blackmore, who was wiping water from his upper lip.

"How much longer before you think you can jump back to Aerdmure?"

He capped his own water skin before answering. "When Jax gets back, I can give it a go. Your wards will stay up until Mehta returns?"

She nodded.

"Let's go over the plan again," Esta said. She had settled into a sitting position against a tree and sat facing Nova, their feet nearly touching.

"Blackmore jumps Jax back to Aerdmure, then takes refuge in our cabin. Jax will send back Mehta and anyone else he can find to help jump the rest of us back. Then we wait for Fynn." Nova's throat caught on the last word when she again remembered that Fynn was chasing down danger. Fear clenched her heart like a vise.

Blackmore's hand rested on her lower arm. "He's smart and he's strong. Have faith."

She blinked at him and swallowed. He was right: There was no point dwelling on what she had no control over. Fynn had said he would find her. He'd told her to keep working on her magic.

She could do that. Couldn't she?

"All right, crew, we're clear," Jax's voice boomed moments before he came into view. "Good job with the wards, Nova. I almost couldn't find you."

"Thanks. Tell my teacher I'm a quick learner." She forced a weak smile at the dark-haired witch, who now stood with his hands on his hips in front of the group. Weariness was starting to take over now that they'd stopped moving. Maybe she'd join Raelyn for a nap…

Blackmore stood quickly. "I'm ready, Jax. Let's do this."

Jax looked at Esta, who nodded to confirm she could take over protection from here. He nodded back and turned to Blackmore, holding out his right hand.

Nova's head tilted against the tree behind her. Her eyelids fought to stay open as she watched her mentor and her father disappear into thin air.

3

NOVA

"Nova? Nova, wake up."

A hand pushed against Nova's arm delicately, pulling her from a dreamless sleep. Her eyes flickered open to find the sun still blazing overhead, but the shadows suggested that she'd been asleep for a few hours. Raelyn was squatting in front of her, a grin sweeping over her face.

"There she is," Raelyn said. She glanced over her shoulder, calling, "She's awake! We're ready."

Nova pushed herself to sit, wiping her mouth with her free hand. "Ready for what?"

Raelyn stood, brushing a curl from her face. "Mehta is here. He brought a friend so we can jump back together."

Right. They were on their way back to Aerdmure. Back to the witches' stronghold village, the home of the witches' goddess, Canta, and her hot spring from which all magic flowed. Back so Nova could continue to learn how to be a wielder while their motley crew also tried to figure out how to cover up the murder of one of Astria's governors.

She drew a deep breath, trying to summon the will to stand and move when her body wanted nothing more than to curl into a ball and continue to sleep until Fynn returned or she realized this was all a horrible dream.

Raelyn extended a hand. "Come on, Nova. We'll be safer there. We can...talk more there."

The realization that she wasn't the only one who had lost someone settled over her like a storm cloud.

Nova turned her gaze up to her sister. "Thank Canta for you, Rae."

She grabbed Raelyn's outstretched hand and stood next to her. Before she could catch her breath, Raelyn's arms wrapped around her and squeezed—hard. Nova fell into the hug, burying her face into Raelyn's hair and breathing in her familiar scent.

How had their world turned upside down so quickly? How were they supposed to pick up the pieces and move on? What would they do after all this played out? Go back to Arkwood, back to teaching, and just pretend it had never happened? What about Blackmore?

Raelyn pulled back, fresh tear tracks on her cheeks shining in the afternoon sun. "We're in this together. Never forget that."

"We've lost so much."

Raelyn bit her lip. "We can hold ourselves together a little longer, sis. Let's get back to the cabin." She slid her hand into Nova's and led her away from their shady refuge and toward a small clearing.

Esta was standing next to Mehta and a female wielder Nova recognized from around Aerdmure but didn't know by name. Her hair was hot pink and cropped short into a pixie style. Nothing about her seemed welcoming; in fact, everything in Nova's bones told her to fear this woman, but she had come to help.

That couldn't be ignored.

"We meet again so soon," Mehta said, his dark-skinned arms folded across his chest in a stance that resembled Esta's.

"So little time and yet so much has happened." Nova sighed, the weight of the transpired events crashing over her.

Mehta held up a hand. "I don't want to know. Jax told me to bring you back. That's what I'm here to do." He indicated the pink-haired wielder. "This is Kath. Between the two of us, we should be able to get you back to Aerdmure in one jump."

Nova's brain was still too frazzled to try to calculate what that meant for Kath's power. But she had a good idea that it meant she was more powerful than Mehta. Her respect for the female rose.

"We're to return you to Aerdmure and not ask questions," Kath said, her voice deep and commanding. "Let's not waste time."

"Why are you doing this for us?" Nova asked. Raelyn and Esta were reaching for Kath and Mehta's hands, but she stood her ground. "We don't even know you, and yet, you're here to help jump us back to Aerdmure, no questions asked?"

Kath rolled her eyes, but Mehta spoke. "We've known Jax a lot longer than you. And there's a certain sense of fraternity that bonds the wielders' guild members together. So we trust Jax. If he says he needs help, but he can't explain why, we will help. If that much wasn't clear to you when I helped you last night, then I don't know what else to tell you."

Nova studied them a moment longer, her eyes darting between the newcomers. But she reached out a hand, closing the loop between Raelyn and Kath.

A moment later, she was whirling. Trees and sky flashed around her until she clenched her eyes shut. Wind whipped her hair into her face, her ears filling with the roar of the gusts.

"Brace!"

The landing in Aerdmure was soft, either because Nova was now more experienced or because Kath's influence made the landing smoother. Nova landed on her feet, her knees barely buckling against the force of the ground. Kath's hand fell away from hers, but Raelyn's held tight.

They stood on the outside of the main town square. The path to the cabin she'd shared with Fynn lay just ahead, and a magnetic pull tugged her toward it.

"Don't forget about curfew," Kath said, wiping her hands together. "I hear you've been gone a few days, but nothing's changed about Blackmore. He's still out there."

Nova swallowed and refused to meet the wielder's gaze. Instead, she asked, "Where's Jax? Is he ok?"

"He's fine." Mehta crossed his arms. "He said he'll meet you for training tomorrow. Sounds like your skills are coming along nicely. Have you thought of joining the guild?"

"The wielders' guild?" The thought hadn't even crossed her mind, not once, since she'd been here. Other than one discussion about meeting more wielders, she'd done nothing to try to learn from anyone other than Jax. "No, I doubt I'm ready for that yet…"

Kath smirked, but Mehta's eyes softened. "Think about it."

Raelyn tugged on Nova's hand. "Let's go, Nova."

Nova looked between her sister and Mehta, offering up a weak smile to the wielder. "We'll see you around."

"Thank you," she heard Esta say to Mehta and Kath as she and Raelyn headed in the direction of the cabin. Nova took off into a run, pulling her sister along with her. Esta's footsteps followed them along the path.

Now that they'd made it back, the events of the past few days crashed down around Nova. She didn't want to talk to or see anyone. She just wanted to curl up in her bed and sleep until tomorrow, with Raelyn by her side.

They rounded the last corner on the path and found the cabin in front of them. The sun was starting to set now, and the enchanted lamps on the front porch were on. Her heart clenched with the memory of everything that had happened in the cabin. She'd imagined returning here *with* Fynn, not without him.

She pulled Raelyn inside, Esta right on their heels. Blackmore was sitting on the couch, clearly waiting for their arrival. He stood when he saw them and hovered in the room awkwardly, like he was unsure what to do or say.

Nova's shoulders slumped. She didn't have it in her to be kind tonight. Her body ached from the lack of sleep, the magic she had used, the emotional injuries she had sustained. Her stomach grumbled, but she didn't even want to think about eating.

"Out." Her voice cracked as she stared at the floor. "Everyone out except Raelyn."

Esta bristled. "Absolutely not, you can't be left alone—"

But Blackmore held up a hand to silence her. "We will be back tomorrow, Al—Nova. Get some rest." He grabbed Esta's arm and led her toward the door. "Oh, and eat. Please."

He gave her one last look of longing, the pleading in his eyes driving a knife into her heart. Then he and Esta retreated from the cabin, leaving Nova and Raelyn alone.

"He's right." Raelyn's voice was barely audible. "We should eat."

Nova glanced at the small dining table and saw it was laden with bread and cheese. Jax must have sent it over. Or, more likely, delivered it himself so Blackmore wasn't seen.

She could hold it together for one slice of bread and one piece of cheese.

Still hand in hand, they made their way to the table and each grabbed a slice, then took the few steps to the bed. Nova plopped down on one side, Raelyn on the other. The wooden frame creaked under their weight, but the bedding was as soft as it had been just a few nights ago when Fynn...

Her thoughts trailed off as her eyes met her sister's. "I'm so sorry, Raelyn. About Luc—"

Raelyn shook her head. "I don't know who that man is—*was*."

"He raised us."

"He stole you. Killed your mother. He nearly killed us."

"But you loved him. We loved him."

Raelyn had no response. She bit a hunk of the bread as her eyes welled with tears.

"We can be glad he is gone and also mourn the father we thought we knew," Nova said quietly, tearing off a piece of her own bread and squishing it between her thumb and forefinger. "We are allowed to grieve *and* feel relieved."

Tears slid down her cheek, landing on the back of her hand. She wiped them away and finally started to eat. Her body reacted instantly: loosening, relaxing, savoring.

"What about Mother?" Raelyn asked, her gaze drifting toward the window above the bed.

"We'll find her," Nova said, surprised to find that she meant it. Not just meant it. *Needed* it. Mother had played a part in the lies as well. Maybe she had more answers. "We'll give her a chance to tell her side."

"Will we tell her the truth? About Father?"

Nova paused, considering. "We need to determine if we can trust her first. If she's covered up his crimes all these years, I have to imagine she'd continue doing so and turn us all in along with Blackmore. But maybe she can be convinced."

Raelyn finished her bread and laid her head on the pillow. "Let's give ourselves this one night to grieve. One night to miss him. And then we promise each other we *will* move forward. We can't let this linger or fester."

Nova nodded and grabbed Raelyn's hand, lying down beside her. "Deal."

They drifted off to sleep, hand in hand, cheeks stained by the trails of tears that consumed them as grief rolled over them like waves.

4

NOVA

"WHAT DO WE DO now?"

Nova took the final swig of coffee from the mug that Raelyn had prepared for her, folding her arms across her chest after she set it down. She'd slept fitfully last night, the only comfort being Raelyn's warm body so close to hers. But between memories of Fynn sharing that same bed and Luc revealing his darkest deeds, sleep had mostly eluded her.

This was not going to be a one-cup-of-coffee kind of day.

Raelyn peeked into Nova's mug and poured another cup from the carafe that sat on the table between them.

"How did you know?" Nova raised an eyebrow at her sister. Had she accidentally spoken that last thought aloud?

Raelyn leaned back in her chair and scoffed. "You think I can't tell when you need another cup? Please. The bags under your eyes are proof enough."

"Ok, moving on from how awful I apparently look today—"

"Not what I said! You just look tired." Raelyn paused for a moment and drew a deep breath. "And, honestly, I didn't sleep well, so I assumed you didn't either."

Nova's black hair fell into her face as she shook her head. "Which brings us back to my question. What now?"

A knock sounded at the front door, startling both sisters. Nova nearly spilled her coffee but was able to use a small gust of wind to right the mug before any drops of the precious elixir escaped. She silently applauded how far her magical reflexes had come. Almost like second nature.

"Open up, it's me!"

The voice was feminine but brash. Tough.

"Esta," Raelyn mumbled as she shuffled to the door to let her guardian in.

But Esta wasn't alone. Blackmore stood just behind her, his gaze cast toward the ground in a show of privacy. He had changed his clothes—where they came from, Nova couldn't even fathom—but that didn't change the haggard look he bore.

"Good, you're both awake and caffeinated." Esta strode into the cabin and made herself comfortable on the couch.

"Good morning to you, too." Nova took another sip of her fresh coffee, staring the elf down.

Her sass earned her a death glare.

"May I come in?"

Nova's eyes wandered back to the doorway, where Blackmore still stood beyond the threshold. Raelyn looked at Nova, searching for permission, and she nodded.

"Of course, Mr. Blackmore, come in." Raelyn shut the door behind him, then crossed the room back to her chair at the dining table.

Blackmore hovered at the doorway, his hands in his pockets. "Please," he said to no one in particular. "Call me Kael." His warm gaze settled on Nova. "That goes for all of you."

Nova's heart clenched. He'd respected her wishes to be called Nova. She could certainly offer him the same consideration.

After all, he hadn't done anything to earn their disrespect.

"Ok...Kael." She cleared her throat and sat up straighter. "Would you like some coffee? Raelyn makes the best in all of Astria."

He grinned. "I can't remember the last time I had good coffee. I would love some."

She stood and offered him her seat, feeling Raelyn's eyes on her the entire time she poured the cup for Kael.

Her father.

The man who had gifted her with her wielder abilities. Her intense and powerful magic.

Because, though she had spent her entire life believing she was a geo-witch like Raelyn, Luc, and Raella Astor—and a weak one at that—she had been living under a suppression spell and was, in fact, a wielder. A rare type of witch with the ability to shape magic to her will, while also commanding all the elements.

Kael closed his eyes and sipped, his lips parting into a grin. When he opened his eyes, they were beaming. "You weren't kidding. How'd you do that, Raelyn?"

"A lady never tells," Raelyn said, though her tone was still filled with the same sadness from last night.

Silence fell over them as the three witches finished their coffee. It hung in the air like a fog, sitting heavily, weighing Nova down. But what was there to say in this situation? Her world had been upended, they were harboring a fugitive, and the country still thought Kael was a mass murderer.

Plus, Fynn was gone.

The holes in her heart were too many to number.

"We were just discussing how to move forward when you both arrived. Any ideas?" Raelyn finally asked, looking over at Esta.

Esta ran her hands over her hair, which was pulled back taut as usual. "We don't go anywhere else or do anything rash until we hear from Fynn. Only then is the coast clear."

"I should probably check in with Silvana at some point," Nova said, remembering the priestess's promise to send for help if they hadn't returned in three days. "And Fynn wanted me to continue lessons with Jax."

"Perfect. I'll go get Jax," Raelyn said, standing and clasping her hands together. "I need to get some air. And I'll stop by the temple to let Silvana know we are back and that you'll check in with her later today."

"Guess I'm going, too." Esta heaved herself off the couch with great effort, repositioning the belt holding her blades in place.

That would leave Nova alone with Kael. Her palms clammed up at the thought of being alone with this man. What the hell was she supposed to say to him? How did one even begin to get to know a father they had been separated from since they were a baby?

"You don't have to, you know," Nova said. "The threat is clearly no longer imminent." She waved her hand at Kael, who smiled meekly.

Esta stopped moving. Nova could almost see the cogs spinning in her brain. "Yes, well...we have to keep up appearances, don't we?"

"Yes!" Raelyn grabbed for Esta's hand to pull her toward the front door. "Whatever the reason, let's get going."

But before Nova could open her mouth to further object, Raelyn and Esta were waving goodbye and closing the front door of the cabin behind them. Nova stood still, her hips resting against the countertop behind her. The same countertop Fynn had lifted her onto to kiss her not all that long ago. One of the first times her magic had surged at his touch.

Stop thinking about Fynn.

He was going to be fine. Dwelling on the separation wasn't helpful.

"I am glad to see that you and Raelyn are so close."

Nova jolted from her thoughts and looked over at Kael, who was watching her expectantly. "She's my best friend," she replied softly. "My everything."

Kael smiled. "I can see that. And I can tell the feeling is reciprocated. I have to admit that even if I couldn't be part of your life, couldn't raise you myself, it brings me great joy to know you now and to see you surrounded by people who care for you."

She blushed, unsure how to respond, so she sipped her coffee.

"I'm not sure how much time we will end up having together since there's every chance I could be caught before Fynn is able to convince Persy and the governors of anything. But in what time we do have, I would love to get to know you. Whatever parts you are willing to share."

Nova's pulse slowed, her mind settling slightly. Kael had so far given her no reason *not* to open up to him or trust him. And he was right. Their time could be very limited. Wouldn't she regret it if she lost him again without ever getting to know him?

So, she took the seat that Raelyn had vacated across from him and looked straight into his eyes. Uncanny, how like looking in a mirror it was.

"How about a question for a question?" she asked.

Those green eyes lit up like emeralds catching sunlight. "Deal."

"You first."

Kael paused for a moment, swirling his coffee and thinking. "What made you decide to become a teacher?"

Oh good, he picked an easy one to start with. She loved nothing more than talking about her students and her profession. "I really loved school growing up. I excelled in most of my non-magical classes and loved learning. I always had a book in hand or was trying to solve one puzzle or another.

"In my last year of grade school, I was given the opportunity to shadow a teacher for younger students and do a bit of trial teaching myself. It just felt...*right*. Like I could take all the expertise, all the stories I had been shoving into my head, and help the other students with my knowledge. Even if I was miserable at spell work, I could do math problems and science experiments like no one else, and seeing the same enthusiasm for those subjects through the eyes of young witches, elves, and humans...there isn't anything better."

"That's beautiful. Seems you've inherited your mother's smarts."

"I suppose." Nova clenched her fingers around the handle of the mug. "What was she like?"

Kael's gaze drifted toward the ceiling, eyes filling with tears.

"I'm sorry, I shouldn't have asked that again—"

"No, no, I want to talk about her. Canta knows she deserves to be talked about." He drew a deep breath. "She was the most beautiful woman I'd ever seen, until I saw you. But you're a spitting image of her, so I suppose that explains it."

His eyes met hers, and her cheeks flamed with heat.

"She was also smart as a whip. I've never met a healer who was as intuitive as she was. She could diagnose an issue often without needing a full examination or any bloodwork. But she was also kind. Every patient she saw got her full and undivided attention. She never rushed them or made them feel like she didn't believe their symptoms. She fought tirelessly to help each one who came her way. Regardless of their race. 'Everyone deserves to live a healthy life,' she would say all the time."

"The world needs more people like her."

Kael nodded. "It does. And it was robbed of her far too soon."

Nova tentatively reached across the table and placed her hand over his. Her magic hummed in response—not the excitement and surges that Fynn could elicit, but a soothing sensation.

Like it was recognizing that it found a kindred spirit.

A family member.

5

FYNN

FYNN HADN'T WOKEN IN this room in decades.

The last time he could remember actually sleeping in his childhood bed was the night before he left for the Academy. And his sleep that night had been as restless as it was last night.

He and Persy had arrived back at the Voss residence mid-afternoon yesterday. His father had refused to divulge any further information about this so-called Defiance. Fynn had peppered him with questions throughout the remainder of the journey back to Arkwood, but Persy had remained tight-lipped, only revealing that it wasn't yet safe to discuss anything further.

Fynn gazed up at the ceiling of the bedroom that seemed to be about half the size he remembered. It was the first time in weeks he'd woken up alone, and his empty arms ached for Nova even while his mind whirled.

What was the Defiance?

What were they fighting against?

Did Persy know this whole time what Luc Astor had been up to? Had he been trying to fight against it?

How did Fox fit into this?

The idea of facing Fox again after all these years had Fynn's stomach knotting. Though human and prone to the effects of age, Fox was physically strong, built almost exactly as Fynn was in terms of muscle and stature. He was also clever. He didn't have the training in combat that Fynn did, but that didn't mean Fox couldn't anticipate his opponents' moves. And he wasn't afraid to go up unarmed against a longsword or magic.

Fynn didn't fear much, but facing his first love's older brother again was something that made the list. It may have been fifteen years since Lena died, but Fynn knew Fox had not stopped blaming him for her death, and he never would. Fox may not have been a true match in strength and agility, but he had the upper hand in emotional warfare.

Fynn pushed back the sheets on the bed and placed his feet on the floor, his toes curling into the carpet. His body was still exhausted after the journey from the lab yesterday and the lack of sleep the night prior to that. Not to mention the fight in the laboratory. But he forced himself to stand. He needed to push through this. Needed to figure out what Persy had been going on about and how this tied back to Astor.

If word got out about Astor's death before they had a chance to change the narrative, it was likely that the initial target would be Blackmore. But Fynn couldn't take the chance that his father would spin tales about it being Fynn's fault.

He'd proven where his loyalties lay in the past. There was no reason for him to change them now.

Dressing quickly in the pants and shirt Persy had given him the night before, his knife belt firmly around his waist and hair pulled back into its usual bun, he made for the kitchen. His stomach grumbled incessantly. There was no point in doing anything else without appeasing that primal ache.

He stepped off the last stair and stopped. Persy was already seated at the large dining table just off the bottom of the staircase. The dining room was ornately decorated, with carvings built into the doorways and wallpaper laced with real gold and silver covering the walls. This room had been his mother's pride and joy, where she loved to host parties, luncheons, or celebrations for Fynn and Aury.

Persy hadn't touched a thing in it since Maura Voss had been murdered.

Thank Dalia.

Persy looked up as Fynn entered the room. "Morning, son. I've prepared some bacon and eggs for breakfast. Please help yourself." He waved a hand at the dishes in front of him, indeed piled high with food.

The seat to his left was already set, so Fynn pulled out the chair and made himself comfortable, the savory scent of the meat wafting his way. He scooped some of the still-warm food onto the plate and began to eat.

"Will you tell me about this Defiance today?" he asked his father. The ache in his stomach was already settling, his mind beginning to whirl again, trying to figure out the next steps.

"I will. But not here. Finish eating and meet me in my study." Persy made to rise from his chair.

"I'm coming now," Fynn said, shoving the remaining eggs into his mouth and picking up a piece of bacon to take with him.

Persy stood, eyebrows raised, but nodded and gestured for Fynn to lead the way.

His father's office was located on the tall and narrow third floor of the house. Each floor only contained two or three rooms, but there were five floors in total, so it was plenty large. As he climbed the stairs, Fynn reminisced about the days that he and Aury would race each other up and down the flights, Fynn always winning thanks to his agility. He couldn't help but grin at the memory, though he also acknowledged the pang of longing for his sister's reassuring presence.

When was the last time he'd seen Aury? It had been far too long.

He reached the third-floor landing and pushed open the heavy oak door that led to the office. Opposite the door was a window that looked over the street below, letting the sunlight stream in over the large desk in the center. Three of the four walls were flanked by bookshelves filled with tomes of all shapes, sizes, and ages. Nova would have loved it here, would have spent hours going through all the books.

Maybe one day he could show her.

Persy stepped around Fynn and took a seat in the large leather chair between the desk and the window. He gestured to the smaller chair in front of Fynn, the one Fynn would sit in as a child when it was time for a scolding. "Please, Fynn, sit."

"I'm good here." Fynn stood at attention, his right hand going to the hilt of his longsword; his left still held that piece of bacon, which he now took the opportunity to eat.

Disappointment flashed momentarily in Persy's eyes before he collected himself and cleared his throat. "What I am about to explain to you cannot leave this room. We will not speak of this anywhere else, even in this house. Understood?"

Fynn rolled his eyes. "Yes. Please just get on with it."

Persy clasped his hands and drew in a sharp breath. "I am part of a secret organization called the Defiance that has been working to subvert Luc's power and restore Astria's government to how it should be."

Fynn's body went stiff. "What? You knew about this—what Astor was doing?"

Persy nodded. "I've known for years. I was not aware that he had finally enthralled all the elven governors until he told us in the laboratory. However, I am part of an active resistance trying to prevent the other governors from turning."

"How—"

"How I knew is not important. What is important is that there are larger forces at play here." Persy leaned forward and placed his arms on the desk in front of him.

"Larger than full government control?"

"We believe so. We believe Luc may have made...plans for his death. Assurances."

Fynn did not like where this was going. "What the hell does that mean?"

Persy's eyes darted around the room. When he spoke again, his voice was even more hushed. "The power that Luc Astor wielded at the time of his death was limitless. He had tested depths of magic that hadn't been explored before, including dark magic. We know the spell he used to enthrall the remaining governors came from dark magic, so it's not a stretch to believe he was experimenting with it in other ways. But there is one...insurance policy, so to speak, that the Defiance believes he may have enacted as well. There are signs that point to it. And now that he is dead, I need to inform the Defiance so priorities can be shifted."

Nothing his father was saying made any kind of sense. Fynn closed his eyes and pressed his palms into his forehead as he shook his head. "I don't understand. What do you mean by 'insurance policy'?"

The sound of glass shattering filled his ears, his hands flying instinctively to protect his face before a gust of wind brushed his skin. He pulled down his hands, and his jaw dropped.

The window behind the desk was completely gone, pieces of glass littering the floor and the desk. But Persy—Persy was also gone.

Fynn ran around the desk, intending to look out the window, but instead found Persy lying on the floor, a large black hole gaping from his chest. Blood poured from the wound and trickled from his mouth. Persy's eyes sought Fynn's, and when their gazes collided, he whispered the words, "Find...Fox."

Fynn knelt, pressing one hand to his father's forehead and the other on his arm. His heart thundered as panic set in. "No, Father, we're supposed to do this together."

"My son. I'm sorry. I'm so, so sorry."

His body stilled as he exhaled his last breath. Persy Voss was no more.

6

FYNN

F YNN HAD NO IDEA how to feel. How to react.

His father had just been killed...right in front of him. But by whom? Or perhaps the better question was by *what*?

Sunlight glinted off the broken shards of glass around him and his father's body, casting light into a room that had been filled with gloom. Emotions warred inside him. Confusion sparred with sadness. Anger dueled with fear. His own body shut down as he processed it all, his shoulders shaking with—of all things—*grief*.

He allowed himself a moment to feel before his Academy training kicked in. After a few meditative breaths, his heart rate slowed and his vision cleared, even if the fog in his brain remained. He stood, drew in one last deep inhale, and let instinct take over to secure the room.

Fynn checked and double-checked that the...thing that had done this was gone and the threat was no longer imminent. But as he frantically scoured the room, looking for any clues, eyes never straying long from the shattered window in case the *thing* should return, he couldn't help but reflect on his relationship with his father.

Persy hadn't always been a horrible father. No, the worst had started after Fynn's mother was murdered. But before that, things were good—great, even. Memories of him and Persy flashed in front of

Fynn's eyes: the two of them camping in the Noriendar Forest for the first time, Persy's face beaming as Fynn graduated from the Academy, swimming together in the sea during family vacations to Adenaport.

He had always hoped that maybe, one day, they would find that relationship again. That ease. That joy. But it wasn't all on Persy. Fynn had been just as detrimental to the relationship in recent years, but that didn't mean he'd completely lost hope for reconciliation.

Now, that would never happen. Someone, or something, had wanted Persy dead. Had wanted him to stop talking. The timing of this attack was no coincidence, of that Fynn was sure. Everything was related: Luc's revelations, Kael's innocence, Persy's death, Nova's—

Nova. Fynn straightened and pinched the bridge of his nose. What if this thing went for Nova next? It had moved so quickly here; could it cover the distance to Aerdmure, or was it confined to a smaller area? How much danger was she in, so far from Fynn's protections? Not that he had any idea how to begin protecting her from whatever had killed Persy.

The chatter of passersby on the street below drew him from his stupor. He shook his head aggressively, throwing out any last thought of anguish for his father. If he wanted to ensure that thing didn't find Nova, there were things he needed to do, people he needed to find.

And he would not let his father's death be in vain. At least he could promise that much.

Fynn returned to his father's body, and his heart broke into pieces all over again. He grabbed a handkerchief off the table and wiped the blood from Persy's face, then closed his father's eyes. A single tear escaped onto Fynn's cheek, but he quickly brushed it away. There would be time to properly mourn Persy later. *After* he was reunited with Nova. He and Aury could plan something special, like the service for their mother.

Hating how many deaths he was now covering up, Fynn wrapped Persy's body in a blanket and carried him downstairs into the basement. Persy was somehow already cool to the touch, but his limbs were still limp, making it easier to transport him. At least in the basement his body would be cooler than upstairs under the window, preserving him until Fynn could decide what to do.

Maybe the Defiance would be able to take care of this. Because right now, Fynn's mind was swimming too much for him to even debate it.

Fox. He needed to find Fox. That was the ticket to getting into the Defiance and figuring out what the hell was going on, what the insurance policy was, and hopefully who had murdered Persy.

And how.

Checking to be sure his baldric was fastened, he drew in a deep breath, the same way he had coached Nova to, and dashed out of the house.

Fynn didn't stop running until he reached the bar he knew was Fox's old favorite.

He allowed himself a moment or two out front to catch his breath, then threw his hood over his head and ducked into the bar, taking a seat at the counter.

The dimly lit bar was nearly empty at this time of the morning, but a few patrons lingered. Most wore hoods as well. A few seats down from Fynn, one had his head resting on the counter, hand clutching a half-drunk tankard. A group of three sat at a table by the door, making enough noise to fill the entire space. The place reeked of stale beer and vomit, leaving Fynn to wonder—for the first time in over fifteen years—what the hell Fox saw in this place.

The barkeep nodded in his direction. He raised a finger, and within a moment, a beer was sliding Fynn's way down the slick, wooden countertop.

Fynn hadn't intended to drink, but once it was in hand, he found himself downing it in one gulp.

It had been a fucking morning, after all.

"Another?" the barkeep asked.

Fynn nodded, and another tankard slid his way.

"Yeah, it's been one of those mornin's, ain't it?"

Fynn's blood ran cold. Did the barkeep know about Persy? Had word somehow gotten out and spread all the way to the south side of Arkwood?

The barkeep approached Fynn, the smell of stale beer and vomit following him. "I'm not much of a government man meself, but still. Gotta respect the man. And now the man's been kilt."

The second tankard was halfway gone, but at the barkeep's revelation, Fynn lowered the mug. "What are you talking about?"

"Ya haven't heard?" The barkeep's eyes widened. He leaned forward, like he was about to spill a roaring piece of gossip. His shaggy hair fell into his face. "It's been all over the papers. That witch governor, Astor, is dead. Kilt by Blackmore methinks. On'y there's no body."

"No body, no crime." Fynn exhaled, fighting to keep his expression cool, a contrast to the churn in his gut and the acceleration of his heart rate. He propped his elbow on the counter, holding his ale up to his mouth for a sip.

"Yeah, that's what me woman says. But that Blackmore bloke is still out there, and he's had it in for the family. I reckon he's done Astor in and made 'way with the body." The barkeep picked up a rag and started washing dirty tankards from the sudsy tub in front of him.

Fynn's elbow slipped off the counter, sending a splash of ale into his lap. He had thought they'd have more time before word got out that Luc was dead. He only hoped that Nova and the rest of the group had made it back safely to Aerdmure and were working on protecting themselves.

"How do they know he's dead if there's no body?" he asked, wiping the damp spot on his pants with the back of his hand.

The barkeep smiled, a few black gaps betraying where he was missing teeth. "His wife. She claims she had some spell or another done what proved it." He shrugged and threw his rag down on the counter. "Would'na surprise me if she done it."

Fynn suppressed the urge to laugh, the image of Raella Astor murdering her husband clouding his mind. Even if he didn't know the truth, there was no way he'd assume that she'd done it. But better for rumors to spiral about her than about himself...

He tapped his fingers on the countertop casually. "Fox Aldon still come in here?"

The barkeep laughed. "Ol' Fox? Haven't seen 'im around for a while now, come to think o' it. He use' ta come 'round once a week or so, but late—"

"Know where I can find him?" It was time to speed along this little interaction. Fynn had bigger things to do.

"Who's askin'?" The friendly tone the barkeep had taken with him when spilling the gossip about Astor's death had vanished, replaced by narrowed eyes and thinned lips.

Fynn pushed himself away from the bar. "An old friend."

The old man hardened his gaze further, then exhaled and picked up his rag again to clean the two tankards Fynn had emptied. "Use'ta live 'round the corner. The red brick house with four floors. Think he let a room on the second floor or summin' like that."

"Thank you, sir." Fynn slapped a few coins—far more than his two ales warranted—down on the counter, tipped his head, and exited the bar.

The humid air blanketing Arkwood was a welcome reprieve from the stale fumes that had wafted through the bar. Summer was approaching its end, but it wasn't going without a fight. There was only about a week to go until the autumnal equinox, but the sun was beating down like it hadn't received that key piece of information.

Sweat started to trickle down Fynn's back as he rounded the corner that the barkeep had indicated and found the four-story red brick house. It was reasonably well-maintained, with a small patch of grass between the stoop and the sidewalk and fresh flowers in the window boxes on the first floor.

Someone still lived here, at least.

All the windows were shut, curtains obscuring the view inside. The mailboxes outside the front door didn't have names next to them, so there was no way to tell if Fox still lived there or which room was his.

Guess I'll have to do this the old-fashioned way.

Fynn traipsed up the stairs and knocked loudly on the door, tensing and curling his hands around the hilt of his sword while he waited. If Fox opened the door and reacted the way Fynn expected him to...

Footsteps sounded off on the other side of the door moments before it creaked open widely.

And, sure enough, there was Fox. As near to a spitting image of Lena as he remembered.

Fynn inhaled, summoning all his courage by turning his thoughts to reuniting with Nova. "Hi, Fox."

"Asshole," Fox replied before angling a punch for Fynn's face.

Fynn deflected with his left hand, drawing his dagger with his right and pushing it into Fox's throat.

Good. Fynn still had the edge on Fox that he had hoped for. At least physically, anyway.

"Good to see you, too. I'm hoping we can talk about the Defiance."

Fox's eyes widened before glancing both ways down the street. He yanked Fynn into the house and slammed the door shut behind them.

7

NOVA

T HE SUN OVERHEAD WAS scorching, unusually strong for this late in the summer.

Nova and Jax had been out in the clearing for only two hours, practicing her wielding, but the heat was unbearable. She'd already had to rework her sun-protectant spell for them because it had worn off so quickly, and their water skins had just run dry.

Though there wasn't a need for a bodyguard anymore, Esta had insisted that Kael go with them just in case, while she stayed behind with Raelyn. Kael had eagerly accepted but, at Jax's request, resumed Fynn's old post at the tree line. Nova agreed that it was safer this way; he could more easily slip into the trees if anyone came upon them.

When she dropped her arm back by her side, her heart leaped. Someone *was*, in fact, coming toward them.

In the distance, opposite Kael's side of the clearing, a small figure dressed in blue approached. Nova fought the urge to turn back and look at Kael, not wanting to draw attention to his location but wishing she knew he was safe. She could only hope he had done the smart thing and hidden.

"Jax," she whispered, tilting her head in the direction of the interloper.

He turned to see what she was indicating. His body went rigid, then instantly softened. "It's a priestess."

"Silvana?"

"I think so."

As the priestess came closer, Nova recognized the gait and outline of Silvana. The high priestess's wispy gray hair and delicate wrinkles came into view moments later, but instead of the all-knowing smile that she usually wore, her forehead was crinkled, and her mouth was pressed into a thin line.

Nova's chest tightened. What could be wrong?

"Hello, Silvana," she said, eyeing the high priestess warily.

"I heard from your sister that you are back and well, but I am happy to confirm that with my own eyes." Sure enough, her eyes twinkled slightly before resuming a deadened stare. "I imagine you have quite a tale to tell, and I, unfortunately, have one of my own. Would you mind accompanying me back to your cabin so we can chat?"

Nova caught Jax's eye, unsurprised to find they were narrowed with the same intrigue coursing through her own mind.

"Jax and Blackmore are welcome to join," Silvana added. "And Raelyn and Esta, of course."

Nova snapped her head back toward the priestess. "Nothing escapes you, Silvana."

The high priestess folded her hands together in front of her hips, a small tilt at the corner of her mouth the only indication of amusement on her face. "Very little does. Initially, when I discovered Blackmore's presence here in Aerdmure, I was concerned, but if he has earned your trust, I would like to learn why."

"We'll go back with you," Jax said, crossing his arms, "but we may not be able to answer all your questions."

"I understand." Silvana reached an arm out in the direction of the cabin, the sleeve of her blue robe cascading like a waterfall under it. How the high priestess could tolerate the heat and humidity with the robe and hood she wore each day baffled Nova. Magic had to be at play. "Please lead the way."

"You start. I'll grab Kael, and we'll catch up to you," Nova said.

Jax nodded. He and Silvana started off in the direction of the cabin. Nova watched their backs for a moment before jogging over to Kael, who poked his head out from around a tree as she approached.

Good; he had reacted as she hoped.

"Everything ok?" he asked, his tone light. "Was that a priestess?"

She nodded. "Yes—Silvana, the high priestess at Canta's temple. She knows you're here, by the way. She must have a one-way connection to Canta with how quickly she learns of things. But she doesn't seem to know *why* you are here. She just said that if I trust you, then she can learn to as well."

She motioned for him to follow her, and they set off toward the cabin, hugging the tree line as much as possible for the shady relief it provided.

"Is that what she wants to discuss? Why I'm here?"

"There's something else that seems more urgent that she wanted to discuss. She didn't give any clues as to what, but judging by her tone and her body language, it's nothing good." Nova sighed. More bad news to take on. There had to be an end to it at some point.

Kael reached over and squeezed her shoulder. "Whatever it is, you aren't alone."

No, she was not, not when Raelyn was around. Jax and Esta had become such a big part of their lives that she may as well include them, too. Even Kael.

And, of course, Fynn. He wasn't here in person, but in spirit. It had been less than two days since they'd parted, but his absence was as noticeable as a missing limb. While her magic today had still been strong, something she was proud of, it was nothing compared to how it reacted to his presence or his touch.

Still, it was important that she practice without him in case...

She shook her head. Wherever he was, whatever he was doing, she hoped he was safe. And that he would return to her soon.

She and Kael caught up to Silvana and Jax shortly before reaching the cabin. After hasty introductions, Silvana ushered them inside with a quick glance over her shoulder back toward town.

Esta and Raelyn were working in the kitchen, starting preparations for dinner in a show of teamwork that just a few weeks ago Nova would not have thought possible. Her lips parted into a smile at the scene: Raelyn chopping vegetables while Esta was deboning a chicken, her forearms covered in juices and grime from the chicken's meat.

Raelyn nearly dropped her knife when she saw the group enter the house. "Oh! We didn't expect you back so soon!" Her eyes widened again when her gaze landed on Silvana. "And Silvana, what a lovely surprise! Please sit." She gestured with the knife toward the sofa.

"Put that down." Nova waved her hands at her sister. "No one wants to end up stabbed."

Raelyn grimaced and set the knife on the counter. She set about clearing off her cutting board while Nova led Silvana to the couch and took a seat beside her. Kael and Jax drew up the chairs from the dining room to sit across from them. Esta scrubbed her hands and arms in the sink, then followed Raelyn to sit on the edge of the bed.

"Everything ok?" the female elf asked. Her brown hair was braided today instead of tied back in its usual bun, her pointed ears sticking out among the strands that had loosened.

"Good question," Jax said, pressing his hands into his thighs. "What's going on, Silvana?"

The priestess straightened out her robes and clasped her hands in her lap. Small wisps of her gray hair fell into her face, but she left them there.

"I am glad that you all made it back safely and hope that at some point I can hear of your adventures." Her gaze landed on Kael before turning to Nova. "But we have received troubling news from the priestesses in the Northern Arkwood temple about dark magic that was detected this morning."

Dark magic; the evil side of Canta's gift was outlawed, with punishments for using it so severe that it had become a thing of myth. Nova couldn't remember hearing a true story about it in her lifetime. To think that someone out there was dabbling in it now, on the brink of Luc's revelation about his wielder magic...

The timing had to be a coincidence.

Luc was dead. Jax and Fynn had confirmed it. There was no way he could be in Northern Arkwood right now, messing around with dark magic. And besides, he was one of the harshest, most outspoken critics of dark magic.

Although, perhaps that had been a façade, just as much as his speeches on equality had been.

"What do you mean?" Kael asked, snapping Nova back to the present. He was leaning forward in his chair, his elbows pressing against his thighs.

"Dark magic is banned!" Raelyn's hand flew to cover her mouth. Her eyes grew as wide as orbs.

Silvana nodded. "It is indeed. And this particular kind of dark magic is one that I thought had been lost to the ages. There are no records of such magic being used in hundreds of years, since the governors were established."

"How do you know what it is then?" Jax's tone was inquisitive but not condescending. He watched the priestess with genuine curiosity.

"As Canta's delegates in Astria, we keep records of all types of magic witches have used. We are the holders of the knowledge of her gift. Some of us priestesses are gifted with the ability to detect various forms of magic, including dark magic. And one of those priestesses at the Northern Arkwood temple alerted us to its presence an hour ago."

"But it was just detected this morning. How did a message get here so quickly?" Raelyn asked.

"They must have other ways to communicate that we don't." Esta sounded annoyed, but her attention was rapt on the priestess, as if absorbing everything she said.

"We do. I cannot divulge all of our secrets, but suffice it to say the news is trustworthy and timely." Silvana drew a deep breath, but when she spoke again, her tone remained calm. "A deocre has been detected in Arkwood."

"A what?" Jax asked the question before Nova could.

Deocre. What a strange word.

It was Kael who answered. "A dark imprint." His voice was breathy, his eyes cast downward. "As Silvana said, it's a forgotten magic—and for good reason. But anyone who researches deep enough could find it."

"What does a dark imprint—a deocre—do?" Nova asked, leaning forward to get closer to Silvana on the couch.

"It's formed when an extremely powerful witch, almost always a wielder, imprints a part of their soul into darkness. The darkness remains dormant until the witch dies, and then the deocre breaks free from the darkness and comes alive." Silvana's voice cracked as she spoke, and her hands began to tremble. Nova resisted the urge to reach out and take her hand.

Kael continued the explanation for her. "The deocre will slowly mature and gain more and more power, until it matches that of the witch who created it and imbued his or her soul within it. It becomes capable of all types of magic, but because of the darkness it's born from, it tends to favor dark magic."

"And it's impossible to reason with. It has no soul. No morals beyond those which its creator had," Silvana added.

Nova tried to piece this information together in her mind. It had to be Luc who imprinted part of his soul into a deocre that was now running free in Arkwood and was predisposed to dark magic. Over time, it would mature and develop power like Luc had...or worse.

She rubbed her palms on her thighs, wiping away the sweat that had started to form, and stole a glance at Raelyn. Her sister's eyes were wide in horror, and her normally bronzed skin had gone pallid.

Jax cleared his throat. "Ok, so we find this deocre and destroy it. How hard can that be?"

"Difficult," Silvana replied. "Deocres are also shapeshifters, so it will be hard to pin down. Right now, it is likely small and potentially not fully corporeal yet, so it may only appear like a wisp of smoke. But over time, it will grow stronger. Just as a child turns into an adult, that wisp of smoke will become a torrent, growing larger and more solid. Eventually, though it may still take its smoky form at times, it will also be able to look more and more like the one from whose soul it derives."

"Like Father?" Raelyn said, a tear slipping down her cheek. She'd come to the same conclusion, then.

Silvana looked at her, eyebrows raised. "Luc Astor is dead?"

The priestess had trusted them with this news and clearly hoped that they would help defeat it. It was only fair that they gave her the same level of trust and revealed the truth—about Luc and Kael—to her.

"Silvana, I think we need to catch you up on a few things," Nova said.

8

FYNN

"THE *HELL* YOU THINK you're doing saying something like that out in the middle of the street in broad daylight?"

Fox had dragged Fynn up the staircase just inside the doorway and into a small studio on the second floor of the row home. The barkeep had been right; Fox hadn't moved. The studio was well-kept: the bed was made, the shelves were neatly organized and tidied, and not a scrap of food sat out on the small countertop in the galley kitchen. If Fynn hadn't known better, he'd have assumed it was staged rather than lived in.

His heart stopped momentarily when he remembered Lena had been the complete opposite, always up to her elbows in dirt and with no patience for keeping a tidy house.

Fox stomped to the middle of the room, then turned back to face Fynn. "Want to tell me why you're here, Fynn? Why you almost ruined everything we've been working on for twenty years with one stupid mistake?"

Fynn looked back over at Fox, whose brown hair was the same shade Lena's had been, his eyes the same shade of mahogany. He was dressed in black trousers and a white T-shirt.

"It was my father's dying wish."

It was all he could bear to say in the moment, pathetic as it sounded. He swallowed a lump that had found its way into his throat, studying Fox's reaction to the news.

The human's eyes widened; his shoulders sagged. "Persy is...dead?"

"As of about an hour ago."

"Shit." Fox turned away and ran his hands through his hair. Then he seemed to remember himself, because he turned back to Fynn and said, "I'm sorry for your loss."

"Consider us even."

"Hardly."

Their gazes collided, Fynn not daring to blink until Fox looked away and collapsed into the small love seat against the back wall of the studio.

"There are things I need to do. People I need to alert. But first, can you tell me exactly how he died?"

Fynn crossed his arms, determined to stand his ground and get the answers he wanted. "Not before you tell me what this secret organization that I can't name is about and why he wanted me to find you. All I know is that he told me you were trying to fight against Luc Astor's power and that he may have had some kind of insurance policy in place in case he died."

"Yes, well, let's be happy *he's* not the one dead."

"Hate to break it to you, but he is." *And I killed him.*

But he didn't trust Fox with *that* information.

The color drained from Fox's face as he stood, arms shaking. "When?"

"About thirty-six hours ago."

"How do you know this?" Fox's eyes narrowed.

No way in hell was Fynn answering that one truthfully. "The barkeep around the corner." He pointed over his shoulder in the direction he'd come from minutes earlier. "Apparently, it's in the newsprints, too, though I haven't had a chance to look into those today. Guess you haven't either."

"Well, then." Fox ran a hand down his face. "We are going to need all the help we can get, and Lena had been begging your father to clue you in for years before she died. Now she can get her wish."

Fynn's whole body tensed. "Lena was part of this, too?"

Fox waved a hand as he turned toward the bookshelf and started rifling through a small chest of papers. "Of course. Her flower delivery service was the perfect cover for delivering messages to those in the Defiance. I believe she even met you during one such delivery to your house?"

Fynn's mind raced back to the moment he had first met Lena. It had indeed been when she delivered flowers to his house. He'd never forget the stunning bouquet of purple and red roses that he'd assumed had been ordered by Persy for his mother. Had those flowers actually been part of a coded message?

"Why wouldn't she have told me?" His voice came out smaller, weaker than he intended. But his head was going to explode from all the new information he'd received over the last three days.

This must be exactly how Nova was feeling right now.

Thoughts of her brought back his strength, his resolve. Lena was the past—Lena was gone. He'd loved her, yes, but Nova—Nova was something else entirely. She was the reason he'd risked everything these last few months. The way she understood him, the way she fought for those she loved...and she loved *him*.

She was the reason he was here. He could use this opportunity to make sure this world was a place where they could be together.

Fox kept rifling through the chest, laying a few pages of handwritten notes on the intricately carved table next to the shelf. "Don't take it personally. We were all sworn to secrecy by the High One. Ah, here we go."

Fox set out the pages and indicated each one as he continued. "The Defiance is a secret organization started by the High One over twenty years ago, when they believed that Luc Astor was playing with magic he shouldn't be. We have slowly grown over the years. Our original mission was to stop the progression of his influence over the other governors, which we succeeded in for a while. But we evolved as Luc's goals evolved. He started restricting wielders, so we pushed back. We helped get wielders safely out of Arkwood, getting them new jobs in Aerdmure or elsewhere in Astria, and tried campaigning against his messaging, with very little luck. Then, when word reached us about this so-called insurance policy, we started researching that as well."

Fynn took a few steps toward the table and glanced at the papers Fox had pulled out. They were timelines. The first entry read, "Suspected date of power acquisition," and the entries that followed indicated dates that suspected governors had fallen under Astor's thrall. One starred entry caught his eye, dated nearly five years ago. The scrawl next to the date read, "Deocre established?"

"What's a deocre?" Fynn asked, tapping his index finger on the entry.

Fox crossed his arms. "That's the insurance policy. An imprint of his soul in a patch of darkness that over time will become a darker, more powerful version of him."

Whatever Fynn had expected Fox to say, that was *not* it. "Excuse me?"

"Yep, it's bad. And it's activated upon the death of the creator, so if Astor is dead, this thing is probably loose on the streets of Arkwood right now. Though if it's darting around like sentient smoke, I have no idea how in Terra's name we are going to find it..."

Fynn's spine tingled as this new information set in. Killing Astor should have been the end of it, should have released the enchantments he had over the other governors, should have set the government back to how it should be. But if this deocre was real, if it was out there continuing Astor's ambitions...

"That's what killed my father." He knew it had to be true; there was no other explanation. Persy's death was unlike anything he'd ever seen, and the deocre was unlike anything he'd ever heard of.

And if it had targeted Persy, there was a good chance it was coming for them next. *For Nova.*

The paper beneath his hand began to crinkle from the sweat forming on his palms. This thing was sentient enough to know the right people to target. How quickly would it locate Nova, Jax, even Blackmore? How much time did Fynn himself have?

Keep yourself alive so you can keep her *alive.*

"We have to hide. Is there anywhere we can go that is protected? That you think it wouldn't be able to find us?" The weak, shaky voice was gone. Nothing but resolve and a small bit of fear fueled him now. He had more questions, wanted to understand more about how he could warn Nova, but an open living room—near a fucking *window*—was not the place.

Fox scrambled to pack up the papers and shoved them in the chest, locking it and pocketing the key. "Yes. We can't guarantee it's deocre-proof since we haven't had one to test it, thank Terra, but it's our best shot at safety. And we can get a message to the rest of the Defiance from there."

Fynn drew in a deep breath. "Looks like we're working together on this."

"Doesn't mean I like you, Fynn." Fox's brown eyes met Fynn's as he smirked.

"Doesn't mean I expect you to." Fynn stared back at him for a moment before adding, "We can get there faster if you let me carry you."

"Fuck that, elf. I'm not some damsel you need to protect." Fox grabbed a backpack that he had stashed under his bed. "And besides, we don't have far to go."

Fynn lifted his arm toward the door of the studio. "Then by all means, lead the way."

9

NOVA

OVA HAD TO GIVE the high priestess credit. She didn't seem at all fazed by their story. In fact, Silvana's face seemed to soften as Nova finished recounting everything that had happened since they had left for Benedict's cabin.

"Canta's bidding makes much more sense now," was all Silvana said in response.

Raelyn had busied herself preparing glasses of water for everyone while Nova was speaking, and Nova didn't blame her. It was hard enough having lived it once, but to have to hear—or tell—the story again, so soon after it had happened...

As soon as she had started speaking, her sister had stood and walked toward the kitchen area, quiet as a mouse with her head down and her curls obscuring her face.

Nova's heart ached. Raelyn needed her.

But right now, she needed to hear the rest of what Silvana had to say.

"What do you mean by Canta's bidding?" Jax asked. He had helped fill in the gaps in the story where Nova couldn't or wouldn't. And she was grateful that he had jumped in without a moment's hesitation, explaining the story as delicately as if it were about his family.

Which, in a way, she supposed it was.

Raelyn finally turned and brought a tray of water glasses over, but her head remained bowed. When she took a glass from the tray, Nova could see the redness that surrounded her eyes, the tracks of moisture that remained on her cheeks.

She reached out and squeezed Raelyn's arm, receiving the smallest of smiles in response.

Silvana ducked her chin in thanks as she received her glass. "This morning, shortly before we received word about the deocre, Canta came to me. She asked me to speak with you today, with all of you, but she didn't say why. Raelyn and Esta stopped by not long after, so I knew you were back, but it wasn't until I heard about the deocre that I connected the dots." She sipped from her glass and swallowed. "I assumed she wanted me to inform you about the deocre, but now—"

"It's because they're linked." Nova's heart started to pound like a drum in her chest. "The deocre is Luc's. It's the only explanation."

The priestess nodded. "Now that we know *who* the deocre is imprinted from, we can begin to guess its motivations. What its goals are."

"How do we stop it?" Jax asked.

Silvana shook her head. "That, I do not know. I am only vaguely aware that it can even exist. Most of the historical records of it were wiped when the governors took over, along with the records of all dark magic. They seemed to believe that if the magic of a deocre—or really of dark magic in general—was forgotten, then no one would dare attempt it. Especially in its foulest forms."

"But that means we also have no knowledge of how to fight said dark magic." Jax dug the heels of his palms into his eyes.

Nova looked over at Kael, who was still leaning forward in his seat, his face an intriguing mask of calm. "Kael, you knew what a deocre was. How? Maybe we can start there?"

He nodded. "My research into the genetics of magic took me deep into the lore of witches. There was only one volume I found that spoke about deocres, and it was brief. Perhaps that was how it escaped the governors' purge unnoticed."

"Maybe that same volume was how Astor found out about it in the first place," Jax said through gritted teeth. "Or maybe the governors have access to books that were supposed to have been destroyed..."

Kael shrugged. "It's possible."

"And it's possible there are other tomes that slipped through the cracks as well," Silvana said. "The upper floors of the temple hold the largest library on witch lore in all of Astria. Normally, it is off-limits to those not sworn to Canta's service. But I'll allow this exception for research purposes. I will inform the other priestesses that your presence is allowed."

She stood to leave, setting her water glass down on the coffee table and straightening her robes. "I do not think I need to tell you, but I would be remiss if I did not." She looked around the room at each of them in turn, then settled her eyes on Nova. "If the deocre goes unchecked, it could be the end of Astria." Her gaze drifted to Jax. "Find out how to destroy it and get rid of it." Then her eyes landed on Kael. "But this information must remain with us."

"Why?" Raelyn said, her voice barely more than a whisper.

"There is a reason the first governors banned dark magic, eliminated all traces of it within Astria. If others find out about this type of magic, they may create their own deocres, and the country will fall to ruin." She sighed, her whole body slumping in the wake of the exhale. "It is best if the citizens of Astria do not know that Luc Astor imprinted himself on a deocre or that the deocre is loose in Arkwood." Her voice hardened as she said, "Destroy it. Cover it up. Save Astria."

And with that, Silvana exited the cabin, her billowing blue robes trailing behind her like ribbons in the wind.

10

FYNN

F OX HAD BEEN RIGHT. Barely a few moments later, Fynn found himself underground, staring at a door that was barely visible in the darkness. Without his elven sight, he wasn't sure he would have been able to see it. And he wasn't sure how Fox could.

Perhaps he had just been down here so frequently he could find it with his eyes closed.

Fox pressed his palm against the center of the faintly outlined doorframe, which glowed with a golden hue in response. The gold flecks traced inward from the outline to Fox's hand until they covered the door completely. Just as the last bit of darkness near his thumb was overtaken, the entire door disappeared, gold flecks and all.

"Come on. Quick." Fox crossed the threshold with one step, and Fynn followed right on his heels.

Quick was right. No sooner had Fynn's ankle crossed the threshold than the golden light returned, followed just moments later by the door. He put a hand up to it, stroking his thumb over the grains of wood. A layer of dirt came off with his hand when he removed it.

Whatever this place was, it had been here for a while.

"Seal it!" Fox's voice reverberated off the cavernous walls that were similar to those of the laboratory Fynn had found himself in before. But it was too dark to see anyone else around them.

A soft flutter of wind tickled Fynn's right arm at the same moment he heard a crackling noise from within the door. It appeared exactly as it had when he had first passed through, but this time, when he touched it, his hand met cool stone.

The last time a door had been barricaded like that in his presence, he'd been at Nova and Raelyn's flat.

Which meant there were witches down here, at least one of them a geo-witch.

However, there was no one in sight. As his eyes adjusted, Fynn could see they were in a hallway, with the faint glow of flickering light maybe a hundred yards ahead. Whispers floated past his ears, incoherent mumbling but enough to identify at least three distinct voices.

Fox turned back to glance at him, his eyes glowing in the faint light of the tunnel. "Follow me."

Fynn nodded, his right hand finding its way to the hilt of his sword again. He wanted to trust Fox, but who's to say what was coming up at the end of the hall? What kind of people would be there? Whether *they* could be trusted?

"This is the home of Defiance headquarters." Fox's words were hushed, his breath ragged. "We try to keep it manned by at least three, one from each race, at all times for emergencies like this one. The witch on tonight is a geo, so hopefully that door-sealing spell will work against the deocre for now."

Fynn didn't like the way his companion's voice quivered slightly, but since he didn't have a better solution, he swallowed the doubt.

They reached the end of the hallway and came upon the room from which faint flickering light had been emanating. Within stood two females—one a human and one emitting the aura of a geo—and...

"Daro?" Fynn's mouth dropped open as his eyes landed on one of the guards who had been assigned to the Astor sisters' flat, the one who had taken over for him the night he had almost lost Nova. The elf's dark hair had grown longer since Fynn had last seen him, thick waves of it beginning to peek around his pointed ears. Though his eyes betrayed a hint of surprise, his lips parted into a smile.

"Fynn. Glad to see you've finally been brought into the fold." Daro made to shake his hand, but Fox stepped between them.

"Glad you both know each other; that makes this quicker." He indicated the two females, starting with the geo. "Fynn, this is Elodie, our resident geo, and this is Ethel. She's the smartest person you'll ever meet, so don't let the fact that she's human make you think you can pull anything over on her."

Fynn crossed his arms. "When have I ever made you believe—"

But Fox waved him away and kept going. "The deocre has been activated. Luc Astor is dead."

Elodie's hand flew to her mouth, but neither Daro nor Ethel showed any reaction to the news.

"And Persy is, too," Fox continued. "According to Fynn, it sounds like the deocre took out Persy as he was trying to tell Fynn about it."

"But why would it have only targeted Persy and not Fynn, too?" Ethel narrowed her eyes at Fynn.

Someone could have knocked him over with a feather. Why *had* the deocre skipped over him? Wouldn't it have been cleaner to kill them both? He hadn't even considered that he could also have been targeted. Now that Ethel had voiced the question, he couldn't believe it hadn't crossed his mind yet.

"It wouldn't have just left you there as a witness," Ethel continued, turning to Fox. "This was intentional. Are you sure we can trust him?"

"I am," Fox replied. Fynn glanced at him quickly, noting the lack of hesitation in his response. So, Fox didn't completely hate him. That was good news. "But you're right, Ethel, there must be a reason, and we will figure it out, but first—"

"We have to alert the Defiance," Daro said.

Fox nodded. "Fynn, what about Persy's...body?"

"It's in the cellar of the house." He wrung his hands. "I suppose we should do something with that as well." A proper burial was what he deserved, but not what Fynn could give right now.

"Take care of that, too," Fox said, nodding at Daro. "Delicately."

"I'm on it. I'll return within the hour." Daro walked toward the hallway, stopping when his shoulder met Fynn's. "Nova and Raelyn?"

Fynn's heart pounded in his chest. "Safe, the last time I saw them." It was the best answer he could give, but it pained him to know so little. He would have given anything to know for sure that Nova was safe. Would have given even more to be with her.

Daro nodded and exited the room, his footsteps barely audible on the dirt floor.

Elodie's soft voice interrupted the silence. "I've secured the defenses here already, but I'll make sure the auxiliary entrances are sealed as well." With a wave of her hand, she followed Daro out of the room.

"Auxiliary entrances?" Fynn asked.

Ethel turned and headed toward a table covered in papers in the center of the room. "This underground hideout was built specifically for the Defiance, but originally there was only one entrance—the one you just came through." She unrolled a large parchment and waved Fynn and Fox over.

"That's why I've always lived there," Fox said as they made their way over to Ethel. "I was right on top of the main entrance for easy access."

Fynn didn't respond, but peered over at the parchment, which was a blueprint for an interconnected tunnel system. In the center of the drawing was a large room, which must be where he was standing now, and one main corridor ran off to the left to an illustration that looked identical to the magical door they had entered through. But there were perhaps ten other smaller passageways leading from the room as well, their endpoints labeled with names like "Park" and "Florist" and—

"Atrium." The word escaped Fynn's mouth in a whisper.

"Yes." Ethel's hand glided over the page, a finger landing on the Atrium label that indicated a door in the basement of the central government building. "Each of these passages is an auxiliary entrance, added on as the Defiance grew. They're portals created by a wielder and only known and accessible by Defiance members, but they all converge here. The door you came through was enchanted by Elodie, our most powerful geo, to allow the same right of access."

"No chance of someone stumbling in here," Fynn said.

Fox nodded. "Correct. Except we aren't sure they will hold against a deocre. As I mentioned, we haven't needed to test them before, but Elodie will shore them up as best she can."

"Until this wielder gets here?"

Ethel scratched her temple. "Ideally. But we haven't heard from him in *weeks*. Maybe months at this point. Last we heard, he was out drinking with friends and disappeared. No one's seen him since."

Something about that story rang a bell, but Fynn pushed it aside for now. That was hardly the most important thing he needed to be focusing on.

"Ok, so Daro is alerting the rest of the Defiance, Elodie is securing the entrances... Then what?"

Ethel looked up at him over the top rim of her glasses. "Well, we wait until everyone arrives, and then we set our plan in motion."

"Care to clue me in on this plan?"

The woman stole a look at Fox out of the corner of her eye. "You were right, he's feisty."

What? When and why had Fox been talking about him?

Fox laughed, then pulled up a chair and made himself comfortable. "What do you want to know, Fynn?"

There were so many things; he didn't know where to start. All he really, truly wanted was to find a way back to Nova, who gave him a reason to live, to *breathe.* Whose intoxicatingly beautiful magic had penetrated his very soul, leaving him in pieces every time their skin collided.

He had come to Arkwood to convince his father not to tell everyone that he had killed Luc Astor. In time, he would have owned up to it, but first they needed a plan. A way to show the world that Blackmore was innocent. That Luc was the criminal the whole time.

Persy would have been a key witness in that testimony. But now, he was dead. Killed by an imprint of Luc's soul, as if it had known that Persy was the ultimate threat to its existence and to Luc's legacy.

Without Persy, clearing his name was going to be a whole lot harder.

But here in front of him now—this Defiance—couldn't they testify to Luc's atrocities? Help others understand why Fynn had needed to kill Luc?

He would win them over. Help them fight this deocre and then ask for their help in return. So that he could live free, without the shadow of fear or guilt over him. So that he could return to Nova, and they could move on from this horrific summer, together.

Fynn closed his eyes, picturing Nova's dark hair floating in the wind, her green eyes glowing with laughter, giving him the strength he needed to keep fighting. With a deep inhale, he opened his eyes and stared directly at Fox. "How many people are in the Defiance?"

"Now that Persy is dead?" Fox paused, doing mental math. "Twenty."

"Twenty? That's it?"

Fox shrugged, but it was Ethel who answered as she crossed her arms. "Not all of them are located in Arkwood either. We've got one in Besa and a few scattered in the smaller villages. But our numbers have been dwindling in recent years. It's hard to keep a secret society running for as long as we have. People tend to die or give up. That's how we lost our Aerdmure and Adenaport members."

"And you don't recruit replacements?" Fynn's confidence in this organization was fading by the second.

Ethel sighed. "We think Astor suspected we were on to him. Recruitment has gotten harder in recent years."

The patter of quick footsteps echoed from the corridor. Fynn's hand reached for a dagger, and Ethel turned to face the newcomer, positioning her body behind the table, but Fox remained seated and simply turned his head to the door.

"It's me!" A soft voice drifted into the room just before Elodie appeared. "All sealed, but Daro should have no problem getting back down with the others."

"Great work, El, as usual," Fox said.

She walked up to the table, her shoulder-length blonde hair hanging ragged in her face and her chest heaving. "But that's not all. I overheard some news as I was sealing the Atrium portal."

Fynn watched her closely, his eyes narrowing. In his periphery, he caught Fox leaning forward, resting his elbows on his knees. Ethel crossed her arms again.

"Go on." Fox's tone was cool, but impatient.

"They've announced—" Elodie drew a deep breath, trying to slow her heart rate "—a suspect in Astor's murder."

Fox raised an eyebrow. "Blackmore?"

Damn it. The Defiance still didn't even know Blackmore's whole story. Fynn made a mental note to remember to clue them in later. Once they'd proven trustworthy, that is.

Elodie shook her head, still working to slow her breath.

"Who, then?" Ethel asked.

Elodie's eyes locked on Fynn's with such a deathly glare that he nearly withdrew his sword. "Him. Fynn Voss is wanted for the murder of Luc Astor."

11

NOVA

THE CABIN AIR WAS stale with silence after the door closed behind Silvana.

No one wanted to make the first move or voice the first thought. Nova stared at her hands in her lap, wringing her fingers involuntarily. She flexed her hands open, then pressed her palms into her thighs, digging her nails into her leggings.

When would the revelations stop?

She would give anything to go back to a few days ago. To tell herself not to go to Benedict's. None of this would have happened if she had just stuck to the original plan—learn how to wield and lay low.

But since the beginning of the summer, her life had been turned upside down time after time, again and again.

Blackmore's escape.

The suppression spell.

The identity of her father.

Luc's death.

And now whatever this deocre monstrosity was.

She didn't fully understand what a deocre was, but Silvana's mandate had been loud and clear. *Destroy it and tell no one.*

Breathe, breathe.

She heard Fynn's voice in her head as clearly as if he were sitting next to her. She closed her eyes and could see his face, feel his touch. Her magic swirled lightly at his memory, but it was nothing compared to how it reacted when their skin brushed or their lips touched.

What was he doing right now? Was he safe? Surely she would know if something had happened to him; her magic would react, her heart would burst. If only there was a way to know for sure. But sending a raven or a messenger was too risky. How could she possibly put into a letter the ache in her chest or the fog in her mind without considering the chance that the letter could be read by the wrong person?

A lump formed in her throat, her eyes burning from the pressure of squeezing them against the pain, but a tear slipped out anyway. The pressure building in her chest grew with her emotions—magic, *power*, trying to find a release.

Nova needed to get out of the cabin before something happened. Before someone got hurt.

She let her eyes open and, without a word to anyone, stood and moved quickly toward the door.

"Nova," Raelyn called out for her, but she didn't respond, just slammed the door behind her as she crossed the porch.

The summer heat was starting to dissipate as the sun moved toward the horizon and the hum of crickets filled the air. Nova's bare feet continued to move, pressing into the warm grass that surrounded the cabin, but her mind and body were not in sync. While her body moved of its own volition, her mind was in Arkwood, with Fynn, remembering the moments they had spent together, wishing he was still near.

He would know what to do. He would have the answers to defeat the deocre. Or at least to whatever their next step needed to be. She hadn't realized the calm, the assurance, his presence had afforded her until it was gone. Without him there to reassure her, the old self-doubt had started to fight its way back in.

The ground around her cleared as she stormed into the trees, roots flattening, branches lifting. *Good,* she thought. *A safe way to let out some of the steam.*

But then her foot collided with something hard, her toe crunching on impact, and a scream escaped her mouth. Her knees hit the ground, that cursed hard ground that she hadn't thought to soften, and her gaze fell on a rock the size of a large rabbit, a small smear of blood now decorating one side of it from where her toe had slammed against it.

"Damn it." Nova curled herself into a ball and leaned back against a tree, not even bothering to glance at her toe. Or try to heal it.

Instead, her forehead fell to her knees, and her shoulders racked with sobs. The magic that had been building inside her beat down the wall she'd built to contain it, the one that *Fynn* had helped her learn to construct, and burst from her in a beam of light, a gust of wind, a rumble of the earth. Relief coursed through her veins in waves as the power continued to emit from her body, as the wind whipped her hair. Nearby, a tree cracked, then the ground rumbled again as it smashed into the earth.

"Nova?"

The hush of the forest returned to her as she reined her magic back in. The wind stopped. The ground stilled. The hazy orange glow from the setting sun overtook the last of her light.

Nova looked up to find Jax standing a few feet away, hands in his pockets, a look of utter devastation plastered to his face. His green eyes were wide, but not in fear, not in anger. With worry.

She wiped the tears off her face. "Hi."

"That was a lot. Back at the cabin, I mean." He shuffled his feet, kicking a small stick with one foot.

"Yeah."

"Mind if I take a look at your toe?"

She'd completely forgotten that she had stubbed her toe so badly that it had bled, may have even broken. Pain flooded back into her body as she glanced down at it and nodded.

Jax took a few hesitant steps forward, then squatted down in front of her. He laid one hand on her foot, and within moments, the pain receded, and the blood disappeared.

"Thank you," she managed to say.

"Next time, do it yourself."

Nova looked up at him, expecting to see his usual stern eyes, but found them still full of worry. A playful smile darted across his lips.

"How in Canta's name are we supposed to fight this deocre, Jax?"

He sat down on the grass beside her and shrugged. "No idea. But I can tell you it's not by sitting in the woods and crying about it. Don't get me wrong," he added when she opened her mouth to protest, "I know the power of a good cry. But tomorrow, we turn our attention to fighting, ok?"

"What do you mean?" Her fingers found their way into her hair, which had come loose from its braid during her escape.

"I mean that you're allowed this moment right now, but tomorrow we go back to the clearing, and we train harder than we have before. You've been through some shit. Let's find a way to use it to strengthen your magic."

Nova blinked as his words set in. "You think I can?"

His brow furrowed, as if he couldn't believe she'd even think those words. "Nova, if there's one thing I know about you, it's that you can do anything you set your mind to."

And there it was. The one thing that she had never believed of herself, but that Fynn had helped her come to realize. Now here sat Jax, telling her the exact same thing, like it was common knowledge.

Maybe she *was* powerful, all on her own. Fynn may have helped amplify her magic, but it was *her* magic, not his. Only she had the ability to wield it. Maybe there were other ways to amplify it. Or maybe she simply needed more training, like Jax said.

She'd promised Fynn she would focus on her magic and continue to get stronger. But if she was being honest, the only person she could promise that to was *herself.* She needed to refocus and listen to Jax. Starting right now.

"Thanks, Jax." Nova managed a smile.

He grinned. "Do you want me to sit with you for a few more minutes? That might be all Raelyn gives us before she stomps out here herself…"

She laughed, perfectly picturing Raelyn's curls bouncing as she ran through the forest looking for them. "Yes, just a few more minutes."

Jax sat back against a tree across from her and closed his eyes. Nova allowed hers to fall shut as well, listening to the sounds of the forest—crickets chirping mercilessly, leaves rustling in the light breeze—and found herself in a meditative state. She remained still until not only was her breath steady, but the wall containing her magic was fortified again, her power singing softly of contentment inside her.

12

FYNN

THREE PAIRS OF EYES burned into Fynn, the heat from them searing a hole in his chest.

How had this gotten out so soon?

He'd left Nova and come to Arkwood to stop this from happening. In the hours since Persy died, he'd lost focus, gotten wrapped up in the Defiance, and didn't stop to think about what other possibilities he needed to consider. What other loose ends needed to be tied up.

But even now, as he racked his brain, he couldn't think of any.

Everyone else who knew the truth was safely back in Aerdmure. Or at least that's what Fynn chose to believe.

That left the deocre. If this...*thing* was an imprint of Luc Astor, it would know who had killed it. It must have found a way to reveal this tiny detail to those with the authority to do something about it.

"All right, Voss." Fox broke the silence, arms crossed over his broad chest. "Explain."

There was only so much he could tell. He and Nova hadn't had a chance to discuss how they wanted Blackmore's story to get out, or what the right way to do that was. Now was certainly not the time to divulge such a huge secret to three people he barely knew and didn't fully trust. But there had to be some kernels of truth from the confrontation in the laboratory that he could share.

He drew a deep breath. "Look, it's not my story to tell—"

"Sounds like it is," Ethel interrupted.

Fynn narrowed his eyes at her. "I assure you it is not. But what I can say is that I was acting in self-defense and in defense of witches I was charged with protecting."

Fox raised an eyebrow and Ethel shook her head. Elodie, however, spoke up. "What in Canta's name could Astor have done to make you *need* to act in self-defense?"

"He attacked his daughters." There—that was as much as he was willing to give.

Fox's mouth hung agape. "You're not serious."

Fynn nodded. "I am. The Astors were—are—being targeted by Blackmore, so I was designated as the elder daughter's protection detail. Turns out the biggest threat was inside the family."

Ethel must have caught onto his wording because she stepped forward and cocked her head to one side. "What do you mean 'biggest'? Blackmore's still out there, and surely he's a bigger threat?"

"Now, yes." The lie tumbled out quickly. "I assure you, in the moment, though, Luc was."

Ethel's eyes darted back and forth, as if trying to deduce whether Elodie and Fox were buying this. But before she could speak, a deeper voice echoed in from the doorway.

"He's right, Ethel."

Daro was back. And he was...agreeing with Fynn?

But the woman didn't falter. Her auburn hair whipped around lazily as she turned to face Daro. "Right about what?"

Daro sauntered over to the group. "He was assigned to protect Nova Astor. I had to...relieve him one night. And we know that Luc was a monster, so why is it so hard to believe he would attack his own family?"

Fynn's heart, which had been thumping furiously moments before, started to slow. He'd known Daro for a while, but only as an acquaintance, so there was no basis for the loyalty or the support he was showing Fynn now. All the same, Fynn was grateful. If Daro's credit got him past this conversation without further questions, then he owed the elf a debt.

Again.

"All right, fine," Ethel said. "Then why can't we just explain what happened to the authorities and be done with this? Get Fynn off the hook so he doesn't need to hide and can help us fight the deocre?"

Daro placed his hands on the table in front of him. "The number one tenet of the Defiance is absolute secrecy. If word gets out that Luc Astor was a monster, that he built a deocre—a long-forgotten magic that I assure you no one wants made public knowledge—then Astria as we know it will fall. The people will revolt. Dark magic will be reborn. And that's if the government doesn't pin everything on Fynn to keep the knowledge secret."

"He's right," Fox added. "Ethel, you know that our goal is to eliminate all traces of Luc Astor's treachery, so that no other tries the same again. We'll have to think of another way to get Fynn off the hook."

"Can we focus on the deocre first?" Elodie asked. "Fynn is safe enough down here with the Defiance until the deocre is caught and destroyed. And then we can figure out how to clear his name without implicating Luc."

As much as Fynn didn't want to admit it, Elodie was right. His criminal record was not nearly as important as the survival of their country and the well-being of its citizens. Elves, witches, and humans alike would suffer if what Daro claimed were true.

"I'll help as much as I can while laying low," Fynn said, trying to erase the sounds of defeat from his voice. His reunion with Nova had gotten a little more complicated.

"Good," Daro said. "The rest are on their way. I was able to make contact with everyone, so I expect they will be here momentarily."

Fox clapped Daro on the shoulder. "Good work. Guess we should set up camp down here for the time being. All of us need to keep our heads down while we figure out how to destroy this thing."

"On it!" Elodie set about bewitching the ground in the room to make an area padded for sleeping and carved what appeared to be a kitchen area out of the stone wall, while Ethel moved the tables into a line along the far wall.

"Fox, wait." Fynn took a step closer to the man before he could walk away, his voice hushed so that the others couldn't hear. "You don't know how to destroy it?"

Fox chuckled. "Oh, Fynn. If we did, do you think we'd be hiding down here, rather than working above ground to lure it? Everything we know about deocres is on the bookshelf over there. We'll comb through it all until someone finds the way to destroy it." He waved his hand at a small shelf with no more than six tomes atop it.

Fynn swallowed. He hadn't anticipated that the Defiance had worked for so long on subverting Luc Astor but had no idea how to handle the dark magic he had spun into existence.

He only hoped they could figure it out before it became too much for them to contain. Before it found its way to Aerdmure.

To Nova.

13

NOVA

NOVA SLID INTO THE chair across from Raelyn, who passed her a mug of lukewarm coffee.

"Sorry, it's not fresh," her sister said with a grimace.

"Doesn't matter. Watch this." Nova cupped her hands around the ceramic mug and held them for a few seconds. Wafts of steam began to cloud the surface of the brew. "It can always be the perfect temperature."

Raelyn giggled. "You know I'll never get over this, you being an absolute *queen* at magic."

Nova hadn't said a word to her sister when she got back to the cabin with Jax last night. In fact, she hadn't uttered a word to any of them. Jax had ushered Esta and Kael out, leaving the sisters alone for the night. Not a moment after the door closed, Nova crawled under the covers and fell asleep.

Now she found herself sipping coffee with a renewed vigor for the fight ahead—a new resolve to tackle her training and to research the deocre.

"I assume Jax will be here soon to start our training session." Nova grabbed a croissant from the platter on the table in front of her and took a large bite out of it.

Raelyn nodded. "And while you're out there today, Esta and I are going to visit the library. We already agreed to split up," she added when Nova opened her mouth to protest. "Your training is just as important as the research. If we split up, divide and conquer, we can do both faster."

She had a point, one Nova didn't have the strength to argue. "Be safe, ok?"

"You know me." Raelyn flipped her hair with her hand. "Always looking for danger." She rolled her eyes in a way only a little sister could pull off, a small smile canceling out the annoyance. "Yes, Nova, I'll be safe. And Esta will be with me. Besides, do you really think anyone—or anything—is going to try to attack us in the temple library?"

Nova shrugged. "At this point, I'd believe anything."

"Well," Raelyn crossed her arms, "they'd have to get past the extra guards around town and at the temple doors. 'Mass murderer' still on the loose, remember?"

A knock sounded at the door. Nova looked over to find Kael and Esta standing on the porch, peering in through the window to the right of the door. Nova waved for them to enter.

"Good morning." Esta strode over and poured herself the last of the coffee, much to Nova's chagrin. She'd been eyeing that for a refill.

"Let me warm that for you." Nova reached out and warmed the mug the same way she'd warmed her own just moments before, earning a smile from Esta. Had she ever earned a smile from Esta before? Her eyes drifted to the scar on the side of Esta's face, the last remnants of the burns she'd suffered at Nova's hand a few weeks ago. She swallowed down the guilt that rose within her.

"Thanks." The elf sank into the couch and sipped her coffee.

Kael once again hung awkwardly near the doorway, hands in his pockets and long hair unkempt. A pang hit Nova's gut when she realized this man was probably sleeping under a tree outside the cabin and hadn't so much as showered since they'd arrived. Nor had he complained about it. But he also couldn't exactly waltz into Aerdmure and ask for a room at the inn—or for a haircut, either.

The one thing he *could* do was shower.

Nova cleared her throat, trying to come up with the best way to word her offer. "Kael, if you'd like, you can shower before Jax gets here."

His dark eyes met hers, a hint of a sparkle shining in them. "I'd appreciate that."

"And maybe we can have Jax bring you some new clothes tomorrow?"

"I'd appreciate that as well."

She nodded at him. "Great. Well, feel free to hop in. There are extra towels in the cupboard in there." Nova waved her hand toward the bathing chamber in the back of the cabin. With a nod, Kael crossed the cabin and disappeared into the chamber.

Nova shifted her gaze back to Raelyn and found her sister grinning foolishly. "What?"

Raelyn giggled. "I just love that you're giving him a chance. After everything he—we, I suppose—have been through, it's nice to see some good happening." She reached across the table and squeezed Nova's hand. "Esta and I can pick up some clothes for him on our way home from the library."

A wave of peace settled into Nova, and she nodded before she took another bite of her croissant.

Raelyn was unusually chipper this morning, especially considering her reaction to Silvana's visit yesterday. Nova was used to her sister's emotions fluctuating like a wave in a stormy sea. She wasn't surprised to see that Raelyn experienced grief the same way.

They'd lost the man they'd called Father, whom they'd grown up revering, loving, trying to make proud. Not only had they lost him; they'd lost everything they thought he was. Nothing about their family life had been true.

And they hadn't even had a chance to speak with Raella about it yet. Did she know? Was she aware of what her husband had done, had been capable of? Had he enthralled her like he had the governors?

There were still so many unanswered questions. In time, Nova supposed, they would get some answers—at the very least, they would have to see Raella again, and probably soon. But others...

She just didn't understand how Raelyn was doing such a good job of masking her devastation or hiding her loss.

However, now was not the time to ask.

Jax arrived around the same time Kael emerged from the bathing chamber, towel-drying his hair and looking refreshed, smiling bigger than Nova had yet seen.

Never underestimate the power of a good shower, she thought.

Raelyn and Esta waved goodbye as they set off down the path to the temple, leaving Jax, Kael, and Nova to head in the opposite direction to the clearing. Nova's water skin bounced against her waist as she walked, the water inside sloshing noisily. She decided to work on her sun-protectant spell while they walked to save time. Yesterday, she'd managed to apply it without needing to touch Jax or Kael directly, a feat she had been most proud of at the time.

That same pride swelled in her chest as she accomplished it again, dispelling any last remnants of the doubt and anxiety that had plagued her last night. She was learning. She was improving.

She was stronger every day.

Kael resumed his position at the tree line when they reached the clearing, while Jax and Nova headed for the center.

"Think you can teach me that persuasion trick of yours today?" That confidence must have bubbled over into boldness because the words tumbled out of her mouth before she could rein them in.

Thankfully, Jax responded with a laugh. "We can try, but I should warn you, it's unlikely to work. Persuasion is a rare ability, even for wielders. I don't actually know any others who can do what I do, and I stumbled into it accidentally. But you probably have your own gift; we just need to find it."

"Accidentally? Now I'm intrigued."

He raised an eyebrow at her. "A story for another time."

She took the hint and dropped it. "Ok, so maybe no persuasion today. What other sorts of abilities are there to test out if persuasion fails?"

They made it to their usual spot, where the grass had been worn into the dirt from their movements over the past few weeks.

"One of the more common ones is jumping, as you know, like Blackmore and Mehta. Another is memory wielding. Wielders with memory powers can modify or solidify their own or others' memories magically."

Nova's hand flew to her mouth. "That sounds horrible."

"Does it?" Jax paused and scratched his chin. "Wielders are good people, Nova. Not all of us are the power-hungry vigilantes Luc made us out to be when he restricted our rights. The memory wielders I've met usually use them to help others heal from trauma or prevent them from forgetting things about people they've loved and lost."

"That's...beautiful." Her voice was barely more than a whisper.

"Told you." Jax smiled. "Another one I know of is amplification. My father could amplify, but I haven't met anyone else who can since he passed."

Nova's magic prickled, warming her already heated body. "Amplify? What does that mean?"

"My father could increase his power whenever he was close to his amplifier. The way I understand it, each wielder who can amplify has a different amplifying object, which can make them temporarily more powerful when it's near. My father's amplifier was an oak tree."

The familiarity of this sensation was sinking in. Had she found her gift? "And could this...object be a person?"

Jax's brow furrowed. "You're thinking of that thing that happens when you're with Fynn?"

Nova nodded.

"It's possible. Though I've never heard of it before, I'm by no means an expert in amplification."

"But it *could* be. It's the closest thing I've felt that resembles a special ability, something you couldn't explain." Her magic continued to prickle, a sure sign they were on to something here...

"Well, we can't confirm it until Fynn's back, so how about we start with the magic we *can* wield?" His foot tapped impatiently.

She reluctantly agreed, but deep down, she knew she was right. Her powers sang when Fynn was near. They were invincible, immeasurable. Any spell she attempted in his presence succeeded. If that wasn't amplification, then she misunderstood what Jax had been trying to describe.

But he was right: there was no point in harping on it now, without Fynn. Her end of their bargain—to keep training—could not be upheld if she daydreamed all day about him or about the effect he had on her magic. She needed to focus.

When the shadows lengthened in the setting sun and Nova's bones were creaking with fatigue, she returned to the cabin with Jax and Kael, able to hold her chin high as she relished in how much she'd accomplished, how far she'd come...and how excited she was to show it all off to Fynn when they saw each other again.

14

NOVA

"HOW DID RESEARCH GO today?"

They were back at the cabin. Jax had gone home, but Esta, Kael, Raelyn, and Nova were eating dinner: a roasted pheasant with mashed potatoes and greens that Raelyn and Esta had picked up at one of the taverns in town on their way home. She couldn't help but notice the new clothes Kael was wearing, thankful to her sister and Esta for finding them.

Nova scooped up another bite with her fork and chewed ravenously, raising an eyebrow at her sister as she waited for a response.

Raelyn pushed her hair behind her ear and took a sip of water. "Unfortunately, we didn't find anything, not even a *mention* of deocres in any of the books we looked at."

"How big is the library?" Nova asked.

"Massive," Esta replied, cutting into her pheasant. "It'll take the two of us weeks to comb through everything in there."

"Weeks we aren't sure we have." The defeat in Raelyn's voice rang through loud and clear.

Nova's shoulders slumped. What would happen if they couldn't find the answer in time? How much time did they even have?

They needed more hands in the library. That was the only way. "Jax and I will come with you tomorrow."

Raelyn's fork dropped. "Absolutely not—"

"Your job right now is to grow your powers," Esta said at the same time.

"But I could go." Kael's voice was quiet but commanding. One that couldn't be argued with. "I'm just spectating anyway. Jax is doing a fantastic job teaching you. I can be more useful in the library."

"Out of the question," Nova said. "We aren't risking you getting caught and turned in. Not until we know that Fynn has Persy on our side and we can bring the truth to light."

Though, with the deocre now their top priority, there was no telling when that would be.

"She has a point." Raelyn shoved a bite of pheasant in her mouth.

Kael smiled. "I can disguise myself well. There's a reason I was never caught." His eyes glimmered with a spark of playfulness as he held Nova's gaze, waiting patiently for her reply.

She placed her fork on the table, crossing her arms. "Fine. But I'm approving your so-called disguise before you leave and have veto power if it's not good enough."

She wasn't sure where this protectiveness was coming from, only that she couldn't stomach the idea of losing him at this point. They'd just found each other, just started to get to know one another, and there was so much more she still wanted to learn.

Raelyn's deep breathing filled the cabin, echoed only by the crickets outside. She and Nova had gotten into bed an hour ago, and though

Nova's body was tired, her mind was spinning, doing everything it could to keep her from sleep.

Lying here was worthless. It was only riling her up more. So, trying as hard as she could not to wake Raelyn, she crept through the cabin to the front door and stood on the porch.

The night air was refreshingly cool as it danced across the bare skin of her arms and legs. Shadows cast by the half-moon covered the small clearing in front of the cabin, lending the crickets privacy as they chirped louder than ever.

Nova let out a deep exhale, then stepped down off the porch and made for the tree line. She had no agenda, no plan for where she was going, only knew that she needed to calm her mind and a walk sounded like the best way to do that.

Her feet were bare, but she didn't mind. The soft ground soothed the soreness that had been growing from constantly wearing her boots, both during training and while traveling to Benedict's and the lab.

What was Benedict doing? Had he survived? Found a way to heal himself fully? She supposed they should check on him sometime, or, at the very least, she should ask Kael what he thought about Benedict. If he was actually seeking retribution from the human.

And what about Raella? Had she found out about Luc yet? A not-so-small part of Nova was dying to speak with Raella about all that had happened. Sure, Raella wasn't her real mother and hadn't necessarily been the most affectionate toward Nova. But at the end of the day, she had still raised Nova. She had been the one to convince Luc to let Nova live. There was a bond there, a tug in her heart, that wouldn't just break. Not in the way it had with Luc.

When her mind turned to Fynn, she walked faster, trying desperately to shut out the thoughts. She didn't think it would take this long for him to find Persy and return. But the fact that he hadn't even sent a message…something had either gone wrong with the plan, or he'd also somehow found out about the deocre and was trying to fight it.

Or the deocre had found him.

No way in hell was an imprint of Luc's soul going to let his killer run free that easily.

Her heart raced, and her pulse thundered in her head. No, Fynn was fine. She would know if he wasn't. She would feel it.

But what if I didn't?

She stopped moving and fell to the ground, her knees colliding with the dirt and her elbows pressing into her thighs as she dug her palms into her eyes, trying to rid her mind of the images of Fynn hurt, Fynn killed.

"Nova?"

She stood and spun quickly, turning toward the voice that called behind her and throwing out a shield of wind like she had the night Luc and Persy had come to call.

But the person standing there wasn't a threat.

It was Kael.

"Oh. Hi." She pushed a strand of hair behind her ear, then wrung her hands together, letting the wall of wind dissipate.

He watched her with a hint of worry in his eyes. "Is everything ok?"

"Yes. I'm sorry if I disturbed you."

Where did he sleep? All she knew was that it wasn't in the cabin, and it wasn't in town. He was probably used to sleeping on the ground after his journey from Mistfell, but guilt crashed over her as she realized she hadn't even *asked* if he was comfortable.

Kael took a small step closer to her. "You didn't. I saw you leaving the cabin and wanted to make sure you were ok. Are you?"

She nodded, her eyes trailing toward the ground. That was a loaded question if she'd ever heard one.

But they were trying to form a relationship. Trying to rebuild the bond between them that had been unwillingly severed twenty-four years ago. The least she could do was answer him truthfully.

"Actually, no. I'm not ok. I could use some company." She looked up and caught his eye, which sparkled with delight as his mouth tipped up at the corners.

"I would be honored."

The idea of where they should go came to her like it had always been there. Like this was why she had gotten out of bed in the first place. "Follow me."

15

NOVA

THEY SETTLED ONTO THE rock formation that overlooked the eastern portion of the Worgreth Mountains, which were arguably smaller than the western. Just beyond the edge of the range, the flat land that stretched out to Arkwood and the ocean peeked through, glowing softly in the moonlight.

"This is beautiful," Kael gasped, the words hanging in the air like mist.

"Fynn and I came here once. After a particularly good day of training, when I was too riled up to sleep." Nova stared straight ahead, not daring to look at Kael, unable to handle the deep sympathy his eyes would be reflecting. His pity would be enough to unleash the tears she was trying to contain.

"You miss him, don't you?"

She nodded. "I wish there was a way to know he's all right. So I can stop imagining the worst."

"I wish I could tell you not to worry, but if you're anything like your mother—which I already know you are—then I know that is a waste of my breath."

She could hear his smile when he said it, though she didn't look his way. Her magic hummed lightly under her skin.

"What I can say is, even though I only met Fynn for a short time, I could see how much he loves you. In his eyes and in his actions. That he'll do whatever it takes to get back to you."

A tear escaped, its warmth sliding down Nova's cheek as she finally turned to look at Kael.

"It was the same way your mother looked at me. The same way I imagine I looked at her." Kael reached out and placed his hand lightly on Nova's shoulder, his thumb rubbing idly along her arm. "It's not the same, but I can get a message to him. He won't be able to reply, but I can let him know you're thinking about him."

Her brow furrowed as she turned to meet his gaze. "What do you mean?"

Kael dropped his hand. "I created a spell, similar to how you've been working on your warding spell, that gives me the ability to send messages to people. They'll feel it like a gust of wind, but the message is delivered into their ear, in my voice."

Her heart stopped. "That's...remarkable."

"It took me years to perfect, but it was very useful once I got it down." He grinned with a worthy amount of self-pride, moonlight dancing in his eyes.

"And you could get a message all the way to Fynn? From here to Arkwood?"

He nodded. "Just tell me what you'd like me to say."

Nova looked out at the mountains again and rubbed her temples. There was so much she wanted to say, but what was most important? What did Fynn need to know?

About the deocre, of course, and how they were looking for ways to fight it. He should be on the lookout for it so he could protect himself.

"Tell him that there is dark magic called a deocre detected in Arkwood, and he needs to be vigilant. Tell him we are looking for a way to stop it and will come to Arkwood once we know." She paused, drawing in a deep breath, then continued. "And tell him I miss him."

The surrounding trees rustled as a gust of wind whistled through them. Nova's hair whipped around her face, her skin turning prickly with the chill.

As suddenly as it came, it disappeared.

"Done," Kael said.

The ache that had been sitting on her chest for the last few days eased. Not entirely, but enough that her shoulders slumped from the release of tension. "Thank you."

"Of course. Now I think it's your turn for a question?"

Ah, yes—a question for a question. They'd been playing this game in the rare free moments they had together. Nova had come to really appreciate these times and had loved getting to know the man who was her father. In her idle time, she caught herself brainstorming questions to ask him at their next opportunity.

So she'd had this one ready to go for a day or two but hadn't yet felt brave enough to ask. Tonight's moonlit midnight hike felt like as good a time as any.

"Let me know if you don't want to answer this one, but...I've been wondering how you were able to escape Mistfell."

Kael laughed, a booming, electrifying laugh that Nova felt in her bones. It was so infectious, she couldn't help but smile, then let out a giggle of her own.

"Why is that funny?!"

His laughter slowed as he drew in deep breaths, then he turned to look at her. "I was expecting something much more personal with that lead-up. But how I escaped...it's not a very glamorous story, but I'm happy to share."

"I'm all ears." Nova shifted her body to face him, resting her elbows on her knees in front of her.

Kael cleared his throat. "Well, one thing to know about Mistfell: It's not guarded by physical guards, except for the warden."

Nova leaned back. "Really? Then why do we hear about Mistfell guards?"

"I think people speak of guards in the loosest of ways. There *are* guards; they are just magical guards, not corporeal ones."

"Like spells? Enchantments?"

Kael nodded. "Some, yes. The witches have set up some of the strongest protective spells I've ever encountered. And, of course, the humans contributed physical barriers: walls so high you can't see the top, trenches along the outside filled with the foulest creatures. But the toughest part to break through was the ancient elven ward.

"The entire fortress is built of an alloy that stifles magic. There is no magic inside the walls; not even the wards and protective spells can reach past the alloy. But that also means that no one inside can perform magic. We are all essentially human once we are imprisoned."

Nova tried to follow. "So, you had to physically get out of the prison fortress before you even had to contend with the magical defenses? And there were no actual guards to fight you, just the warden?"

"Exactly. And the warden has a fairly regular sleep schedule. All the inmates know when he's asleep, because you can bet that's when most of them try to escape."

She gasped. "More prisoners try to escape?"

"Oh yes," Kael said. "Almost all do at some point. But if they get past the wall, they are nearly all caught or driven mad by the enchantments and defenses on the outside. Even those who can do magic.

"But the witches' magical defenses had a fatal flaw, one I hoped for but didn't know about for sure until I landed on the other side of the wall. They're meant to capture and detain people who are guilty. The spells latch onto even the smallest fraction of your mind that betrays your guilt for what you've done and exaggerate it. They use it to cause pain to make you stop moving and retreat straight back to the warden's clutches. The few I saw return from escape attempts weren't the same mentally, even if they were physically unharmed."

His words hung in the air as Nova imagined him in a metal fortress surrounded by humans, witches, and elves who had all been driven out of their minds, who were no more than a shell of their former selves.

"But you weren't guilty," she whispered.

That's when he smiled. "Correct. While the spells fought me, and I could feel them trying to claw into me, to get into my mind, there was nothing for them to latch on to. Nothing but the love and the yearning I felt for you, which, if anything, seemed to repel the spells. By the time I got through them, I made it to the trenches and felt my own magic start to stir back to life.

"It was very little at first. It had been suppressed for so long that I had assumed it was lost forever. But when I felt that first wave, despite how small it was...it was like finding a piece of my soul. As it filled me, I felt more alive. I felt stronger, though physically I was still quite weak.

"The magic that came back initially was enough to get me through the trenches unscathed, but that was all it was. I burned through it quickly. It was hours before I felt any whispers of my power again, and by then, I was long gone. Looking back, I'm thankful it was only a small amount of power. The burnout didn't exhaust me as much as it had before...Mistfell."

"But what about the elven ward?" Nova asked.

"Ah, yes, the other side of the trench. I made it through alive—tired, weak, depleted, but alive. I knew, however, that there was one last hurdle. Unfortunately, I had no idea what it was. No one had ever made it that far before. I stumbled through the trees, thankful it was summer because, given I was so far north, it was still bone-chillingly cold. Exposure would've claimed me had it been any other season. I knew I didn't have much left in me before I needed to stop and rest or find something to eat. But there was no way in hell I was stopping before I passed whatever the last hurdle was."

Kael stopped to draw in a deep breath. Nova waited silently for him to continue, wanting to give him the space he needed to process what he had been through and to decide what to share.

"I kept walking, trying to summon any drops of magic I could to keep myself warm. And just when I felt like I could go no further, like I was going to collapse, I spotted the most beautiful grove. Pink, purple, and blue flowers danced in the breeze, which suddenly felt *warm*. Their stems were waist-high, their leaves luscious and green as the trees are here.

"I should've known right away that flowers that grew like that, so far north, couldn't be harmless. That the fruit they bore, the pollen they deposited, had to be enchanted. But it took longer than I care to admit to realize that I was facing frost blossom."

Nova gasped, her hand flying to her mouth. Frost blossom was a product of the Noriendar Forest, known for its hallucinogenic properties. Some liked to take it as a drug. But it was incredibly dangerous, so much so that the governors centuries ago had put limits on how much could be sold to one buyer. Taken in the tiniest of doses, it could leave the user in a state of absolute bliss, transcending the here and now and landing somewhere in between. But many had accidentally gone too far, overdosing on the frost blossom and losing their memories, their sense of self. Permanently.

Growing frost blossom was restricted to only those elves in the Noriendar Forest who went through significant training to do so. And harvesting it—well, she'd never seen it, but she'd heard that the process was extremely intricate.

She couldn't imagine what a field of frost blossoms could do to someone.

"How did you escape?" Her hand drifted from her mouth to the braid that had fallen over her shoulder.

Kael looked at her. "Frost blossom works by removing your memories. I could feel them—my memories—swirling around me, trying to escape." He shivered. "But one seemed to jump out at me. One of your mother, telling me about other healers who were exploring microdoses of frost blossom as a means of trauma recovery. They needed a way to be able to test the dose, but if they went too high, they needed to have a way to counteract the effects."

"You remembered her telling you the antidote?"

He shook his head. "Not exactly, but I remembered her telling me there *could be* an antidote. I don't know that one was ever fully developed. But it was enough for me to realize what I was walking through. To know what lay in store for me if I kept going unprotected.

"There was very little magic left in me at this point. I could almost feel the Noriendar Forest starting to pull on my power the same way the alloy prison had. But to get through the frost blossom, I needed to summon every bit of wind magic that I could to create a barrier between myself and the pollen in the air."

Nova's palms were sweating as she took in every word. "How'd you do it?"

Kael's gaze drifted downward, but his mouth curved into a loose smile. "I thought of you. Of seeing you, meeting you, of how much joy that would bring me. Of how much I wanted to learn about you, not just for myself but for Wynna. Familial bonds run deep in magic; that's why twins have stronger magic together than apart. I pulled on those familial bonds, on that knowledge that you were alive and the truth could be set free, to keep my mind focused on the present. Once I felt like my mind had cleared enough and I had a strong enough barrier, I ran as fast as my feeble body could carry me, drawing that barrier around me the entire way."

A tear slid down Nova's cheek as she imagined Kael—not the groomed, well-fed Kael she'd come to know from the last few days, but a scrawnier, rougher version—running for his life through what appeared to be an oasis but was actually a death trap. Kael, using every bit of energy he could to focus on *her*, so he could get through.

"Once I got through and into the Noriendar Forest proper, I collapsed. I crawled to a cave and hid myself for a full day to allow myself the time to recover. By then, I knew they'd be after me and I needed to get out of Noriendar so I could use magic again, but I also needed my strength. I bided my time, foraged and hunted, exercised as much as I could, until my body felt stronger. I had waited twenty-four years to see you again. There was no point rushing into things, only to get caught in a silly mistake before I could find you."

Nova reached out and took Kael's hand, enjoying the warmth it held, but also noting the calluses, cuts, and scrapes. This was her father. The man who had fought through trenches, poisons, and traps just for the chance to see her. Who had used the idea of her not once, but twice, to get past the wards and escape Mistfell.

Who wanted nothing more than to be there for her when she needed him. Like he was tonight.

"Thank you for sharing that story with me, Kael," she whispered.

"Thank you for asking about it." He squeezed her hand. "Maybe one more easy one and then I can walk you back to the cabin?"

Nova yawned, then nodded.

"Ok." He chuckled. "What are some of your favorite things?"

She smiled, picturing the seaside cottage and the waves rolling on and off the beach. The children coming into her classroom on the first day of school, wide-eyed and eager to learn, fresh from summer break. Evenings with Raelyn, curled on the couch, sharing gossip or silently reading novels, their legs intertwined. The way a cup of coffee filled her soul every morning, giving her the grace she needed to start her day.

The way Fynn's violet eyes sparkled like midnight when he laughed, or when he was about to kiss her.

So, she told him. She told him about all those things, ready to fully embrace this new relationship, to let him in.

To see where these familial bonds that ran deeper than magic could take them.

16

Nova

Two witches stood outside Nova's door. Not one. Two.

Jax had brought a friend.

"Mehta?" she asked, wrinkling her brows as her gaze shifted between the two wielders on her porch.

Mehta smiled, his dark arms crossed over his chest. "Morning, Nova. Good to see you again."

"You, too." Nova closed the door behind her as she stepped onto the porch. Kael and Raelyn were still inside, getting ready to head to the temple. If Mehta saw...

She flashed what she hoped was a warning glare at Jax, but he just rolled his eyes. "What are you doing here?" she asked, returning her focus to Mehta.

But it was Jax who answered. "I asked him to come help today. You're doing so well with a single opponent. I wanted to up the ante a bit."

"You want me to fight...both of you?" She didn't like the sound of this. Not. One. Bit.

He was right that she was doing well enough on her own, but the idea of bringing someone new into their training regime and the risk it presented if one of them said the wrong thing...or if Kael was seen...

He should've run this by her first.

"It'll be fun." Mehta flashed her a smile, his white teeth contrasting brilliantly against the darkness of his skin.

"Fun. Sure. That's a word." She heard the scrape of a chair and footsteps moving from inside the cabin. They needed to get off the porch—and fast. "All right, let's see what you've got. Come on."

Nova pushed between the two of them, looping her arm through Jax's and pulling him along with her.

He stumbled over his feet down the stairs and toward the trail as he tried to keep up and turn himself around. "Nova, wait, what—"

"What were you thinking, Jax?" she whisper-shouted at him. A quick glance over her shoulder showed that Mehta was following them but not close enough to hear. "Bringing him that close to...you know..."

Jax scoffed. "If there's anyone in the world I trust, it's Mehta. He—"

"Maybe you trust him," Nova spat, continuing to pull him along the trail, "but it's not your secret to tell."

"He's powerful, Nova. Maybe he could help with the—"

"Shhhh." She stopped moving, yanking him in front of her. "You heard Silvana as well as I did. Tell no one...and maybe you trust him, but I don't know him well enough yet to say I trust him with the secret that could take my real family back when I only just got it."

Nova dug her foot into the ground and clenched her fists. The fact that Jax thought he had the right to just bring another person into this without asking first made her blood boil.

And, evidently, the look she bestowed on him worked because he took a step back and held his hands up. "Ok, ok, I'm sorry. You're right."

Footsteps approached from behind them. "Everything ok?" Mehta asked, his voice silky. He raised an eyebrow at them.

Nova schooled her expression into one of sweetness and smiled at him. "Of course. Let's go and see what you've got for me."

Three hours later, Nova regretted allowing Mehta to come along. He was good—really good—and fast. While keeping up with Jax had gotten easier, partially because she'd learned his tells and could anticipate his movements, adding Mehta into the mix challenged her in a whole new way.

Which, she supposed, was the point.

But she was exhausted and sweaty, sore from being hit with spell after spell that she couldn't dodge or block. She'd gotten in a few good deflections early on, enough to bolster her confidence, but fatigue had set in, hampering her reflexes.

"Break, please." She held up her hands in surrender, then hinged at the waist and gripped her knees.

"There's only one hour 'til lunch, Nova. Let's power—" Jax started to say, but Mehta cut him off.

"A break is well earned. Let's take ten."

If it were possible to send a rush of magical gratitude, Nova would have. Jax hardly ever let her take breaks. Maybe it was worth having Mehta here if only for that purpose...

"Fine. Ten." Jax started walking off toward the trees.

"Where are you going?" Mehta called after him, but all he received in return was a middle finger.

Nova collapsed onto the ground, folding her legs under her and leaning back on her palms. "Has he always been this...I don't know, rigid? Stubborn?"

Mehta joined her in the grass and chuckled. "The short answer, yes."

"And the long?" She raised a brow.

"Too long for ten minutes."

Ah. Ok. Not going there today.

"You know," Mehta continued, "it may not feel like it, but you're doing really well. I'm impressed with what I've seen today."

If she hadn't already been so warm, Nova was sure her cheeks would have flushed. "The beating my body has taken would suggest otherwise."

He chuckled again. "We've all been there. It gets easier, though. Stick with it." He took a swig from his water skin. "Listen, I'm sorry for intruding today. Jax and I were talking last night at the guild, and I offered to come help. We used to train together and teach other wielders together, so it seemed like a good idea at the time. But I could tell from your face this morning that I was wrong."

Nova took a deep breath, partially to help her heart rate slow but also to give herself the time to collect her thoughts. She had to admit that she'd learned a lot today, and they were only halfway through the session. Having a second instructor was beneficial, and perhaps she hadn't been fair to him this morning. She wasn't ready to trust him with everything like Jax was...yet. But she wouldn't mind continuing to get to know him.

"I overreacted. I'm sorry." She flashed him a weak smile, all she could muster at the moment. The corners of his lips turned up in return. "I appreciate that you came."

A cloud passed overhead, darkening the clearing and offering them some reprieve from the sun. Jax had yet to reappear from the trees into which he'd disappeared.

"Any fun tricks you can teach me that Jax can't?" Nova asked.

His smile spread wider. "I think the only thing I can do that he can't is jumping, which unfortunately isn't something that can be taught. Jax has explored depths of magic and wielding that I haven't had the chance to yet."

The way his tone dropped off at the end suggested there was a story behind why that was, and that it wasn't a happy one. But Jax had emerged from the trees, striding toward them with determination, and she didn't have the chance to follow up.

"Uh-oh," Mehta said, "he's back from relieving himself and ready to go with a vengeance. I'm glad I'm on his side and not yours right now. Might be better off running for it, Nova."

She couldn't help the laugh that escaped her. Mehta shook his head, his curly black hair falling into his face as he tilted his chin down to hide his own laugh.

Jax stopped in front of them. Nova tried to clamp her mouth shut and suppress the laugh, but the look on Jax's face just made it worse. "What's so funny?"

Mehta stood, and Nova followed suit, pressing her lips into a thin line to contain any further giggles. "Nothing," she said, dusting her hands off.

Jax narrowed his eyes on her before turning to Mehta, who responded, "Your hair looks nice."

The laughter that erupted from Nova earned her a magical blow from Jax that she was unprepared to block, but it had been worth it for the moment of levity and the utter scowl on Jax's face.

17

FYNN

F YNN SLAMMED THE BOOK in front of him shut with a groan and cradled his head in his hands. His hair, loose today because he was beyond caring, fell into his face, blocking his vision of the room around him.

"Fynn?" a soft voice said from somewhere on his left. He'd been here long enough now to recognize it as Elodie's. In the three days he'd been down here, in the Defiance's makeshift underground headquarters, she'd been one of the few who had been consistently kind, trusting, and unafraid of him.

The remaining members of the Defiance who lived in Arkwood had arrived that first night, all eyeing Fynn, the newcomer, warily. All they'd known about him was that he was wanted for Luc Astor's murder and he may have been what triggered the deocre's release. He couldn't blame them for not fully embracing his presence, even with Fox and Daro's commendations.

He lifted his head and looked at Elodie, who was hunched over her own book, but her eyes were peeking up at him. They'd spent the better part of the last three days taking turns poring over the scant collection of books and planning their next steps, trying to figure out how to contain and destroy the deocre, but so far had come up short.

"You ok?" Elodie asked, one eyebrow raised.

What a stupid question. Was he ok? No, of course he wasn't fucking ok.

He had uncovered a secret powerful enough to throw Astria into revolution.

He'd learned of a cover-up plot that landed an innocent man in prison for twenty-four years.

He'd been separated from the woman he loved while a monster of unknown proportions threatened her safety.

He'd watched his father be murdered by said monster.

And now, he was nowhere close to finding a way to deal with it and get back to Nova.

No, he wasn't even close to ok.

Plus, there had been that voice he'd heard the first night here. A whisper, really, carried on a cool breeze that shouldn't have found its way down here. No one else had seemed to hear the voice that claimed to be a message from Nova, that told him it missed him and was searching for a way to defeat the deocre. It was certainly just part of his imagination.

There was no way she had found a way to communicate like that. He'd never heard of such a thing.

He pushed himself back from the table and stood. "I need a walk. Some fresh air."

Fox had warned him about going above ground, given the target on his back, so he hadn't left their underground lair since he arrived. But it had been quiet since then, the scouts in the group bringing back no news of any more sightings or attacks from the deocre, life in Arkwood seemingly returning to whatever normal was with the manhunt for Blackmore—and now Fynn—still ongoing. Surely a few moments outside wouldn't hurt.

"That's not a good idea." Elodie pressed down the corner of her book, marking the page and closing it. "If you're caught—"

"I know the risks, but I also know that I'm going stir-crazy down here."

"I'll go with you." Daro approached from where he had been standing with Fox and two others around the map table in the middle of the room. "Safety in numbers. And to make sure you find your way back in."

Fynn didn't love the idea of company, but if that's what it would take… Besides, Daro had become more of an ally over the last few days than Fynn had anticipated. Perhaps he had misjudged the elf before getting to know him.

So he nodded, trying to portray gratitude in his gaze.

"Fox, we'll be back," Daro called to their leader. "Going to scout above. I'm taking Fynn."

Fox looked up, his jaw falling open but not responding. After a few breaths, where Fynn could almost see the cogs in his mind spinning, he nodded. "All right, but at the first sign of trouble—"

"I know," Daro said. "We'll come back down."

Fox nodded, then turned back to the maps on the table and began pointing at something, speaking in a hushed tone.

Daro grabbed his baldric from the hooks that hung along the wall near the door and fastened it around his waist. "You'll want yours, too," he said to Fynn as he tightened the buckle.

A burn of irritation ignited in Fynn's chest. "I know." But he checked himself. Daro had been nothing but nice and was just looking out for him. He would do well to remember those breathing exercises he had taught Nova to help her control her power.

Inhale, exhale. Breathe, breathe.

He grabbed his own belt off the wall and fastened the buckle. When he was sure it was secure, he looked up at Daro. "Let's go."

Daro nodded and led him out of the room, with one last wave back at the small group still assembled around the various tables. Only Elodie watched them and waved back; the rest were either huddled with Fox or crouched over books, scratching notes on parchment. Fynn tipped his chin at her and slipped through the doorway.

When they first arrived, Fox had brought him through the hallway to the left, but Daro turned right when he exited the chamber, continuing down a long, arched hallway, quiet, flickering torches lighting their path. It was unnerving how quiet it was down here, just a little below Arkwood's bustling streets. What else went on below that Fynn had no idea about?

"This way." Daro turned at a fork, taking the right path again, his voice echoing off the stone walls. "We'll come up near the park, as good a place as any for you to get some fresh air."

The park. The last time Fynn had been in the park was when he'd brought Nova back after her attack. When he had taken her back to help her process the trauma as much as to help him process the anxiety that had pressed on his chest since he woke up and realized she was gone. Or the fear that had enveloped him when he'd found her, struggling, after following her scent through Arkwood. His body had sprung into action to save her, almost of its own free will.

She was safe now, he reminded himself.

After what felt like hours of walking in silence, they came upon a staircase built into the stone wall of the tunnel. At the top stood a door, shut and locked from the inside with complicated locking mechanisms that Fynn had never seen before. Magical locks, probably, put in place by the Defiance's wielder. But Daro approached them and unlocked them all with ease, clearly having done it before.

"Out, quickly, and stay quiet for now." Daro held the door open for Fynn to pass through.

The threshold opened into another staircase that led to what appeared to be a small stone cabin. With only one room, it was surrounded by fogged glass windows on two sides, enough to let in the natural light of the sun, but not so transparent that anyone outside could see in. A solitary door that had clearly seen better days stood on the wall in front of him. Chunks of wood were missing from the face of it, the four glass windows lining the top of it cracked but somehow still in place, and an odd arrangement of circles etched into the frame above.

"What is this place?" Fynn whispered. The cabin's floor was stone but covered in so much dirt it was hard to know for sure. The musty air, probably filled with mold spores, made Fynn's nose tickle with the promise of a sneeze. Guessing that Daro would drag him back down the stairs if he let it out, Fynn held the bridge of his nose, trying to keep the sneeze down.

Daro emerged up the steps behind him. "It's an old guardhouse that was abandoned decades ago. The High One recommended we use it as one of our first entrances to the underground. From the outside, it's so inconspicuous that it's never been an issue." He opened the door for Fynn to exit the cabin.

Sunlight and fresh air streamed in, hitting Fynn like a boulder. He breathed in deeply, savoring the smell of the flora in the park, a stark contrast to the dank air from the underground hideout. With an exhale, he crossed the threshold.

He was surrounded by willow trees, their long, dangly branches brushing against the grass, providing cover to hide the cabin but letting through enough sun to warm and light the space. It was a small sanctuary, the sounds of Arkwood—the clopping of horse hooves, the chatter of strolling citizens, the bellows of merchants hawking their wares—barely making it through, so they must have been far enough from one of the paths through the park.

This was all he needed. The breeze in his hair, the warmth of the sun's kiss on his skin. His muscles instantly relaxed—his mind, too. It was easy to get caught up in the fear, in the unknown while trapped underground, but out here...out here, it was just like any other day.

The last time he'd been out in the sun like this, simply for the sake of enjoying nature, had been with Nova in Aerdmure. Fynn loved the way sunlight glittered as it reflected off her emerald eyes, the way she always thought to protect his skin with her clever spell before protecting her own. He could picture the two of them strolling hand in hand through this park one day, all memory of the *first* time they'd been here overrun by the more cherished memories they'd create.

"Better?" Daro asked from behind him, snapping Fynn out of his daydream. He turned to find a smile on Daro's face.

He couldn't help but be grateful.

"Yes, thank you."

Daro leaned back against the stone wall of the cabin. "It's secluded enough that I think we would all be safe enough to come up here, but especially you. As long as we don't stay too long and you stay under the willow, I don't think anyone will find you here."

No sooner had he said the words, though, than the sound of footsteps—many footsteps, many *running* footsteps—ricocheted in Fynn's ears. Based on the way Daro's body stiffened, he'd heard them, too.

"He's somewhere over here!" a voice called. "Split up!"

A second, deeper voice called, "Don't let the elf get away!"

"He's likely armed," the first one said. "Be prepared to cast your spells!"

There was no way they were coming for Fynn. No way had they detected his presence here already, had known he'd just stepped out from underground, from outside the enchantments protecting them below. Those voices...they must have been tracking someone else.

But then again, there was already magic at play here that Fynn had never imagined in his wildest dreams. If the deocre was tracking him, if it was targeting him...

"Fynn Voss, we know you're out here!" the second voice boomed. "Come quietly or we will be forced to use magic!"

Fynn's eyes met Daro's, his heart thumping wildly in his chest. "Are they—"

"Inside, quick," Daro hissed, his eyes sweeping the area. "Downstairs."

Fynn didn't need to be told twice. In a flash, he ran into the cabin, back down the stairs, and through the hidden door, until he was across the threshold and in the tunnel again, Daro hot on his heels.

Thank Dalia they had the same agility powers.

Daro closed the door, quickly but quietly, and reworked the locks on the inside. It wasn't until the last one was fastened and the elf turned back to look at Fynn that his heartbeat began to slow.

That had been close. Too close.

"How the hell did they find me?" he whispered, his breath ragged.

Daro shook his head. "Your guess is as good as mine. There must be some kind of tracking magic that they've put on you." He ran his hand across his forehead. "Fuck, this is worse than we imagined."

If Fynn couldn't go above without getting caught, if he was trapped down here until they figured out how to defeat the deocre—how long would that be?

He had a sudden understanding of how Nova and Raelyn must have felt, trapped in the flat all those weeks ago.

"You're telling me. We've got to figure out how to defeat this thing...and fast." With that, he turned on his heel and stalked down the tunnel, back to the chamber where he could only hope the answer lay.

18

Nova

NOVA WIPED THE SWEAT from her brow, but not before some of it trickled into her eye, the saltiness stinging.

She groaned and pressed her fingers into her closed eyelids, trying to rub out the pain. Her other hand was raised in front of her, her palm facing Jax. "One second!"

Jax didn't reply, but she could picture him standing across from her, hand on his waist, tapping his foot impatiently as he was wont to do.

Today, they were working on her reflexes—how quickly she could defend or block his spells. It was hard work, physically and mentally, and she had developed a newfound appreciation for how Jax and Kael had fought Luc back in the lab. They had moved instinctually, throwing out spells left and right to block or attack like it was second nature. While she was delighted that certain spells were becoming second nature to her, her reflexes were not the fastest.

Still, she was proud of how far she'd come in so little time. And that progress was enough to motivate her to keep going, especially since Jax wasn't going easy on her.

Her eyes flickered open, blinking a few times to see clearly again. Sure enough, there he was, exactly as she had expected.

"Ready?" He was wearing a sleeveless tunic today, and the tops of his olive-toned shoulders looked a little pink. Her sun-protectant spell was wearing off. Or perhaps the sun was extra strong today. Good thing they were almost done with their lesson.

The day was brutally hot.

Nova nodded. "Sorry, sweat got in my eye." She picked her water skin up off the ground and tried to sip from it, but it was already empty. Throwing it back down, she added, "Is it extra hot today or is it just me?"

"It's not just you. Now, assume your position. Let's get in five more before we head back." Jax wedged his left foot into the grass behind him, his hands out in front at chest height, ready to spar.

Five more. That was it. She could do five more.

Although, she had to admit that sitting in the cool library at the temple was starting to sound like it had been the better idea. She wondered how it was going; had they found anything? Kael had been going with them for the last few days. His disguise was so impressive, Nova asked if he could teach her how he did it. Between that and the messaging spell, she was in awe of her father. His power was immense, and he had explored depths of magic she wasn't sure even Jax had.

The first morning he went to the temple, he'd emerged from the bathing chamber completely unrecognizable. He looked like any young man, having lost about twenty years, his hair darker and shorter. Even his voice was pitched slightly lower. If it weren't for the green eyes that twinkled at her knowingly, she probably would have thought it was someone else entirely.

Hopefully, with three sets of eyes looking through the books, they could uncover something today, even if the three days prior had resulted in nothing.

Lost in her thoughts, Nova had forgotten to assume her defensive stance before Jax struck. And so, when the force of whatever spell he threw her way hit her square in the face, she flew off her feet and landed hard on her ass. She shrieked as pain erupted in her cheekbone. Her fingers met something warm and sticky when she pressed them against the injury to quell the pain.

Blood. She was bleeding from a gash just below her right eye.

"Shit!" Jax ran over, squatting down next to her and pulling her hand away. Her gaze lingered on her hand as he held it, at the blood coating it. More blood than she could have thought possible from one cut. What kind of spell had he hit her with?

His thumb pressed into her temple, and she winced, recoiling from his touch. "I'm sorry, Nova. You'd been doing so well, I thought I'd try something new. Where were you? You didn't even react, didn't try to duck or block..."

Warmth was weaving its way from where he pressed his thumb into her head and through her cheek. "I was lost in my thoughts." She winced again as the warmth—Jax's healing powers—found its target and started working to seal the wound.

His eyes found hers. "Fynn?"

"No, actually. Kael." Although, now that she thought about it, it was good neither of them was here right now, or Jax would probably need his own healer. Kael hadn't been happy to learn that they were working on defensive maneuvers and spells because he was worried Nova would get hurt, but he didn't put up much of a fight, understanding the benefits. Fynn, though...maybe he would have also understood, but at the first sign of Nova hurt, he would have made sure Jax hurt just as much.

The warmth from the healing spell slowly dissipated, and Jax drew his hand back. He sat on the ground in front of her. "He's been going to town for three days now without any issue. I'm sure he's fine."

"I'm not worried about him. I just want them to find something." And it was the truth. Her clean hand pressed lightly into her cheekbone, where the gash had been. There was a small, warm, raised line of skin there now, healed but sure to leave a small scar. "What spell was that?"

"One I've been working on." Jax bit his lip. "One that I haven't yet tried outside the guild, and now I see isn't ready."

Her eyebrows raised. "You used an experimental spell on me?"

"You've been doing so well in blocking and agility, I didn't think it mattered what I threw at you," Jax said. To his credit, he did look a little guilt-ridden, like he held some remorse for his actions.

"What's this spell supposed to do?"

He crossed his legs underneath him and leaned back on his hands. "It's supposed to open so many wounds on my assailant that they end up losing too much blood to continue. Lucky for us I didn't attempt the full force of the spell..."

Nova tilted her head to the side and asked, "Death by a thousand cuts?"

He chuckled. "Something like that." Once his laughter had subsided, he continued, "We'll call it for today. You need to get cleaned up. You ok to walk back?"

"It was one small cut, Jax." She rose to stand, Jax mirroring her actions. "Yes, I'm fine."

They started off in the direction of the cabin. Jax had taken to walking her home now that Kael was not accompanying them. As much as she hated to feel like she needed a protector, and though there hadn't been any indications of the deocre making its way to Aerdmure yet, she appreciated his company nonetheless, especially today. When she was alone, her thoughts tended to wander to Fynn, and that didn't usually end well.

How was it possible to miss someone so much? To feel like part of your soul, part of your very essence, was ripped from you? Like you were no longer whole?

Jax's voice interrupted her thoughts before she could go much further. Thank Canta. "It will probably leave a scar. I'm usually able to heal well enough so that wounds don't scar, but this spell...there's something about it. I haven't quite figured it out, but there's something in the way I've woven it and the way it splits the skin that makes it hard to completely heal."

She turned to look at him, squinting against the late afternoon sun slanting over his shoulder. "It won't completely heal?"

"No, no." He shook his head furiously. "I just mean it leaves a mark. It will scar, and I think the scar is related to the magic that opened the wound in the first place." He paused and drew in a breath. "I'm so sorry. I shouldn't have used that spell without warning you first."

"Yeah, well, I shouldn't have let my guard down." She punched his arm playfully. "Don't beat yourself up about it. I'm fine. There's nothing wrong with a little scar."

No one else was home when they made it back to the cabin. Jax offered to stay to help Nova clean up, but she waved him off. She'd never known him to feel this remorseful. Normally, when he knocked her down or got through her defenses, he would just keep trying harder, would push her harder. But something about drawing blood had been different. Hopefully, tomorrow he'd be back to normal. She didn't need him treating her like glass if he expected to teach her anything.

She wet a rag and stood in front of the small mirror. Dried blood covered one side of her face and her hand, some even having trickled down onto her shirt. It was barely visible on the black, but if someone looked close enough... She'd have to change once she cleaned up. It would be better if Raelyn and Kael didn't see the extent of the damage.

She wiped up the blood, needing to rinse out the rag a few times before she finally got every last speck off her skin. The remaining scar, a small pink line that ran along her cheekbone, was maybe half an inch long.

She sighed.

It would be difficult to hide, but then again, maybe she wouldn't try to hide it. Maybe she could wear it proudly, a symbol of her new life, her new power, her new identity. A reminder of everything she had lost, but everything she had gained as well.

19

FYNN

FYNN VOSS WORKED WITH a renewed vigor as he continued assisting with the research over the next few days. The threat was now real, immediate, and if he had any hope of getting back to Nova, he had to figure this out.

So far, he and the Defiance members had skimmed through all the books in the underground headquarters once. And so far, there was nothing to suggest that the books contained anything about deocres, let alone how to defeat and destroy one. The other members had taken turns sneaking out to libraries, temples, the Atrium...wherever they could scout for more books to bring back. But, of course, since they had to be discreet to avoid unwanted attention, their efforts were mostly for naught.

To ease the cabin fever, Fynn had taken to jogging up and down the hallways. Daro initially wanted to accompany him, but once Fynn promised that he wouldn't pass through a single door, he acquiesced. Now these jogs had become Fynn's chance to clear his mind while keeping his body active. When the time came to fight this demon, he didn't want atrophy to be the reason he couldn't keep up.

And, luckily for him, the tunnels were quite extensive. Each door-way had its own passage, and since it traversed nearly all of Arkwood, the total distance Fynn could cover in a single run was nearly ten miles. Of course, he completed that distance easily, but he didn't have any issue running them over and over...and over again.

He had just returned from one such run—sixty miles today—and was filling a glass of water in their makeshift kitchen. The glass was gone in one gulp, so he refilled it and grabbed a piece of fruit from the counter next to the water barrel.

There was no running water down here, but a hydro among them had been able to pipe in water from a stream. In fact, each member had found a way to contribute, even if only by taking out waste and shopping for food. So far, none of them had been targeted by a tracking spell. That privilege was reserved only for Fynn.

He pulled aside the chair that had become "his" and plopped down next to Elodie, downing the second glass of water.

"Good run?" she asked without looking up from her notes.

"Mmmm," Fynn responded, mouth full of fruit.

The geo's spine straightened. "Fox!" She whipped her head around to look for their leader. Fynn's heart raced—what was she summoning him for? Had she found something?

He tried to lean forward to look at what she'd written, but Fox was there a moment later, hunched over Elodie's shoulder, blocking his view entirely.

She pointed to a line in the book next to her notes with one hand and to a scribble on her notes with the other. "I've read this passage a million times and didn't think anything of it. But today...I don't know. Maybe I'm just getting desperate, but I'm seeing a link here I didn't before."

Fox didn't respond right away, his eyes darting back and forth across the text in the book before skipping over to the scrawled note and reading that, too. The lines in his brow deepened as he read.

Had Elodie actually found something?

Without taking his eyes off the page, Fox said, "So you're thinking we need one of each and the combined strength would do it?"

Elodie nodded vigorously. "You interpret it the same way I do. But—"

"How do we find them?" Fox met her gaze, his eyes wide.

Find them? One of each? What were they talking about?

Elodie shook her head. "I have no idea. The annals haven't been maintained in…"

Fox's face paled. "Twenty years." He drew a sharp breath between his clenched teeth. "And we can't assume he didn't wipe them out further back."

Enough was enough; Fynn needed to know what was going on.

"What are you talking about?"

Elodie and Fox both snapped their heads up to look at him like they had completely forgotten he was right there. Her mouth fell open, but no words came out, and her eyes flicked up to Fox's, as if waiting for his permission.

The human stood and rubbed the back of his neck with one hand. "Elodie is onto something. Except what she has found…it will be nearly impossible to confirm. Impossible to trace. Because the annals are no longer accurate."

It was common knowledge that the governors had stopped maintaining the annals about two decades ago. There was a massive library in the Atrium just for their storage and safekeeping, enchanted with aero spells so the pages of the tomes didn't dry or wither and the ink didn't fade. Though genealogy was an important part of Astrian culture, particularly for witches, maintaining the annals took time, space, and magical effort, which the governors declared a waste of resources.

"Astor." The realization hit Fynn like a ton of bricks. Luc was behind all of this. "They stopped maintaining them twenty years ago...around the same time Luc started stealing power."

Fox's mouth twisted into a wicked grin. "Good, you're catching on. Yes, the High One clued us in to it years ago, thinking it might be important, but until now we weren't sure why he would do that. What Elodie just found, though..."

"What did she find?" Fynn leaned forward, trying to read the pages, but the writing was too small, and he was still too far away.

"El, I think we need to alert the High One," Fox said, completely ignoring Fynn. "Once we run this by the High One and get their thoughts, we can share it with the group. Since you found it, would you like to do the honors?"

Elodie nodded as she tucked her notes into the book as a placeholder and closed the cover. Fynn caught the title—*A Study of Ancient Magicks*—before she pulled the tome to her chest. "I would. Should we go now?"

"They wanted to be alerted as soon as anything was found, so yes, let's go." Fox finally turned to look at Fynn again. "Can I trust you and Daro to hold down the fort until we return? I'm not sure how long this will take."

Fynn stood. "Of course, Fox, but can't you just tell me—"

"No, Fynn." Fox shook his head but kept his gaze locked on Fynn's. "The High One, as our leader, gets to know first. They decide if we do anything with this knowledge, if we take action."

"But we could start getting ready. We could be doing something, not just sitting here waiting for you to return." He could start figuring out what it would take to get back to Nova. His hands trembled with the urge to contribute *something*.

"No, Fynn," Fox repeated, his voice harsher than before. "The time will come for us to make moves, but that time is not now. You're new, so you aren't as used to how we work. All decisions go through the High One before any of us hear about them. It's how we've maintained secrecy for so long, and we aren't about to change that now. You will wait. Come on, El."

Fynn clenched his hands into fists, slamming one on the table. "How do you even know where to find the High One? If no one knows who they are—"

"Fynn." Elodie placed a hand over his fist. "We've developed codes over the years. We have ravens that are trained to find the High One, even if we don't know who or where they are. Usually, we send a message, and, if necessary, the High One arranges a place to meet. Somewhere dark, where faces cannot be revealed. Fox or Persy are the only ones ever to speak directly with the High One."

"Come on, El," Fox repeated through gritted teeth.

"He deserves to know," she said, removing her hand from Fynn's.

"He deserves to let us get on with our business."

With that, Fox turned and walked toward the doorway. Elodie offered Fynn an apologetic look before pushing back her chair, tucking the book under her arm, and jogging after Fox. The two disappeared into the corridor, off to find this mystical "High One," leaving Fynn to sit and wait, to continue doing nothing to get him back to Nova or to clear his name.

20

Nova

"**W**HY DON'T WE TAKE the rest of the day off? Grab some lunch in town?"

Nova stared at Jax like he had grown another head. "Excuse me?"

Jax let out a low laugh. "You've progressed so well. You've blocked every spell I've thrown at you the last two days with ease and have even started throwing them back at me. A break is well earned."

It seemed like he meant it. The smile that spread across his face was genuine. And he was right—she *had* come a long way since he had given her the scar under her right eye that still itched slightly. She'd gotten quicker, her reflexes developing nicely and her endurance even more so.

But Jax never suggested they take a break. He'd only ever given her one day off for Canta's Festival, with the exception being their excursion to Benedict's and the lab. But was that really a day off?

"Are you drunk?" she asked, a hint of sarcasm in her tone.

"Not yet." Jax winked, then waved his arm. "Come on, I'll buy you an ale."

Without waiting to see how she reacted, he pivoted and started walking through the grassy clearing toward the trail that led back to Aerdmure. Nova stood still for a moment, until she was convinced this wasn't all a ploy to catch her off guard, before she gave in and followed him.

She ran a couple of paces to catch up to him. "If I beat you to town, you can buy me two," she said, barely catching his eyes widening before she sprinted off ahead of him.

"You're on!" His voice carried on the breeze, his footsteps picking up pace as they raced to the village.

Nova dared a glance back and saw he was gaining on her, so she summoned her magic and put up her favorite wall of wind between the two of them. The roar of the wind filled her ears, the breeze blowing loose strands from her braid across her face. She turned back around, a grin spreading wide on her face.

"Cheater!" His voice sounded slightly farther away, and his footsteps slowed as he tried to find a way around the wall.

Her foot caught in something thick, something sticky, and she nearly toppled over from the loss of momentum. When she looked down, she found her foot had been trapped in a small patch of quicksand. *Quicksand?! Where did that come from?*

"Now who's a cheater?" she said as she yanked her ankle from the trap.

Jax caught up to her and laughed so hard that he nearly had to stop to collect himself. He slowed enough that, when she found her footing, she was able to bolt off after him and overtake him again.

"See you there!"

They stumbled into the busy tavern a few moments later, Nova just a few paces ahead, but both of them collapsed into fits of laughter as they took a seat at the bar. Other patrons watched them warily, going momentarily silent before resuming their meals and conversations, having decided that the two who stumbled in were harmless. Nova's body shook as her lungs tried to keep up, to keep oxygen flowing through her body despite the run and the laughter that followed.

She hadn't laughed like this since they'd come back to Aerdmure. It was refreshing. This feeling...this was something she needed more of.

"You owe me two," she managed to say between gasps of breath, looking over at Jax as he sat on the barstool beside her.

His cheeks were flushed slightly pink from exertion, and his green eyes were wild with glee. Apparently, he had needed this laugh, this moment of fun, just as much as she had.

"Fine." He signaled to the bartender to bring them two drinks. "One now, one after we eat."

The petite female geo tending the bar slid two tankards of ale their way. Jax caught them both, passed one to Nova, and held his up for a toast.

She raised an eyebrow. This was going to be good.

"To people who don't play fair." He clinked his tankard against hers.

But she couldn't take a sip because she was consumed by another fit of giggles.

"Fancy seeing you two here," a familiar voice rang out from the doorway.

Nova managed to collect herself enough to stop laughing and turned to face the voice, her eyes widening. "Mehta, hi! Care to join us for lunch?"

The way his eyes darted toward Jax's momentarily before coming back to hers...there was something in that gaze. What was it?

"No, I—"

But Jax interrupted him. "Sit, Mehta." He gestured to the empty barstool on Nova's other side.

Mehta stood for a moment, his narrowed eyes on Jax, but he responded, "All right, if you insist."

Yes, something was definitely going on here. They'd been friendly just the other day at training, and yet today was...different.

Nova sipped her beer, then leaned back slightly so the two male wielders could see each other. They seemed to be purposefully avoiding looking at one another, Jax staring up at the ceiling and Mehta signaling to the bartender for a drink.

All right, give them a drink or two. Then she'd start asking questions.

Once Mehta had his ale, he turned back to Nova, pointed to her scar, and said, "What happened to your eye? That wasn't there last time I saw you, was it?"

"Nope." She glanced quickly at Jax. "This one got a spell on me during training the other day. A new spell he's been working on himself."

Mehta's forehead wrinkled as his eyebrows knit together. "You're trying *new* spells on her now, Jax?" He took a long swig of his ale.

"She's advanced enough to handle it." Jax's tone was firm, defensive.

"Yes, clearly." Mehta rolled his eyes. Nova pretended not to hear the jab, downing a large portion of her beer instead.

The bartender came by to take their orders for lunch, then set about preparing the meals.

"So," Nova started, trying to break through the tension that was settling in around them and find the levity they'd shared a few days ago. "Mehta, how did you figure out you could jump?"

She'd asked the right question, because his dark eyes lit up. "Funny story, actually. I was about thirteen, and my parents had locked me in my room for breaking some rule or another. I was so mad that they were going to make me miss a camping trip with my friends, so I stewed about it on my bed for a while. Apparently, I stewed hard enough to make myself jump, because next thing I knew I was at the campsite, scaring my friends half to death with my sudden appearance."

"Yeah, Bodhi nearly shit his pants," Jax added without looking at them.

Nova whipped her head around to look at Jax, her braid falling over her shoulder in the process. "You were there? You two go that far back?"

Jax just sipped his beer. "Oh, I was there."

The bartender set their food—grilled chicken with vegetables—in front of them. Jax reached for a chicken leg and bit down, tearing the meat from the bone in one pull.

"Anyway," Mehta continued, picking up his fork and knife to cut into the chicken. *Like a civilized person,* Nova thought. "My parents were even more furious when I got home. They were so mad at me for jumping—in the middle of my punishment, no less—that they had anti-jumping wards placed around the entire house."

"They trapped you at home?" Nova took a bite of the vegetables, the heat burning her tongue slightly. She chased it with a sip of cool ale.

If Mehta was put off by her deeply personal question, he didn't show it. "I was adopted. My parents didn't know I was a wielder when they took me in, and once my powers revealed themselves, they did everything they could to keep others from finding out. For my protection."

"Bullshit," Jax said under his breath, barely audible over the hum of the tavern at lunchtime. Any residual humor in his body from their run was gone, replaced only by tension and angst that Nova could have sliced through with a dagger. "They always wanted to suppress you."

Mehta sighed and set down his fork. "Jax has never believed that my parents were worried about me. He's always felt they were trying to force me to be something I'm not. To keep me from my full potential."

"Because it's the fucking truth!" Jax slammed a palm on the counter, then downed the rest of his beer. The barkeep looked their way with wide eyes, shaking her head as she returned to her work.

Nova stared at Jax for a moment before turning away to focus solely on Mehta. *Parental suppression of your true identity*—now that was something she could relate to. That was something she could talk about. But it also seemed like there was more to this story. "And what's your truth, Mehta?"

He finished the rest of his ale, signaling to the barkeep for another before he responded. "It's not a good time to be a wielder. The government regulations, the fear-mongering...I can understand why they did what they did."

"And that's where we will always disagree." Jax's teeth were clenched together, his gaze still everywhere but on Mehta and Nova.

"Ok," Nova said, raising her voice slightly. "What am I missing here?"

She moved her head from side to side, looking between the two male wielders, waiting for one of them to speak first. It didn't matter which one—there was clearly something going on between them that needed to be hashed out.

Mehta drew in a deep breath and sighed. "It's the one thing we've never agreed on. It's the thing that drove us apart."

His voice was laced with sorrow, with heartbreak, and his gaze drifted toward Jax with something like love and grief mixed up in his eyes.

Wait—had they been...together?

"He...saved me. Jax is the one who came and risked everything to pull me out of that house when I was eighteen. Brought me here, helped me learn how to be a wielder, just like he's doing with you." Mehta hung his head, his palms pressing into his thighs as he continued. "I owe him everything for that."

The favor Jax called in to have Mehta jump them to the lab. This was it. Jax had saved him. Had taught him. Had allowed him to become the best, most powerful version of himself, the same way he had done with her. The same way he *continued* to do with her every day.

Her gaze slowly wandered over to Jax, who had his elbows on the bar, his palms digging into his forehead as he stared at his lap. She hadn't seen him this emotional since the day they'd gone through Margot's journals together.

"But," Mehta continued, wiping his palms on his pants, "he could never get past the forgiveness I offered my parents. That I wanted to rebuild a relationship with them." He lifted his head and turned toward Jax, looking over Nova to meet his gaze. "If you could give them a chance—"

But before Mehta could finish, before Jax could answer, the door to the tavern burst open with a slam. Nova's head whipped instinctively toward the sound, but she caught Mehta's exhale and slump as she did. Her heart ached for him, but only for a moment because—

"There you are!"

Raelyn came bounding through the tavern, Esta and Kael, still in his disguise, close on her heels. Her sister's face was flushed, her curly hair blown back from her face like she'd been running.

Raelyn? Running?

"We've been looking everywhere for you," Raelyn said as she approached, folding her arms across her chest. "The clearing, the cabin...finally, Esta thought maybe you'd be in town, which was ridiculous, but apparently not *that* ridiculous—"

Kael cleared his throat.

"Right." Raelyn straightened and let her hands fall to her sides. "We were at the temple, and Silvana came up to us, saying she had an urgent message for us."

Nova's pulse started racing. Was it Fynn? Was he ok? Was he on his way? Or was it something more sinister? Had the deocre attacked?

But it was Jax who collected himself enough to speak. His face had been rearranged into its usual mask of indifference and arrogance, a stark change from the raw emotion he'd let loose just moments ago.

"What did it say?"

Raelyn grabbed Nova's hands. "Mother has summoned us. To the cottage." She paused and drew in a deep breath, a mischievous grin spreading across her face. "She has something she wants to tell us. About Father."

21

Nova

M OTHER MUST HAVE FOUND *out about Luc's death. She must know.*

Guilt crashed over Nova like a tsunami. If she hadn't already been sitting down, she would have crumpled under the weight of it.

She should have prioritized Mother. She and Raelyn should have sent word to her, should have tried to get her to come to Aerdmure. Everything had happened so fast, and despite the revelations about Nova's true parentage, despite Raella not always treating her with the most love and respect, Raella had still raised her. Had still lost her husband.

She deserved better from her daughters. Didn't she?

"When can we leave?" Nova asked, staring into her sister's dark brown eyes that seemed full of joy more than anything else.

Raelyn continued to beam. "First thing tomorrow. Silvana is arranging horses for us, so we don't have to walk. If we move swiftly, we can be there in three days."

"Let's get back to the cabin." Nova jumped off her stool, releasing her sister's hands. Under her breath, she added, "We can talk more freely there."

To her surprise, Jax followed suit, throwing a few coins on the counter as he stood. "I'm coming, too." Nova's eyes flicked over to Mehta, who turned back to his now-empty plate and shook his head almost imperceptibly. There was unfinished business here. She wouldn't push Jax today, but maybe she could get him to open up on the journey, or while they were in Adenaport.

"Good. We can continue my training once we get there." She studied his gaze, looking for any signs of the emotions he had borne just moments ago, but all traces were gone, replaced by his usual stoicism. Turning to Kael, she added softly, "I assume you are coming, too?"

He smiled. "Where you go, I go, Nova."

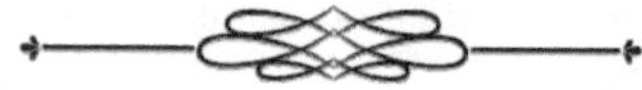

A few hours later, Nova stuffed as much as she could into her pack, déjà vu sweeping over her. Had it been only a week ago that she had done this to go find Benedict?

Had it only been a week since she'd seen Fynn?

Her heart ached for him, so much that her shoulders sagged under the weight of it. What if he came back to Aerdmure, and they were gone? What if he was on his way now? Leaving would only prolong their separation.

But it was the right thing to do. Seeing Mother, learning what she had to say—it could all be relevant. It could be helpful to their fight against the deocre. Maybe Mother knew what Luc had been up to. Maybe she had even worked with him on it. If they could get any bit of information out of her that pointed them in the right direction, the trip would be worth it. And they could always come back to Aerdmure if she proved unhelpful.

Or if it proved to be a trap.

The thought had crossed Nova's mind once the initial shock had worn off. There was a very real chance that Mother had summoned them to Adenaport under the guise of needing to tell them something, when the deocre was actually with her or, worse, controlling her. How far was it willing to go to protect itself?

Would the imprint of Luc's soul hesitate to harm his wife and daughter?

Of course, it wouldn't hesitate to kill Nova, but Raella and Raelyn *had* to be safe from its wrath. Despite Luc attacking Raelyn in the lab, she still believed that Luc would never seriously hurt his own flesh and blood. Maybe she was being naive. There'd been a lot of that lately.

Regardless, she wasn't going to Adenaport without an escape plan or back-up, in case things went south and their lives became threatened. Especially Raelyn's. Jax and Esta were obviously going to be critical for protecting her sister, and Nova's training had only increased her confidence in her abilities.

Plus, Kael would be with them. How they would explain his presence to Mother was something they would need to figure out on the way there. But if Mother knew what Luc had done, how he had turned on Kael, that Kael was innocent...well, then it could end up being a reunion of long-lost friends.

Nova straightened as Kael passed through her mind. Since he had started going to the library, she hadn't gotten to see as much of him or spend much time with him. And she'd completely forgotten, until just now, that he had the ability to send messages.

She dropped her pack to the floor and turned to face the kitchen. Kael stood there, preparing dinner while she, Raelyn, and Esta packed. He was currently hovering over a chopping block, directing a knife to magically slice the vegetables. His movements were so natural, so choreographed, it was hard to believe he'd been imprisoned and not regularly cooking for nearly two and a half decades.

Maybe he'd been the chef of the family. She'd have to remember to ask him.

But now, she had more important things to ask.

She moved past Raelyn, who was mumbling under her breath as she knelt to fish something out from under the bed, and toward Kael in the kitchen.

"Can you send another message to Fynn?"

Kael jumped, turning to face her with wide eyes. The knife fell to the counter, the spell that was controlling it having broken when she startled him.

"I'm so sorry!" she said. "I didn't mean to scare you."

He placed a hand on her elbow. "I'm a little jumpier than I used to be."

Right. Mistfell probably had that effect on people. Nova made a mental note to be more cautious around him, to announce her presence better in the future. She opened her mouth to apologize again, but he smiled, dropping his hand and waving it back at the knife, which resumed its task.

"You want me to let Fynn know we are moving?"

Her heart skipped a beat. He already knew her so well. "If you don't mind."

"Not at all. In fact…" The knife finished its chopping, and Kael moved it to the sink, wiping his hands on a towel before continuing, "I've been working on an amendment to that spell. I was going to tell you soon, when I was sure it was ready, but now is as good a time as any to try. I think I can send a message that *you* speak, so Fynn would hear it in your voice."

Nova's hand flew to her mouth, the tension that had been building in her heart now rushing to a lump in her throat. Fynn could hear her voice. He'd know the message was from her and that she was well.

She would've given anything to hear his voice, so she could only imagine how he'd react to hearing hers.

"Do you want to try it?" Kael held out a hand, his eyes shining with pride that he could do something for her.

Nova nodded, placing her hand in his, the warmth from his hand engulfing hers. "Thank you, Kael."

"Anything for you." He blinked away a tear, then closed his eyes and drew in a deep breath. "Whenever you're ready, just think the words you want him to hear in your mind."

She studied her father for a moment as she tried to find the right words to say to Fynn. After a week apart, there was so much she wanted to tell him, so much she wanted to convey. But she needed to be concise to ensure that the whole message was received.

So, a moment later, she closed her eyes, too. Fynn's face swam in the front of her mind, those midnight eyes flecked with stars, that long white-blond hair blowing in an invisible wind, as she used her magic to push a message through her hand into Kael's, and then—hopefully—to Fynn.

22

FYNN

FYNN WAS PACING THE cavernous chamber when it happened.

Yesterday, when Fox and Elodie returned from delivering their message to the High One, bringing with them good news, the group had decided that they earned a day off. Some—those lucky ones who didn't have a target on their back—decided to go above ground for the day, while others were celebrating with whiskey below.

They'd done it.

They'd found the way to defeat the deocre and delivered the message to the High One, who would now put a plan in place. Fox still hadn't shared what the book had said, on the High One's orders apparently, but his ebullience was contagious. Whatever had happened during their meeting with the High One, it had been very good.

But Fynn wasn't in a celebratory mood. Of course, he was happy they'd found a way to quell the threat of the deocre, but he still didn't know what that actually meant, what it would cost. Would it be easy? How much time would it take to execute?

How much longer before he could finish what he came here for? Before he could return to Aerdmure and reunite with Nova?

Which is how he found himself pacing, thinking of her, willing his heart not to shatter, when he felt it again. That breeze. The same exact breeze that had tickled his skin just a few nights ago when it told him Nova was safe. But this time...

His spine straightened, and he stilled.

A different voice carried over the wind this time. A voice he'd recognize anywhere. A voice that could bring him to his knees.

Nova.

There was no mistaking it. This message was from her.

Fynn, we are moving to Adenaport. Mother has summoned us, and though part of me fears it's a trap, I think we could learn something important, too. Find us at the cottage, Fynn. I love you. I miss you.

The breeze and the echo of her voice in his ears stopped as abruptly as it started. He whipped around, grasping frantically at nothing but air as he tried to find that voice and bring it back.

It had gone too quickly.

"Fynn?"

The drawl of Elodie's voice brought him back to the room. He looked over his shoulder to where she, Fox, and Daro were standing around the table of maps, and found three sets of eyes staring at him. Fox's eyebrows were halfway up his forehead while Daro wore a smirk of amusement.

Fynn must have looked ridiculous, chasing after and grabbing nothing but air.

"Did...any of you hear that?" He turned his whole body to face them, his eyes darting among theirs, looking for a sign, for any indication, that they'd heard it, too.

Fox crossed his arms, but his eyebrows didn't lower. "Hear what?"

"That voice?" Even he had to admit that he sounded crazy. He should've kept his damn mouth shut.

Elodie, Fox, and Daro exchanged glances with each other. Great, now not only did they think they had a murderer among them, but also a psychopath who heard voices.

To his surprise, Elodie stepped forward. "I didn't hear a voice, Fynn. Whatever you heard must have been meant for your ears only."

Well, he could've told her that much already. But at least she didn't think he was crazy.

"Did you recognize the voice?" Elodie took another step, slowly making her way closer to Fynn.

He nodded, recalling the words that voice of silk had spoken in his mind just moments before. The pressure in his chest built up so much that he thought he might burst. "Nova."

Elodie stepped closer, placing a delicate hand on his arm. "Is there anything in the message that we should know?"

Fynn lifted his gaze from the floor and met Elodie's brown eyes, grateful that she was not demanding he share the entire message. But was it worth sharing that they were moving? That Raella had summoned them? It was likely that Raella wanted them together to mourn the loss of Luc. But Nova had mentioned a possible trap—good; she was being smart. Did that mean she didn't fully trust Raella? Did she think that Raella could be involved or controlled by the deocre?

It really wasn't so far-fetched.

"She and her sister are moving to Adenaport. Their mother summoned them." The words were barely more than a whisper, but the light squeeze on his arm told him that Elodie had heard.

"We'll find a way to get you there soon," she whispered in reply, a hint of a smile gracing her lips. "Fox will need to tell us how to get you past the wall first."

"The wall?" He raised a brow at her. No one had mentioned anything about the wall to him yet, not in the entire week he'd been down here. "What's going on with the wall?"

"The High One has been working on fortifying it," Fox responded, his eyebrows finally returning to their usual place. He pulled out a map from the bottom of the stack and placed it on top, motioning for Fynn and Elodie to come closer. "They have been working to build enchantments around the wall to prevent the deocre from crossing it." His index finger traced the circular line of the wall that ran along the outer border of Arkwood on all sides, crossing over the river twice.

"They want to trap the deocre in Arkwood? Endangering everyone here?" Fynn couldn't believe it. The havoc—the *destruction* the deocre could wreak...

But Fox then pointed to the rest of Astria, the part that lay outside the walls of Arkwood. "No," he said. "They want to prevent it from destroying all of Astria. Keep it in Arkwood, where it will be easier to find, easier to contain, easier to track. If it gets beyond the wall, it could become impossible to locate and destroy."

He made a fair point. And Fynn had to admit that it made him feel better about Nova's safety, too. If the deocre couldn't get out of Arkwood, she was safe.

"How good are the enchantments?" he asked, glancing between Fox and Daro.

Daro shrugged. "They haven't let the deocre escape yet, but we also don't know if it's tried or if the enchantments have been tested. But we do know that, unfortunately, they prevent anyone from leaving...easily."

The moment of relief passed as quickly as it came. At any moment, the deocre could become strong enough to test the enchantments. At any moment, Nova could be in danger again.

He slammed a hand on the table. "I need to get to Adenaport."

"And risk getting caught again?" Daro asked. Though his tone was incredulous, his posture was relaxed. "I don't think that's a great idea, Fynn."

Elodie looked up at him. "I know you want to get to Nova, Fynn, but we need a plan. It's not good rushing out there without a plan, just for you to get caught and never even make it to her."

Never.

Never make it to her.

He could have vomited at the thought, but he held himself together. Pressing his palms into the table of maps to steady himself, he said, "Then where do we start?"

23

Nova

"**I** SEE THE TOWN!"

Raelyn kicked her heels into the side of her black mare. It picked up its gait, pushing into a canter, leaving a cloud of dust behind the pair as they made their way into town.

Next to her, Nova heard Esta groan before clicking her tongue and forcing her own steed after Raelyn.

They'd been traveling all day, keeping to the main roads despite having Kael with them. He remained in disguise, pretending to be Nova's bodyguard, a fictional male of his own creation named Will. For the first half of the ride, Nova had remained tense, ever fearful that each village they passed on the way to their first stop, each citizen or nomad they came upon on the road, would recognize "Will" for who he was and turn him in.

But no one had given him a second glance. In fact, no one seemed to care at all about the crew of five that was traversing Astria from Aerdmure to Adenaport. Either because they were used to travelers, or because fear around Blackmore's escape was still so heightened that people kept their heads down, going about their business as quickly as they could.

Nova had to admit she was relieved that they'd made it to the small village of Granby, where Silvana had arranged for them to stay for the night. In fact, Silvana had taken it upon herself to arrange the whole journey, sending word ahead to three inns that they would be able to stay in each night.

"I don't want you to worry about finding a safe place to stay," she'd told them when she stopped by the cabin last night to say goodbye. "You've enough on your plates to be getting on with as it is."

Nova knew she'd been referring to saving Astria from the deocre, coming to terms with Luc's atrocities, and finding out Nova's real identity. Silvana hadn't needed to voice any of it because the tension was palpable enough. The weight of it all hung heavily over the group like a storm cloud.

But for now, Nova only looked forward to getting off this goddess-damned horse, letting her hips relax, and eating a proper meal. As she and her horse crossed into the town, the smell of a wood-fired grill hit her like a wave, her stomach grumbling in retort.

She looked down the main thoroughfare and saw Raelyn and Esta not far ahead, dismounting at the entrance to a large building with a wooden sign bearing a pig on it. The Pig's Tail. That's what Silvana had said the inn would be called. An odd name for an inn, Nova had thought at the time, but right now, she couldn't have cared less.

The main road was lined with wooden buildings, most two to three stories tall, and citizens of the town were out in full force, enjoying the early evening reprieve from the late summer heat in the shadows cast down from the enormous deciduous trees that lined the street. Horses pulled carts up and down the road, but there were no carriages here. There was no need for carriages when the town was this small and walking everywhere was the norm. If Nova had to guess, only a few hundred people called this place their home. Mostly humans, if what she saw as they made their way to the inn was any indication.

"I'm *dying* for a drink," Raelyn said, tying her horse's reins to the porch post as Nova dismounted.

"I'm dying for dinner." Nova unbuckled her pack from the back of the saddle and slung it over her shoulder as Kael and Jax tied their horses up beside her. "Or a bath."

Raelyn laughed. "Dinner first. Come on!" She turned and bounced up the two steps to the porch, then pushed open the swinging doors of the main entrance, Esta and Jax following closely behind.

Nova was about to follow when a small tug on her elbow stopped her. Whipping her head around, she readied herself to attack until her eyes met a pair that looked just like hers. Despite the disguise, he always kept his eyes the same.

"If it's ok with you, I'll take dinner in my room tonight?" Kael asked. "I could use the break for my magic. The constant use of this spell is wearing on me."

Not to mention he hadn't slept in a proper bed in decades. When she had realized how well his disguise was working, she tried to convince him to get a room in Aerdmure, rather than continue to stay in the woods near the cabin. He'd waved her off, saying he was fine, but she had a feeling he just hadn't wanted to be that far from her.

Honestly, she had been glad to know he was still close.

Nova exhaled and smiled. "Of course. Let's go see the innkeeper. I'd like to drop my bag in my room anyway."

The first floor of the inn was a bustling tavern filled with wooden tables and chairs haphazardly strewn around the open room in between the large posts that held up the ceiling. Evening light streamed in from the windows on the front and side walls, but lamps hung from the ceiling as well. Raelyn, Jax, and Esta were making themselves comfortable at a table near the back of the room. The smell of roasted chicken, stew, and…something sweet made Nova want to join them, but she forced herself to turn toward the innkeeper's desk at the left of the entryway and ask for the keys for her and Kael's rooms.

Her voice trailed off as her gaze landed on a poster: one with Kael's face on it, very much like the ones she had seen all over Arkwood. It hung on the wall just over the innkeeper's shoulder. Her spine straightened. She chanced a quick glimpse at Kael and saw his eyes widen. So he'd seen it, too.

But then his eyes turned to her. One corner of his mouth ticked up into a reassuring smile, and his hand gave hers a quick squeeze.

He didn't look anything like the man in that poster right now. *Calm down, don't make a scene.*

"Ah, yes, Ms. Astor and friends, welcome," the elderly man behind the desk said as he shuffled through his box of metal keys. "I must extend my condolences on the death of your father." He straightened, plucking a key from the box and handing it to her.

Her body tensed, not entirely sure how to respond. She held out her hand for the key and mumbled, "Thanks."

"I do hope they catch that elf who did it," the gray-haired man continued as he dug around for Kael's key. "'Tis a shame that he went the way he did."

Nova froze, her gaze sweeping toward Kael, but he remained unchanged, his face relaxed, his body loose as he held out his hand for his own key. Once he had it, he looked at her, his head shaking almost imperceptibly when he saw the shock on her face.

"It's very troubling for her to talk about," Kael said gently to the innkeeper. "Thank you for the keys." He put a hand on Nova's back, guiding her over to the staircase, then up the stairs to the hallway containing their rooms.

She wasn't sure how her feet were moving, how she found the right door, but she was sure she wouldn't have if it weren't for Kael. Her mind was swarmed with thoughts of Fynn, of the fact that he was now being targeted for Luc's death. And he was in Arkwood, where it would be all too easy to track him.

Metal clanged as Kael inserted a key into a door to her right, then the squeal of rusty hinges filled the hallway as he pushed the door open. He pulled Nova into the room after him. Her eyes took a moment to adjust to the low light.

The dark curtains around the single window in the room were drawn, casting the room in dark shadow, but Kael quickly lit the lamps on either side of the bed with a wave of his hand. The glow illuminated a single bed in the middle of the small room and a bureau with three drawers opposite the window.

Tiny, but sufficient for the night.

Kael set down his pack, his gaze resting for a moment on the bed before turning to Nova with something like excitement in his eyes. She wished she could match it and join in the thrill of a room all to himself, but her thoughts were still a tangled mess of worries.

"They're after Fynn." Her voice cracked as she spoke, barely audible above the noises from the tavern below. "He went to Arkwood to prevent this from getting out, but it got out anyway." He must not have been successful at convincing Persy. What did that mean about what was happening to Fynn right now?

A lump formed in her throat, one she unsuccessfully tried to swallow down. Her eyes prickled with tears.

Kael was there in an instant, pulling her close to him. He was tall—tall enough that her head barely hit his shoulder—so she found herself nestled into his chest, his arms wrapped around her back, one hand resting on her hair. His embrace made her feel...content. Like a purring cat had curled onto her chest. This was the first time they had hugged, but it would not be the last.

A father's hug, like she had never experienced before.

Protective. Soothing. Full of love.

Breathe, breathe, she reminded herself. She had much better control of her magic than she did even a week ago, but these emotions were fuel for its fire burning inside her. The last thing she needed was to cause a scene with her magic erupting in the Pig's Tail.

But the single breath was enough. Or maybe it was the comfort of the hug. Her magic responded more quickly than it usually did, settling down into a soft purr in her chest.

"We don't know all that the deocre is capable of." When Kael spoke, his chest vibrated against her cheek. "It's possible Fynn did get to Persy, and they're trying to sort it out, but the deocre got word about Fynn out in the meantime. The innkeeper said they're still looking for him. Which means they don't have him. He's *safe*."

She drew her head back sharply to meet Kael's eyes and found that he had transformed into himself again. He must have seen the worry in her eyes because he let out a low laugh and said, "The door is closed. I wanted you to see *me* right now."

As the initial shock of seeing him wore off, the impact of his words set in. Fynn hadn't been caught yet. Fynn was still safe as far as she knew. In the moment, she'd been so consumed with fear, she hadn't comprehended the full extent of what the innkeeper had said.

Nova wiped a tear from her cheek. "You're right. He's still out there. He'll find a way to get to Adenaport." His Academy training would be put to the test, but he'd make it.

Kael let his arms drop back to his side, a chill brushing over Nova's skin where theirs no longer met. The purr in her chest turned to a hiss, but she managed to still it with her breath and sheer will.

"Go," he said, a smile on his face. "Get some food with the others. I'm sure Raelyn is wondering where you are."

She nodded and turned to the door to leave. "I'll bring something up for you."

"Don't worry about it. I'll be asleep the moment I hit that pillow." She looked back just in time to see him gaze at the bed longingly.

His eyes slowly turned back to meet hers, and heat rose to her cheeks at being caught watching him. But his gaze was soft, gentle, like coming home.

Just before she left, she met his eyes and said something she'd been wanting to say for a while. "Thank you...Father."

She didn't stay to see his reaction. But as she turned back to the door, she could've sworn that, out of the corner of her eye, she saw his mouth drop to the floor.

And, indeed—when she brought up a shepherd's pie for him to eat an hour later, he was fast asleep, snoring in his bed, the ghost of a smile still etched on his face.

24

Nova

THE STAIRS CREAKED UNDER Nova's feet as she padded down them the next morning in search of coffee. She'd woken up refreshed but sore. Coffee wouldn't fix the soreness, but it would help prepare her for another day in the saddle.

The tavern was mostly empty, save for one female standing near the bar. Esta. It was odd to see her alone. She didn't usually let Raelyn out of her sight.

"Morning," Nova said as she sidled up next to Esta. The elf cocked an eyebrow, probably at the rasp in her voice. She cleared her throat and tried again. "Good morning."

"Good morning." Esta took a sip from her steaming mug. The smell hit Nova's nose like an oncoming carriage, awakening the side of her that clamored for the brew every morning.

Thankfully, there was a carafe of it and a few extra mugs on the bartop. Great hospitality if Nova had ever seen it. She poured herself a mug and asked, "How is the coffee here?"

Esta shrugged. "It's not Raelyn's."

Nova snorted. "No. There is no comparison to Raelyn's." She lifted the mug to her lips and sipped. The hot drink scorched her tongue, making her blink furiously as it trickled down her throat.

"It's hot," Esta warned.

"Thanks for the heads up." Nova wiped the tears that formed in the corners of her eyes. She'd give it a minute before she sipped again. "Where's Rae?"

Esta nodded toward the stairs. "Still sleeping. I didn't want to disturb her."

"We'll have to soon," Nova said, tapping her thumb on the handle of her mug. "Need to get back on our way." She glanced over her shoulder toward the windows that overlooked the shady dirt road outside. Very few people were out this early. The sky was still a grayish blue, the sun barely above the horizon.

"She needs to rest." Esta's voice was harsh enough that Nova flinched. But in the next breath, Esta's face softened, her chin tilting down. From this angle, Nova could clearly see the scar on her temple, which, once again, sent her heart into a guilt-ridden spiral. Esta muttered into her mug, "I mean, we all do."

Nova took another sip of her coffee, more tentatively this time. It didn't burn and instead went down easily. *Much better.* "I'm going to head back up and get ready." She took a step away, then turned back toward Esta, the guilt forcing her to say something more. "Hey, Esta?"

The elf's brown eyes met hers.

"Thanks for taking such good care of her. Of Raelyn. She's not always the easiest to get along with, but you've made it look effortless, even if it didn't start that way." She smiled, but didn't wait for Esta to reply before heading back toward the stairs, mug in hand.

An hour later, Nova, Raelyn, Jax, Esta, and a disguised Kael set off again toward Adenaport. Nova was pleased they'd gotten on their way early, even if Raelyn had grumbled at being woken up "so goddess-damn early." They had a lot of ground to cover to make it to the next town Silvana had arranged for them.

She couldn't remember the last time she'd ridden a horse for this long, and her hips and back were feeling it. Try as she might to summon any kind of magic that would soothe her aching body, she was unsuccessful and had to resort to "sucking it up," to quote Raelyn.

"There really isn't any magic for it," Jax said, falling behind the others, riding beside her. "Just so you know. Don't feel bad about it."

"I just thought with my mother's healer magic, I'd be able to do something..."

Jax laughed. "It's been centuries, and even the healers haven't figured out how to solve pains for horseback riding. Don't you think it'd be well-known if they had?"

She pursed her lips, unwilling to admit he was right.

The other three were far enough ahead of them to be out of earshot but still within sight. The late morning sun had crossed the tree line, shining right in Nova's eyes. She put a hand to her forehead to shield them and turned to face Jax.

There was something that had been bothering her about their conversation with Mehta in the bar back in Aerdmure. Something unresolved that she couldn't help but feel like she wanted to fix.

"So," she began. Jax narrowed his green eyes at her, almost like he knew what she was about to say and was begging her not to. But she pushed on. "You and Mehta?"

He turned back, his gaze now facing forward, his eyes turned down against the sun. Silence reigned for so long, she wondered if he had even heard her or if she should drop it, but just when she was about to trot up alongside Raelyn, he spoke. "We were together for about five years. He ended it with me because I didn't want him to forgive his parents, but he did, and we couldn't move past it."

"It's really none of my business—"

Jax scoffed. "Then why are you asking me about this?"

"Because, believe it or not, Jax, you're my friend, and I generally like it when my friends are happy." She paused, watching him, but he didn't speak. Their horses continued moving forward together at the same pace. "It was clear there are still feelings there even after all these years."

Silence again. But was that redness building on Jax's face? From anger or embarrassment, she couldn't tell, but his normally olive-colored skin was definitely reddening.

"Our first big fight," Jax's voice was barely above a whisper, "that's how I discovered my persuasion abilities. I accidentally used it against him to convince him to stop talking to his parents. I realized right away what had happened but hadn't yet learned how to reverse it." He drew in a deep breath and then exhaled. "I have to be careful with my power. It took me a long time to learn to control it, to not use it against people I care about or for the wrong reasons."

Nova wound the reins she was holding around one hand, reaching out with the other to squeeze Jax's arm. "If there's anyone who can relate to that, it's me. You're not a bad person, Jax."

They rounded a bend and found themselves deeper in the trees, now fully shielded from the sun's light by the canopy.

"I wanted to use it on his parents." Jax finally turned to look at her again, his eyes blazing. "To persuade them to see sense, to let him be who he wants to be. Who he was born to be. But he wouldn't let me."

"I don't blame him—"

"Neither do I, Nova. But I was desperate. I could feel him slipping away from me..."

His voice trailed off as he glanced forward at their companions. Nova followed his gaze, expecting to find them focused on the trail or a tree up ahead, but instead it appeared his eyes were boring into the back of Esta's head, like he wanted to try out that new curse on her.

But, just as quickly as his gaze had turned feral, it softened again. "His adoptive parents are elves."

She whipped her head around to face him, her braid falling over her shoulder. "That's why you don't trust Fynn. Why you have a hard time with Esta."

His immediate dislike of Fynn. Mehta's reaction to Fynn the night he had jumped them to the lab. It all made sense now.

"I hate that it affects me the way it does, but when you see someone you love struggle so hard with...a specific race, it has an impact on you."

Their horses rode on in silence for a few moments, Nova's brain whirling with the new information. She'd just unlocked new personal details about Jax, the wielder who had taken the time to train her and help her for nothing in return. Her heart ached for him, for the past trauma he had borne, not only for his mother's death and his father's ensuing deterioration, but also for the heartbreak he had suffered.

"Hey, slowpokes!"

Nova looked up to see Raelyn waving at them from her saddle.

"Hurry it up or we'll be out here all night!"

Nova waved her off. "We're right behind you! Keep your eyes ahead before you fall off your horse again!"

Raelyn pouted and spun her head back around, straightening her shoulders. Nova smiled, remembering very clearly the moment she could never let her sister forget.

Jax's voice brought her back to the present. "She fell off her horse?"

"Oh yes, when she was about seven."

"Seven?" He raised a brow. "That was a long time ago."

Nova shrugged. "There are some things you never quite get over. That moment has been cemented in my mind ever since."

Jax just glared at her.

"What? She wasn't hurt. She fell in a mud puddle, despite her geo powers being well enough developed by then to have corrected that before she landed. We all thought it was funny, and it's my job as her sister to remind her of her past faults."

A small pang lashed at her stomach as the memory took shape with more clarity in her mind. Mother and Luc had been there. Mother had gotten off her horse immediately and run to Raelyn's aid; Luc had stayed atop his, watching the scene from above, a look of amusement in his eye that matched Nova's.

They'd laughed about it together later.

What a difference time had made. Had that been a rare moment of Luc setting aside power and manipulation to...laugh? Had there been a true bond between them, even if only for a moment?

"Anyway." She needed to change the subject. Needed to stop feeling anything for Luc right now, at least until they had answers from Mother. "Tell me more about Mehta. How your relationship developed."

"His family—" Jax said, his voice cracking. He cleared his throat and started again. "They were a safe haven for me after my mom died. When my father was off dealing with the aftermath, I was at Mehta's, shielded from the worst of it. We had always been friends, he and I, but those formative years after her death are what took us...further.

"But, as you can imagine," he continued, "after the camping trip, we couldn't see much of each other. We tried finding different ways to communicate, tried to find ways to still see each other, but his parents found out and put a stop to it. I'm sure to this day they consider me a bad influence. And maybe they're right." His mouth ticked up into a meek grin.

"It sounds to me like 'bad influence' is just one side of the story," Nova said. "The other is someone who's caring, loyal, and protective of someone in need."

Jax let out a low laugh, and at the sound, Nova exhaled a breath she hadn't realized she'd been holding. "And you, Nova Astor, have a knack for always saying exactly the right thing."

Heat rushed to her cheeks. She kept her eyes trained ahead on the rest of their group, nearing where the tree line opened into a grassy field a few hundred feet ahead. "I don't know about that."

"Somehow you've got me talking about something I haven't spoken to anyone about—except Mehta. Something I've always felt horrible about because I couldn't get Mehta to see my side of the story. But you're right. There are two sides."

Nova unwound the reins from her hand, rubbing at the red marks the leather had made on her wrist. "Maybe," she said, "and hear me out here. Maybe you can give Mehta another chance to tell his story when you get back to Aerdmure. Maybe you can give Fynn and Esta a break and treat them like the rest of us."

Jax paused for a moment, his gaze trained on the path ahead and his brow furrowed as he pondered Nova's words. Had she gone too far? She truly only wanted to help.

"I don't know, Nova." He looked at her with a glimmer of mischief in his green eyes.

She tilted her head to the side, an invitation for him to continue.

"I can probably work on it, but...you think Fynn will forgive me for that scar?" His gaze fell to her cheekbone, where the faint pink remnant from days ago was still visible, but his mouth broke into a wide grin.

"Oh, I'll make sure of that." She winked at him, then kicked her heels into her horse's sides. "Come on—race you to the clearing!"

Her horse picked up its pace, Jax's laugh drowned out by the sounds of hooves on dirt as she sped off with him following close behind.

25

NOVA

T HE ROAD AHEAD WAS familiar, one Nova had traveled count-less times before, most recently just a few months ago with Raelyn. Now, instead of summer kicking off, it was winding to a close, darkness setting in earlier and a chill hanging in the air long into the morning. Soon, the leaves would start to change, the autumn rains would come, and school would start back up. A new classroom full of students.

But none of that mattered right now because the cottage was in sight, and that meant answers.

Or, at least, she hoped it did.

She pulled her horse to a halt at the head of the group, Raelyn stopping next to her. Her sister bent down to pat her mare's neck. "Good girl, almost there," she said in a sing-song voice.

Nova inhaled deeply and exhaled as the rest of the party stopped behind them. "This is it."

"This is it," Raelyn echoed.

"Everyone remember the plan?" Nova turned her head to check with her companions and was met with nods. "Let's hope Mother is on our side, but just in case—"

"We know what to do." Jax straightened his spine.

Raelyn reached out and took Nova's hand. "Together?"

"Always." She smiled, meeting her sister's gaze.

Raelyn leaned closer, her curls tickling Nova's cheek as she whispered into her ear, "And soon Fynn, too." She pulled away with a squeeze of her hand and then kicked her heels inward, urging her horse to the end of their journey.

A now-familiar lump formed in Nova's throat, but she swallowed it down. There hadn't been any news from Arkwood, any whispers or even rumors that Fynn had been caught, so for all she knew, he was safe. For now, she had other things to focus on.

Like Mother's story.

Esta and Jax trotted past her to follow Raelyn, but Kael pulled up beside her. "I'll be just over the dune. Come find me when...if it's safe."

Nova nodded, unable to form words. They had agreed that it wasn't safe for Kael to come with them into the house for the time being—even disguised. Until they knew what side of the story Raella Astor was on, there was no reason to put Kael at further risk.

If things went well, and on the off-chance Mother was on their side, then a reunion with Kael would probably be welcome. And Nova would be more than happy to facilitate that.

Kael gave her a smile, his green eyes glittering, before he steered his horse off in the opposite direction, through the brush toward the beach. She watched him until he disappeared, then set off toward the house.

The squeak of the front door opening caught Nova's attention as she was tying her horse next to the others. She glanced up and locked eyes with Mr. Larson, who had poked his head out, likely to see what the racket outside was. The four horses had not been quiet, especially when the only other sound that could be heard was the rolling crash of the waves on the other side of the house.

Mr. Larson's eyes widened as he flung the door open wide. "Nova? Raelyn? Is that really you?"

Raelyn squealed and ran up the short steps to the door, throwing herself into his arms like she had on their last visit. Nova grinned and followed her sister up the stairs, motioning for Jax and Esta to do the same.

"Hi, Mr. Larson. Long time, no see." Nova hugged him once Raelyn stepped aside. "This is Esta, Raelyn's guard, and Jax, my trainer."

Mr. Larson nodded to Jax and Esta, then looked back at Nova and Raelyn, his eyes full of what could only be described as wonder as they darted between the two of them. "There is so much to catch up on. Come, your mother is in the living room."

He turned and crossed the threshold back into the house as Nova's pulse began to race. Whatever they were about to learn from Mother...it had the potential to be even more life-shattering news. Though she'd had three days to mentally prepare for it, was one ever really ready?

Her hand found Raelyn's. Her magic swirled within her, not like the fiery power she felt when Fynn touched her, but more like a reassuring squeeze, giving her the extra boost she needed to take a step toward the door, pulling Raelyn in behind her.

The living room was in the back of the house, its entire rear wall a line of floor-to-ceiling windows that opened toward the beach. The sun was setting outside, and the sheer curtains hanging over the windows filtered out the darkening hues streaming in. Mr. Larson had already lit the lamps in the room, their silent flames giving off enough light for Nova to see her mother—or was she just Raella?—standing near the windows, staring out at the sea.

At the sight, Raelyn let out a squeak and dropped Nova's hand, running for her mother, who turned around at the sound. Raella's arms opened wide to welcome Raelyn in, her eyes brimming with tears and her face, usually pristinely made up, blotchy and puffy.

Seeing her tugged at Nova's heart harder than she expected. More than she cared to admit.

"My girls." Raella's voice cracked as she embraced Raelyn. Her eyes closed for a moment before opening again and directing their gaze right at Nova. One arm released from Raelyn, waving Nova in.

Despite everything she had learned and that had transpired, despite the way that Raella clearly favored Raelyn all her life, this woman before her was still the closest thing Nova had to a mother. She was the reason Nova was even alive and had not been killed when Luc arrested Kael.

And if Nova was being honest with herself, right now, there was nothing she wanted more.

She exhaled loudly and ran into the empty space next to Raelyn, wrapping her arms around both of them. Warm, wet tears trickled down her cheeks as she inhaled Raella's floral scent.

"My girls," Raella said again, her breath warm against Nova's ear. Her chest shook through a sob. "We have so much to discuss, but I am just so happy you both are safe."

She pulled back, glancing first at Raelyn and then at Nova, who brushed tears off her cheeks.

This didn't appear to be a trap.

This was a mother who had lost her husband and wanted her family together again.

"Mother—" Raelyn started, but the elder witch held up a hand.

"Please, Rae, let's sit. Invite your guests in. Mr. Larson will bring us drinks." Mother motioned at the sofa and the armchairs set up in the room, all facing out toward the windows. Nova had spent many a summer day reading on that couch. She and Raelyn had made forts out of its cushions as witchlings.

Now it looked old and tired.

Raelyn ran her hands across her cheeks and bowed her head as she retreated toward the door, returning a moment later with Esta and Jax.

"Esta." Mother approached and took Esta's hand, holding it and squeezing it with her own. "Good to see you again. Thank you for all you've done for my daughter."

Esta simply nodded, stepping back against the wall, ready to observe and act if needed.

"M-Mother." Nova's voice cracked at the word that stuck on her tongue like sap. But she brushed that aside and beckoned to Jax. "This is Jax. He's been...training me."

Mother's eyes lit up, her pallor starting to fade, skin returning to its normal hue. "Jax, it's so good to meet you. I can't wait to learn more about what you and Nova have uncovered together, what you've taught my special girl." She squeezed Nova's arm and grinned.

Mr. Larson entered then, carrying a tray with a pitcher of what looked like iced tea and five glasses.

Mother turned to him and clasped her hands. "Perfect timing, Mr. Larson. Yes, one for everyone, I think," she said as he began to pour the tea and hand the glasses out. Once he had finished and they each had a cool glass of tea in hand, she sat in the purple armchair that had always been hers. "Thank you, Mr. Larson, that will be all for tonight."

He bowed and left the room, closing the door behind him. Nova took a seat on the couch next to Raelyn, while Jax took the black armchair. They all somehow managed to avoid the brown chair that had always been Luc's. She sipped her iced tea, savoring the balance of sweet and refreshing after the journey they had endured over the last three days.

Mother cleared her throat. "I imagine you're all exhausted and would prefer to sleep, but there is much we need to discuss, and I'm afraid it cannot wait."

The voice was clearly Mother's, but the tone—that was not her usual tone. Instead of dainty, it was strong. Instead of compassionate, it was hard. Like the tone she might have taken when scolding—not that she had ever done much of that.

This was a side of Mother that Nova wasn't sure she had ever seen. She cast a wary glance at Raelyn, but her sister was staring straight at Mother, unblinking.

"We need to start with your father. He was not who the world thought him to be—"

Jax scoffed, earning a raised eyebrow from Mother, but she didn't bat an eye before continuing.

"I don't know all the details of his death, or even what you know. But I know that Fynn was involved, and if he was involved, I assume you were all there. I would like to hear that story, but first you must hear mine."

She set her glass down on the coffee table situated between the couch and the armchairs, wiping the condensation that had transferred from the glass to her hands on her skirt. "Your father betrayed our people. He betrayed our country. But most egregiously, he betrayed those that we loved, those we counted as family. And I have been doing everything in my power for the last twenty-five years to not only contain his power, but to stop him."

Whatever Nova had been expecting Mother to say, that was not it. This time, when she looked at Raelyn, Raelyn looked back, her mouth agape and her brown eyes wide.

Mother smiled. "Yes, I know it's shocking. I've put on quite a good show, so, to the world, I was just an oblivious wife. I don't think even Luc suspected. But I wasn't acting alone. I formed a group, a small group of those I could trust that has slowly grown, and that's how we uncovered Luc's largest secret." She paused, drawing in a sharp breath, her gaze floating around the room to each of her daughters and their friends in turn. "He delved into magic so dark he could never come back from it. He found a way to immortalize himself. He made what's called a deocre."

The room fell into a deafening silence.

26

NOVA

"**Y**OU KNOW ABOUT THE deocre?"

Raelyn's voice was weak, weaker than Nova had ever heard it. Her sister's skin had gone entirely pale, but she'd somehow found the will to speak.

Nova, on the other hand, couldn't find any words. Her mind was racing. Her mother *knew* what Luc had done. Knew what he had set in motion. And not only that—but she had conspired with others to try to stop it? Nova pressed a finger to her temple and closed her eyes.

More fucking family secrets.

"I do." Her mother's voice wafted through the room, still stronger, more forceful than Nova was used to hearing it. She blinked her eyes open but kept them narrowed as she watched the woman across the room from her. "I had hoped to have it destroyed before it could be...let loose. But, unfortunately, you all took care of Luc more quickly than I anticipated."

"You know how to destroy it?" Jax asked, leaning forward to rest his elbows on his knees.

Mother nodded.

Jax hung his head. "Then why didn't you do so *before* Luc...died?"

"I didn't know then." Her eyes began to water, tears threatening to spill out. "Had I known, I wouldn't have hesitated to get rid of it, even if it meant risking the Defiance's anonymity. I only just found out when the Defiance discovered the method, buried cryptically in an ancient text. Or at least we suspect that's what they found."

"You suspect?"

"Jax," Nova hissed, glaring in his direction. Now was not the time to insist on definitives and conclusives. If Mother had an idea, they were in a better position than they were ten minutes ago.

He put his hands up in defeat and leaned back in the armchair.

"Tell us, Mother." Nova directed her gaze back at the woman who raised her. The woman who had so much more explaining to do. But that could wait until they'd saved Astria. And Fynn.

Her mother sighed, a single tear sliding down her cheek. "This is where I'm stuck. It seems that we need one person from each race to fight the deocre. It can only be defeated by a human, a witch, and an elf coming together to fight as one to overpower it."

"Well, that shouldn't be too hard, right?" Raelyn said, a small amount of life coming back into her voice. "We've got two here. And I'm sure we can find a human in Adenaport who would help us."

But the look on Mother's face made Nova's stomach curdle. It wasn't that easy. There was something else, something she hadn't yet told them that would make this more complicated.

"What are we missing?" Nova said, meeting her mother's gaze.

"They have to be descendants of the goddesses."

Silence hung in the air like a fog, muting even the sound of their breath.

"The annals," Raelyn whispered.

Mother nodded as realization dawned on Nova, her mouth dropping open. "Luc was the one who stopped maintaining them," she said. Jax groaned, and she swore she heard Esta spew a string of curses. "He knew if the annals weren't maintained, if the histories of our lineages weren't up to date, then it would be more difficult to figure out who was a descendant of the goddesses."

"It does seem that way." Mother finished her iced tea and set the glass down in front of her. "So, first, we need to find out who the descendants are. Then we can recruit them to our cause."

"But why?" Raelyn knelt in front of their mother on the floor, clasping her hands together. "Why does it have to be the descendants? Why can't it just be any witch, human, or elf?"

It was Jax who spoke first, his voice hollow and full of reckoning. "The deocre is the darkest form of magic in existence. It would take the power and the might of the three most powerful in existence to extinguish it."

"And without the goddesses themselves..." Nova added, her voice trailing off as she met Raelyn's eye.

"It has to be their line." Raelyn pressed her forehead into her mother's knee. " What do we do now? Where do we even begin?"

Mother gently lifted Raelyn's head to meet her gaze. "We will sleep and reconvene tomorrow. But first, I believe you have your own stories to share. And perhaps a new friend to bring inside." Her eyes sparkled as they met Nova's. "I have a lot to apologize to you both for."

Half an hour later, their glasses were refilled, and Kael Blackmore now stood in the room with them. Nova had gone to retrieve him, Jax in tow. "For your protection," he'd said. She didn't argue. It was dark, and Fynn's voice in the back of her head told her not to be reckless.

Even if this was her happy place, the idea of going somewhere alone right now...

Mother's eyes, which only moments before had been dry, brimmed with tears again at the sight of Kael. She seemed torn between wanting to reach out and hug him and being wary of how he would react to her. Understandably so. Even though Nova and Jax had caught Kael up on the walk over, there hadn't been enough time for him to process the new developments.

"Kael." Her mother's voice was muffled by the hand clamped over her mouth.

The corner of his mouth twitched. "Raella."

The next moment, Mother was in his arms, wrapping hers around his torso and pulling him into one of the hugs that Nova liked best. Kael's eyes widened at first, but then he settled into the embrace. A single tear slid down his cheek, and, based on the way her shoulders were trembling, Nova assumed her mother was crying as well.

They'd been *friends*. They'd both cared so much for Wynna, probably still did.

Nova forced down the lump that burned in her throat.

"I'm so sorry," her mother said, pulling away and looking up at Kael. "About Wynna, about everything. You have to believe—"

Kael moved his hands to her shoulders and met her gaze. "I do. Trust me, I do. It sounds to me like we've both been imprisoned in a way. You've been working to right some wrongs, and for that I am grateful. I want to hear more about what you've been doing and how we can help."

Mother nodded, dropping her hands to her sides and stepping back from Kael. Raelyn, who was standing next to her, took her mother's hand in her own and squeezed.

Nova's heart lurched in a way she couldn't quite describe. Seeing her remaining family—all the odd bits and pieces of what she could somehow call a family—together in one room was a sensation like no other. If only Wynna could be here. If only Fynn were here.

"It's getting late, Kael," she said, moving her gaze from her mother to her father. "We won't get anything done overnight, but we *are* safe here. We all need to rest. With clear heads tomorrow, we can start to plan."

"How do you know we are safe?" Kael raised an eyebrow.

It was Jax who answered. "I've put up some protective enchantments. It wouldn't hurt if you wanted to add some, though. And Nova as well." He glanced at Nova, who nodded.

They had no idea what they were up against with the deocre—what it could break through, how far it could travel—but they could use all their available resources to keep themselves as safe as possible.

"Mother and I can barricade the doors and windows as well," Raelyn said. "No one will be able to come in or out while we're sleeping."

Kael's eyes were still wary, but he nodded. "It's the best we can do."

Moonlight trickled in through a crack in the curtains, casting the room in an eerie shadow. Thoughts of her bed upstairs consumed Nova as exhaustion overtook her body.

"Before we turn in," Mother said as the group started to head toward the door, "I would like to know...what happened."

Of course. Mother still had no idea the truth about what had happened in the cave. What had happened to Luc. Her husband had died, and—regardless of what their relationship had become over the years—at some point, she must have loved him.

Nova drew in a deep breath, the soft touch of Raelyn's hand on her back steadying her. "Kael lured us to the lab." She deliberately left out how; it wasn't important and would just cause more worry. "He explained to me, Rae, and Fynn what had transpired, how Luc had tricked him and sent him to prison. How Luc had my…Wynna killed. And the rest of their partners."

"Then Father caught up with us," Raelyn said, wrapping her arm fully around Nova. Her voice was surprisingly steady, considering how distraught she had been in the days after. "And explained the rest. How he had changed his powers and made himself into a wielder. He—" She paused, catching Nova's eye. Nova slipped her hand around Raelyn's back so they were now linked, supporting each other as they always had.

Raelyn swallowed and continued. "He attacked us. All of us. Even me."

Mother's hand flew to her mouth, a tear falling down her cheek. "Were you hurt? Any of you?"

Nova shook her head. "Nothing some healing spells couldn't fix. We were fortunate that we outnumbered him."

"So who…" Her mother's eyes darted between the two sisters before looking around at Esta, Jax, and Kael, too.

"Me," Jax said, stepping forward and crossing his arms. "And Fynn. I will spare you the details, though."

Nova watched her mother's reaction, studying the look on her face. To her credit, she didn't lose composure. She didn't even shed another tear. Apparently the emotion was reserved for Raelyn and Nova, while Luc would get none. Instead, Mother's face hardened into a mask of strength, one Nova had never seen her wear. Gone was the socialite who was more concerned with appearances and being "seen." She'd been replaced by something different.

Something like a warrior. A leader.

Mother opened her mouth to speak, then closed it. After another beat, she tucked her chin to her chest and said, "Thank you."

Nova shook her head, sure she'd heard incorrectly. Her mother was looking right at Jax, and there was no mistaking what she'd said.

Raelyn stiffened beside her, clenching Nova's waist tighter. "Thank you?"

Mother's gaze turned back to the sisters, but her expression didn't change. "Yes, thank you for doing what I've been too cowardly to do for twenty-five years. There was no other way to end this, even if it meant the deocre awakened. Now we just need to hope we can fight it before it gets too powerful."

"You've known Father would need to die for my entire life?" The voice that had been so strong before cracked now. Nova tightened her arm around Raelyn in an effort to provide the steadying force that her sister always gave to her. "Why couldn't you have told me? What if I could have helped?"

"Oh, Rae." Mother took a step closer, reaching for Raelyn's free hand. "I thought maybe, as you aged, being a father would change him. Or I hoped it would."

"But it didn't." Raelyn averted her eyes. Behind them, floorboards creaked under Esta's shifting weight as the elf stepped closer.

"I think he loved you in his own way. And I never thought he would have harmed you. Hearing that he did only proves he was too far gone to be saved."

Nova looked between her sister and the woman who had raised her, seeing her mother in a whole new light. Whereas it had been easy to discount Luc as her father, Raella was a different story. There had been moments, particularly moments when Luc wasn't around, that had been wonderful, where she'd been an exceptional mother.

Now it made perfect sense why. She didn't want to let Luc know that she was working against him. That she disagreed with his suppression of her powers, his incarceration of Kael, and the destruction of his family and friends. That she knew what he had planned and, apparently, had a cohort of people trying to minimize his power.

Raella Astor had been putting on a show for twenty-five years. And had done a damn fine job of it. This woman had done everything in her power, including belittling herself, to keep Nova and Raelyn safe. To try to keep Astria safe.

She was a hero.

She may not have given birth to Nova, but she'd earned the title of Mother.

Nova reached her arm out, wrapping it around her so the three witches were again enveloped in a hug. Raelyn let out a gasp as she squeezed, while Mother planted a kiss on each of their cheeks.

"My girls," she said. "I love you both so much. We will endure this. We will survive. And when we do, we will be *free*."

Freedom meant different things to each of them. For her mother, it meant being able to live as herself outside of the shadows, no longer living two lives and hiding from her daughters who she was deep down.

For Kael, it meant living outside of Mistfell. Being granted the pardon he deserved and settling into life again. Learning how to be a father.

And for Nova...she hoped it meant that Fynn's name would be cleared. That the two of them could explore their new love further without the presence of an outside threat. That they could look toward the future together without needing to hide.

Without Fynn close, it was becoming harder and harder to imagine, but as she nestled into the arms of the two women who loved her the most, she was beginning to feel like anything could be possible.

Like the three Astor women could take on the world.

27

NOVA

NOVA'S PACK SLID OFF her arm and onto the floor of her cottage bedroom. The last time she'd been here was before she heard about Kael's escape. Before her world turned upside down.

Before Fynn.

It looked exactly as it did when she'd left, though the bed was now made, the only sign that Mr. Larson had been here. The armoire that she kept filled with clothes stood to her left, next to a full-length mirror that hung on the wall. She pulled open the armoire door and peered in. Her clothes were there, linen and cotton dresses to one side, tunics on the other. Just the essentials, and hardly what one could call a full wardrobe, but it would do for now.

"Knock knock," a voice trilled from the doorway. Nova shut the armoire door and found her mother standing there, a curved finger raised to tap on the door. Her eyes were puffy, but she bore a smile. "Can I come in?"

Could she? While Nova was relieved to learn about her mother's true involvement—or lack thereof—in Luc's plan and proud to learn that she'd actively fought against Luc's transgressions, she still hadn't been the most...motherly. Moments here and there did not make up for a lifetime of hurt, even if that hurt was in the name of a greater good. In the name of staying alive.

Right?

Her mother stretched her arms out wide, and Nova's body acted of its own accord, pulling her toward the motherly embrace. She buried her nose in her mother's hair and inhaled. That scent carried a wave of nostalgia with it, a memory of hugs and consolations from years past that had helped Nova get through the harder times in her childhood.

Perhaps Raella Astor hadn't been the best mother to Nova, but maybe she had been the best she could be.

"Yes," Nova murmured. Her mother's body relaxed as she gave Nova another squeeze. Then she pulled back, leaving her hands on Nova's arms.

"Thank you."

Nova guided her over to the bed, where they sat, side by side, on the edge.

"Nova," her mother began, folding her hands in her lap, "I owe you a thousand apologies. Perhaps a million. I know I treated you poorly, and I hope you believe me when I say that I hated doing it."

Nova stared at her own hands, which were pressed into her thighs. Her eyes began to burn with tears.

"Every time I looked at you, I saw Wynna. One of my dearest friends. Your laugh is just like hers. And you're as smart, if not smarter, than her. Your compassion for those less fortunate mirrors hers. There is so much of her in you, and sometimes I admit I resented you for it."

A tear slipped down Nova's cheek, dripping onto the back of her hand.

"But that resentment was misguided. In the same moments it would rear its ugly head, I would remember *why* you were with us. *Why* she was dead. And then I would channel that anger elsewhere."

"The Defiance?" Nova asked, her voice shaking.

Her mother sighed. "Eventually, yes. But it took a while to build up that organization and to find people I could trust. All the while, I worried I was damaging *our* relationship beyond repair."

Another tear joined the first one.

Her mother pushed the hair back from Nova's face, tucking it behind her ear. Then her fingers gently pulled Nova's chin to the left until their eyes met.

"The truth is, Nova, that I've loved you since the moment you were born. I remember how it felt when Wynna first let me hold you, like you were already part of my family. I delight in seeing you and Raelyn so close because it was all I ever wanted, all Wynna and I talked about my entire pregnancy. I could never be the mother to you that Wynna would have been, but in the moments when Luc wasn't looking, I tried to channel her. I tried to make you feel like you belonged. Like someone cared for you."

Memories of those exact moments flashed before Nova's eyes. Some from as far back as she held a memory, some more recent. As hard as it was, she *did* believe that Raella Astor had tried her best. That she had acted as she thought best.

Maybe a part of Nova just desperately wanted to cling to the idea of having a mother and all that came with that title. Maybe that's why she was finding it so easy to forgive.

"I remember." Nova's voice cracked. Her mother wiped a tear off her cheek with her thumb. "I remember you being there at all the big moments, and he wasn't. When I completed my schooling. When I started teaching. When I successfully completed my first spell."

"I was particularly proud of that." Her mother grinned. "I'd been so worried that Luc's suppression spell was too good. The thought of Kael and Wynna's daughter having no magical ability at all sickened me. When you grew that first flower, small as it was…I'll remember that day for the rest of my life. It shows up in all my happiest dreams."

Nova placed her hand over her mother's. "You did what you had to do. You put on a hell of a show. And because of that, I'm alive. Because of the game you played all these years, I'm here today to learn about the real me and the real you. Thank you."

And she meant it. In a way, learning why she'd always been treated differently was the greatest relief of her life. It didn't erase the decades of emotional turmoil, but it was a step toward learning how to process and move past it.

Her mother bit her lip. "And I'm sorry. Endlessly and unabashedly sorry."

Nova swept her mother into a hug, wrapping her arms around her torso and breathing in that familiar scent again. Her body trembled just as much as her mother's did, the tears now falling in earnest.

"It's ok," Nova whispered into her mother's hair. "You saved my life."

Her mother squeezed her tighter. "I don't deserve that. And I don't deserve this, but I'm going to ask anyway." She pushed herself back from Nova, their gazes meeting. Tears continued to fall down Nova's cheeks, and her heart rate quickened as she awaited her mother's request. "Can we start a new chapter? I won't ask you to forget everything that's happened before today, but I'd love the chance to move forward, earn your trust, and be the best mother I can be for you."

How many times had Nova wished she could hear those words? How many nights had she fallen asleep wondering what she had done, why she didn't earn the same love from her parents that Raelyn had? How often had she wondered what was wrong with her?

And now she knew—nothing was wrong with her. Nothing at all. It hadn't all been in her head, but there had been love behind it. That same love now had a chance to come forward and shine.

Nova nodded, grabbing her mother's hands and forcing her mouth into a smile.

"I'd like that."

28

FYNN

THE PLAN WAS TAKING shape.

Daro was going to accompany Fynn on the escape mission to Adenaport, but Fynn had grown used to the other elf's company and realized he didn't mind. Plus, his agility matched Fynn's—almost—so he was the only Defiance member who could keep up with the parts of the plan that required them to run.

"The new moon is in two days," Fox said as the group ate dinner. They'd taken to eating while standing since they spent most of the day sitting and poring over books.

"If we find anything you need to know, we will send a message," the leader had said before shooing Fynn away from the table where Elodie and Ethel were sorting through the tomes.

Elodie had shot a look of apology his way.

"I think you should try to escape then."

Fynn whipped his head around to look at Fox, diverting his attention to the present.

Fox must've mistaken the look on his face for apprehension because he continued, "Witch magic is at its weakest during the new moon. The enchantments along the wall as well as the deocre will both be impacted, giving you the best opportunity to escape."

"And you'll have the cover of darkness," Elodie added, setting her now-empty plate in the washbasin.

Fynn snorted. "I've never believed that lore about magic at the new moon. It's never been proven. It's just something we tell kids in bedtime stories."

"But if there's a chance it's true..." Fox shrugged. "You're welcome to stay here and hide as long as you'd like, but I thought you wanted to get to Adenaport."

"I do," Fynn replied, so quickly that his tone was harsher than he'd intended. He took a deep breath and tried again. "I do. Two days sounds like as good a time as any to try."

"We've still got a little work to do to hammer out the plan," Daro said. His fork clinked against his plate as he set it down. "We'll have to work more diligently."

Fox looked over at Elodie. "El, switch tasks for a few days and help the elves. You know these tunnels and the layout of Arkwood better than anyone."

Elodie grinned and met Fynn's gaze. "Happy to."

From the moment he'd shared the message that he'd heard from Nova, Elodie had become one of his closest friends here. She was naturally kind, not quick to anger, and incredibly brilliant. She alone was responsible for ensuring the structural integrity of their cavern and the tunnel system, and she did so *easily*. Looking at her, one would have no idea there was a constant pull on her magic, holding this place together.

The smile Fynn returned came more easily than expected. In two days, he'd be on his way to Nova. In two days, he'd be out of this underground dungeon.

Two days.

He could do two days.

Elodie approached to take his empty plate, then Daro's. She added them to the washbasin with her own, then returned to his side. "Show me what you've got so far."

29

NOVA

NOVA FOUND KAEL STARING out toward the sea the next morning. He held a cup of coffee in one hand and had the other in his pocket as he watched the waves rolling in and out across the sand through the sliding doors at the back of the house.

How majestic that must have seemed to him after years in the cold, dark prison.

"Morning," she said as she came to stand next to him.

His green eyes met hers, his face breaking into a wide grin. Since he'd joined their crew, he'd started to gain weight. His cheekbones no longer stood out as prominently, his eyes didn't appear as sunken, and his arms and legs were not just skin and bones. He'd also trimmed his beard and brushed his hair, though it was still long enough to tie back into a small ponytail at the base of his neck.

And, though the lines on his face betrayed his age, his eyes sparkled with the youth and vigor she was used to seeing in her students.

Mistfell hadn't broken him.

"Hi, Nova." He passed the mug of coffee her way. "I had this prepared for you."

She took the mug from him, the warmth of it seeping into her palm as she wrapped her hand around it. He'd been keeping it at the perfect temperature for her.

"Thank you." She sipped, drinking in Chef's familiar blend of brew and instantly feeling the change in her body. "Is anyone else awake?"

Kael shook his head. "Not that I've seen. The kitchen was empty when I went for coffee, too."

Odd. Chef was always up at the crack of dawn. "Maybe Mother sent all the staff home?"

They were trustworthy, but some secrets weren't meant to be shared unless absolutely necessary. And the cottage could certainly function without the staff for however long it took them to figure out the next steps.

Something passed over Kael's eyes. Nothing more than a shadow, but enough that Nova caught it. She refocused her gaze, looking outside as a gull landed on the deck and let out a squawk before taking flight again.

"Does it bother you that I call Raella 'Mother'?"

That had to be what had caught Kael off guard. It was a perfectly understandable reaction to hearing your daughter, whose mother had been killed, calling the wife of her murderer "Mother."

Nova's life had become a series of very tangled webs.

There was no point trying to tiptoe around feelings when the webs were so muddled. Better to just get things out in the open.

"You caught that?" Kael sighed, but Nova kept her focus on the view outside. "It'll take some getting used to, but Raella was your mother's best friend. It sounds like she has done her absolute best to protect you and to fight against Luc over the years." He paused, taking a deep breath. "Wynna would be happy to know that Raella is who you bestow the honor of that title to in her absence. I...I just need a little more time to process it."

"Honestly, so do I." Nova took another sip of her coffee. "The family I thought I had just two weeks ago...it doesn't exist anymore. Turns out it never existed. And now I have this mismatch of people that I care for. How do they all fit together?"

"You." He caught her eye and grinned. "You're the glue that holds this misfit family together. And, just so you know, even a family not bound by blood is still a family." He winked at her, but there was a sadness behind his eyes. A family he was missing.

"Your research partners were like your family, weren't they?"

He nodded, casting his gaze toward the floor and clasping his hands behind his back. "I feel bound to Jax almost as if he were my own son, because of what Margot meant to me."

She reached out her free hand to squeeze his arm. A barely imperceptible pulse of *something* tickled her fingertips as she did so, but she ignored it. Probably just a chill from the morning air.

"You're a good man, Kael Blackmore."

He looked at her, his lips parting as if he had something to say and his eyes widening, but before he could voice anything, the door behind them slammed open.

"Good morning, you two!" Raelyn said in her ever-chipper tone as she strode into the room, Esta hot on her heels and looking like she could barely keep up. "Who's ready to save the world?"

Breakfast ended up being prepared by Raelyn and Esta, since their mother had indeed sent all staff home, including Mr. Larson. The group was settling down to eat the small feast of scrambled eggs and buttered toast when Jax posed the question that was on all their minds.

"So, how do we find these descendants?"

The impossibility of the task ahead of them hit Nova like the waves she'd been watching mere minutes before, knocking her down beneath the surf until she was drowning under its weight.

She took another sip of her coffee to swallow down the egg that had become lodged in her throat.

"We're going to need to get the annals. See how far back we *can* trace the lineages and then go from there," Raelyn said, setting down her fork. "Esta and I broke in once. I'm sure we could do it again."

Esta, standing against the wall behind Raelyn, rolled her eyes. "That was a completely different circumstance."

"And how are you getting into Arkwood?" Jax asked, one eyebrow raised.

Raelyn slumped back in her chair and crossed her arms. "Fine, let's hear your ideas then."

Nova had one. It had come to her as she was falling asleep last night, and there was a chance, though small, it could work. "We could visit Terra's temple in Adenaport. See if the priestesses know anything, at least about Terra's human descendant."

Kael coughed and dropped his fork onto the table with a clink. "Wait, *what* exactly are we looking for?"

Oh, right. Nova and Jax hadn't had time to fill him in on every part of their discussion with her mother before they'd returned to the cabin. In the...excitement, they must have forgotten to mention that they knew how to defeat the deocre.

"Mother's secret organization, the Defiance, figured out how to defeat the deocre," Nova explained. "But we need a descendant from each of the goddesses. And we have no idea who those may be."

However she had expected him to react, laughter—big, booming laughter—was not it. And yet that's exactly what he was doing right now, his left hand clutching his stomach and his head tipping back.

"I'm not sure what's funny about this," Esta grumbled.

Mother shot Esta a warning look, then looked back at Kael. "Kael? Care to explain?"

He collected himself and drew in a deep breath before lifting his head, a huge smile plastered to his face. "I can make this a little easier for us."

His gaze met Nova's again, those green eyes sparkling with joy this time.

"We've got two of Canta's descendants right here."

"Us?" Nova asked, her heart starting to race. They were descended from Canta? Were the stories about wielders being her direct descendants true, then?

She tore her gaze from Kael's to look at Jax. He caught her stare and held up his hands. "Not me. My ancestors immigrated here from the West about a century after the war. They worshiped entirely different gods back then."

Ok. So ignore that theory then.

Mother smiled and Raelyn cheered. "Oh *hell* yes. One down already."

But Nova didn't share her sister's joy. The thought of going up against the deocre, of being one of the three who could—who *must*—defeat it in order to save Astria, made her want to run into the Worgreth Mountains and hide with the nomads. She'd only come into her power two months ago. Despite how much she'd learned, there was no way she was ready to take on the most powerful form of dark magic.

Kael must have sensed her fear, or maybe it was etched all over her face, because he said, "I can be Canta's descendant. It would give me a chance for true retribution."

Right. Because the deocre was essentially a living embodiment of the darkest part of Luc's soul. Another reason Nova wasn't certain she was capable of destroying it.

Bile rose in the back of her throat.

"Excuse me." She bolted up from her chair, which overturned with a thud against the floor, and ran for the back deck, desperate for the salt air that smelled like Fynn and provided her the comfort she so craved.

Kael's voice trailed after her, but she slammed the sliding door shut behind her and drowned it out. Her feet carried her down the steps and into the sand, where she collapsed, squeezing her eyes shut. Her magic ran rampant, pushing at her skin, trying to find an outlet. The sand clenched in her fists warmed from pulses that escaped before Fynn's voice entered her mind.

Breathe, breathe.

Briny sea air filled her lungs on her first deep inhale, the breeze blowing tendrils of her black hair into her face. A wave crashed nearby as she pushed the breath back out, the hum of the tide advancing and then receding helping to soothe her pulse.

The sand in her hands cooled again, matching the ambient air.

Nova glanced up, looking toward the water. The sun was bright, but a few clouds hung in the sky, including one that obscured its blaze for now. The day would be cooler, despite the humidity that hung in the air, because summer was ending. Autumn was arriving, and with it, colder days, even in Adenaport.

The sliding door to the porch squeaked open behind her. Nova twisted to see who was emerging, relieved to see it was Raelyn. Her curly hair bounced as she skipped down the stairs—how could she *skip* given everything going on?

Maybe Nova could find a way to steal some of her sister's incessant optimism.

Raelyn plopped in the sand next to Nova, crossing her legs in front of her and placing her hands in her lap.

"Will you tell me what's bothering you?" Raelyn asked kindly as she brushed a lock of hair behind Nova's ear.

Nova sighed. "Why does it have to be us? Why are we the descendants?"

"Would you prefer it was a random witch we didn't know and had to try to convince to help us?"

Fair point. It was easier that someone who was already aware of the deocre and the risks it posed was the one they needed. Silvana had warned them to keep this close to the chest. She'd said there could be dangerous ramifications if the public found out about the deocre, about what dark magic could do.

"No, you're right," Nova said. She shifted her position, so instead of kneeling, she mirrored Raelyn and dragged her fingertips through the sand. "But I just found Kael. What if I lose him again?"

What if I have to step in and do it instead?

Raelyn stopped her fingers' wandering, instead lacing them through Nova's. "What if this is what needs to happen so the two of you can continue getting to know each other? He's never had a chance to prove himself as a father. I bet he's thrilled to have this one."

Yet again, Raelyn spoke true. *When did she become the wise one?*

"But it's not the only thing that has to happen for us to become a normal family—whatever that is. There's still the matter of proving his innocence to the world."

"Yes." Raelyn shrugged. "But we can't do that if the deocre destroys the world first."

Nova looked over at her sister, the grin on Raelyn's face almost masking the hurt that lurked in her big brown eyes. They'd both been through it the last few weeks. They'd both lost. But they still had each other. It was obvious that Raelyn was trying to hold it together for Nova's sake this morning when, inside, her heart was just as shattered.

"I think," Raelyn continued, "that we've earned something fun. We've already found one-third of the people we need, we've been traveling for three days, and we've hardly had any time to spend together, just you and me."

Nova straightened her back, unable to help the smile that took shape on her face. "I think you might be onto something. What did you have in mind?"

A gull cawed nearby as a family of them passed overhead. Raelyn's lips stretched into a wild grin as she used the hand still intertwined with Nova's to pull them both upright.

"We never got that spa day we were supposed to have, did we?"

30

NOVA

"Appointment for Raelyn and Nova Astor."

Raelyn looked at the woman standing behind the small reception desk at their favorite day spa in Adenaport. She'd gone into town herself yesterday after the conversation at the beach and demanded they rearrange their books to accommodate the sisters.

Apparently she'd told the receptionist that she and Nova desperately needed a day away after their father's death, and the human women who ran the spa were sympathetic enough to oblige.

The receptionist checked their names off in her appointment book, smiling at them. "Follow me."

The spa was a large, circular hut with individual treatment rooms along the outside and a large open space in the middle containing a pool. The roof was thatched, which kept out the sun and the rain and maintained a comfortable darkness inside.

The receptionist led them to the changing room, where they removed their clothing and donned gray robes and slippers before making their way to the lounge chairs by the pool. They had time to relax or go for a swim in the heated water before their treatments started.

As Nova collapsed onto her chair, she drew in a deep breath, the scent of eucalyptus and lavender filling her nose. If the trickle of the small waterfall that fed the pool wasn't serene enough, the oils they used in the treatments permeated the air, leaving tranquility in their wake.

Or maybe it was just Nova they had that effect on.

She glanced over at Raelyn, who was reclining in the chair next to hers, eyes closed and lips tipped up into a smile.

Nope. It wasn't just her, then.

"Hey, Rae?" Nova whispered. Her sister cracked one eye open and looked in her direction. "Thanks for suggesting this. It was a good idea."

She hadn't realized how much she needed this time with Raelyn until the suggestion had been made, and then she'd found herself genuinely excited about something for the first time since Fynn had left for Arkwood. She and Raelyn had been separated for most of the summer, and since they'd come together again, they hadn't really had a moment alone that wasn't punctuated by grief or some other interruption.

In the absence of Fynn—or, if she were being honest with herself, even with him around—she needed her sister. Their bond was irreplaceable. How ridiculous that she'd thought, for even a moment, that not actually being related by blood could tear them apart.

"I know," Raelyn said, grinning wider. She opened both eyes and rolled to her side, propping her head up on her hand as she looked at Nova. "I've got the best ideas."

Nova laughed. Raelyn always knew how to get a smile out of her.

"Nova, how are you?" Raelyn asked once Nova's laugh had died off. "Like, not just right now. How are you *really*?"

As much as she didn't want to talk about this, Nova knew she needed to. And if there was anyone she could talk about it with, it was

Raelyn. She drew in a deep breath, summoning all her willpower. "I miss Fynn."

"A lot," Raelyn added. A statement, not a question.

Nova nodded as a small lump formed in her throat. Visions of the elf passed through her mind: the smile on his face first thing in the morning, the way his hair fell down his neck when it was wet, the abs—*all* the muscles, really. Her power danced in her core, excited at the prospect of Fynn, while feeding off her emotions as usual. At least it was becoming easier to control.

"Yes, a lot."

"There's something special between you two. More than just a romantic bond."

Nova rolled to her left side to face her sister, pulling her braid over her shoulder so it lay in front of her. "It seems that way. I'm not sure why my magic reacts the way that it does when he touches me. Even Jax said he's never heard of it." The lump grew, Nova's voice cracking before she could swallow it down. She forced the surge of magic within her back down as well. "I just hate that I have no idea if he's safe. If I'll ever see him again. What if we never find out what happened to him?"

"We will." Raelyn reached out and took her hand. A wave of peace overtook Nova, her magic instantly settled and...was it *purring*?

She'd noticed the tranquil effect of Raelyn's touch a few times before, but, perhaps exaggerated by the atmosphere in the spa, she noticed it felt stronger. It wasn't unlike the way her magic reacted to Fynn's touch, but instead of growing more agitated, it calmed. It still felt...stronger.

Raelyn furrowed her brow. "What's wrong? Your face..."

"I never noticed this before, at least not like right now, but my magic reacts to your touch, too." To test her theory, Nova pulled her hand away, letting it find its way to the tail of her braid to twirl the hair. As suspected, her magic riled up, ever so slightly, but also…weakened.

Well, that was interesting.

"When I moved my hand away, it felt different. Weaker. The effect isn't the same as it is with Fynn, but it's still there."

"Maybe it is like I thought." Raelyn's eyes widened. "Maybe it is that you can absorb power from others through contact."

Nova shook her head. "No, I don't think that's it. I don't feel anything when anyone else touches me. Or at least…not that I've noticed." Though she'd sure as hell be paying better attention now.

Raelyn stuck her hand back out, and Nova intertwined their fingers again. The sensation returned almost immediately. How had she not noticed it before?

"It's more subtle. But it's there," she said.

"Subtle?" Raelyn laughed and rolled onto her back, her hand leaving Nova's and coming to rest on her stomach. "Not usually an adjective people use for me."

"Raelyn?"

The sisters looked up, finding a human woman in a brown robe similar to theirs standing at the other end of the pool. Nova recognized her as the massage therapist that her sister usually visited when they came to this spa.

"I'm ready for you now," the woman said, bowing her head.

"We'll talk more later," Raelyn said as she stood and made her way over to the therapist, leaving Nova alone with her thoughts.

A dangerous place to be.

Nova held up her hand, drumming her fingers in the air, wondering what it was that caused her to react this way to Raelyn. And why it was the same, but different, from how her magic reacted to Fynn. Once they were back at the cottage, she'd talk to Jax, see how they could experiment with it in her training, which he insisted would resume tomorrow. Maybe he already had some ideas.

Nova's ability was seeming more and more like the amplification that Jax's father had, but instead of just Fynn, it was strengthened by multiple people. Was it *everyone*? And if not, then who? And why?

Her masseuse, a human she'd seen a few times named Mandy, came to fetch her a few moments later. Fortunately, during the massage she was able to completely tune out her thoughts, dropping into that meditative state that Fynn had talked about being just as healing as magic itself.

"That was *exactly* what I needed," Nova said an hour later as she shuffled toward the pool. Raelyn was already there, this time sipping on hot tea with her feet dangling in the water. Another mug sat beside her, which she offered up to Nova.

"I knew it would be. And here's part two."

The aroma of the coffee hit her before she could even peer into the mug. "Mmm, yes, the perfect part two."

She dipped her feet in the heated water slowly, the heat providing an extra dose of warmth to muscles that had been worked during their massages. Mandy had, unsurprisingly, found a number of extremely tense knots all over Nova's body. After a brief scolding about the need for rest and stretching, she went to work massaging out as many of them as she could until Nova was as sore as she was after a training session with Fynn and Jax...but also luxuriously devoid of tension.

Her feet dangled listlessly in the water as she sipped the coffee.

The coffee tasted *exactly* like Raelyn's. Nova swallowed the warm brew down, then turned to her sister, open-mouthed. "You did something to this."

Her sister just winked. "I'll never tell."

"What would I do without you?"

"We've discussed this before." Raelyn took a sip of her tea. "You'd be incredibly lonely and grumpy from the lack of endless entertainment and caffeine I provide you."

"Yeah, but it's more than that, Rae. You know that, right?" She wasn't sure why, but it was suddenly very important that Raelyn understood just how much she meant to Nova. How much Nova needed her in her life. "You've always supported me. Lifted me up. Never let me feel like I was less...like others did."

Raelyn shrugged, but her eyes were sparkling. "That's what sisters do. I could say the same for you."

Nova nudged her playfully with her elbow, and Raelyn nudged her right back.

"So," Nova said, forcing her tone into something more serious, "how are *you*, really?"

Raelyn cast her gaze toward her feet, which were crossed at the ankles under the water. A loose curl fell into her face. After a few moments during which Nova wondered if she needed to repeat the question, or potentially even disregard it altogether, her sister finally spoke.

"Grief is a weird thing." She reached up and pushed the errant curl behind her ear. "You know, this is the first time I think I've ever truly felt it. And it comes in these enormous waves, where it's crippling, like I can't *breathe*, but then it's gone. In those moments, I remember all the awful things we've learned about Father, and I berate myself for even feeling that grief. He doesn't...deserve it." Her voice cracked.

Nova reached out a hand and rubbed it along Raelyn's back. "You're allowed to feel both grief and anger. *I* feel both."

Raelyn nodded, a tear streaking down her cheek. "There were good moments, too, weren't there?"

Were there? Maybe if Nova racked her brain enough, she could find them. Certainly there were good moments with Mother, but Luc?

Yes. There *had* been good moments with Luc. She'd been so consumed with the bad memories and the recent revelations that she'd forgotten them. But now that Raelyn brought it up, how could she forget the sandcastles he had built with them when they were kids? Geos had the ability to morph and shape sand in incredible ways, so their castles were enormous. Taller than she'd been as a child, taller even than Luc. He'd even built them each their own room in one castle, where they'd insisted they spend one night. Despite the enchantments he'd put on the castle to shore it up, it couldn't withstand the tides. The sisters had come running into the house shortly after midnight, soaking wet and doubled over with laughter.

Luc had been waiting up for them, a wide grin on his face. He'd clearly expected that very outcome.

Or what about the time he'd brought them to the Atrium with him? Nova and Raelyn had been teenagers then, eager to learn more about what he did every day at work. Mother had convinced him to let them skip school and accompany him. Though the work he did was tedious and boring—one of the many reasons Nova had not pursued politics herself—he'd shown them off to everyone they came across, and he'd given them both special tasks. Nova's had been delivery of interoffice mail, which on any other day was probably delivered magically, but she'd enjoyed the freedom it gave her to roam the halls and the proud look Luc had worn when she'd asked to deliver more...

Were those moments real? Had Luc actually cared about her? Surely there was something to be said for raising a child from a toddler, watching them grow and accomplish new things, that made a parent grow *some* type of feeling for the kid? Despite how it had started and ended, had there been times along the way when Luc had loved her, or at least liked her?

No sooner had the thoughts crossed her mind than a swarm of guilt buzzed around her stomach.

Here she was trying to find the good in Luc when her real father was alive and well and had suffered at Luc's hand. Shame on her.

She didn't realize she had closed her eyes until she opened them again and found Raelyn's hand waving in her face. Turning her head, she found her sister staring at her, her eyes narrowed and all signs of the grief from moments before gone.

"Where'd you go?" Raelyn tilted her head to one side.

Nova rubbed her forehead. "Sorry. I was trying to remember the good times with...Luc. But then I thought of Kael and guilt took over." She smiled weakly at Raelyn. "Told you. I feel both, too."

"Oh, Nova." Raelyn pulled her feet out of the water and turned to sit facing Nova, her legs crossing in front of her. Nova shifted her seat to meet her, tucking her robe over her legs to dry the water dripping off them. Raelyn grabbed her hands, causing that wave of calm to wash over Nova, her power humming along happily.

"It's quite a mess that our lives have turned into, isn't it?" Raelyn asked.

Nova looked up and met her gaze. "It is. And I think there's more of a mess coming."

"But we'll get through it. Like we always do—together."

"Always."

Footsteps echoed behind them as another patron entered the pool area, taking a seat on one of the lounge chairs and paying them no mind. But they no longer had the privacy they'd had a moment before. Nova jerked her head toward the exit, and Raelyn nodded before they both stood and went to change.

The visit had the effect that Nova had hoped it would. It hadn't solved her problems—not even close. But it had given her a sense of peace, of hope. And it had given her and Raelyn the moments of emotional clarity that they had needed to experience. Together.

31

FYNN

FYNN WAS READY.

The plan was set, and he felt as good about it as he could. Elodie had reviewed it, Fox had reviewed it, and both thought it was solid.

Daro gave them about an eighty percent chance of escape.

"Only eighty?" Fox had asked him with a smirk.

The elf had shrugged. "More if we actually knew what we were up against. But the unknown of the deocre has to account for something."

The dark spirit was continuing to lie low. The Defiance scouts that went above ground once a day for updates or to bring down newspapers reported that the city had mostly gone on as normal. Raella Astor had left Arkwood, though they knew that based on Nova's message to Fynn, and despite the official mourning period ending, no election processes had convened for Luc Astor's now-vacant seat.

Fynn had a strong suspicion that the deocre was to blame for that. Which is why they needed to act. If it continued Luc's vision of overpowering the governors...

He shoved the last of his meager supplies into the pack he was carrying for their journey. It was small, barely large enough to hold a change of clothes and some food, but he'd have his weapons on his person, and running with large bags was difficult. Better to keep it small and be more agile.

Slinging the bag over his shoulder, he approached Fox. "One last chance to tell me what we need to do to defeat this thing before we go."

"Not gonna happen, Fynn." Fox pressed his lips together into a fine line.

"What if we can do something to help from Adenaport? There's strength in numbers. We can cover more ground—"

But the human just shook his head, sending Fynn's blood straight into a boil.

"Fuck your pride, Fox. This is the future of Astria we are talking about."

"This isn't about my pride, Fynn." Fox rolled his shoulders back, standing taller, though he still didn't match Fynn's height. "This is a direct order from the High One themselves."

"Fuck the High One, then."

With that, Fynn turned toward the door, hearing but not comprehending Fox's mumbles. Probably cursing him for his insolence. Whatever. Hopefully this was the last time they'd have to be in the same room together anyway.

He joined Daro by the entrance to the cavern. Elodie and Ethel were standing with him, exchanging goodbyes. "Remember, exactly two hours from now—" Daro was saying before Ethel cut him off.

"Yeah, yeah, we know. We got this, trust us."

Elodie turned to Fynn when he walked up. "Take care of yourself. And this one, too." She pointed her thumb over her shoulder at Daro.

Fynn found himself smiling despite the angst lingering from his conversation with Fox. "Thanks for everything, Elodie. I hope to see you on the other side of this."

She reached out and embraced him. The hug was familiar, like the ones he'd received from his sister, Aury, full of companionship and concern. When she pulled away, she whispered, "Go get your girl."

His smile widened further as the thought of Nova—her eyes, her scent, the sound of her voice—filled him with the strength and courage he needed to start this journey. If all went well, he would be with her the day after tomorrow.

All would go well.

"Let's go, Fynn."

He looked over at Daro, who was standing with one foot out the door, surveying the corridor beyond, as if he expected something to be lurking there. With one last nod to Elodie and Ethel, Fynn stepped past the women and stopped next to the other elf.

"I'm ready."

"All right. This is the end of the line," Daro said, patting the wall in front of them with his left hand. His right held a torch—they each had one—because these tunnels were so far out that they weren't regularly patrolled or lit.

Fynn cast his torch around, taking in the cramped area where they'd ended up. There was no other way out besides the way they came, except for the wooden door above their heads. The walls around them were just packed dirt, held up only by Elodie's enchantments.

If they'd followed the map correctly, this trapdoor *should* let them out within a mile of the Lesser Western Gate, the closest they could get to one of the gates in Arkwood's city wall. The same gate he and Nova had passed over a few months prior on their way to Aerdmure. It wasn't the closest part of the wall to Adenaport and would add time to their journey, but its proximity to the tunnels and Fynn vouching for its lack of guard made it an easy choice.

Daro set his torch on the ground. "Boost me up."

He would go up first, because, as far as they were aware, his appearance would not set off the silent alarms that Fynn's would. The last thing they needed now was the deocre detecting Fynn's presence and ruining the plan before it truly started.

Fynn set his torch down opposite Daro's, shadows dancing from the flickering flames along the walls, and laced his fingers together to provide a step. Normally, supporting the other elf's weight would be trivial, but after nearly two weeks underground, his muscles ached under the strain.

Fortunately, Daro got the hatch open quickly and pulled himself out. The night was so dark that the opening didn't provide any additional light. Only the twinkle of the stars could be seen from where Fynn stood, the new moon doing its job and offering them darkness as cover.

"Put out the torches," Daro whispered down to Fynn as he looked around. Fynn rolled them in the dirt, fully extinguishing them.

He wasn't one to be afraid of the dark, but seeing a long, empty tunnel stretched out behind him with no idea what might be lurking within it was unsettling. Even if it was the same tunnel they had just traversed. Instead, he focused his attention back up the hatch and toward Daro.

"Clear?" he asked in a whisper.

Daro continued to survey for a moment, staying low to the ground, before nodding. He looked down at Fynn. "Clear. I can see the wall in the distance. We have full line of sight to the gate."

Good. All they needed to do was cross the wall...

"Now we wait for the signal," Fynn said. It should come any minute now if they'd timed it correctly. And he was sure—Elodie was sure—they'd timed it correctly.

Not a moment later, a blast went off on the other side of the city, followed by the blare of a horn.

"Now!" Daro reached down a hand for Fynn to grasp. Fynn wrapped his hand firmly around Daro's wrist, then pressed his feet into the wall to help him climb up. Within seconds, both of them were sprinting off toward the wall.

Less than a mile was easy. They'd be there before he could even start to get winded.

Daro had been right—he was just as fast as Fynn, keeping up with him easily. They made it to the wall and scrambled up, landing on the wide parapet.

The same parapet on which Fynn had stood when he'd looked over Arkwood with Nova.

That night had been quiet, the only noises this far out the sounds of crickets and the occasional owl hooting nearby. But tonight...

"Wait," Fynn said, grabbing Daro's arm to stop him before he crossed the parapet.

"Wait? We are so close, Fynn, come on, we just need to get down—"

"Something's wrong."

Daro stopped, his body going rigid. Fynn released him and turned back to face the city, his mouth dropping open at what he beheld.

Red and orange flames licked the northern part of the city, the part where the Voss household had been. The part where elves usually lived.

And not small flames. If they could see them from here, they must have spanned multiple city blocks.

"But that's not—" Daro said, his hand covering his mouth.

"No, it's not."

Elodie and Ethel had planned to set off a diversion in the southeastern part of the city to lure the deocre and the city guard away, giving Fynn time to escape. They hoped the deocre would think he'd surfaced there. They'd even taken one of his old shirts in case his scent was what lured the demon.

But that was planned in an area where it wouldn't actually hurt anyone. And an area far from where the fire was burning right now.

"No accidental fire would cause that," Fynn said, trying to steady his voice. "No witch could cause that so quickly either."

"The deocre." Daro's voice was barely more than a whisper.

It had finally attacked. Had it chosen this moment specifically, knowing Fynn would see it? Had it been aware of his plan all along? Or had this been a coincidence, the new moon giving the deocre the darkness it needed to move more freely around the city? Had the deocre chosen this night for the same reason they did?

"We have to go help," Fynn said.

"That's the dumbest thing I've ever heard you say," Daro replied with a huff. He stood next to Fynn at the edge of the parapet, his arms crossed, eyes focused on the scene unfolding in front of them. "What would this whole escape have been for if we go *back*? What would you even do?"

"There are people dying—*elves* dying. Probably because of me, because the deocre is trying to get to me. I can't just sit here and do nothing." He hiked up a knee to place it at the ledge of the wall but was quickly brought back down by Daro's hand on his shoulder.

"Don't be a dumbass." Daro pulled Fynn around to face him and dropped his hand to the hilt of his sword. "You aren't doing nothing. You're escaping to get back to Nova and the rest of your group. And then continuing to fight this thing, from a place where you can make a difference and not be stuck in a cave all day."

Fynn clenched his fists. Daro was right, but it went against everything he stood for to just let people suffer. Especially elves.

They might not all get along, but they generally had each other's backs.

Daro's eyes bore into his. "Besides, the hardest part is yet to come. We aren't in the clear yet."

Another explosion blasted behind them. Both of them turned sharply toward the sound, toward the flames.

"It's closer." Fynn's voice was thin, hushed.

This time, the blast had been close enough that the shockwaves in the earth beneath them had shaken the wall on which they stood. Were the attacks coming *for* them? Was the deocre causing as much destruction as it could on the way to them?

"We've got to go," Daro said, his voice harried as he turned to face the other side of the parapet. "We still need to break through the wall enchantments."

And hope to all three goddesses that the enchantments worked to hold in the deocre, too.

As hard as it was to draw his eyes away from the destruction before him, Fynn managed to divert his attention and met Daro at the edge.

He stuck out a hand, expecting to feel some sort of force or resistance that they'd have to fight through. Some physical manifestation of the spells. But he only met air and nothingness. "It doesn't feel any different than it did last time."

"Let's hope that doesn't mean there's nothing there." Daro took a step up onto the ledge so that he was standing above Fynn at about chest height. "I'll try first."

Another rumble and explosion shook the wall under them. Fynn chanced a glance over his shoulder, his pulse quickening. Again, the attack was closer. There was no mistaking it now.

The deocre was cornering them.

He glanced back at Daro, meeting the other elf's stare. Daro's dark eyes narrowed, and his face turned into a mask of resolve as he started to climb down the wall.

Only to stop not even two steps down.

"What's wrong?" Fynn asked. Their eyes were level now. He could've grabbed Daro by the shoulders and shoved him off the wall if he'd wanted.

Daro scratched his ear. "I found the edge of the enchantments. Time for Plan A."

Plan A had been Elodie's idea. Initially, they'd had a different method in mind for getting past the enchantments, using knowledge that Defiance scouts had managed to find. But the knowledge was sparse since getting to the wall was time-consuming and being in the open for as long as a real research mission required was dangerous.

Once Elodie had joined the team, she'd reviewed the information and proposed an entirely different plan. One that both Fynn and Daro thought was smart enough to try first.

Daro loosed a dagger from his belt, holding it firmly in his right hand while maintaining his grip on the wall with his left. He reached out the dagger but couldn't fully extend his arm without meeting the same resistance that he'd met with his feet. He began to trace it with the dagger, testing it for weaknesses, for holes that the pinpoint of a dagger could fit through.

"The deocre isn't corporeal…yet," Elodie had said. "The defensive spells guarding the wall are likely more for containing something that isn't smart enough to look for flaws. It would have no way of feeling around for a small hole and would only be able to exit through a large enough one for it to sense."

If they could find a hole, there was a *chance* that they'd be able to use a dagger to cut into the barrier and make a hole big enough for them to get through.

And then hope that the enchantment was smart enough to seal itself.

"It should be," Elodie said. "The High One and their counterparts would have been stupid not to make it self-sealing in case anything were to happen to it. Waiting for a witch to come around and fix it—or even to assign someone to inspect it—would have been a waste of resources."

And a draw of attention, which they were still trying not to do.

But now that the deocre was attacking, how would the Defiance react? Would they have to announce to Arkwood, to Astria, what was behind the attack?

At the same moment that thought crossed Fynn's mind, another explosion jostled them. The ground shook so violently that he instinctively reached out to grab Daro's wrist, without even considering that Daro couldn't really fall anywhere. He winced and let go, but didn't bother looking behind him. The shock had been so forceful, the deocre had to be close. Each attack seemed to bring it exponentially closer.

They were running out of time.

Daro continued to wave his dagger around, with slightly more vigor than before. Beads of sweat formed on his brow—from exertion or adrenaline, Fynn couldn't tell. So far, Daro had come up short.

"Start on Plan B." Daro had to raise his voice slightly over the rush of wind that was now blowing in the first tendrils of smoke from the attacks behind them. "I'll keep looking, but it'll be better to work in tandem."

Without hesitation, Fynn nodded and ran across the parapet to scale back down the wall. It went against every nerve in his body to leave Daro alone in the middle of an impending attack, but Plan B was to try the gate, so he had no other choice.

He sprinted for the gate, waving his hand to try to dissipate some of the smoke swirling around him, and reached it within moments. The old gate was made of solid iron, woven into an interlocked pattern of squares that he could barely fit an arm through. The top arched into the stone surrounding it and the spikes along the bottom had long been overtaken by the brush growing along the wall.

More importantly, there was no sign of a lock in sight.

Fuck.

Without a lock, Plan B would not work. He gripped two of the bars and tried to rattle the gate. It didn't budge. He tried to lift it. Again, nothing.

The next explosion was so close that his elf ears buzzed incessantly, even after the blast died away. What little light the stars emitted was now completely drowned out by the smoke. If it weren't for his elf eyesight, he'd have been completely blind. The temperature in the air plummeted. Gusty wind blew over his arms.

The deocre was coming.

Suddenly, Fynn's vision descended into total darkness.

Scratch that. The deocre was *here.*

Before he could even start climbing back up the wall to join Daro, he was slammed into the stone, his head cracking against it so forcefully that stars swarmed behind his eyelids. Fynn collapsed to the ground on his hands and knees, rubbing the back of his head.

His fingers met something warm and sticky.

Shit.

He didn't feel dizzy, so he probably wasn't concussed. If he could just get past this wall, he would heal.

He crawled back toward the gate, desperate for one last attempt to get out. For one last chance to get to Nova.

His ears were still ringing, his heart pumping, as he fumbled on the ground where the gate met the grass. If the lock wasn't visible, maybe it was buried. He brushed stones, thorns, and weeds of all kinds before finding a lump in the ground.

Could it be?

He pulled his knees under him and hunched over the spot, digging furiously with his hands. They moved at lightning speed as his hair whipped around his face in the wind. Just when he was about to give up and try to get back up the wall again, his fingers scraped metal.

A lock!

He gasped, inhaling a large puff of smoke that burned his lungs. But there was no time to dwell on the pain or the coughs now racking his body. He needed to get that gate open.

Using his hands, he felt around to determine what type of lock he'd found. Locks and knots had their own course at the Academy, one Fynn had particularly enjoyed. This one was familiar, but ancient, proof of how long the gate had been in disuse. It was an older design that, thankfully, wasn't sealed by witch magic.

He ran a finger along the edge of the lock, searching for a seam. Locks of this type were made in two halves of metal that were welded together with the locking mechanism inside. If a knife tip was inserted in just the right way, the two halves could be wrenched apart and the lock undone manually.

Another inhale, another cough. The air was as cold as Besa in winter now.

His body shivered, but it wasn't entirely related to the cold.

The ringing had left his ears, only to be replaced by whispers. Whispers that he couldn't quite make out but sounded familiar. Like they came from a voice he knew…

Ah-ha! He'd found it.

Shutting out the voice, he focused all his concentration on the lock, leaving a finger on the weak spot while he removed a dagger from his belt. He stuck the point of his dagger into the fault, wedging it in as best he could despite the fact that it was clearly too big.

The wind continuously blew his hair into his face, but what did it matter? He couldn't see for shit anyway. He could fix that once he'd gotten past this goddess-forsaken wall.

With a barely audible *click*, the lock came apart. Fynn's heart leaped. He cast the top portion aside and set to work on undoing the lock, silently thanking the Academy for teaching him to do exactly this. Just because he hadn't picked this exact type of lock in years didn't mean it wasn't so ingrained in him that he couldn't do it in mere—

Another *click* and the latch of the lock sprang open.

He was getting out of here.

As he started to heave the gate open—no small feat considering its weight and how lodged into the ground it was—his mind flashed to Daro. They'd agreed if they became separated at any point not to go back for the other, but that was easier said than done. He should try to go back…

"You will pay for what you've done."

Fynn froze.

The whispers. They were back and close enough to comprehend now.

Sorry, Daro. All thoughts of chivalry died with that whisper.

With a groan and another burst of adrenaline, he thrust the gate all the way up, dashed through the opening, and slammed it back down behind him. The holes in the weave of the iron wouldn't keep out the deocre, or at least he had to assume they wouldn't, so he ran like the wind down the short, dark hall ahead of him.

The smoke was starting to get to him, his lungs and eyes burning from the exposed contact. He needed fresh air. *Now.* Tendrils of the smog followed him into the corridor, expanding to fill the space around him and engulfing him entirely. Covering his mouth with his hand, he bowed his head and closed his eyes. Not like he could see anything anyway. The sooner he could get to the other side, the—

His body slammed into something solid with such force that he needed another moment to collect himself. With a quick brush of a hand through his hair, he could feel that the blood from his head wound was already scabbing over and drying. *Good.* Now he could focus on getting this other gate open.

This gate of solid steel.

Fortunately, its durability meant there was hope it would seal out the deocre. Unfortunately—and exactly the reason why this had been Plan B—they had not been sure whether this gate *could* be opened.

It had long been rumored that the Lesser Western Gate had gone into disuse because of this very door. That the witches who had guarded it had magically sealed it so that no one could get through. It didn't even require a lock because of how strong that magic was.

Fynn and Daro had been holding on to hope that the rumors were either false or that time had worn the magic down, making it easier to open.

Elodie had laughed in their faces.

It was her laugh that Fynn heard echoing through his head now. The rush of the wind had died out slightly and the whispers were again unintelligible, but her laugh reverberated above it all.

His hand traced along the edges of the gate. There was a small gap between the wall and the gate, enough to confirm that the gate was not attached. It could move if he could open it. But there was no trace of a latch, a hinge, a lock...anything that would indicate *how* to open it.

"You will not elude me."

The whispers were getting closer again. *Fuck fuck fuck.* He needed to get out of here, and *fast*. There was no way to know if Daro would make it out at this point, but if he didn't—and Fynn didn't either—no one would have any idea what happened to them. Nova would have no idea...

Nova. He was doing this to get to her. To be with her. He needed her like he needed air. If he could just get to her, they could make this right together.

It was her eyes, her laugh that he thought of as his hands furiously traced every inch of the wall for something—anything—that would let him through. A cough clenched at his chest as the smoke trailed in, and a shiver raced down his spine in the cold.

Nothing. There was absolutely nothing.

"There you are."

Fynn whirled around, still unable to see anything but the darkness engulfing him. But that whisper had been so loud. And now he recognized the voice.

Luc Astor's voice.

The deocre had found him. Cornered him.

His hand flew to the hilt of his longsword by instinct only. The weapon would do nothing for him against this being of smoke and air.

Images of Nova continued to flash through his mind, sending his heart racing. He was utterly trapped with no way out, and the deocre was here to exact its revenge.

But he wouldn't go down without a fight.

He still had his agility and his elf senses. He wasn't entirely defenseless.

He could run. Get as far away from this gate and from Daro as possible, lure the deocre away. Daro would follow the plan, get to Adenaport and explain what happened. Maybe he could even get a message to the Defiance somehow. Maybe Fynn could outrun the deocre and find a way to sneak back into the tunnels. But could he attempt that without the deocre following him and gaining access to the tunnels? Was it worth the risk?

"You are mine."

Just as Fynn was deciding which way to run, metal shifted and groaned behind him. A small beam of light—faint, though in this darkness it could have been the sun—illuminated his feet.

He spun around ninety degrees, not wanting to leave the deocre at his back—especially not when it was essentially in this tunnel with him—to find the gate *lifting*.

But entirely too slowly. The smoke was unbearable now, and the chill...

He had no idea who was here to save him, but he did know he wasn't getting out unless he helped.

"You cannot escape me."

But he could damn well try.

Fynn stooped down and slid his hand under the gate, using the strength of his legs to help hoist it up. Once it rose to knee height, a new voice rang out. Another familiar voice.

"Roll through, you idiot!"

Daro!

Somehow Daro had made it through and had come back for him. Somehow Daro had gotten the gate to open and was saving him.

Warm summer air tickled Fynn's lower legs as it blew into the tunnel and tried to overtake the smoke and the chill.

He was going to be free!

Quicker than lightning, he threw his body to the ground and rolled under the gate. The last sound he heard before Daro dropped the gate again was the murderous scream of a dark force that had been outdone.

32

FYNN

ALL FYNN WANTED TO do was lie there and breathe in the fresh air. Inhale the aroma of the wilderness. Let his body savor the oxygen and pump out the remnants of the smoke that scorched his lungs.

But, of course, there was no time for that.

His body was hacking out coughs when Daro grabbed his arm and yanked him upright. "We have to make it to the forest, to the next part of the plan, before we can stop. Can you run?"

Fynn nodded, but the coughs continued. It wouldn't be pretty, but he could do it. "How did you—" He couldn't even finish the thought; his lungs betrayed him again, and the coughing resumed.

"I'll explain later," Daro said, straightening his belt. "Follow me."

The dark-haired elf cast one more look over his shoulder at the wall behind them, then sprinted off toward the woods. Fynn looked back once, too, at the enormous stone wall that looked completely normal from this side. No signs of smoke, no sign of the utter darkness that had consumed him on the other side.

Either the deocre was gone or the protection spells weren't just keeping people in. They were showing the outside a perfectly normal city. An illusion.

With one last deep inhale of clean air, he sprinted off in the direction that Daro had gone, pushing past the burn in his lungs and the minor ache in his head, until he was alongside the elf, and the two ran side by side, not stopping until they reached their safe house.

"What is this place?"

Fynn and Daro had entered what appeared to be a rundown old hut, probably left over from a brief nomadic settlement. It was only one room—one bare room—with no windows. But it was also nearly overgrown with ivy and brush, making it almost invisible to anyone passing by.

Daro had pointed out the markings etched on the front door. It was nothing conspicuous, but to those in the Defiance, the three circles—two adjacent to each other with one balanced atop them, the same Fynn had noticed in the shack back in the park—would mean safety. Trust.

Daro closed the door behind them as silently as he could and pulled down a wooden bar to latch it. "This is one of our outposts. We have a few scattered throughout the woods around Astria. Places we could hide when we felt there was pressure building in Arkwood or when we risked discovery. We've even used these to follow Luc Astor around, keeping tabs on him as he traveled the country."

Amazing. This underground network had existed for decades, had been following Luc's every move, and he'd had no idea. It was nothing short of amazing.

Whoever the High One was had done their job well.

"So, we're safe here?"

Daro shrugged but began loosening the belts holding his weapons in place. "Safe enough. We'll rest here and try to make progress tomorrow."

They had no way of knowing if the spells tracing Fynn's presence were confined to Arkwood or if they'd extend along the border wall. Obviously the deocre was well aware Fynn had escaped, so would it alert the guards stationed outside the city? *Could* it alert them?

It was risky to move during the day, but even riskier to move at night. Sure, they had elf eyesight and hearing, but these woods were still quite dark. They'd more easily be able to spot and fight assailants during the day.

Fynn started to unstrap his belts, too, but left his longsword attached. "I'll take first watch." He moved closer to the door, but stayed inside, as they'd already agreed.

Daro sat down in the far corner, leaning into where the two walls met, and closed his eyes.

"How'd you do it?" Fynn knew he should let Daro rest, but there was no way he could sit there for hours without answers.

Daro tilted his head forward and sighed. "I found the hole about three minutes after you left. It wasn't easy to get my dagger into, but I managed. I could see the deocre approaching, though, and I knew there was no way you'd get back up, or even hear me call you." He stretched his legs out long, placing his hands on his thighs. "I went through, and the world righted itself. I couldn't hear, see, or smell the deocre anymore. I didn't feel the cold anymore. I looked up at where I'd fallen through and watched as the darkness disappeared. It resealed itself like we hoped."

Good; that was good. And it made sense. Plan A had worked. "But then how did you open the gate?"

Daro paused, his brow creasing, as if trying to determine the best way to explain it. Or to decide if Fynn would even believe him.

"I had help."

"Help?" That had not been the response Fynn had anticipated. "From who? No one else was there."

"From Dalia." Daro stared straight at him, watching his reaction.

Fynn managed to keep his face still, despite the storm raging in his brain. "The goddess Dalia?"

Daro nodded.

Fucking hell. These goddesses were silent for centuries and now—*now* Dalia and Canta decided to show up and start looking out for them? Did Terra have something up her sleeve, too?

Through his teeth, Fynn managed to say, "What did she do?"

"She told me to lift the gate."

Fynn waited for Daro to continue, but he didn't. "That's it?"

Daro nodded. "That's it. I ran to the gate, lifted it, and out you came." He leaned his head back against the wall again, letting his eyelids drift shut.

Fynn sighed. He had more questions, but Daro needed to rest, and he probably wouldn't know the answers anyway.

Somehow, the elven goddess had been watching out for them tonight and had intervened to save his life. Because, in the back of his mind, he could only assume that the goddesses had a hand in the protection enchantments around the wall. Maybe Dalia was even the one who resealed Daro's tear.

But why had she come to Daro? Why not tell Fynn to open the gate? Maybe she couldn't get beyond the barrier herself. Had Arkwood inadvertently become a godless city through the enchantments, or did the deocre keep the goddesses out?

These questions and more filtered through Fynn's mind as he started his watch. It wasn't until his thoughts shifted to Nova that he finally breathed deeply, his heart started to slow, and his mind cleared. He was just over twenty-four hours from being reunited with her. From seeing her, holding her, smelling her.

He couldn't get there fast enough.

33

Nova

"**N**ow that you're done being *pampered*, can we get back to training?"

Nova, sitting at the breakfast table, looked up at Jax. He'd just returned from dropping his breakfast dishes off in the kitchen. He leaned a shoulder against the doorframe, his arms crossed and one leg bent over the other at the ankle.

Her neck and back were tender from Mandy's massage yesterday. Despite drinking copious amounts of water as instructed, it hadn't helped. The muscles that Mandy had smoothed out needed more time to repair themselves.

Nova bit back a retort about how far from pampering the trip to the spa had been and instead nodded. "Wielder training, though. Not physical."

"That's Fynn's job anyway."

She averted her gaze, staring at her half-empty plate. "I know."

Jax didn't move for a second, as if he realized he'd struck the wrong chord and wasn't sure what to do next. Luckily, Nova's mother and Raelyn entered the room at that exact moment in such a flurry of motion that Nova dropped her fork. Jax straightened so fast that she was reminded of Fynn's agility.

"It's happened," Raelyn said, her gaze on a piece of parchment in her hand. Upon closer inspection, Nova saw tears trailing down her cheeks, her eyes red and her skin blotchy. While Mother wasn't crying, she had a look of trepidation that Nova had never seen on her before.

Nova pushed herself up from her chair to run to Raelyn, taking her sister's hand and hoping she could pass some of the calm she felt on to her. "What happened?"

It was Mother who answered. "The deocre attacked Arkwood last night." Her eyes darted between Nova and Jax, who had come to stand a few paces behind Nova.

"Attacked? What do you mean?" Nova asked. But in her gut, she knew what it meant. Death. Destruction.

Her blood went cold.

Raelyn held out the piece of parchment. "A raven delivered this just moments ago."

"From who?" Nova took the parchment slowly, turning her gaze to her mother. "Your secret organization?"

Mother nodded. "The Defiance managed to get a raven out in the early hours of the morning. They didn't even bother with our usual code."

Nova raised an eyebrow. "I thought they didn't know who you were?"

"They don't." Mother smiled meekly. "But that doesn't mean a raven can't find me."

Nova looked down at the note in her hand. As she read, a shadow fell over the note...Jax, who had come to stand next to her, was reading over her shoulder.

Arkwood is under attack. The northern neighborhoods. Many elven casualties. The governors are calling it a wielder attack.

She turned the note over, expecting more on the back, but finding it blank. "That's it? That's all we get?"

Her mother pulled it from her hand. "It's all that was safe to write in a letter. I'm sure we will learn more from the newsprint. And I may need to return to Arkwood to learn the finer details myself."

"You can't!" Raelyn dropped Nova's hand and grabbed her mother's arm with both hands. "It's not safe for you—for *anyone*—there. What if this was just the beginning? What if there are more attacks planned?"

"We have to know more if we are going to strategize and fight it." Mother patted Raelyn's hand. "If I leave today, I can be back tomorrow."

Raelyn's eyes flicked to Nova's, begging her to intervene. Nova didn't like the idea any more than her sister did, but they now lived in times where hard choices had to be made. She and Fynn had made the hard choice to split up. Hopefully her mother would come back to them.

"Go," Nova said. "But don't linger. Do you need to take Jax or Esta with you?"

"Training, Nova," Jax said with a snarl. He tensed beside her.

She waved a hand at him. "Kael can train me while you're gone."

"I'm better on my own," Mother said. "Less likely to get caught, or to be asked questions, than if I'm caught with a counterpart." She'd already told them how she'd let her bodyguard go after Luc's death. He'd apparently put up a fight, claiming that Blackmore was still loose and more dangerous than ever, but she still managed to persuade him to leave so she could get back to her secret meetings.

Jax relaxed beside her, his breathing audibly slower than it had been moments ago. Nova kept her eyes on her mother and nodded. She was still getting used to this stronger, more forceful side of the elder witch, but she needed to trust her.

Mother turned to Raelyn, whose face was a perfect display of shock and betrayal. "Come, Rae, you can help me pack a small bag." She pulled Raelyn with her from the room, leaving Nova and Jax alone once more.

"Training is now more important than ever, don't you think?" Jax said, a hint of scolding in his voice.

Nova looked over her shoulder at him and crossed her arms. "No. If anything, finding the other two descendants is now the most important. But I'll meet you on the beach in half an hour."

She needed to talk to Kael before they got started. He hadn't made an appearance for breakfast yet, but she had an idea where she might find him.

As suspected, Kael was sitting on the deck, facing the ocean, a mug in one hand resting in his lap. Nova watched him through the glass door, hating that she had to break up his serenity with the news she was about to share. But he would find out eventually.

With a sigh, she pushed open the sliding door and stepped out into the breezy morning air.

He looked up, smiling when he saw who had found him. "Good morning."

"Looks like I figured out your secret for a quiet morning," she replied, sitting in the wicker chair next to his.

"It's just that I didn't think I'd ever be here again. Especially with you." He brought the mug to his lips, sipping reverently.

Her heart warmed, her magic singing happily underneath her skin. "Soon, we can do this, *and* you'll be free."

His eyes darkened as he cast his gaze back out to the ocean. "We'll see."

Nova furrowed her brow at his ominous tone. Where had his optimism for a future together gone? Given how little time they'd yet had, she was surprised at the way her heart tightened at the thought of that dream not playing out.

She inhaled deeply, pressing her hands into her thighs. "There's news from Arkwood."

Kael's eyes darted back to her. "Oh?"

"Yes. An attack, on the northern neighborhoods. Mostly elven casualties."

His mouth dropped open, his free hand rubbing at the rugged facial hair growing on his cheeks and chin. "How many?"

She shook her head. "We don't know yet. Mother received a raven from the Defiance. She's going to sneak back into the city to figure out what happened and why."

"Alone?"

Nova nodded.

"Is that wise?"

She shrugged. "She says it's safer that way."

Kael frowned at the breaking waves. "What can we do?"

"Jax wants to keep training today, and I suppose I should since I've now missed quite a few days." And she needed an opportunity to speak to him about the connection to Raelyn anyway. "I'm hoping that Rae and Esta can do some digging into the other two descendants."

"I'm sorry I didn't tell you, by the way," Kael said quickly.

"Tell me what?"

"About your heritage from Canta."

"Oh. Right."

He sighed and leaned forward, placing his mug on the ground next to him. "It isn't necessarily a secret, but we didn't go around flaunting it either. It comes from my father's side. He had a book full of the lineage from Canta down to me, tracing the whole family over the centuries."

"What happened to that book?"

"No idea. I imagine it was destroyed or taken when they went through our house after I was sent to Mistfell."

So much of Astria's history, lost at the hands of a greedy politician.

"Is there anything else about our family that I should know?"

He smiled, his green eyes sparkling with the reflection of the morning sun on the water. "Lots. But nothing important to this fight."

She understood. There was more he could tell her, more he wanted to tell her, but right now he couldn't. It was still too hard for him to discuss.

Nova stood up to head back inside and change before Jax found her and began berating her for not being ready. "Would you like to help with training today?"

Kael stretched his arms above his head, then stood to join her. "Wouldn't miss it."

34

NOVA

NOVA HAD BEEN ABLE to convince Raelyn and Esta to go into town and visit Terra's temple. Their goal was to find out whatever they could about Terra's living descendants and hope to the goddesses that the priestesses there knew something.

She'd expected one or both of them to grumble about it, but Esta actually looked thrilled to be getting out of the house, with a task to do. And Raelyn had wanted a distraction from thinking about the danger their mother was putting herself in. So the two of them set off around the same time that Mother departed, but in opposite directions.

That left Jax, Nova, and Kael alone at the cottage. They stood on the beach, sun-protectant spell applied and dressed for training. Jax led Nova through some warm-up spells. It had been almost a week since their last session, so he insisted she ease back into the training mindset. She disagreed, ready to go, but she also knew better than to fight him.

After an hour of mindless spell work—of summoning wind to blow the sand into shapes, of wielding fire to light up the darkness Jax cast, of sprouting grasses and vegetation along the dune line—Jax decided Nova was ready to return to more complex spell work.

But she had another proposal in mind.

"What if," she said, placing her hands on her hips, "the three of us work together to figure out how we can create defensive spells against the deocre?"

Kael smiled, while Jax furrowed his brow and said, "We've already got defensive spells up around the house."

"I know." She tried her best to keep her tone sickeningly sweet. "But what if we could protect the whole town? The whole country?"

Jax pinched the bridge of his nose between his thumb and forefinger. "That would take an insane amount of power."

"But we have three insanely powerful witches right here." Nova waved her hand to indicate the three of them. "I know I'm not quite at the level of power the two of you are—"

"You are—" Kael started, but Nova held up a hand to silence him.

"No. I'm not. But there's something about Fynn and Raelyn that makes me more powerful."

"Raelyn, too?" Jax asked, his eyes widening.

"Wait," Kael said, crossing his arms. "What are you talking about?"

"I noticed back in Aerdmure, once Fynn and I...got together, that my power strengthened when he touched me." If she was honest, it started long before their first kiss, but that information didn't seem relevant at the moment. "In the last few days, I've noticed the same thing happening when Raelyn touches me. It feels entirely different, but it's the same effect."

Kael's eyes widened as he marveled at the revelation. "Fascinating."

"Amplification." Jax muttered the word with his gaze cast down at the sand, his hand rubbing at his temple. Nova could almost see the gears turning in his head.

Kael turned to face him. "Like your father."

He nodded, not looking up. "But I've never heard of an animate object being the amplifier, let alone two."

"Could it just be anyone with magical power in general?" Kael asked. He approached Nova and held out an arm. "Try me."

Unable to determine a reason not to, she placed her left hand on his arm and gripped it firmly. A tickle shot up her arm, not unlike the way her magic usually reacted to his touch, but she'd assumed that was more related to their blood relationship. Magic recognizing where it came from.

She closed her eyes and tried to focus on the feeling, tried to force the tendrils of magic pooling around his hand into her core like they did of their own accord with Raelyn and Fynn. But it wouldn't budge. It stayed where it was, almost surface level, not something she could wield.

With an exhale, she opened her eyes and dropped her hand. "There's something, but not amplification."

A shadow of something—disappointment?—crossed over Kael's face, so quickly that Nova almost missed it. Her heart sank. He'd been hoping he could prove as valuable to her as Fynn and Raelyn.

"So, not just anyone, then," he said, his tone a little more somber than it had been just a moment ago. She wanted to reach out, to hug him, to assure him it didn't mean anything about their relationship, but something held her back. Instead, she bit her lip and remained in place.

"No, not just anyone. There must be something that Fynn and Raelyn have in common that we aren't seeing." Jax started pacing in front of them.

A thought occurred to Nova. Far-fetched but not without potential. "Maybe something related to nature? Raelyn is a geo, and elves are the most in tune with the earth around us. Fynn was telling me about Dalia's Festival, which is entirely—"

"Not a bad thought." Jax stopped pacing and finally looked back up at her. "Let's test it when Raella is back. She's also a geo."

"Or with Esta," Kael said.

"I'll try both." Frustration was starting to build inside her, her stomach turning in knots. Didn't they see that *what* caused the amplification wasn't the point? "But isn't knowing that two of them *can* amplify me enough? That should make me at least equal with the power you two have. Which means that we can then be strong enough to cast a larger spell, maybe over all of Adenaport to start."

Jax chuckled. "You know how to dream big."

"I spent my whole life doing nothing but dreaming. When there isn't much you can do, your imagination runs wild dreaming up the things you wish you could."

She hadn't meant the words to be said with such venom, but, goddess-damn it, she was tired of people telling her she couldn't do things. Her whole life had been a mash-up of "maybe a simpler spell" and "let's focus on other skills." Not once had anyone looked at her and told her, "Go ahead and try," and truly meant it.

At least, not until Fynn.

As visions and memories of him crossed her mind, the magic churning in her gut burned brighter, hotter. Almost as if he were right there with her. Part of her wished she could just unleash the pent-up magic, the fury building within her, but what had the last months of training been for, if not to master control?

Instead, she closed her eyes and repeated the mantra Fynn had taught her: *Breathe, breathe.* Over and over again, she repeated the words, focusing on her breath and slowing her heart rate. On making sure her magic stayed contained.

Little by little, the meditation worked. When she opened her eyes again, her heart settled, and her magic calmed from a flood to a trickle.

Kael and Jax were staring at her—Kael with a look of concern and Jax with a look of amusement.

"You back?" he asked, his mouth ticking up on one side.

"We're trying it," she said through her teeth, staring him dead in the eye. "We're trying it today."

Kael reached an arm toward her. "Maybe we should take a br—"

She stepped to the side, out of his reach. "No. We are doing this. Now."

The two male witches exchanged a glance, as if trying to decide who was going to stand up to her. In the end, neither did.

35

FYNN

THERE IT WAS. IN the distance. The cottage.

The sun was setting behind them, a deep golden glow cast along the horizon ahead, which stretched out over the quiet ocean. Clouds overhead blocked out any sign of the stars or the waxing moon, and the incoming breeze smelled of rain.

But Fynn didn't care. He'd be inside soon. Out of the storm and in the arms of Nova Astor.

Though he'd never seen the cottage before, he knew this was the right one. The Defiance had records of all the Astor family properties and had willingly given over the address when he and Daro left. Thank the goddesses for that, because otherwise he would have had to inquire in town, and who knew what kind of suspicions that would've raised.

A drop of rain landed on his cheek. He wiped it away, drawing in a sharp inhale. After almost three weeks apart, the anticipation of seeing Nova again pulsed through his body, sending his heart racing and his mind whirling. By forcing himself to breathe, he reminded himself of the meditation he'd worked on with her.

"That's it, then?" Daro asked, stepping up beside him. The other elf fidgeted with his longsword as he took in the sight of the cottage, which, in truth, was a complete misnomer.

The Astor cottage was nothing short of a mansion, particularly for Adenaport standards. Though only two floors, eaves and gables on the roofline made it clear that a full attic sat at the top, and the outside was surrounded by a covered porch. Sheer curtains were drawn over most of the windows, enough that light could get through, but Fynn couldn't make out any distinct shapes inside.

No light shone through the second-floor windows, implying everyone inside was downstairs. Perhaps they were sitting down for dinner.

"Fynn? Is this it?"

He startled, having forgotten that Daro was still there, waiting for an answer while his mind was stuck on picturing Nova clinking glasses with Raelyn to start dinner, her cheeks flushed from the glass of wine she'd already finished.

Fynn cleared his throat. "Yeah. I think so."

Thunder rumbled in the distance. Out over the ocean, heat lightning lit the sky, momentarily illuminating the gathering clouds. More raindrops fell onto the elves.

"Let's get on before this turns into a proper downpour." Daro struck off in the direction of the house. Fynn inhaled deeply again, following him.

The wind picked up, blowing loose strands of Fynn's hair across his face, nearly obstructing his view when the front door to the cottage flew open and two figures ran out onto the porch. One, the taller, was leading the way, her curly hair bouncing as she ran along the porch, dragging the other, just slightly shorter, with a dark braid trailing behind her.

Fynn's heart stopped.

Nova.

Thunder cracked as he tried to call out her name, drowning out the sound.

The sisters were running toward the back of the cottage, likely to watch the storm, and would disappear from view in seconds. A lump had formed in Fynn's throat at the sight of the woman he loved, and he found he no longer had the words to try to get her attention.

Idiot. Are you agile or not?

Next thing he knew, he was standing beside the porch, rain now falling in earnest as he pushed loose strands of hair from his face and tilted his gaze up to the two witches standing just slightly above him on the porch.

Green eyes that sparkled like emeralds bore into his, widening into shimmering orbs as Nova beheld him standing in front of her.

"Fynn!"

He intended to run up the stairs to meet her on the porch, but somehow—stunned as he was to now be within reach of her—she beat him and met him on the sand, rain soaking her hair and tunic. She threw herself into his arms, wrapping her legs around his waist and burying her face in his neck.

He pressed his nose into her hair, inhaling the lavender scent coming off her in the mist of the rain, and he instantly relaxed, his mind settling, his pulse slowing.

"Oh my goddess, Fynn."

Her voice was a sweet melody in his ear. He laughed, stroking her hair with one hand while keeping the other firmly clasped around her back.

"Nova." Her name escaped his lips in a breath, barely audible over the building storm.

She pulled her head back so those green eyes he loved getting lost in were blazing into him once more. Her hands found his cheeks, her thumbs brushing away drops of rain.

He was vaguely aware of Daro now standing next to him, of Raelyn standing on the porch, beaming. But the heat of Nova's body pressed against his, of her very presence in his arms, consumed him, blocking out the rest of the world until it was just the two of them and the storm.

"You found me," she said in that voice he would never be able to get enough of. Breathy, full of exhilaration.

"I told you nothing could keep me away."

His lips crashed against hers, unable to wait another moment. His fingers combed into her hair, pressing her against him so he could deepen the kiss. Thunder rumbled around them, the ground trembling. Somewhere, a voice shrieked and laughed.

Nova's tongue parted his lips, and he allowed her in, basking in the feeling of being back with her, of kissing her again. How good—how right—it felt, to be this close to her.

He'd known love before, but he'd never experienced this. What he and Nova had...it was different. More raw. More ethereal.

Still holding on to her, he took a step forward, then another, until they'd reached one of the porch columns, and he pressed her back into it. Tilting her chin just slightly, he kissed her further, deeper, the little whimper she let out in response sending shockwaves through his body.

Her hands drifted from his cheeks down to his arms, giving him room to bring his hands to her neck, his thumbs tracing her jawbone on either side as their tongues continued to collide.

Someone nearby cleared their throat, bringing Fynn back to the present and forcing him to reluctantly tear his lips from Nova's. The abrupt separation left him empty, until he glimpsed the joy in her eyes, the redness around her mouth from his kisses, and his heart filled again.

"Can you at least come inside and get a room?"

Fynn smiled, not moving his gaze from Nova as he responded to her sister. "Go away, Raelyn."

Nova smiled and let out a giggle as the ground stopped rumbling, her head falling back against the column behind her. The storm raged on, both of them thoroughly soaked. Tendrils of hair stuck to Nova's neck and forehead. Fynn had never seen anyone so beautiful.

"You don't want to go inside and get dry?" Nova asked him quietly, so that Raelyn and Daro, who had moved to the porch to escape the storm, couldn't hear.

Fynn leaned forward and whispered in her ear, "I'm not ready to share you yet." Her body shivered, a response that delighted him. "And, besides, I like you *wet*."

"Go away, Raelyn," Nova said, squeezing her legs tighter around Fynn and nipping at his ear.

This time, it was Fynn who let out the low laugh. "You too, Daro," he called to his companion as he leaned in to claim Nova's mouth again.

But before his lips found hers, her head jerked around to face the two on the porch. "Daro?"

The dark-haired elf wiggled his fingers at her. "Nice to see you again, Nova."

Nova turned to look back at Fynn, and though there was still so much love, so much *joy* in those eyes, he could tell the spell had worn off. Something had changed.

Their moment of reunion was over.

He sighed, her body slumping against his. Taking a step back, he pulled her from the column and let her legs fall from his waist. "I'm not done with you yet."

The corners of her mouth twitched up into a smile, her green eyes twinkling. "I'm not done with you either, Fynn." Her hands slid down his arms until they met his, their fingers interlacing. "But it looks like you've got as much to catch me up on as I do you. Let's get dried off, have a chat, and then I'll show you where you'll—*we'll*—be staying." She winked, pulling him along behind her toward the porch stairs.

"Don't think for a second that I'm letting you out of my sight, Fynn Voss."

His heart purred in content.

36

NOVA

NOVA CROSSED THE THRESHOLD into the living room at the back of the cottage, pulling Fynn along behind her. Her hand hadn't left his since they'd intertwined them moments ago, her body refusing to be parted from his.

He was here. He was actually here.

Flutters of magic danced through her—that wonderful, powerful feeling she'd been missing for weeks. His touch was a drug she couldn't get enough of, a drug she now had in glorious supply.

"I'll grab the others," Raelyn said, closing the sliding door behind her, forcing out the sounds of the storm. She headed for the dining room, where the two of them had left the others mid-meal to go watch the storm together.

Nova nodded but didn't speak, her tongue still tied from the shock of seeing those deep amethyst eyes reflecting lightning back at her just moments ago. Of finding Fynn—*her Fynn*—standing right below her on the porch, his shirt clinging to his chest in the rain. Those muscles she loved pushing against the wet fabric.

Just as she couldn't let him go, she couldn't take her eyes off him either.

"You're a wielder now, right?"

A deep voice cut across the room, jarring her from her thoughts and her reverie. A voice she remembered and didn't think she'd hear again. Her eyes flicked back toward the sliding doors, where lightning flaring outside illuminated Daro, the elf who had stood in for Fynn one night and left a sour taste in her mouth.

"Yes," she replied, intentionally keeping her tone curt, as he had with her.

He waved his hand at the puddle around his feet, then indicated the one forming under hers and Fynn's. "Care to dry us off?"

"Oh!" In the excitement, she'd forgotten that they were still soaked and had trailed in the water from outside. She looked back at Fynn, who grinned and shrugged. "Right, yeah, let me do that."

With a wave of her hand in his direction, a blast of warm wind blew Daro dry, the puddle at his feet evaporating. He shook the hair out of his ponytail and combed his fingers through it.

"Thanks."

She nodded, then turned and did the same for Fynn, her heart clenching as those muscles returned to their hiding spot beneath his dry shirt. There would be time to explore them later. All of the time, actually, since he was never leaving her side again...

As she was finishing off drying herself and redoing her braid, the rest of their cadre swarmed into the room. Kael swept Fynn into a hug, then Esta took her turn. The female elf eyed him up and down, as if inspecting for damage, but, finding none, she retreated with a nod to let Jax through.

"Welcome back." Jax stuck out a hand to shake Fynn's.

Fynn quirked an eyebrow, but took Jax's hand and nodded. "Thank you. Glad to be back."

Raelyn flitted around the room, lighting the rest of the lamps before turning her attention to Fynn. "Ok, ok, now that everyone's here and happy, let's settle in for story time."

Nova pulled Fynn to sit next to her on the couch, catching his gaze in the newly lit room as she did so. All of the tension, the unease, the worry that had blanketed her since Fynn had left disappeared like a weight lifted from her chest. Seeing those eyes, that smile again...it was enough. It was all she needed.

Until that smile turned into a frown, and his eyes darkened.

His thumb reached up and brushed under her eye, where she'd nearly forgotten a new scar lay. "What happened?"

Her gaze darted to Jax, who sat opposite them in the armchair that her mother usually occupied. The other wielder tensed, sensing how this was going to go, and started rubbing his temple with his fingers.

Fynn followed her gaze, then snapped his eyes back to her. "What did he do to you?"

"Nothing, Fynn." She reached out and took his arm to hold him back as he tried to stand. "I'm fine."

"What," Fynn wrenched free from her grip and stalked over to Jax, towering over the seated witch, "did you do, witch?"

Jax held up his hands. "We were training, just like you asked us to. Things got out of hand—"

"Out of hand?"

"Fynn!" Nova stood and grabbed him, using all her strength to pull him back down on the couch with her. "We were practicing using defensive spells, and Jax got one through on me. He healed me instantly. I'm fine." She reached up and touched his cheek, pushing it gently so his gaze met hers again. "I'm fine. Truly."

His shoulders dropped slightly. Turning his gaze back to Jax, he said, "If you ever do that again—"

"He won't."

This time, it was Kael's voice that interrupted. Nova and Fynn turned to look back at him where he leaned against the wall by the sliding doors.

"We all need to trust each other. We're on the same side here. Bickering amongst ourselves will only make it easier for the deocre to defeat us."

Silence fell over the room as the group digested his words.

"He's right," Nova said, squeezing Fynn's hand but looking at Jax. "We need each other. We've got research to do, spells to build to defeat this thing and to protect Astria. Fynn," she turned her gaze back to those violet eyes, "let this go. I promise, I'm fine. Ok?"

He stared at her for a moment, then nodded.

Nova breathed a sigh of relief. Fynn's reaction was almost certainly rooted in his fears about not being able to protect Lena and his mother. But this was a step in the right direction to proving that she could defend herself, that he didn't need to worry so much.

Exactly like she had promised him before they had parted.

"Good, now, where do we begin?"

Jax waved a hand at Daro. "How about introductions?"

After introducing Daro to the rest of the group and bringing Daro up to speed on Kael's story, Fynn and Daro explained what they could about the Defiance, their research into the deocre, the tracking spell on Fynn, and the attack.

"You were the reason the deocre attacked?" Nova gasped, her hand flying to her mouth.

"My escape was, I suppose." Fynn hung his head. The guilt was clearly weighing on him. Nova fought the urge to pull his head into her lap and brush her fingers through his hair to soothe him.

There would be time for that later.

"Because the deocre is targeting you for Luc's death?" Jax asked.

Daro and Fynn both nodded.

"So it could be after me too?"

"It's possible," Daro said. "Best you don't step foot in Arkwood for now."

"Wasn't planning to, but that certainly complicates how this ends." Jax stood and walked toward the glass doors, peering out over the ocean that was still wild from the disappearing storm. "Even if we destroy the deocre, we still need to find a way to clear mine and Fynn's names."

"Let's focus on one thing at a time," Kael said. "End the deocre. Then worry about the fallout from Luc's death."

Nova nodded in agreement. Focusing on too many things at once had led them down a tumultuous path to begin with, and to what end? What had they gained?

"How do we take it down, though?" Fynn asked. "Fox wouldn't tell us. He insisted that was information only for the High One."

"Good thing we know the High One, then," Raelyn said with a giggle.

Daro leaned forward. "What?"

"Oh yes, did we forget to mention? Our mother is the High One."

Nova could have sworn waves of shock vibrated through the room. Daro's mouth dropped to the floor, while Fynn shook his head, mumbling incoherently under his breath.

She put a hand on his shoulder to steady him. "Fynn?"

His head stopped moving. He lifted his gaze to meet hers. "Sorry, I just didn't see that one coming."

She laughed. "Trust me, neither did we."

"Does that mean you know how to defeat the deocre?" Daro asked, bringing them all back to the topic at hand.

"Yep," Raelyn said brightly. "And we are one-third of the way to being ready to fight it."

Daro leaned forward more, waving his hand as if gesturing for Raelyn to continue. But Raelyn simply looked between Nova and Kael.

Fine. She'd just tell them herself.

After a sharp inhale, Nova said, "We need a descendant of each goddess to defeat the deocre. Mother knows the spell we need to do once we've identified the descendants, but first, we need them to willingly participate."

Daro froze, while Fynn asked, "And you've already found one?"

"Me," Kael said. "My family is descended from Canta."

Fynn's hand tensed in Nova's. "Which means..."

She nodded. "Yes, it means I am, too."

"But don't worry, I'll be doing the fighting." Kael smiled at Fynn, whose grip slackened slightly.

He nodded at Kael, then looked back at Nova. "So we just need a descendant of Terra and Dalia?"

"Yes," she responded. "Raelyn and Esta have been searching the records in the Adenaport temples for Terra's, but maybe you or Daro have ideas for how to find Dalia's?"

"I do."

Daro had unfrozen and was walking toward them with long strides, his face paler than usual.

She furrowed her brow. "Care to share?"

He swallowed, stopping his prowl to stand behind the armchair Jax had vacated. "I'm a descendant of Dalia."

Nova's mouth dropped open, her gaze flicking over to Raelyn, whose eyebrows had risen nearly to her hairline. She started to clap excitedly as Esta grumbled behind them.

"Guess we have two-thirds now."

37

NOVA

Nova's pulse drummed elatedly at Daro's revelation. If he was right—and why would he lie about that?—then they were one step closer to their goal. Now they just needed to scour the temple archives and find Terra's descendant.

Fynn was here. They'd found another descendant. Things were starting to look up.

Her magic thrummed inside of her, itching for a moment of release to revel in her excitement.

"The gate..."

Fynn's voice brought Nova's focus back to the room, and her magic quieted. He was staring at Daro, but his eyes were glassy, like he wasn't fully present. The flicker of the lamp cast shadows across his face.

"What gate, Fynn?" she asked.

Daro answered, leaning with his elbows on the back of the armchair. "The gate we escaped Arkwood through. Dalia helped me open it to save Fynn."

"Dalia...spoke to you?" A memory flashed through Nova's mind—more than one memory, actually. A memory of Silvana on her first day in Aerdmure, mentioning that Canta had warned Silvana of her arrival, asked her to prepare to host her. Then a second memory from when they'd left for Benedict's cabin of Silvana speaking in a tone she'd never heard before. Speaking about descendants.

Canta had been speaking through Silvana to Nova. Canta had told Nova what they needed to do.

Our children will right the way.

"It wasn't the first time, but it doesn't happen often," Daro said. His eyes moved between Nova and Kael. "Does Canta speak to you?"

"Yes," Kael responded, so quickly that Nova's heart skipped a beat. She turned to look at him, her brows furrowing. "Most often while I was in Mistfell. Telling me to hold on. I think she was watching over my escape, too."

He hadn't mentioned that detail when they spoke about his escape previously. Maybe he hadn't wanted her to think he was crazy, or he hadn't wanted to overburden her by sharing too much of their family history at once.

She shook her head to clear those thoughts and returned her focus to Daro's question.

"Not directly to me, but through the head priestess in Aerdmure, yes."

Maybe Silvana hadn't wanted to overwhelm Nova with her heritage before she'd had a chance to hear it from Kael. Could she now expect a direct visit from Canta?

Her body shivered. Fynn wrapped an arm around her and pulled her in close enough for her to breathe in his warming cedar and sea-breeze scent.

There was something so...*right* about that scent here in Adenaport.

"Well, great!" Raelyn said, pressing her hands into her thighs and standing. "Now we've got two. Mother will be thrilled when she gets back tomorrow night." She turned to face Esta. "Think the priestesses will let us in for a late-night research session?"

Esta uncrossed her arms and stepped forward. "I think we can make them."

"I'll come this time," Jax said, following Esta and Raelyn out the door.

Maybe he wanted to be helpful, or maybe he just wanted to get away from Fynn in case he sought retaliation for Nova's scar. She couldn't tell, but also didn't care, burying her face deeper into the elf's chest. The others could go and try to find answers.

Tonight was about her and Fynn.

Kael must have become very adept at reading her already because he gestured for Daro to follow him out of the room, acting as the gracious host. "Daro, I think there's one last guest room we can get set up for you…"

Daro exchanged a glance with Fynn, who just nodded at the other elf, before following Kael out of the room and up the stairs.

"And then there were two." Fynn's chest vibrated against her cheek as he spoke.

"Finally." She tilted her head up to look at him, letting her lips brush against his. "Want to go for a walk?"

Fynn laughed, and she was reminded why it was one of her favorite sounds. Goddess, she'd missed that laugh! "You and your walks."

She beamed at him.

"Yes, Al, let's go for a walk."

Her heart fluttered as his nickname for her passed his lips, but she collected herself enough to stand, grab a blanket from near the couch, and lead him back outside and off the porch, onto the sand.

"First rule of beach walks," she said, turning to him and tucking a loose white strand of hair behind his ear, "is shoes off."

"Yes, ma'am," he said, releasing her hand to undo his boots and drop them by the stairs. The few seconds it took felt like an eternity, but once his fingers were safely linked in hers and her magic was humming happily, she breathed easily again.

The storm had passed, but a few clouds lingered, making the beach quite dark. Nova found a piece of driftwood, then conjured a small fire to turn it into a torch, so they could better see as their feet traversed the wet sand. Ghost crabs scurried around ahead of them, scared off by the light of the fire but still anxious to find dinner now that the rain had stopped.

"I've missed you so much, Fynn," she said as they walked northward, hand in hand. "Not knowing where you were or what you were doing or if you were safe nearly drove me mad. Catch me up, tell me everything. Did you find Persy? Did you get him to agree?" Nova looked up at him just in time to see a shadow pass over his eyes. She bit her lip. *Too far.* "Or maybe just start with how are you?"

He rubbed the back of his neck with his free hand. "Not great. But better now."

She squeezed his hand. "Me too."

"Persy is dead."

Her feet stopped moving. With their hands connected, she yanked him to stop beside her. The torch tumbled to the sand, snuffing out, as she pulled him into a deep embrace. "Oh, goddess, I'm so sorry, Fynn."

"The deocre," he whispered into her hair.

She pulled back, looking into his watery eyes. "No."

He nodded. "He wasn't a great father. We had our disagreements, but then I found out he had been in the Defiance all this time, fighting for a better world, and it just isn't fair that I didn't get to know that side of him. That he hid it from me."

"Not fair at all." He'd never spoken about his father with such emotion. Had he even had time to grieve Persy's passing? Or had he been in survival mode, much like she had been? "But you now get to carry on the best of him."

He smiled at her weakly. "I'm trying." He picked up the extinguished torch and handed it to her. She relit it, then laced her fingers back into his.

They continued walking as he told her about how he'd found Fox and the Defiance. Nova was shocked to hear that Lena had been part of it, that she *and* Persy had managed to hide it from him for so long.

Nova wasn't the only one dealing with an upheaval of everything she thought she knew about her family and her loved ones.

They reached a point where they could barely make out the lights from the cottage and stopped. Any farther and they risked moving outside the protective boundaries that she, Jax, and Kael had worked hard to put in place.

Nova doused the torch's flame, laid out the blanket, and then guided Fynn to the ground, where they sat facing each other with their legs crossed, their knees touching and their hands folded together.

"I got your messages," Fynn said, rubbing his thumb over the back of her hand.

They'd worked! Her mouth spread into a wide grin. "You did?"

He nodded and smiled back. "It's how I knew to come here. But they also helped keep me going. I'd replay them over and over in my head, especially when they came in your voice."

"I hope they made you feel less alone."

He pulled her into his lap, with her legs hooked around his waist. "They did. But let's not have to do that again."

She pressed her forehead against his, feeling his warm breath against her lips. "You have a deal."

His lips collided with hers before she could prepare herself, sending her magic into a frenzy, pulsing through her fingertips and into his back.

"Fuck, I forgot how good that feels," he whispered against her lips.

She kissed him again, harder, deeper this time, letting the power flow through her hands and into him. He pulled the ribbon out of her hair, letting her braid free. They stayed like that for a moment, the cool breeze off the ocean swirling their hair together in a contrast of light and dark, and the rolling ocean waves, still rough from the storm, drowning out all other noise.

Fynn leaned forward, settling Nova onto her back on the blanket, not breaking the kiss. He pressed his hands to the ground on either side of her shoulders and unfolded his legs so that his knees framed her hips.

It was a perfect moment, like something from a dream. To be here, in her most happy place with the person who made her the happiest—who made her feel whole—was all she could have ever hoped for. All her worries, all her fears and doubts about what the future held, fell away as she explored his body with her hands, pulling his shirt off over his head so she could finally get to those muscles she loved.

"Fynn," she breathed as his kisses made their way down her neck. Her skin broke out in goosebumps.

He stopped instantly and met her gaze, his breath as heavy as hers.

"I've missed you. So much."

He leaned down and kissed her collarbone, snaking one hand under the edge of her tunic and placing it on the bare skin of her waist. "I missed you, too."

"I want this. Now."

His head drew back sharply, white-blond strands of hair tickling her cheek as they hung over her face. "Here?"

"I can't think of a better place." She smiled at him, tucking some of those strands behind his ear again.

He was quiet for a moment, his violet eyes filled with longing as they glanced over her face. "You can still do that ward?"

She laughed, pulling herself forward to kiss him and summoning the magic in her core that would envelop them, making sure that no one could see or hear them.

"Done," she whispered in his ear.

He tore off her tunic in a frenzy, planting kisses on her mouth, her chest, trailing down her body until he reached her navel, and he worked her out of her leggings.

Within moments, they joined in the last way possible, the only way they hadn't yet explored. And as they did, the stars twinkled brighter, the wind stilled completely, and the earth rumbled gently around them as the magic of their union spread from Nova, through Fynn, and into the world.

38

FYNN

"WHERE WERE YOU LAST night?"

Raelyn's voice echoed from down the stairs. Fynn couldn't yet see her, but he could picture her with her hands on her hips, her head tilted to one side as she stared Nova down.

Sure enough, when he reached the landing of the staircase just behind Nova, there she was: exactly as he'd predicted.

"We, uh..." Nova stammered, her cheeks flushing. He loved when they did that, especially when it was because of him.

Raelyn's eyes widened as her mind went to places that were likely true, but Fynn jumped in to stop it from going too far. "We went for a walk. To catch up."

They certainly had caught up—on everything that had happened since they'd parted, yes, but also emotionally. Physically.

Twice on the beach and then once more when they snuck back into the quiet house hours later.

As suspected, it had been worth every minute of the wait. He'd do it all over again if it achieved the same result as that first time they had made love. It was a memory he would never forget.

"A walk?" Raelyn tapped her forefinger to her chin, raising one eyebrow. "Sure, ok, a walk."

Nova looked up at Fynn, those bold green eyes nearly making his knees give out. Something about those tired, puffy eyes...knowing that he was the reason behind them...it was enough to drive him crazy.

Then she smiled and winked at him, and he had to reach a hand to the banister to steady himself.

Luckily, Raelyn didn't seem to notice. She was rocking back and forth on her heels, bursting to share something.

Nova started down the stairs. "Ok, what is it, Rae?"

Fynn followed close behind her, just as curious as she was. He stood behind her at the bottom of the staircase, his hand finding its way to her lower back.

"Well, I wanted to tell you right away last night, but you weren't here. I waited up for you, but apparently you like really *long* walks, so I fell asleep before you got back and—"

"Rae, you're standing between me and coffee, so please, just out with it."

"We found a clue to Terra's descendant!" She clapped her hands and straightened her back, waiting for Fynn and Nova to react.

"That's great—" Fynn started, but Nova grabbed his hand and dragged him off toward the dining room.

"A clue," she said over her shoulder, "can wait until after caffeine."

Raelyn groaned and chased after them. "But you're going to want to hear this!"

Fynn followed Nova across the threshold to the dining room, which he hadn't yet visited since he arrived. Though the Voss household in Arkwood had a stately dining room, and he was sure that the Astor penthouse did as well, he was pleasantly surprised to find that the one in the cottage was...quaint.

Along the wall was a buffet, which held trays of food and a carafe of coffee. The smell of freshly baked waffles filled the air. A small table set for four sat in the middle of the room.

"Who made breakfast?" he asked no one in particular.

Jax pushed his way into the room, carrying another stack of waffles on a plate. Through the door that closed behind him, Fynn caught a glimpse of the kitchen.

"I did," the male witch said. "My mom's old recipe. I know it by heart."

Add that to the column of things he never expected from Jax.

Jax set the platter down, then pointed to the carafe. "Fresh pot for you, Nova. Raelyn, Esta, and Kael already killed the first one."

"Thanks, Jax." Nova started pouring herself a cup, not even bothering to sit before taking the first sip. Fynn loved the way she closed her eyes to inhale the aromas wafting out of the mug with each sip. He had to force himself to tear his eyes away and bring his attention back to Raelyn, who was standing, arms crossed, at the threshold.

"Good now?" Raelyn snorted.

"Good now," Nova replied. "Do we need to sit down for this?"

Raelyn sighed. "Not funny. But no, it's not *that* big of a clue. We started looking in a new section last night and found an ancient text. The dates on the spine indicated it was from before the war, back in the timeframe the goddesses would have walked the world."

Fynn poured himself a cup of coffee as he listened.

"The book appeared to be a diary, written by someone claiming to be Terra's daughter."

"Ok," Nova said, setting down her mug and grabbing a plate. "But what is the actual clue?"

"Well, we have her name! So if we know her name, maybe we can trace her lineage down as far as possible through the annals—"

"No." Nova turned abruptly to face her sister. "We aren't risking anyone else going into Arkwood."

Raelyn leaned against one of the dining chairs, sticking out her bottom lip and donning those puppy-dog eyes. "But Esta and I did it once—"

"That was before there was a deocre on the loose attacking the city." Nova turned back to the tray of waffles and forked one onto her plate. "There's no way to guarantee your safety."

"Nova, come on," Raelyn groaned, rolling her eyes.

Nova set her plate on the table and pulled out a chair to sit. "We'll find another way."

Raelyn looked at Fynn for support, but he only shrugged and shook his head. No way was he getting on Nova's bad side when he just got her back. Besides, he knew firsthand what it was like back in Arkwood. Hell, there was a personal tracking spell on him. He certainly didn't want to go back and wouldn't subject anyone else to that either.

"I'll ask Mother when she gets back later." Raelyn's eyes lit up. "Or maybe I can get a raven into town to tell her now, and she can find a way to check before she comes back. Or get her Defiance people to look into it." She turned and left the room, calling for Esta to join her.

"Good, now I can finish my breakfast in peace," Nova mumbled, taking a bite of waffle. While she chewed, she looked over at Fynn and Jax, who were still standing. "Was I too harsh?"

Jax shook his head, and Fynn said, "No, you're absolutely right. We'll find another way. If there's a tracking spell on me, it's possible there's one on you all as well. Or at least on Jax."

"Tell me more about this tracking spell." Jax raised an eyebrow as he pulled out the chair across from Nova and sat.

"Sure." Fynn's hand reached for the hilt of his longsword but met only air. He hadn't yet donned his baldric today. "Anytime I would go above ground in the city, I would be instantly found, by either guards or the deocre itself."

Nova dropped her fork with a clatter against her plate. "Fynn, how did you—"

"We found out the hard way, but luckily, I managed to escape both times. Thanks to my agility...and Daro's help." He wasn't so proud that he couldn't admit when he'd needed help, and besides, he'd come to appreciate—if not like—Daro.

"So," Jax leaned forward to rest his elbows on the table, "if I follow correctly, the deocre has a tracking spell on you because of Luc. Which means it's likely that it would have one on me, too. But it hasn't found us because of the enchantments and wards protecting the city?"

Fynn nodded.

Only the two of them knew exactly what had happened down in the laboratory with Luc. Before they'd resurfaced, they vowed never to speak of it to anyone, and though Fynn had initially been inclined not to trust Jax, he had seen the resolve in the wielder's eyes that night. They were in this together. They'd killed Luc together.

They would either go down or find a way out of this together.

If he'd been told that he'd be bound to this witch the first day he'd met him, when he'd initially sensed that Jax was no friend to elves, he'd have laughed. But that was the thing about time and circumstances. It often led to places you never imagined going.

"All right then." Jax ran his hand through his hair, which was no longer cropped as close to his scalp as it usually was. Small curls were forming in its new lengths. "Thank you for letting me know. I will stay away from Arkwood until this thing is dealt with."

"As much as I don't like this tracker at all," Nova said, leaning back in her chair with her mug in hand, "it is nice to see the two of you getting along."

Fynn chuckled but caught Jax rolling his eyes. Though there was still the issue of his attitude toward elves, Jax wasn't all bad. He'd been an excellent teacher for Nova and had helped them immensely when it came to uncovering the truth about Kael and what had happened to the laboratory. And Jax's mother. Once he'd realized that Jax wasn't a threat to him for Nova's affection, Fynn had started trying to warm to the witch.

That is, until he saw that scar. Fynn's eyes flickered over to Nova's cheek, where the small crescent scar was barely visible in the shadows cast on her face by the morning light. But just as his temper was starting to flare, Nova's voice grounded him.

"Maybe you should explain a little bit about your history with elves, like you did for me." Nova was looking directly at Jax, her eyes full of compassion but also determination.

Whatever it was that she wanted Jax to tell him was important.

Fynn sat in the chair next to Nova, his mug of coffee now empty.

Jax inhaled deeply, his chest rising as he lowered his gaze to the table. "I've not been the most welcoming to you, Fynn, and for that I apologize. I haven't had the...best experiences with elves in the past. They hurt someone who was important to me. And you look particularly like the one that delivered the news of my mother's death."

Nova reached over and took Jax's hand. "Mehta is *still* important to you."

Mehta? The wielder who jumped them to the lab?

Fynn recalled a memory of Jax, the night of the festival, telling him *"She's not my type,"* then going back to join a group of friends. One of the witches at the table had been someone who looked like Mehta, though they hadn't known him at the time.

Had they been...together?

As if sensing where his thoughts had gone, Nova caught his eyes and nodded, almost imperceptibly.

Ah. So she had uncovered something new while he'd been in Arkwood.

"Regardless," Jax continued, completely unaware of the silent exchange between Fynn and Nova, "I just want you to know that I'm sorry. You're not like those elves I knew, and you don't deserve the way I treated you."

Fynn was glad he was sitting because he could've been knocked over with a feather. "I appreciate that, Jax. And I'm sorry for whatever those elves did that hurt Mehta."

Jax kept his gaze on the table and nodded.

Some wounds were harder to heal than others, something Fynn was well aware of. Persy had left this world while Fynn was still angry at him for something that was beyond his own control. Fynn had been holding a grudge against him for fifteen years, and what good had it done? All it did was create a rift in their family, alienating him from the ones who were supposed to love him the most.

Persy hadn't been a bad person. He just hadn't been Fynn's mother. No one could replace her. And when she died, Fynn needed to pin that grief on something. On *someone*.

He placed his hand over Nova's and squeezed, giving her a weak smile before looking back at Jax. "Don't let grudges and grief hold you back from someone you love. Take that from someone who learned the hard way and ran out of time."

Jax finally looked at him. It was impossible to miss the gratitude that shone in his eyes. "I never thought I'd say this, but you're right, elf." He cracked a smile before standing to retreat from the room, calling over his shoulder as he left, "Training starts in ten, Nova."

But Fynn could tell from the look in her eyes that she could not have cared less about training. In that moment, it was plainly obvious that she was simply happy. And he couldn't blame her. For the first time since Persy had died, he felt it, too. There was a chance they'd get through this. They'd all come out stronger, better.

They still had hope.

39

NOVA

NOVA STILL COULDN'T BELIEVE the conversation that had transpired between Fynn and Jax this morning. Still couldn't fathom that they were starting to become...friendly? She'd never imagined anything close to that for them. Though they'd shifted from their initial dislike to a tolerance around the time that Jax had revealed he was Margot's son, she never thought they'd get to a point where they helped each other willingly.

But that short conversation had been healing for both of them. She sensed it in their changed demeanors. Fynn's shoulders had relaxed, the tension he'd been holding in his back since he arrived disappearing almost entirely. And Jax—well, the fact that he admitted Fynn was right indicated that he seemed keen to repair things with Mehta.

It was all enough for her to glide through training that morning.

Kael had not participated today, but Fynn resumed his post watching over the training. It helped that they hadn't been able to keep their hands off each other for long, which made all of her spells easier to wield. Her heart swelled at the thought of how much easier building the protection spell would be with Fynn here. And maybe she could convince Raelyn to join in, too, so she could utilize amplification from both of them...

That would be a task for after lunch. Right now, she was famished, and the sandwiches that Kael had brought out for them looked delicious.

"Were you the chef of the family?" she asked him after she'd savored the first bite.

He'd brought down a blanket for them to sit on and enjoy the beautiful weather following last night's storm. It was cooler than it had been since they'd arrived, a sure sign that autumn had begun, but there wasn't a cloud in the sky. Nova sat between Kael and Fynn, while Jax and Daro, who'd been observing training from the porch, sat opposite her.

It had gotten easier to talk to Kael about what had been, what could have been. She found that the more he revealed, the more she wanted to know, and the more she could imagine her life as it would have played out without Luc's interference.

Kael laughed at the question. "I've dabbled and know my way around the kitchen. But your mother had a way with food that I never did. Sandwiches, though? That I could do well enough."

"Sandwiches hardly require any sort of skill," Jax said, his tone playful.

"Exactly."

Nova grinned. On top of learning more about Kael, she'd loved getting to see this more playful side of him. Three weeks of a new kind of freedom had done wonders for him. He'd healed, physically and emotionally; maybe not fully, but enough to laugh. To know joy.

"Are Raelyn and Esta back yet?" she asked him. Training had taken place on the beach and lasted all morning, so she hadn't yet seen if her sister and Esta had returned from sending a raven to Mother.

Kael shook his head.

"Where did they go?" Daro asked. He'd been the last to emerge this morning, when the coffee had already been cold and the last waffle was no more than soggy mush. By that point, training was about to begin and Raelyn and Esta had already departed, so he hadn't had a chance to catch up on the morning's events.

"She said they had a name they wanted Mother to look up in the annals. The name of Terra's daughter." A seagull touched down nearby and squawked, begging for a scrap of bread. She shooed it away with a small blast of magic.

"It shouldn't have taken this long to send a raven..." Fynn's voice trailed off as his gaze shifted toward the house.

Daro shoved the last bit of sandwich in his mouth and stood. "I can run into town to find them."

"Thank you," Nova said. She hadn't even noticed the worry that had settled into her chest until Fynn had voiced the concern. Daro could run to town and back quickly, with news that they were fine...or not. "Check the temple, too, if they aren't still at the post office."

He nodded and dashed off, kicking up sand as he went.

"Did she mention the name before she left?" Kael asked. "Maybe I can send a message to her."

Nova's mouth dropped open. How had she not considered using Kael to send the message? "I should've thought of that." Her fingers reached for the end of her braid, lacing through the loose strands. "I admit I wasn't the nicest to her about it this morning; I didn't even think to ask for the name."

A hand rested on her lower back. Fynn's. The warming comfort of his touch washed over her, soothing the guilt that had been building over her treatment of Raelyn. Coffee or not, she should've been kinder to her sister.

With one last tug on her braid, she let her hand drop.

"They'll be back soon." Kael cast a sympathetic smile in her direction. "We can ask then. And Raella should be back tonight, correct?"

Nova uncurled her legs, stretching them in front of her, enjoying the light tug on her hamstrings. "If all goes well, yes."

Jax stood, dusting his hands on his pants. "Well, let's get back to training. Kael, if you're staying, we can start back on the protection spell."

"Count me in," Kael said, collecting the scraps and empty plates on the tray he'd brought the sandwiches out on. "I'll drop these inside and be right back."

Fynn stood and reached for the tray. "I can do it. You stay and get started."

"You're not going anywhere." Nova grabbed his forearm and pulled him back down into the sand. "I just got you back. I'm not letting you out of—" She stopped and bit her lip. *Oh, for Canta's sake.* Even to her own ears she sounded like a lovesick teenager.

Jax rolled his eyes, but Fynn and Kael laughed.

Nothing was going to happen if he just went inside for a minute or two to clean up from lunch. He wasn't going to disappear while doing dishes. But still. She'd been parted from him for long enough, and after...last night...she just wasn't ready to let him out of her reach yet. Her arm snaked around his elbow, pulling him closer, and she schooled her face into a mask of resolve. *Might as well commit to the role.*

With a twinkle in his eye, Kael said, "I've got this." Then he shuffled back up the sand toward the cottage.

Once he was out of earshot, Jax snorted. "Real cute, Nova."

With a flick of her wrist, she sent him flying backward into the sand. Not hard enough to hurt, but hard enough to send a message. It worked: Jax righted himself and chuckled. "Point made."

Something tickled her ear, and a moment later, Fynn's voice whispered, "Now *that* was cute, Al."

"Maybe in another day or so, we'll be ready to start casting this spell over parts of the city."

Nova, Fynn, Jax, and Kael found themselves each with a glass of ale on the back porch of the cottage to cap off the training session. The waves were lightly rolling along the edge of the surf, and a tuft of cloud would pass by now and then in the late afternoon sky.

"You think so?" Nova asked Jax, her voice laced with hope. They'd been working so hard on it. She was proud of them, proud of herself, in a way she hadn't been before. This spell was so much more complex than the ones she'd built to ward herself. There were a number of times today when she'd needed to take a break, but now that Fynn was here, those breaks could be shorter. One kiss, one hug from him, and she instantly felt replenished.

Jax shrugged. "We've got to start somewhere. I was thinking maybe the temple and the immediate vicinity—"

"The temple!" Nova sat upright like a bolt of lightning. "They should be back by now, shouldn't they?"

Daro had returned briefly to let them know that he'd found Esta and Raelyn back at the temple, then he'd returned to help them search. But he'd promised they'd be back in time to help welcome her mother home. Now that the sun was beginning its descent, that could be any minute.

Right on cue, a female voice drifted their way, carried on the breeze that blew off the ocean. The same breeze that reminded Nova of Fynn's scent. A second female voice followed it, and though she couldn't make out the words, her spine instantly softened.

Esta and Raelyn.

Moments later, the two of them, followed closely by Daro, came around the back of the house and stepped onto the porch.

"Thought we might find you here," Raelyn said, placing her hands on her hips. "Hope you didn't drink all the ale."

Kael laughed. "There's more inside."

Daro motioned toward the sliding door. "I'll grab some. Three?" He looked between Esta and Raelyn, who both nodded, Raelyn more eagerly than the elf.

"No sign of Mother yet?" Raelyn asked, looking directly at Nova.

"Not yet." Their mother had said she'd be back in a day, but since they hadn't heard anything from her, was it possible that she'd gotten held up? Trapped? Captured by the deocre?

Nova had no idea what the deocre would do to her mother. If it was a reincarnation of Luc's spirit, would it recognize her as his wife and treat her kindly? Or would it recognize her as the one behind the Defiance and try to destroy her? Pushing those thoughts aside, she turned her attention back to the group.

"She's smart. She'll be ok," Kael said, probably noticing the worry that she was sure was etched all over her face.

Daro slid back onto the porch, three ales in hand. As he passed them out, Fynn said, "I still can't believe how much she was pulling strings behind the scenes. This whole time, she was putting on the world's greatest charade."

"If you'd told me three months ago that Raella Astor was the High One," Daro said as he leaned up against the railing, "I'd have laughed in your face. She's played her part well."

"I wish she'd let us in on all of this sooner," Raelyn said. Her brown eyes focused on Nova, who couldn't help but share the sentiment. How much of this could have turned out differently had their mother brought them into the Defiance and allowed them to help?

"My girls, I was trying to protect you."

Nova stood as her mother's voice carried toward them across the sand. Raelyn shrieked and bounded down the steps. "Mother!"

For there she was, standing right below them on the beach, unharmed and whole. Looking just as she had when she left.

Nova handed her ale to Fynn and ran after Raelyn, until the three of them were arm in arm again, just as they had been the first night they'd arrived at the cottage.

Her mother's hand rubbed up and down her back. She kissed Nova's head and then Raelyn's, then pushed them back slightly, so they could see each other's faces.

"Let's get inside," she said, her voice not wavering one bit. But her eyes were full of exhaustion. Had she slept at all? "We have much to regroup on."

40

NOVA

"How were things in the city?" Nova asked. She handed her mother a glass of ale, then settled down onto the couch between Raelyn and Fynn.

Her mother had taken her usual spot in the armchair, while Kael, Daro, and Esta stood along the walls. Kael was closest to the sliding doors and had his gaze set on the ocean outside, though his posture indicated he was listening intently.

"Not great." Mother's tone was...defeated. That was the only word Nova could come up with to describe it. What had she witnessed? "The Defiance is completely overwhelmed with trying to help those who lost their homes or loved ones."

Raelyn stiffened and started to open her mouth, but Nova quickly put a hand on her knee to silence her. There would be time to share what she'd found, to ask about their raven, soon. For now, they needed to allow their mother to speak.

"I didn't venture into the impacted neighborhoods to see the devastation firsthand, but what they described to me...it's awful. Hundreds are dead. Even more are displaced and now living on the streets. And they've realized they can't leave the city, which, frankly, I knew would come sooner or later, but I hoped it'd be later."

"How is that being explained?" Esta asked, her tone accusatory. Raelyn flashed her a look. She cleared her throat and continued, this time a little more subtly. "All those elves with nowhere to go, unable to leave the city to try to make it to Besa to find shelter."

"I understand your concern, Esta," Mother replied. "Don't think that I wished for them to suffer, nor do I want this to continue. But we have to keep the deocre a secret. If it gets out to the public, who knows what could happen."

Esta snorted, crossing her arms and looking to Daro or Fynn for support but finding none.

To her credit, Mother ignored the jab and continued, "As you can probably imagine, it's become quite a nightmare for the Defiance. The deocre appears to have kept all of the governors under Luc's thrall, so we can't even try to get to them. They're acting like nothing is wrong, probably on the deocre's orders."

"The Defiance will continue to fight until the end," Daro said, sticking out his chest proudly. Had the whole situation not been so grave, Nova might have found his arrogance funny.

Of course, it hadn't been funny a few months ago, when he'd forced her to keep her bedroom door open all night, but she was willing to let bygones be bygones. He had brought Fynn back to her, after all.

"Fox is feeling the loss of Balthazar, though. Having a wielder among the ranks of the Defiance in Arkwood would make it much easier to protect the citizens. The other witches are doing what they can, but against a deocre, they are limited." Mother's shoulders sagged as she let out a sharp exhale.

"I could go."

Nova had nearly forgotten Jax was in the room. He'd been uncharacteristically silent for the entire conversation, but now he stepped forward out of the shadows. She gaped at him.

"What about our spell? What about my training?" she hissed at him. "You've made it very clear *that* is the most important thing right now. That you didn't want to go anywhere near Arkwood."

Jax shrugged. "Kael can continue it. Now that Fynn is back, you have him to help with protection as well. Not that you need it," he added quickly after seeing her mouth open to protest. "There's more than enough power, both magic and mind, here to build the spell and to research the last descendant. If I can be of help in Arkwood, I should go."

"Jax, that would be—" Mother started, only to be cut off by Nova.

"No, that would be stupid. Mother going was one thing. You...you haven't been to Arkwood in years. You don't know your way around; you don't know anyone there. Just finding the Defiance tunnels could expose you to so much danger."

"Especially if the tracker is involved," Fynn added.

"Yes!" Nova put a hand on his leg, squeezing his thigh in thanks. "The deocre could find you instantly, Jax."

"We don't know that for sure." Jax started to pace the room in front of the sliding door. The light coming in from the sunset through the floor-to-ceiling glass cast him in an eerie glow.

"We know it enough—"

"Nova."

She pivoted to face her mother, who was wearing a delicate smile but whose eyes matched the tone she'd just used: cold.

"If we want there to be an Arkwood to go back to after this, they need help. Jax can help."

No, no, no. She would not let Jax risk his life in this way. Couldn't they see how stupid this plan was? "Could they find another wielder? It sounds like they used to have one..."

"He disappeared a few months ago. Went out drinking with friends and never came home," Daro said. "Fox gave up searching for him because he was afraid to draw attention to a missing wielder when Luc was on high alert already given this one's escape." He pointed a thumb toward Kael.

"Guilty," he said, wincing.

Nova's heart started to race as pieces fell into place in her mind. A missing wielder...a few months ago...Kael...

Her hand found its way into her braid, untying the ribbon holding it together and unweaving the strands. "The attack in the park."

Fynn tensed and sat up straighter.

She shifted her gaze to Kael. "We thought it was you, but you never would have ordered an attack on me."

"You were attacked?" Kael pushed himself off the wall, as if he'd activated a primal fatherly instinct to protect her. Good thing the threat had long since been extinguished.

Nova nodded, her hair soft between her fingers. Comforting. "Back at the beginning of the summer. By a wielder."

"Nova." Raelyn's tone was wary. "Why would a wielder from the Defiance attack you?"

"Maybe he thought he could bring me into the Defiance. Get me to join the ranks and act as an insider? Or maybe he knew the truth about Kael and wanted me to know." To be honest, she could think of many reasons, each just as likely as the last.

"But again, why attack you?"

Nova bit her lip, racking her brain for a response. Thankfully, Daro answered. "He had...his own way of doing things. If it was Balthazar, he probably did have good intentions but liked putting on a show to get his point across."

Even if this was the real story behind her attack, the reason why the Defiance no longer had a wielder, there was one more part of the story that wasn't adding up to Nova.

"You were there," she said, staring down Daro with what she hoped was intimidation. He'd seen the wielder lying on the floor of her flat before Luc had taken him away. How had he not recognized Balthazar? How had he not reported this to the Defiance? "You would have recognized him, but you let the Defiance go on wondering what happened. How do we know you aren't a spy? That your loyalty doesn't actually lie with Luc?"

"Whoa, Nova." Fynn grabbed her wrist as Daro took a step forward, his hands clenched into fists and betrayal raging in his eyes. "Daro, stop." The other elf stopped moving toward her but didn't relax. "I beat that witch to a pulp after what he did to you. There was no way anyone could have recognized him. And what I've seen him do the last few weeks, what he's helped me do...no, I trust him. He isn't a spy."

Fynn's grip on her wrist loosened slightly, but his hold was still enough to fuel her magic. It swirled within her, feeding on the emotion that had been building within since her mother's return.

Breathe, breathe.

She squeezed her eyes shut and allowed herself to sink into Fynn. "You're right. I'm sorry, Daro." When she opened her eyes again, Daro had retreated to his spot along the wall, his fists no longer clenched. His eyes softened slightly as he nodded at her.

"Well, now that's settled." Jax looked back at Mother. "I can leave tomorrow if you tell me where to go and are sure they will take me in."

Mother nodded appreciatively. "Consider it done."

"Mother." Raelyn's voice sounded so fierce that Nova jumped slightly.

Mother turned her head to face her daughter and smiled at the look of determination she found there. "Yes?"

"What about the annals? Can you tell us about that now? Did you get our raven?"

Mother's eyes widened. "Raven? No, I didn't."

Nova's stomach turned to stone. If Mother hadn't received the raven, where had it gone? Who knew they were searching the annals? Goddess-damn it! If she'd thought to use Kael's messaging spell instead, they wouldn't be stuck in this situation.

If it somehow landed in the hands of the deocre—did it even have hands?—they would be royally screwed.

Raelyn groaned and put her head in her hands. "We had a lead."

"We found the name of Terra's daughter in the temple," Esta said. "We had hoped you might bring back the annals so we could look for the lineage and find out if her descendants are still alive."

"You...sent a letter with that information?" If possible, Mother's eyes widened more. Her glass started to shake in her hand.

"Of course not," Esta spat. "We obviously don't have an established code, but all we did was request an annal. We did not write the name in the letter."

"Still..." Mother's voice trailed off. She set her glass down on the small table next to the armchair and pressed her palms to her thighs.

"We knew the danger of sending it, Mother." Raelyn's voice was desperate. "But we believed if you could bring back the annal, it would solve this last part of the mystery."

Mother drew in a deep breath, then sighed it out. "What was the name?"

Raelyn blinked, momentarily stunned by her mother's tone. "What?"

"The name, Raelyn. What was the name you found at the temple?"

"Oh." Raelyn clasped her hands together and slouched. "Marella Hollis. Terra's daughter was Marella Hollis."

A choking sound by the door drew Nova's attention away from Raelyn to Kael, who had started coughing.

"Hollis?"

She turned back to face her mother, whose face was now unnaturally pale.

"Do you...know that name, Mother?" Nova asked.

Her mother's eyes slowly shifted toward Kael, widening as they went. He met her gaze with a furrowed brow, his own eyes teary from the coughing but glistening with...resignation?

Fynn stiffened beside Nova, his hand curling around hers when she asked again, "Do you know someone with the name Hollis?"

Without breaking Kael's stare, Mother replied, "We do."

Raelyn clapped her hands together. "Oh good! Now we can find the third—"

But Kael shook his head, rubbing a hand to his temple. "We can find the third. But it won't necessarily be good."

"Who is it?" Jax inquired. He shifted his weight uncomfortably as he looked from Mother to Kael.

Kael sighed and groaned. "It's Benedict."

41

Nova

"BENEDICT...LIKE, YOUR FORMER PARTNER?" Nova's mind was swirling as she processed this revelation. As the realization of what lay ahead of them settled in. "Like, the guy who blew up his house with us in it?"

"He did *what*?" Mother's hand flew to her mouth.

Nova waved her off. "We can explain more about that later."

Kael nodded, scratching his chin. "Yes, that very same Benedict."

"No," Raelyn said quietly, wringing her hands. "It can't be. Esta and I looked Benedict up to find where he lived. His last name is—"

"Aldon," Esta finished. She had come to stand right behind Raelyn, fury blazing in her eyes.

"He took on a new name once the research started," Kael explained. "He claimed it was for privacy, and I didn't think anything of it. We all hoped that our names would be well-known one day. I couldn't fault him for wanting to change something to protect himself."

"Any chance he has brothers, sisters...cousins?" Nova asked. She bit her lip and hoped to Canta that someone said yes.

But Mother shook her head, and Kael replied, "No. He was an only child and never spoke about any extended family. His parents are both deceased."

"Surely Marella has more than one line? There could be other descendants out there without the last name Hollis." Raelyn spoke hesitantly, but her voice was also full of hope. And Nova could understand why. The last time they'd seen Benedict had not gone well and had ended even worse. Raelyn had been injured and kidnapped after he'd blown up his own house. While Nova certainly had no desire to see him again, she couldn't even fathom how Raelyn was feeling.

Nova pulled her hand from Fynn's and grasped Raelyn's instead, giving her sister a gentle squeeze to combat the slight shake coursing through her.

"It's possible," Mother said.

"But could take ages to find and trace." Kael crossed his arms, a wave of regret washing over his face. "As much as we all hate it, Benedict is now our only shot at stopping the deocre before it does any more damage."

Benedict was their last chance at destroying the deocre. The man who had tried to kill them. Who had betrayed her parents and turned the whole research team into the governors for extermination. He was the one they now needed in order to save the country.

If that wasn't a cruel twist of fate, a wicked trick of the goddesses, Nova wasn't sure what was.

Kael stepped forward and straightened. "I'll jump to him tonight, see if I can bring him back."

"I'll go with you." The words tumbled out of Nova's mouth before she could give credence to the idea. She meant them, nonetheless.

Kael gave her a tired smile. "I would love that, Nova. However, I can only jump one person. I wouldn't be able to bring you both back."

Her heart sank, even though he was right. Fynn wrapped an arm around her, letting his hand rest on her hip, where his thumb began to trace circles.

"But don't worry," Kael continued. "I'll be swift. I'll remain hidden. I eluded capture on my own this long; one more adventure won't be difficult. And if anyone can reason with Benedict, it's me. Or, at least, it *should* be me."

"Well, that settles it," Mother said, though her voice wasn't filled with conviction. She got to her feet. "Let's get you and Jax squared away with supplies for your journeys and then you can be on your way, Kael."

Kael nodded, following her out of the room, toward the kitchen. Jax trailed not far behind.

"I'll be the only wielder left," Nova said, the realization hitting her like a fast-moving carriage. "If anything happens to the protections here, it's all on me."

"First of all," Raelyn said, turning to face her, "that's irrelevant because you could power these wards on your own, easily. Second, you've got me and lover boy here to help give you a boost when you need it." Raelyn winked at Fynn, who chuckled. "And lastly, what are the rest of us, chopped liver? You're not the only one here who can fight, Nova."

"I'm still learning how to do all of this." Nova buried her face in her hands. "I'm still trying to figure out what my limits are, to understand the depths of my power."

"We all—well, ok, not Daro, but the rest of us in this room—saw you fight Father in the lab." Raelyn's voice took on a soothing tone. She placed her hand on Nova's knee. "You've got it figured out. You're just still working on believing in yourself. We believe in you. And we need *you* to believe in you."

"She's right," Fynn said, squeezing Nova ever so slightly. A shiver raced down her spine. "And besides, Kael shouldn't be gone too long. With any luck, he'll be back later tonight. Worst case, tomorrow."

Nova inhaled a deep breath. Her magic was still running wild in her veins, feeding on her emotions, her anxiety, her fear, but it wasn't as hard to control as it had once been. The change had been slow—so slow she hadn't even noticed until this moment. But it was there. Her control was there, without even needing conscious effort.

They were right. On all counts. She *could* handle this just fine until Kael came back. And, eventually, Jax would return, too. Jax, who had helped her get this far. Who had coached her and helped her even when she hadn't been the easiest student. Who had no one in the world anymore, but still wanted to do something to help, something to make the world that had turned against wielders better.

He was a good person. He deserved better than the hand he'd been dealt.

An idea popped into her mind. She stood quickly, and with a hurried "Be right back," she left the room in search of Kael.

She found him leaving the kitchen with a backpack of food slung over his shoulder. His eyes widened when he saw her standing before him in the dining room.

"Nova." His face relaxed. "I wouldn't have left without saying goodbye, you know."

"Can you do me a—oh." She paused as his last words set in. "I, uh, wasn't worried about that." His face fell slightly. She clenched her hands into fists and bit her tongue. *Stupid, Nova, stupid.* "I mean, obviously I wouldn't have wanted you to go without saying goodbye. I don't trust Benedict around you, and I don't like you going alone, even if I understand why."

He walked toward her and put his hand on her arm. "I'll be ok, Nova. I have every intention of coming back in one piece. With Benedict in tow so we can get rid of this goddess-forsaken spirit monster."

She couldn't help the smile that spread across her face. "Good. But before you go, can you do me a favor?"

"Of course." He dropped his hand from her arm, then took the pack off his shoulder and let it fall to the ground. "What's up?"

Nova looked over her shoulder to make sure no one was within earshot, or at least not a certain someone. Then she leaned in toward her father and said, "I need to send someone a message."

42

NOVA

"WHAT WAS THAT ALL about?" Fynn asked as he pulled the sheets back from her—*their*—bed and sat, leaning against the headboard.

Nova finished redoing her braid, then turned to face him. "What was what about?"

He waved his hand toward the door. "Running off while Raelyn was trying to comfort you."

"Oh." She sat down next to him, curling her legs underneath her. "I wanted to ask Kael to send a message to someone."

"To whom?" Fynn raised an eyebrow.

Though she desperately wanted to tell *someone* her plan, it was better kept a secret for now. "You'll see. Hopefully."

Kael had departed just after dinner, which had ended up being a rushed and hurried affair. Jax planned to leave at first light. Mother had retired to bed earlier than usual once Kael left, claiming exhaustion that no one doubted.

Once they heard the click of her mother's door closing, Fynn had met Nova's gaze and cocked his head toward the staircase. An invitation to follow him. Her skin had tingled with goosebumps the entire way up the staircase and into their room, particularly when he closed the door behind them.

But then he made it clear he wanted to talk. At least, *before* they got into anything...else.

"You're up to something." Fynn grinned, his eyes sparkling. The sun outside hadn't yet fully set, but the room was dark enough that Nova had lit a lamp when they entered. The shadows it cast across the room danced in his eyes.

"Nothing bad, I promise. Something for Jax. A thank-you of sorts." For everything he'd done for her. For helping her. For supporting her.

Fynn raised a brow, clearly skeptical. "Now is hardly the time to be writing thank-you notes, Al."

She shrugged and grabbed one of his hands in hers. "I'm playing a long game with this one."

Fynn let out a low laugh. He put his free hand behind his head, then reclined against the headboard. "How are you?"

She traced circles on the back of his hand with her forefinger, her gaze drifting down to watch the movement. "Better. I overreacted earlier."

"It was a lot to take in all at once."

"Story of my life recently," she mumbled, hoping he didn't hear.

His hand slipped from hers, floating to her chin. He gently pushed her face up to meet his gaze. "You're stronger than all of this. You've handled this with such poise. Such grace. I am in awe of you."

Guess he heard. Heat rushed to her face. She wanted to escape his gaze, but his hand stayed firm under her chin. "It hasn't been easy."

Fynn's eyes locked with hers. "No one would assume it has."

"I just hope it's over soon." She hated how her voice cracked as she spoke. "I want to go back to normal."

"Normal." Fynn dropped his hand, taking hers in it again. "I wonder what normal is like for Nova Astor."

"Boring, I assure you." She smiled, tilting her head to one side. "You'll probably tire of me quickly. Run off to find some other witch in need of saving."

"Never."

He pulled her in closer to him, until she was straddling his lap. Her magic hummed inside her, happy to be so close to him. She pulled at the ribbon holding his hair so his white-blond tresses fell around his face and began to run her fingers through it.

"Watch what you promise," she said quietly as the soft locks brushed over her skin. "I'll hold you to that, Fynn Voss."

"Easiest promise I've ever made."

He leaned forward and kissed her, framing her face with each of his hands as he pushed his body into hers. She let her body soften as it melded with his, falling into the kiss with everything she had. Her hips ground into his, feeling him harden beneath her.

All her worries and doubts evaporated as she let herself be consumed by Fynn. By what he promised, what he signified, what he meant to her. Never in her wildest dreams had she pictured this—*him*—as her future. As part of her story. And yet here he was.

Her hands found their way under his shirt, lifting it up. For the briefest moment, their lips parted, enough for her to pull the shirt over his head before slamming them back into his. Soon, her tunic was off as well, and in the next breath, all their clothes were cast aside on the ground in a heap.

Fynn picked her up and flipped her onto her back. His eyes roamed her body as he hovered over her. "You're beautiful, Al," he purred. "Absolutely breathtaking."

She thanked him by pulling him down on top of her, reaching between them to guide him to her entrance.

If Kael came back tomorrow, if Benedict agreed to help them, there was a good chance they'd confront the deocre within days. And while they all hoped for the best outcome, they were going up against the unknown. There was a good chance that the other side of that confrontation may look very different than today.

And she'd be damned if she was going to leave anything unsaid. Anything undone. Nova would treat each moment, each kiss, each touch with Fynn like it could be her last.

So, with that thought in the front of her mind, she let her magic flow freely through them as they made love that night, turning it into an experience she was sure neither of them would forget.

Nova was awake. But why?

She peeked an eye open. Darkness still engulfed her room, so it wasn't morning yet. Fynn's warm, firm body was pressed against hers, his steady breaths indicating that he was still deep in sleep. Whatever it was that had awoken her hadn't disturbed him.

Then she heard it. A creak on the stairs. A whispered voice.

Were Kael and Benedict back already?

Torn between the desire to go see how they had fared—to lay eyes on her father herself to be assured of his safety—and the desire to stay there, warm and comfortable in bed with Fynn, she made no move to stand up. Her eyes started to drift closed again, her mind making itself up.

But then the creaking got closer, louder. It definitely sounded like two people. Two large people. The sound stopped just outside her door.

Her heart started to race in her chest. Kael's room was on the other side of the hall. There was no reason for him to stop here if it was him—

The door flung open, but in the darkness, she couldn't see who stood there. In the time it took her to leap from the bed, a husky voice said, "It's the elf. Get him!"

Finally, the intruders came into focus. Two enormous men—their auras giving them away as pyros—made their way into her room, approaching Fynn, who was still fast asleep.

Damn him and his deep sleep!

Nova summoned as much of her power as she could and flung it out at the men. They froze in place, faces twisted in surprise as they spotted her, but one broke through the curse and started charging for her.

"I'll get the witch, you get—"

"The hell you will!" She took a step forward and raised her arms to cast the curse again. This time, both men froze, completely immobilized but able to speak. Her chest heaved as she attempted to calm her breath now that the threat appeared under control, but she didn't lower her arms. "Who are you?"

"Wouldn't you like to know, pretty little witch," the first man said. He gave her a disgusting grin that displayed a few gaps where his yellowed teeth had fallen out—or been knocked out. His eyes were dark and beady in the glow of the starlight trickling into the room.

Fynn rolled over and blinked open his eyes. "Nova?" His eyes, dark as midnight in the dimness, widened when he beheld the two frozen men that stood near the threshold. In a flash, he was standing next to Nova, his sword unsheathed and pointed directly at the intruders. "Well done," he whispered to her.

"Someone had to save your sleepy ass," she retorted, throwing a smile at Fynn. She meant it in jest, but as soon as she said it, she worried she'd gone too far. That she'd brought up memories of Lena, of the night she was attacked in the park.

He met her gaze, and after a moment, his face softened. "I suppose I've earned that given my track record."

She breathed a sigh of relief. "Mmhmm." With a wave of her hand, she lit the lamps on either side of the bed, illuminating the two pyros as she turned her attention back to them.

They were both filthy, as if they'd been on the road for days and hadn't bothered to bathe. Their faces were smeared with dirt, their clothes caked with mud. And the stench coming off them... If she hadn't heard them first, she surely would have smelled them coming.

"I'll ask you one more time," she said through her teeth. "Who are you and what are you doing here?"

The smaller pyro spat in her direction, earning him a prick on the cheek from Fynn's sword.

"Answer her," Fynn growled, leaving the tip of his blade against the man's face, a drop of blood pooling on it.

"We was sent by the governors, wasn't we?" he said, his jaw clenched and his eyes on Fynn's sword. "To get the witch and the elf what killed the other governor."

Nova met Fynn's gaze. Was he thinking what she was thinking? The governors had found them, which meant the deocre knew where they were, too. And even though the deocre couldn't get past the wall—for now—it had still found a way to attack.

They were out of time. Thank goodness Kael would be back soon with Benedict...

She turned back to the men, drawing in a deep breath to still her mind. "How did you find us?" And how did they slip past the protections they had set up around the cottage?

"I 'eard somefink about a raven from Adenaport. Then it wasn't hard, was it?" The older one licked his lips. "You took over the dead governor's house."

"The dead governor was my *father*, you imbecile," Nova spat, fury roiling in her gut that she had to continue playing up that farce. It was nearly enough to overcome the guilt that washed over her again for not thinking to use Kael's ability to send her mother a message. That lost raven *had* cost them in the end...

The man laughed. "And you let your boyfriend kill 'im?" The smaller one joined in the laughter, but the movement earned him another nick from Fynn's sword, another bead of blood. He clamped his mouth shut.

"Someone's coming," Fynn said, not taking his eyes off the two men.

The footsteps reached Nova's ears a second before Jax crossed the threshold, Daro close behind.

"Look at that, Ed, a two-for-one," the larger man said when he recognized Jax.

Jax's pupils flared as he scanned the room to take in the scene. Behind him, Daro had his sword out already. He pushed past Jax to stand in front of the larger man so that both of their intruders were now cornered by an elf.

"What the hell is going on in here?" Jax asked, settling his gaze on Nova.

His appearance should have calmed her, but instead it riled her up more. Her magic was swarming inside of her, the freezing spell not using up enough of the power. It wanted to do more. It wanted to hurt. To maim.

To *kill.*

These two men wanted Fynn and Jax. Wanted to take them back to Arkwood, where they would be executed.

She'd be damned if that happened on her watch.

"It seems," Nova began, her voice cool as ice, "that the governors have sent these two to hunt down you and Fynn. Though why they'd send two of the most helpless witches I've ever seen, I have no idea. They couldn't even sneak into the house undetected."

The larger pyro clicked his tongue. "Got through your wards, though, didn't we, Ed?"

Ed's toothless grin widened as he nodded slowly.

Panic flooded Jax's eyes for a moment, receding as quickly as it had come, leaving them vacant and distant. Maybe he was checking to see if the wards were in place...

She should have done that already. Stupid of her not to have thought of that. But her magic was overcome with something else right now, her thoughts entirely elsewhere.

"The wards are gone," Jax said.

Fynn straightened while Daro pushed the tip of his blade into the larger man's chest.

"Oi, watch it!" the man said, but Daro ignored him.

"What do you mean, the wards are gone?" Daro asked, not taking his eyes off the pyro.

Jax shook his head. "They're gone. Not a trace of them left that I can feel."

"Go put them back up." Nova almost recoiled at the veracity in her tone. "We can handle these two."

Jax narrowed his eyes but nodded and sprinted for the stairs.

For the first time, real fear seemed to settle on both of the pyros. Their pupils widened as they watched her. Was it fear of her? For some reason, that delighted Nova. Sparks flew off her hands as she stepped around the bed and came to stand between Daro and Fynn.

"Al?" Fynn's voice was gentle, as if he was trying to coax her off a ledge that she was willing to jump from. Which, she realized, she was. "Breathe, Al."

She blinked, looking at him, seeing herself reflected in his dark eyes and in the mirror hanging on the wall behind him. Except she didn't look like herself.

Her eyes were dark—not a trace of green remained—and blood-shot. Her skin had gone pale, contrasting with the darkness of her hair and eyes.

Her breath came out in shallow pants as she registered what she was seeing. What she had turned into. She had no idea how to escape it.

"Come back, Nova. Breathe."

Her eyes flicked to Fynn's, the use of her name drawing her attention back to the scene around her. He was looking at her with compassion, with love, but with the smallest hint of fear as well.

She'd let her power overcome her so much that she'd *scared* him.

Nova drew in a deep breath, Fynn following suit. As she exhaled, he exhaled, not breaking eye contact with her. His unwavering presence helped to bring her heart rate down, helped bring the room back into focus, and they breathed together in sync until her mind cleared and her magic retracted into her core. A quick glimpse in the mirror showed that she looked normal again.

Thank Canta.

A small tug on the spell she'd wielded to freeze the intruders proved it was still taut. Somehow, she'd kept that branch of her magic intact. Despite nearly being overcome, she'd protected her friends.

"You good over there?" Daro asked. He was staring at them with his eyebrows furrowed. "We still have a situation here." He jerked his sword toward the man closest to him.

"I said watch it!" the man shrieked, unable to move to deflect the jab. The tiniest pinprick of blood started to stain his tunic.

Daro turned back to the man. "You think you're going anywhere after this? No, just make yourself comfortable for your last moments."

The man's eyes widened further, but he stayed silent. Ed, next to him and still frozen, howled. "I don't want to die! Oh, Canta, save me!"

"I think Canta's on the other side of that argument," Daro said under his breath. He looked back at Nova and Fynn. "You good?"

Nova nodded, unable to find her voice. Her hands trembled as she took a step backward. The bed met the backs of her legs, and she collapsed onto it, attempting to steady herself. But she couldn't shake the guilt and the *shame* engulfing her as bile rose in her throat. How could she have let herself be so overcome with power that she'd become...a monster?

Had she really been ready to attack? To kill?

Fynn knelt in front of her, taking her hands in his. "Would you like me to have Raelyn sit with you for a bit?" He spoke to her without forcing her to lift her gaze, and she was eternally grateful for that. She wasn't sure she could stomach the look she'd see in his eyes.

Nova nodded, understanding what he meant when he asked that. Why he couldn't stay himself. Raelyn's presence would help, at least until she could fall asleep again.

"I'll be right back." Fynn stood, planting a kiss on her head as he did. "Daro, get that one out back. I'll meet you there shortly with this one."

Tendrils of black hair hung in Nova's face, obscuring her view of whatever it was that Daro did, but she heard a thud, followed by a grunt, and then a groan. Ed started to protest again, but another thud shut him up.

Daro must have knocked them out.

His footsteps retreated from the bedroom, heavier than normal; Nova assumed he was carrying one of the pyros on his shoulder.

"Nova!" Raelyn's voice entered the room. A heartbeat later, her floral scent hit Nova's nose. The bed creaked under her sister's weight as she sat down next to Nova, pulling her into her arms.

Nova rested her head on Raelyn's shoulder and allowed herself to be held. She clenched her eyes shut.

"I'll be back as soon as I can," Fynn said, heaving the other pyro over his shoulder. "Stay with her, Raelyn."

"Always," she whispered into Nova's hair.

The door shut with a quiet click behind Fynn, and finally—*finally*—Nova could breathe normally again. With a deep inhale, she pulled herself away from Raelyn and crossed her legs underneath her, keeping her eyes closed to fight the pressure building behind them.

"What happened?" Raelyn asked, her voice laced with hesitation. "I woke up to Fynn shaking me, saying you need me. Who was that man?" She curled her legs under her and took one of Nova's hands in hers.

Nova chanced a glance at her sister, whose brown eyes were wide and eager. "Pyros, sent by the governors, or so they say, to bring in Fynn and Jax." She pushed the loose hair behind her ears so she could see Raelyn more clearly. Her sister's hair was flat on one side from sleeping, and her eyes were smudged with kohl she hadn't removed well enough before she went to bed.

Raelyn's back straightened. "No! How did they get past the wards?"

Nova shook her head. "No idea. The wards disappeared. Jax is putting them back up now."

"Did something happen when Kael left?" Raelyn paused, then gasped. "You don't think the deocre could have…"

"That's my fear. That it removed the wards, which means it can extend its power beyond the walls even if it can't physically get beyond them yet."

Raelyn squeezed Nova's hand. "Did they hurt you? Did they hurt Fynn?"

"No, we're all fine." When she said it, she realized it was true; she felt fine. Or at least much closer to fine than she had been minutes ago. The room was in clear focus, and her mind seemed sharp as could be expected at whatever ungodly hour it was. "But I think I let my power overcome me. I…became something else. I lost control." Her voice was so quiet, it was possible that Raelyn hadn't even heard her, but she couldn't bring herself to repeat it. To admit again what she had let happen.

Honestly, life was so much easier when she had less power.

But Raelyn had clearly heard her, because she responded, "No, you didn't."

Nova furrowed her brow. "You didn't see me, Rae. I looked horrific. Like I'd been possessed."

"But if you'd truly lost control," Raelyn took Nova's other hand in hers, "something far more catastrophic would have happened. Maybe you would have hurt Fynn or Daro. Or yourself. Maybe you would've killed one or both of those pyros—"

"I wanted to," Nova said through clenched teeth.

"But you *didn't*." Raelyn brought their joined hands to her chest. "You're still here. You're still you."

"Only because Fynn brought me back."

"No one can bring a witch back from the depths of her power. Maybe seeing him triggered you to come back. Maybe something he said reminded you of why you needed to regain control. But ultimately it was *you* who regained that control. *You* who made sure you owned your power and not the other way around."

She was right. If Nova had been thinking clearly, she'd have remembered that, too. That if a witch sinks too far into her power and lets it consume her, she can't come back unless she chooses to.

But just because she had chosen to this time didn't mean she was willing to risk it happening again. She would fight for control more than ever before and train harder to maintain it.

Nova yawned. Exhaustion crept into her body so that all she wanted to do now was curl up and sleep. Maybe she'd wake up and find this had all been a dream.

"Will you lay with me until Fynn comes back?" she asked as she pulled her hands away from Raelyn and crawled to her pillow.

"If I wasn't so concerned about what the two of you had been doing in this bed, I'd offer to lay with you all night." Raelyn plopped down next to Nova, a wide grin plastered on her face.

Nova couldn't help but smile through another yawn. "Ha, very funny, Rae."

"I'm just glad you're finally getting some." Raelyn rocked her hips back and forth. Nova groaned and slapped her, but Raelyn didn't stop. "Fynn is such a snack. I could not have held out as long as you did."

"Shut up," Nova groaned. She rolled onto her side so she faced her sister, who finally stopped gyrating. "But also, thank you."

Her eyes drifted shut, but she managed to stay awake long enough to hear Raelyn's reply.

"Always, Nova."

43

FYNN

"IS THERE ANYONE ELSE working with you?"

"We was alone, I swear on me life!"

Fynn wasn't sure whether to believe Ed or not. He was standing just behind Daro, who had already taken care of the other man. His body lay next to Ed, a deep gash across his throat and blood spilling out along the sand around him.

He hated that it had come to this. That in order to clear his name of one death, they needed to kill more. Sure, he and Daro had killed enough over their lives, but always in the line of duty. Always in the name of defense.

These men believed they were acting on the governors' orders. They truly believed they were doing something right. And killing them didn't sit well with Fynn.

He pulled Daro aside and lowered his voice. "Is there another way?"

"Not one that is foolproof." Daro crossed his arms. "We don't have a wielder who can do memory magic. Even if we did, it wouldn't surprise me if the deocre could still find what had been erased."

Fynn nodded and approached the pyro.

Ed was still completely frozen where he lay on the beach. Fynn couldn't help but be proud of Nova's spell work, even if he was still concerned about what it had taken to get her there. He'd seen a witch overcome only once in his life, and Nova had come dangerously close to making that twice. He couldn't—*wouldn't*—let that happen again on his watch.

He just needed to watch her more closely. Learn her tells and the signs that she was going too far. And then help her understand them, too.

"Please, *please.*"

Ed's begging brought Fynn back to the scene in front of him. To the job that needed to happen here so he could get back to Nova. She was safe with Raelyn, but it still pained him that he wasn't there with her right now, helping her through this himself.

"Just do it, Daro," Fynn growled. He was ready for this to be over. They hadn't gotten any more information out of either of the pyros since they'd brought them down here, either because they were truly ignorant or they were enchanted into not speaking more. Fynn suspected the latter, which didn't help the guilt already growing inside. But without a memory wielder, they had no way to break through that enchantment.

These men had tried to capture him. Might have even tried to kill him. There was no reason to feel guilty for protecting himself. Or for protecting those he cared about.

Daro turned to him, his eyes glistening in the glimmer of moonlight shining from the sky. "You want to do the honors?"

"Allow me." Jax's voice rang out behind him. Fynn turned to find the wielder stalking across the beach toward them.

Fynn called to him, "The wards?"

"They're back," Jax said, coming to stand between Fynn and Daro. "I couldn't figure out what caused them to dissolve in the first place, but maybe this one knows." He turned his feral gaze toward Ed, who let out another howl.

"Kael better get Benedict back here fast. This thing is coming for us." Fynn turned to look at Jax, but Jax only had eyes for the pyro. With a snarl, he whipped his hands in the air. Not a moment later, Ed's scream filled the air as his skin ripped open with a thousand tiny cuts.

"The fuck—" Daro started, but Jax held up a hand to silence him.

"How," Jax ground out as Ed wailed, "did you get through our wards?"

"Canta save me!" Ed cried, his eyes rolling back in his head.

Jax approached until he was nose to nose with the pyro. "Tell me how, you fucking asshole!"

This has gone far enough. Fynn stepped forward. "Jax—"

"How?!"

Ed's head dropped forward onto his bloody chest. "Canta, please." His voice was now no more than a whisper.

Without a word, Fynn stepped forward, ignoring Jax's protests, and stabbed his sword into the pyro's heart. Ed choked and sputtered, his eyes flaring wide—was that gratitude?—before drawing his last breath and going still.

Good fucking riddance.

He withdrew his sword and wiped it on the dead man's tunic before sheathing it. Then he rounded on Jax. "What the hell, Jax? We could have learned something from him *without* torturing him." Fynn narrowed his eyes on the wielder. He'd been starting to trust the guy, but now...was that the spell that had caused Nova's scar? If so, he wanted to flay the witch alive for the damage he *could* have caused her.

Jax didn't respond.

Better to let him calm down. They didn't need two witches losing control tonight. Fynn started back toward the house. "I'll send Esta to help with clean-up."

"Where are *you* going?" Daro called after him.

Fynn stopped and looked back. His shoulders sank a few inches as the realization that the threat had passed—at least for now—finally set in. "I'm going to check on Nova. She nearly lost control."

Jax, who had been staring at Ed's body, visibly shaking in anger, whipped his head around to catch Fynn's gaze. "Is she ok?"

Fynn nodded, watching the wielder warily. "Raelyn is with her now."

"I'll help with clean-up." Jax sank to his knees in the sand, exhaling sharply. "No need to send Esta."

Daro caught Fynn's eye with the briefest of nods, as if signaling he was ok with Jax's help, before Fynn turned back toward the house. He drew in a sharp breath as he crossed the threshold into the living room and made his way toward the staircase, pushing the intrusive thoughts about the pyros, about Jax's behavior, out of his mind.

There was only one thing that mattered right now.

Fynn looked up the stairs, where he could see the faint strip of light coming from under the door to his and Nova's room. Either she was still awake, or the sisters hadn't bothered to turn the lamps off. He trudged silently up the stairs, nodding at Esta once he reached the top. Esta had woken when Daro did but stayed back with Raelyn until Fynn fetched her. Then she'd taken up post in the hall to guard the three Astor women.

"Any sign of Raella?" he whispered to her.

Esta nodded. Her hair, which was nearly always pulled back, swung freely around her face. "She poked her head out shortly after you went down. I told her what I knew and insisted she stay up here. I don't think she liked it..."

"Go tell her the threat has passed, and Jax restored the wards. I'll send Raelyn back to you momentarily."

Esta nodded curtly, then headed down the hall and knocked lightly on Raella's door. Fynn watched her enter before turning to his own door and slowly opening it.

The sisters were in bed, Nova asleep with her head in Raelyn's lap, and Raelyn stroking her hair. His eyes met her brown ones when he entered the room, closing the door behind him.

Keeping his voice low, he said, "Is she ok?"

Raelyn nodded and smiled. "She is. Exhausted, but ok."

Fynn breathed a sigh of relief he didn't realize he'd been harboring. He approached the bed and sat near Nova's curled legs. "Do you want to stay with her tonight? I can take the—"

But Raelyn shook her head vehemently, curls bouncing in her face. "No, Fynn. If she wakes and finds you aren't here after what happened tonight...I know she'll assume the worst. She'll want you here. She *needs* you."

"She needs you, too."

She smiled weakly, stifling a yawn. "Not in the same way."

He pursed his lips. "I don't want to take away from what you two have."

"Trust me," Raelyn said with a wink, "you can't."

His eyes met hers for a second as he nodded in understanding. Nova needed both of them, but for different things. She needed Raelyn for the comfort, for the history, for the family that she provided. But she needed Fynn for the steadiness, for the future that came with him. There was more than enough room in her heart for them both.

Raelyn gently slid Nova's head off her lap and onto the pillow next to her. Slowly, she swung her legs from the bed. Only the slightest creak of the mattress gave away her movements. Nova stirred lightly, tucking her hand under the pillow, but didn't wake.

"Good night, Fynn," Raelyn whispered, patting his arm before exiting the room.

Fynn turned back to the raven-haired witch lying on the bed before him. The one who had captured his heart from that very first day at their Arkwood flat when he'd seen just how strong her bond was with her sister. He and Aury had a bond like that once. Though they'd grown distant over her time in the navy, he knew that they'd both still drop everything if the other one needed them.

Someone like that was capable of immense, powerful love. That's what he had seen in Nova. That's what he had come to feel for Nova.

He lay in the bed next to her, curling his body around hers. She nestled into him, tucking her head toward his chest and weaving one leg in between his thighs. As he drifted off to sleep, breathing in her lavender scent and listening to the soft drumbeat of her heart, he knew for certain that this was the last woman he would ever love.

44

NOVA

"**N**OVA, FYNN!"

Nova peeked an eye open. She was met first by the sight of Fynn's chest as he started to stir, pulling her in closer. But when she lifted her head slightly to look toward where the voice had sounded, she found Raelyn poking her head through the doorway.

"Morning, Rae," she said, her voice husky with sleep. How long had she been out? After those middle-of-the-night...adventures, she had wanted nothing more than to sleep for days. She didn't even remember Raelyn leaving and Fynn coming back.

Apparently thinking they were decent enough, Raelyn entered the room, looking behind her as she did. "Kael's back," she said, approaching the foot of the bed.

Nova sat upright, Fynn following right behind her.

"Benedict?" he asked.

Raelyn nodded.

They had all three descendants! Thank the goddesses.

Nova pushed aside the thoughts about the descendants that had been stewing in her mind since last night to focus on the here and now. "And did Jax leave yet?"

"No." Raelyn shook her head. "He decided not to go now that we are so close, and after last night…"

Nova understood. It didn't make sense for him to leave anymore. This whole…situation could all be over soon, and they could all go to Arkwood to help. "We'll be right down," she said, pushing back her quilt to step out of the bed.

"Coffee's waiting!" Raelyn said as she left the room, closing the door behind her.

Nova found a pair of her Aerdmure leggings and a gray tunic in her wardrobe, pulling them on as quickly as she could. The air had turned chilly, autumn now fully set in, so the long sleeves kept her warm against the brisk morning air. She was running a brush through her hair, the strokes rushed and violent, when Fynn grabbed her arm.

She looked up at him, letting her hand holding the brush fall to her side. "What?"

He was looking at her like she might break. Like it was all he could do not to wrap his arms around her and hold her together.

"Are you ok? After last night?"

Wasn't that the question of the year? *Are you ok, Nova?* She wasn't quite sure how to answer, other than to be brutally honest, as they had always been with each other.

"No. But I will be. I know what I need to do to get control. I know what it feels like to be close to the edge. I'll be able to pull myself back if it happens again." She turned back to the mirror and started brushing again, more gently this time. "For now, we need to focus on the deocre. On what the next steps are now that all the descendants are together."

Kael, Daro, and Benedict. They had all the pieces they needed, but what now? What exactly did they need to do?

One aspect of it had been eating at her all morning, like a bug bite that wouldn't stop itching. It was ridiculous, but if she was being honest with herself, the idea was one she'd been shoving down into the deepest depths of her conscience for days. After last night's display of her power and the fact that she could amplify off two people...

"I...think I should do it." She met Fynn's gaze in the mirror. He wrapped his arms around her waist and stood behind her, resting his chin on her shoulder.

He raised his eyebrows. "Do what?"

"Take Kael's spot in the trio of descendants."

His hands gripped her tighter, spinning her to face him so they were chest to chest. "What?"

"Kael is powerful, but I have the potential to be more powerful. I can draw power from Raelyn and you to boost what I already have." His hands squeezed even tighter, sending her magic into a dance, as if to prove her point. "And we need every ounce of magic we can get."

His eyes darkened and his lips parted, but he didn't speak for a moment. He stood preternaturally still, almost like he'd stopped breathing, before he finally spoke. "But last night... Nova, if you lose control again, if the deocre is faster than you... I can't let you do this."

"You can." Her eyes bore into his own. "You will."

He stepped back from her, pinching the bridge of his nose between his thumb and forefinger. "Where is this coming from?"

"It's been somewhere in my mind since Kael told me I'm a descendant." She took a step toward him, placing her hand on his arm. She hated seeing him like this. She hated even more that she was the one causing him pain. But she had to make him understand. "And then last night, the way my magic held on instinctually against the pyros, even when I lost control, combined with the fact that I can amplify..." *Breathe, breathe.* "It just got me thinking—"

"Two stupid pyros are not nearly the same as what we expect from the deocre. You want to put yourself in danger?" He pulled his hand away from his face, revealing the tears brimming in his violet eyes. She nearly gave in at the sight.

"Of course not, Fynn."

He ran a hand through his hair, still tousled from sleep, and turned away from her again.

"Look, let's talk to Kael and see what he thinks. But I just feel like it needs to be me. Like that's why I have this...amplification."

He laughed. "You're starting to sound like an elf with this talk of *fate*."

"Fynn—"

"Nova." He turned and looked her dead in the eyes, his use of her actual name, not her pet name, freezing her. "You are my *world*. You are what lights up my nights and what gets me out of bed in the morning. I've watched the women I love die and couldn't do a damn thing about it. Now you expect me to watch you go take on the darkest magic this country has seen in centuries, knowing full well I am defenseless to do anything if it attacks you?"

She crossed her arms. "You don't believe in me."

"I don't believe in you?" He barreled toward her, his hands gripping her just above her elbows. "When have I ever made you feel like I didn't believe in you? Nova, there is not a doubt in my mind that you *can* take on the deocre, but do you *need* to? Kael is willing and capable. There's no reason to put yourself in harm's way—"

"So you'd be ok with him getting hurt, but not me."

"Fuck. *Yes.*" He lowered his face so close to hers that their foreheads touched. "When you get hurt, I can't breathe. I can't think. All I want is to destroy whatever it is that has caused you pain, and in this case, I *can't*. I'm powerless—"

"But I'm not." Nova held his gaze. She understood him, truly she did, but she also understood herself. "Fynn, my whole life, I have been powerless. I've sat by and watched others do everything, dreaming of when it would be my turn. You told me to leave in the lab, and I left. But this time, I'm asking you to let me have this chance." She cupped his cheek with her hand, wiping away an escaped tear.

He closed his eyes. His shoulders shuddered, but he stayed quiet. He didn't object further, yet he also didn't acquiesce.

"Will you think about it?" Her hand moved from his cheek into his hair, the locks soft between her fingers. Goddess, she just wanted a million more days of running her hands through his hair.

He didn't respond right away, and she let him collect his thoughts while she continued to weave her fingers into his hair. His fears were valid. In fact, they mirrored her own. Part of her was terrified of what would happen if she let herself take on too much power and couldn't fight back. Or if she *couldn't* destroy the deocre and the power she took on wasn't even enough.

But on the other hand, she had the ability to summon more power than Kael did. And she had just as much of a personal vendetta against Luc and all this deocre stood for. She'd been robbed of the chance to play a part in Luc's death, for which she was mostly grateful. But wouldn't it feel good—wouldn't it feel *right* to play a part in the destruction of his one last stand?

Fynn sighed and opened his eyes. His lips brushed her forehead.

"I'll think about it."

Everyone else was already in the dining room when Nova and Fynn arrived, the small space entirely too crowded. Jax, Daro, Esta, and Raelyn were seated at the table, empty plates and half-drunk mugs in front of them, while her mother, Benedict, and Kael hovered along the wall by the door to the kitchen. When her mother saw them enter, she ran over to Nova, pulling her into an embrace.

"Oh, Nova, I heard about last night. I'm so glad you're all right."

Nova buried her face into her mother's neck, inhaling her sweet scent and allowing herself the moment to sink into the comfort only a mother's hug could provide.

She pulled away after a moment and flashed a weak smile. "Me too."

Mother patted her cheek, then stepped back so Kael could also hug her.

"I felt awful when I heard. I know I had to leave, but the timing—"

"Was good," she said, squeezing his arm, savoring the now-familiar tingle of his touch. "If you'd been here, they would've probably seen you, too. Maybe even tried to attack you first."

He exhaled, searching her eyes for something. But then he took a step back and turned to Benedict. "It took some convincing, but he's here to help."

Benedict cowered where he stood, his beady eyes darting around the room, his hands unable to keep still.

"I managed to get him to believe that by helping with this, he'd be absolved of all the wrongs he committed in the past."

Nova couldn't have cared less. If Kael had needed to drag him back here by his hair, she wouldn't have cared. As long as he was here.

No amount of help would absolve him of what he did to her mother, to the rest of the lab partners, in her eyes.

"Good." She turned to her mother. "So now what? What do we need to do?"

Raelyn stood from the table, taking her plate and mug with her. "First, you and Fynn need to eat. You need coffee. And then we can talk."

Nova sat at the small table, her mug empty and her plate half-eaten. Fynn had barely touched any of his food, choosing to push it around the plate instead. Was he nervous? Was he still trying to process what had happened last night?

Then she remembered. He'd had to kill the pyros. She needed to ask him about that. Even though it hadn't been his first kill, taking someone's life couldn't have been easy. And he hadn't allowed her to ask about Luc's death.

"Now, Mother," Raelyn said from where she stood beside Jax. "Tell us what's next."

Mother was sitting across from Fynn at the small table. She set down her mug and sighed. "We have all three descendants. Each will be required to make a...donation to bring down the deocre. And then Canta's descendant, in this case Kael, will cast a curse to kill it."

"What kind of donation?" Fynn asked. He'd stiffened in his seat. Nova looked at him, trying to get a read on his thoughts, but he didn't meet her gaze.

"Well, first, just blood—"

"Just...just blood!" Benedict wailed from his corner. "He didn't say anything about blood."

"Shut up," Mother spat in a tone she could only have learned from Luc. "It's just a small amount of blood. But the combined blood of the goddesses is needed in order to power the spell that the witch will cast to destroy the deocre."

Benedict wailed again, continuing to fidget in the corner with his hands pressed to his face, but Kael kept close to prevent him from trying to run. Not that he'd get far before Fynn or Daro caught up with him.

"That doesn't sound so bad," Daro said, crossing his arms. He was standing with Esta by the door to the hallway, not technically guarding it, but certainly appearing that way.

Where Benedict had seemed crazed at the idea of spilling his own blood, Daro seemed almost relieved. Nova supposed he'd been imagining much worse, though she honestly hadn't given any thought to what would come next. But Daro was right: donating a few drops of blood didn't sound too bad...

"And what's second?" Kael asked.

Mother traced the handle on her coffee mug. "It's not entirely clear. The text the Defiance found only said a 'donation of blood and other.'"

"'Other'?" Daro asked, his hands falling to his sides. "Surely it's not a donation of our *life*?"

"And if it was, would that change your position?" Mother asked him. Her voice was delicate, but her face was full of fire. "Would you not give your life to save your people, your country?"

Daro didn't answer, but a shadow of something—fear? shame?—passed over his face.

"For what it's worth, I don't think it's a donation of life," Mother continued. "That seems a sure way to end the line of descendants and prohibit future generations from destroying the worst of evils."

Nova breathed a sigh of relief. She had a good point. But if it wasn't death, then what?

"Power."

Kael had whispered the word so softly, Nova almost didn't hear it over Benedict's whimpering. But as soon as the word clicked in her mind, she knew he was right. A donation—or, rather, a sacrifice—of their power would be exactly the price that would need to be paid to defeat this ultimate darkness.

"Power?" Raelyn asked, rubbing at her ear. "Is that what you said?"

"It makes sense," Jax said as he started to pace the room. "The only way to destroy the raw dark power behind a deocre is with more power..."

"Ok, so that makes sense for witches," Raelyn continued, tapping her forefinger to her chin. She looked at Daro. "And I suppose you have your agility, which could be construed as power." Then she turned to Benedict, Nova following her gaze to the man trapped in the corner, who had only ever wanted power because he had none of his own. "But what about him?"

Benedict kept his eyes on the ground to avoid the stares of everyone in the room. Nova's heart almost went out to him in that moment. Almost.

But he spoke, his voice sounding stronger than she'd yet heard it as he made his declaration of allegiance. "The pursuit of power. The desire to harness magic. The ability to work with runes. That will be my sacrifice. I will be truly human."

That hardly seemed a sufficient sacrifice in Nova's mind, but if that was what he would willingly give—and he did seem more than willing now—then she supposed it would work.

A sacrifice of power would mean she'd never have to worry about being overcome again. She could go back to living as she had before: regular, average Nova without her wielder powers. Powers that were still so new to her anyway. That sacrifice would be worth it.

It was the final straw in the decision she'd already made.

"I'll do it," she said, not letting the quiver in her body carry into her voice. "I'll fight the deocre."

45

Nova

"Excuse me?" Raelyn shrieked, taking a step forward. Jax grabbed her arm and pulled her back.

Nova winced, not at all surprised by her sister's reaction, but startled just the same. She stole a glance at Fynn, whose eyes glistened as he dipped his head into an almost imperceptible nod. He reached over and grabbed her hand.

"Nova, we discussed this," Kael said, his eyes wild. "I can take this on. *Let me* take this on."

But Nova shook her head, the long, dark hair she hadn't braided this morning framing her face as she turned to face her true father. "You've given enough. It's my turn. And with my amplification, I can overpower the deocre. I know I can."

Kael ran a hand through his hair. "But is it necessary? If we have all three descendants, do we need *extra* power?"

"It certainly wouldn't hurt." Mother smiled at Nova, her eyes twinkling with a mixture of pride and fear. "I didn't want to ask you to do this, but I've been thinking along the same lines myself. The descendants alone are not guaranteed. Using Fynn and Rae to amplify you—"

"Amplification from people?"

All eyes turned back to Benedict, who had spoken loudly, though there was still a tremor in his voice. He turned away slightly.

"Not any people," Nova said, eyeing him closely. Did he know something she didn't? He'd certainly studied the lore of magic more than anyone else she knew, more than most witches probably ever had. Maybe he had the answers to her amplification.

"People you...love?"

His eyes met hers, gray clashing with green. In that moment, she realized he was right.

The reason her power responded to Raelyn and Fynn's touch, but to no one else's, was because of the reciprocated *love* between them. Because it knew when she was near someone who cared for her, someone who would protect her and look out for her because they loved her as much as she loved them.

She grabbed her mother's hand. Mother flinched, her eyes widening in surprise from the contact, but then settled, squeezing Nova's hand in return. The slow intensification of her magic under her skin was different from Raelyn or Fynn's touch, but maybe that was because the love was different. It was slower to grow, more complex, slightly hidden still. But it was there.

Proof that Raella Astor had always loved Nova as her own daughter, even if she hadn't shown it. Proof that Raella had done just enough to garner Nova's love, too, without raising suspicion under Luc's watchful eye.

But with Kael—it hadn't worked yet. She didn't love him yet. It reacted to his touch, sure, but so had it reacted to Fynn's touch long before she realized she loved him. Maybe there was still a chance it would work someday...

She closed her eyes, searching her memory for more supporting evidence. Like those times growing up when she'd caused accidents, things she now believed were lapses in the suppression spell. Raelyn had been touching her those times. The night she'd broken the suppression spell completely, Raelyn and Fynn's hands had been steadying her.

Her magic was amplified by love. It always had been. Even when she didn't think she could be loved.

"He's right," she breathed, her eyes opening and darting from Fynn to Raelyn. "That's what it is—that's my amplifier."

Jax had stopped pacing and stared at her, his hand in his hair. "Remarkable. I've never heard of anything like that."

"It's rare," Benedict said, ducking his head. "But not unheard of. Especially in Canta's line."

"It does have to be me, then. It was always meant to be me." Nova looked at Kael, whose lips were parted slightly, his eyes wide and watery. "Kael—Father—I know you wanted to be able to do this for me, but I need to do it. I *want* to do it."

"You've just found your power, and it's beautiful. Don't give it up—"

She shook her head. "I lived without power my entire life. At least now I'll be able to feel proud about my lack of magic, rather than weakened." Even if she couldn't tell anyone *how* she'd lost her powers, she would know. Raelyn would know. Fynn would know. Everyone who counted in her life would know.

The rest never knew she was a wielder anyway.

Kael glanced at Fynn, whose hand was still in Nova's. "Are you ok with this?"

Fynn sat up straighter and squeezed her hand. "I am. But don't think for one second I would send her in there defenseless. Even after she has amplified, I plan to stay right beside her, ready to step in if needed."

Kael stalked forward until he was right next to Nova. He knelt and placed a hand on her arm. "I will, too. I'll be ready to step in if needed."

She looked down at where his hand rested on her sleeve. The same sensation she'd felt on the beach a few days ago came flowing back into her, but there was a hint of something...*else*. Was there love growing between them? Did they just need more time?

Unfortunately, it seemed time was the thing they lacked the most.

"Nova." Her mother's voice drew her attention back to the rest of the room. "Are you absolutely certain?"

Nova looked around the room, at this group of people, a collection of all three races that had come together to save their country—their fellow witches, elves, and humans—from an unspeakable dark force. These people had changed her life over the past few months, and those were the kinds of bonds that didn't break overnight.

Raelyn, Fynn, Mother, and Kael certainly weren't going to go anywhere when this was over. Even Jax, if he couldn't train her, could still be counted on as a friend. Esta may be a grump, but she and Raelyn had developed such a bond that Nova was willing to look past that. Daro was proof that first impressions weren't always correct, and they had bonded as descendants of goddesses. Then there was Benedict, whom she was still certain she'd never forgive, but if he continued his quiet life in the mountains and never hurt another person again, she'd feel good about bringing him into this. And allowing him a shot at personal redemption.

These people had her back, and she had theirs. Not only could she do this for herself; she could do this for them. For their protection. For their futures.

Nova met her mother's brown eyes, eyes that for so much of her life had hardened, but today they beamed with love and pride in a way she'd seldom seen growing up.

"I'm certain." Mother's shoulders dropped with relief, but Kael hung his head as Nova continued, "Now, how do we catch a deocre?"

46

FYNN

Though he'd been surprised by Nova declaring her desire to take on the deocre so soon after she'd initially proposed the idea, Fynn couldn't help but smile. He'd thought about what she'd said. She did need to be the one to do this. Her amplification was only part of the reason, though; she needed to fight this thing for *herself*. To prove to herself what she was capable of. This was about *her* and no one else.

It had pained him to agree to the switch from the original plan, but seeing her in attack mode last night had changed something in him. In *her*. He saw a new fire there, a fire that was fighting for justice and wouldn't be extinguished until it had seen its mission through. If Nova hadn't been allowed the chance to play some role in Luc's demise, it would fester and eat at her for the rest of her life.

And since he hoped to be around for the rest of her life, he didn't want to see her beautiful soul turn into something ugly.

He could set aside his fears if it meant that she had a chance to be something great.

Now, Fynn stood back to watch as Nova, Raelyn, Raella, and Jax set up what was to become the battleground on the beach. Tomorrow would be the day the deocre was destroyed.

They'd decided that somewhere in the open, away from the eyes of the town, would be best, and the ocean provided an excellent barrier on one side. The witches were using their magic to smooth out the sand in places while also building dunes along the remaining three sides of the arena and magically fortifying them.

Footsteps approached from behind. He turned to find Kael walking his way, his hands in his pockets and his posture resigned in a way Fynn hadn't seen since they'd first laid eyes on him in the lab a month ago.

"Everything ok?" Fynn asked. Given the circumstances, he knew the question was ridiculous.

"Please tell me you didn't put her up to this," Kael said as he came to stand next to Fynn. His gaze was focused on the four witches building the arena, but Fynn didn't miss the tension radiating off his body.

"We haven't known each other long, but you should know me better than that," Fynn said, mustering every last bit of confidence he could before speaking again. "I know, and I think you know, too, that she needs the opportunity to prove herself. She's lived her whole life in the shadows, believing herself to be something she's not. Now she finds out who she really is but is too sheltered by people like you and me to do anything with that or test the limits of what she was born to do. We took that from her with Luc. I can't live with myself if I take that opportunity for her to embrace her true self again."

Kael was silent for a long moment; the waves and the occasional incomprehensible voice carried on the breeze were the only sounds around them. At last, he nodded and turned to look at Fynn. "It's a hard truth, but you're right. I'm glad she has you." He tilted his head to one side. "Promise me, come what may, that you'll be there for her. Look out for her, love her, protect her?"

Fynn smiled. He couldn't help it. It was a vow he would happily make over and over again. "I promise you, Kael. I will guard your daughter and her heart for the rest of my life."

Eyes glistening, Kael rested a hand on Fynn's shoulder. "Thank you." He turned back toward the house and walked away, leaving Fynn alone again with his thoughts.

As he looked back at the witches, who were nearly finished now, the smallest tinge of regret tore at his heart. He hated, more than anything in the world, the idea of Nova putting herself in danger, the idea of her going into this battle unprotected. The idea that there would be nothing he could do to intervene—because what good was a sword and agility against a being made entirely of dark magic?

But he had to shove that selfish part of him down and let Nova do this for herself. For Astria. So that they even had a shot of an *after*.

He sighed and let his hands fall to his sides, his right resting on the hilt of his sword.

After.

Even if—*when*—the deocre was gone, there was still the matter of Blackmore's innocence and Luc's murder to deal with.

In order to prove Blackmore's innocence, they'd need to expose Luc's crimes, as well as his wielder abilities and what he'd done with them. So far, the attack in the city was the only public display that anything had changed, and they'd bought into the belief that wielders had been the cause. Trying to change the story now would be difficult, despite how much he hated the lie.

And who was to say that there wasn't another corrupt governor among them who wouldn't try to get Kael to change their powers? The cycle might never end...

Without Kael's innocence being proven, there was no way for Jax and Fynn to prove they'd killed Luc in self-defense. That his murder had been just. Which meant that, until one of them had a brilliant idea, he and Nova couldn't have an after. He'd remain on the run and in hiding.

Look how well that had treated him so far. At least whatever was tracking him should die with the deocre.

Should.

"Fynn? What's wrong?"

He blinked. He'd been so lost in his thoughts that he hadn't even noticed the witches leaving the site and approaching. All four of them now stood before him. Nova took a step closer, reaching for his hand.

He imagined never being able to look into those emerald eyes again. Never being able to run his hands through her silky raven hair. Never feeling the heat of her skin on his or the way she clenched around him right before she...

Then and there, he resolved with a renewed vigor that they would figure this out. There would be an after. No matter what it took.

That thought in mind, he smiled and laced his fingers with hers.

"Nothing. Nothing at all."

47

NOVA

DINNER THAT EVENING WAS a quiet affair. Only half of the group could fit around the dining table, so Fynn, Nova, Raelyn, and Esta had chosen those seats while the rest of the group sat in the living room. Nova was happy to see Fynn eating, but she couldn't get his expression on the beach earlier out of her mind. Something had been bothering him. He'd been so deep in thought, but about what?

She was certain that, despite saying he supported her choice, he was worried. It must have taken a lot for him to get over his inability to protect the women he loved and willingly allow her in harm's way. If something happened to her, how would he cope? Would he be riddled with more guilt than he could handle?

She forced those thoughts into the deepest recesses of her mind. Though she'd initially been hesitant to take on the deocre, the more she'd thought about it—and she'd thought about it a lot—the more excited she became.

The end of all of this was near.

The end of her insurmountable power was near.

She could make a difference in the lives of Astrians, maybe use this as a step toward true equality.

Because she realized today that ultimately that was her passion. If—when—she made it through this, she wasn't going back to teaching. She wasn't yet sure how, but she could never live with herself if she didn't fight for true equality.

Wielder restrictions lifted.

Prejudices slashed.

Better integrations of Arkwood's neighborhoods.

Maybe it was a far-fetched dream. Maybe it wouldn't even happen in her lifetime. But if she could lay the groundwork for future generations to carry on, she'd have accomplished something great.

Without the help of magic.

Nova sat back in her chair, her face softening. She glanced at Fynn next to her, allowing herself a moment to imagine their future together. They could live here in Adenaport—they both so loved the beach—or maybe back in Arkwood, helping to rebuild the northern neighborhoods that had been destroyed. In autumn, they'd visit Aerdmure to see the brilliant display of color from the changing leaves, always staying in *their* cabin and sitting on that little outcrop of rocks they'd discovered.

Would they have kids? While half-witches were common among humans, it wasn't the same for elves. They rarely married outside their own race. What would that mean for their children? Would they have pointed ears and magic? Would they live a normal lifespan but have heightened senses? No matter the outcome, if they were blessed with a family, their children would come into the world with so much love and would hopefully grow up in a world where no one cared what race they were or how much power they had.

A tiny Fynn was dancing around her mind when the real Fynn caught her eye. He leaned toward her and whispered, "I'd love to know what thoughts are giving you that smile."

She turned her face so she could reply in his ear, "When we get through this, I'll tell you."

He grinned and leaned back, forking his last bite of fish.

"You two really know how to make me want to vomit," Raelyn said, sticking her finger in her throat mockingly. Esta snorted and sipped her wine.

Nova's smile spread wider. "I hope you find this level of happiness one day, Rae, so I can throw those words back at you."

"Cheers to that." Raelyn held up her drink. Fynn clinked his glass with hers.

Esta stood so fast, Nova could've sworn she'd somehow gained Fynn's agility. With a crash, her chair toppled to the floor. She threw her napkin down on the table and stormed out of the room. The creak of the front door opening and then closing followed her footsteps.

"What the hell was that about?" Nova asked, her fork hovering in midair.

"I think I know." Raelyn's face paled as she stood, more carefully than Esta had. Her hand shook as she pushed her chair to the table.

"Be gentle with her," Fynn said, setting his glass down.

Nova looked between Fynn and Raelyn. What did they know that she didn't? What had they been keeping from her?

Raelyn nodded, then followed Esta onto the front porch.

"Ok, what's going on?" Nova asked once it was just the two of them left.

Fynn sighed and leaned back in his chair. "I've suspected for a while. But I wasn't sure until I saw that reaction."

He was still speaking in riddles. "Suspected what?"

He looked her dead in the eye. "That Esta is in love with Raelyn?"

"She...what?" Nova racked her brain for how she could have missed this. She remembered remarking on how much it seemed Esta had come to care for Raelyn when Raelyn had been taken by Kael. How she knew intuitively that Esta would take care of Raelyn once they got out of the lab, even if she herself wasn't there to watch over Raelyn.

But how had she missed that Esta had developed feelings for her sister? Why hadn't Raelyn said anything?

"I suspect that Raelyn does not reciprocate." Fynn turned to look at the doorway through which the two females had just passed. "And that Raelyn's words about finding love may have set Esta off."

"Well…yeah." If Raelyn knew that Esta was pining for her and had turned her down, then Esta's reaction to Raelyn's words was warranted. Raelyn wasn't one to be openly cruel, but sometimes she did forget to filter before she spoke. "I should go talk to her." She started to stand, but Fynn grabbed her wrist, chuckling.

"Al, she's a big girl." He guided her back to her seat. "She doesn't need her elder sister stepping in. Let her handle it herself."

Nova rolled her eyes, but he was right. While her reflex may have been to run to Raelyn's side, to be of some kind of help, this wasn't a situation where she could do much. Raelyn needed to decide for herself how to handle this.

"How long have you known?" she asked Fynn as she returned to the bite of fish that she'd abandoned a moment ago.

"Known? All of one minute, like I said. But suspected? Since the night they went to that gala with Raella back in Arkwood."

The night she'd been attacked in the park.

That night, Raelyn had gotten dressed, had primped herself up more than she had the entire time the elves had been with them. Esta had been surprised that they were going anywhere at all and had hastily changed into her own outfit for the gala, but now that Nova really thought about it, maybe the surprise that had been etched all over

Esta's face hadn't been because they were going to the gala as much as it was about how stunning Raelyn had looked.

"All this time, I thought Esta was just a grump and that's all there was to her."

Fynn laughed again. Apparently, he found this whole situation—and especially Nova's ignorance of it—incredibly amusing. "This may surprise you, but Esta has smiled more about Raelyn than in the entire time I've known her. Which, granted, isn't that long, but long enough."

Nova let her fingers wander to her braid, twirling it absentmindedly for a moment before she caught Fynn raising an eyebrow at her. "Can't a girl play with her hair in peace?" She began to exaggerate the twirls.

"Not you, no. It usually means you're nervous, or...deep in thought."

She ignored him but let her hand drop. "I've never asked, but how long have you known Esta?"

"Not as long as you'd think." He scratched at the stubble growing on his cheek. "She's about fifteen years younger than me, so we never overlapped at the Academy. But we've crossed paths in various posts over the last ten years."

"And has she always been this..." Nova waved her hand in the air, the word she needed escaping her. "I don't know, miserable? I mean, really, I could count on one hand the number of times I've seen her smile."

"I think," Fynn said, running a hand down his cheek, "that recent...circumstances have put a strain on all of us. Maybe she doesn't handle stress or being out of her routine as well or in the same way as we do."

He had a point. She leaned back in her chair, her gaze settling on the doorway again, and crossed her arms.

Despite the fact that she'd always pictured her little sister with someone who had the exuberance to match Raelyn's, Nova couldn't get past the idea that maybe Esta would be good for Raelyn. Maybe she could help ground her—although the idea of a geo-witch needing grounding was enough to make Nova smile.

She turned back to Fynn, another humorous thought crossing her mind. "What do you think Luc would have said if he'd known that his daughters would both end up with their elven bodyguards at the end of this?"

Fynn's eyes sparkled as he let out a booming laugh. Nova joined him, letting herself enjoy this moment of joy, of lightheartedness, before tomorrow arrived along with the darkness they would be summoning.

48

NOVA

RAELYN APPEARED BACK IN the house half an hour later, at which point Nova and Fynn had joined the others in the living room to review the plan. But one look at Raelyn's beet-red face and her wild eyes, and Nova was leading her back out of the house and onto the sand, grabbing a shawl off the back of Mother's chair as she left.

The evening had a distinctly autumn bite to it, the breeze steady and cool. The moon was just starting to peek over the ocean, leaving a trail of light reflecting in its wake. As if anticipating what lay ahead, the ocean was raucous, waves pushing in close to the dune line in fast succession. Nova looked down the beach toward where they'd constructed the arena earlier and saw that their enchanted dunes were holding strong against the surf that threatened to plow them down.

Raelyn's hand warm in hers, she led her sister to the arena. Nova could just make out the sound of the sliding door opening and closing behind them, and with a quick glance over her shoulder, she saw Fynn step out onto the porch, hand on his sword.

Good. He could watch them from there, but still give them their privacy.

Once they reached the arena, Nova pulled Raelyn down on the sand with her and took her other hand.

"What happened, Rae?"

Raelyn tilted her chin toward the sky. "What happened is I'm an ass." A single tear trickled down her cheek.

Nova didn't say anything more, just rubbed her thumb in circles over her sister's wrist, waiting for her to continue.

"Esta loves me. She said she wants to be with me after all of this is over, and I just...I don't know, Nova." She brushed away another tear with the back of her hand. "Do I feel something for her? Sure, maybe. Do I feel love? No, I don't think so."

"That doesn't make you an ass."

"But I wish I *could* give her that. After you and Fynn left for Aerdmure, and it was just Esta and I...We really bonded. We worked well together. We had a mission. It was *fun*. But now, after losing Father, after learning all these truths...I'm not the same person I was then. And if I'm not even sure who I am, how can I be sure what—or who—I want?"

Nova was silent for a moment, inwardly happy to hear her sister voice the concerns that Nova suspected she had been masking. "No one is making you choose right now."

"Esta is." Raelyn's eyes found Nova's and hardened.

Nova bristled and pulled back slightly. "She gave you an ultimatum?"

"Not in so many words, but essentially, yes." Raelyn tucked a stray curl behind her ear. "She said there's really no reason for her to be here anymore, which is true, I suppose, since we don't need guards anymore. She told me that if I can't give her a reason to stay, then she's leaving." She paused and exhaled sharply. "Tonight."

"Oh, Rae—"

"I don't want to hurt her, and I want her here, but not for the reasons she wants me to want her here." Raelyn buried her face in her hands. "It's stupidly selfish of me to even want her to stay at this point."

Nova pressed her fingers into the cool sand, the wind whipping her hair into her face. "What do you want? Deep down, what is it you want right now?"

Raelyn peeked through her fingers. "Aside from this deocre to be utterly destroyed tomorrow?"

"Yes, besides that." Nova's heart stopped for a moment. Hopefully she would be the one to deliver that wish. "What do you want for *you*?"

Raelyn let her hands fall back into her lap, her gaze wandering around the dunes that towered on all sides of them. From where they sat, they couldn't see the waves, but they could hear them. It was a symphony to which they'd had deep conversations, so much like this one, many times throughout their lives. Memories flitted through Nova's mind as she waited for her sister to reply. Memories of them sitting on this very beach, discussing one teenage melodrama or another. Discussing Nova's lack of power, her parents' mistreatment of her. Or Raelyn's misgivings about not achieving the same high marks that Nova had in her non-magical courses and feeling like she had too much invisible weight on her shoulders to carry on the family legacy.

A cloud passed in front of the moon, casting them in darkness, their shadows elongating and almost disappearing entirely.

When Raelyn finally spoke, her voice was raspy and barely audible over the wind and the sea. "I want to get through this and then find myself again. I want to work on me, before I can work on me *and* someone else, regardless of who that someone else may be." She brushed away a tear. "I need a chance to properly grieve, I think, before

I'll be ready to do anything else." Raelyn lifted her gaze to meet Nova's, her brown eyes watery and pleading.

More than anything, Nova wished she could take this pain away from her sister. To remove all sense of hopelessness and grief and desperation that she could see plastered all over her face. But the only way Raelyn could get through this was on her own. Nova would be there to support her in whatever way she could.

"I think you have your answer, then," Nova replied, pulling Raelyn in close and pressing her lips to her sister's hair. Raelyn's body shook as sobs racked through her, the grief she'd been suppressing—they'd both been suppressing—coming to a head and forcing itself out in the way only grief can. Nova held her, allowing her to cry, to feel, to be, as the wind continued to whip around them and the clouds overhead thickened.

"I'm so scared for you." Raelyn's voice was muffled against Nova's shoulder. "What if—"

"Shhhh," Nova said, rubbing Raelyn's back in slow circles. "No what-ifs." They'd been circulating through her own mind enough. But she'd successfully put aside the doubts. Putting voice to those what-ifs now would only bring those doubts back to the surface.

Raelyn's body shook. "But, Nova, I can't do life without you. You're the other half of my soul."

Tears burned in Nova's eyes. She clenched them shut to force them back. "And you're the other half of mine. The best part to have come out of this whole mess that Luc created is the relationship I have with *you*." *Breathe, breathe.*

The first drop of rain landed on her cheek like a delicate caress from Canta herself. Nova pushed Raelyn back from their embrace and whispered, "I think we need to head back."

Raelyn looked up at the sky, as if noticing the brewing storm for the first time. "I suppose we should. And I should talk to Esta." She brushed away the tear tracks that stained her cheeks.

The sisters stood and, hand in hand, walked back toward the cottage, where Fynn was still waiting on the porch. But before they reached him, Raelyn turned back to Nova, her eyes puffy and blood-shot, and said, "We stick together, come what may, right?"

Nova pulled Raelyn back into a hug, despite the rain picking up and beginning to soak them while they stood there. As she inhaled her sister's sweet floral scent, feeling more at peace than she had in weeks, she whispered, "Always."

49

FYNN

"**E**STA'S GONE."

Fynn sat down on the bed next to Nova, who was still lying there despite having been awake for a good half-hour already. He held out the mug of coffee he'd brought with him.

Today, he would do whatever Nova asked, whatever she needed. Coffee was just the first thing.

"*Gone* gone?" Nova sat up, taking the mug from him and holding it up to her lips. One waft of the brew, though, and she paused. "Wait, this is Raelyn's. She made coffee despite Esta leaving?"

Fynn nodded. "I ran into her in the kitchen. She insisted you would get nothing but the best today."

His stomach curled into knots at the idea of what was going to be happening out on the beach in a few short hours. Well, as long as everything went according to plan, that is. Raella had sent a coded message via raven to the Defiance yesterday to ask them to remove the spells on the wall at noon today, effectively allowing the deocre free roam. Kael had wanted to send it, but Raella had insisted they wouldn't trust such a message, and Fynn agreed. Now it was only a matter of time before the deocre would make its way to them. It already knew where they were. The pyros were proof of that.

Nova, Benedict, and Daro would be ready to meet it in the arena when it arrived. They'd give their blood donations as soon as it descended on them, then Nova would cast the spell. Fynn, Raella, and Raelyn would be right behind her, ready to assist with amplification.

It was almost too simple. Which was why Fynn's body was so tense, why his stomach roiled with nausea. There was so much that they couldn't predict about this dark spirit; they had to keep it simple. Had to be ready to improvise at a moment's notice.

"Of course she did," Nova said, bringing his focus back to the room. "She's a master at emotional suppression." She took a sip and sighed. "I can't believe Esta actually left, though. Especially given what we're doing today."

Fynn hadn't asked what the sisters had discussed on the beach last night. It wasn't his business. But he did wish he'd had a chance to speak with Esta before she'd fled into the night. To convince her to stay.

"We'll get through today, and then I'll go find her," Fynn said. He pressed his hands to his thighs and stood.

"I know your heart is in the right place, Fynn," Nova said, taking another sip, "but please don't. Let Raelyn figure this out for herself."

He turned to face her and saw her emerald eyes full of love. While he may have an entirely different bond with his own sister, he could understand the desire to both protect a sibling and allow them to flourish on their own. Nova's compassion and deep understanding of her sister was one of Fynn's favorite things about her. One of the things that first drew him to her.

He held up his hands in mock surrender. "You're right. I won't intervene." He looked outside the window while Nova finished her coffee. The storm from last night had tapered but the wind was still fierce, pushing against the windows of the cottage with every gust. "Three hours until the wards fall."

Nova set the empty mug down next to her and finally got out of bed. Fynn marveled at her confidence, the way she held her head high, not a tremble or a shake in sight as she padded over to the armoire and opened the doors.

This was a completely different woman from the one he'd met in Arkwood just a few months ago. How lucky was he to have witnessed her transformation? How lucky was he that this woman loved him?

She flicked through a few of the tunics and dresses hanging on the rack, then turned back to him with a twinkle in her eyes. "Come here, Fynn." She beckoned him with her finger. "Let's find the perfect outfit to slay a monster."

Nova stood in front of the mirror in a white dress, her hair cascading down her back. The dress had been pushed against the wall of the armoire, but as soon as Nova had seen it, she'd gasped and reached for it. She quickly donned it, her eyes widening as she beheld herself in the mirror, her shoulders softening.

It wasn't elaborate. Rather, it was a fairly standard dress. But on her—the way she carried it confidently—it was the most beautiful dress in the world.

It also made him want to rip it off her.

The silver material glittered with something he'd never seen before, some kind of magical sparkle that was woven into the light, nearly sheer fabric. The sleeves fell to her wrists, ending with a cuff, and the waistline and bodice were cinched tight. His favorite part, though not necessarily the most practical for battle, was the plunging neckline in the front and back. The V shape in the front connected just below her breasts, while in the back...it soared all the way down to her waist. He could see where the skin of her back poked out from under her hair.

"Stunning," he said breathlessly as she studied herself in the mirror.

She swayed her hips from side to side, the loose skirts of the dress swishing around her legs as she did. "This dress...I got it a few years ago on a shopping trip in town." Nova twirled, the skirts billowing, before she stopped in front of the mirror again. "The fabric was one of a kind, and when I tried it on...Fynn, it's the most comfortable thing I've ever worn. And it has always felt like it was made for me."

Just like the dress at Canta's Festival, he remembered.

"I think it's perfect." He strode over to her, standing behind her and placing his hand on her back, her hair finding its way between his fingers. "You look radiant. Confident." It was a different type of armor.

Green eyes met his in the mirror. "I feel confident whenever I'm with you, Fynn."

His heart melted right then and there. Unable to help himself, he pulled Nova into an embrace, burying his face in her neck and inhaling her sweet lavender scent. She wrapped her arms around his back and tucked herself into his chest.

He refused to allow any intrusive thoughts today. No. In a few hours, they'd be back here, ready to figure out the next part of the plan: how to exonerate Kael, Jax, and himself.

There was no other option. No other result he could live with.

Nova pulled away slightly to look up at him, and his resolve turned molten. How he was supposed to let her walk into the face of the worst danger he'd ever known when he couldn't do a damn thing about it...

But the way she held herself higher these last few days, the way she'd committed to this valiantly on her own, the way she smiled at him right now—there was no way he could possibly prevent her from doing what she wanted to do.

Fynn slid a hand up to rest on her cheek, his thumb stroking the buttery-soft skin just below the new scar that still angered him. "No matter what happens today—"

"Fynn," she warned, but he put a finger to her lips to stop her.

"Let me get this out." He took a deep breath, then met her gaze, aiming to speak directly to her soul. "No matter what happens today, I want you to know that I am with you. I am yours. Wholly, truly, and irrevocably. If this is the last moment I get alone with you, I need you to know that, no matter what cruel twist of fate it was that brought us together, I would write it the same way a hundred times over just to get the moments I've had with you. What we have...I've never felt anything like it, and I know I never will again. So, thank you for giving me the time that we've had together. For sharing this part of your journey with me. For letting me love you."

Nova swallowed, and her eyes glistened. *Fuck.* He hadn't meant to upset her. He only wanted to get it all out there before... "Fynn, I—"

"NOVA!"

The sound of Jax's voice—Jax's *angry* voice—bellowed up the stairs. Startled, Nova wrenched herself from Fynn's grasp. She looked utterly confused, her brow furrowed and her lips parted. He could've cursed Jax then and there for breaking up this moment.

She sighed, then stepped forward and brushed a kiss against his cheek before she whispered, "There's more I want to say, but I'll save it for after. Just know, Fynn, that I love you endlessly and absolutely."

Her breath on his ear...it was enough for him to want to curse Jax again, pull that dress off her, and push her back onto the bed.

But Nova stepped past him toward the door, grabbing his hand and pulling him along on the way out of the room. They didn't have to go far to see what Jax was yelling about.

At the bottom of the stairs stood Jax, his hands balled into fists and his face red with fury. Behind him stood another male—a dark-skinned, dark-haired male wearing a smirk. Fynn recognized him, and his hand reached for the hilt of his sword before he could stop himself.

"Oh!" Nova gasped. She descended the stairs quickly, moving as if on air. Fynn followed right behind her. Why had it sounded like she wasn't at all surprised this witch was here?

Nova breezed right past Jax and wrapped her arms around the newcomer. Fynn froze. Was there something he was missing here? The last time they'd seen him, he'd jumped them to the lab, but now she seemed much more familiar with him.

Of course, she'd had almost two weeks in Aerdmure before coming here. Perhaps they'd crossed paths then. Gotten to know each other better.

Fynn swallowed down the lump of jealousy that rose in his throat. *Don't be a child*, he scolded himself.

Nova pulled back, looked up at the witch, and said, "Welcome to Adenaport, Mehta. You're just in time."

50

Nova

He'd come! The message Nova had asked Kael to send to Mehta had not only worked but had summoned the wielder here to them.

She'd wanted him here for Jax, so they could resolve once and for all this issue between them. Before whatever it was that would happen in a few short hours. But now that Mehta was here, before the deocre, he could help the cause *and* spend time alone with Jax. It was a win for everyone. Except maybe Jax, if his current beet-red expression was any indication.

"What the *fuck* did you do, Nova?" She'd never seen him look so angry. A few weeks ago, the look on his face might have made her cower and run, but now...

"I had Kael send Mehta a message before he went to get Benedict. At the time, I thought he could talk you out of going to Arkwood, but seeing as how he didn't come right away—"

"Sorry about that." Mehta rubbed the back of his neck.

Nova waved him off. "It's better this way, actually. Plans changed after the pyros found us."

"Pyros?" Mehta's eyebrows raised.

"There's a lot to catch you up on." Nova flashed him a smile. "Jax can do that while the two of you work on a protection spell for the town."

They'd decided last night that while they engaged the deocre in battle, the town of Adenaport would need protection. But Nova was needed in the arena, and Kael flat out refused to leave her, so that left only Jax to weave the protection spell they'd been working on. Now that Mehta was here, though, he could help. The spell wasn't perfect, but with two wielders rather than one, it would be a hell of a lot stronger.

Jax moved his body, now flush against her chest, his nose nearly touching hers. Fynn shifted next to her, a warning growl escaping his lips.

"You brought him here, closer to the danger, rather than leaving him safe in Aerdmure? Are you insane, Nova?"

She stared into Jax's eyes as she replied, "Nothing like facing death to make you realize what truly matters...and what doesn't."

He was silent for a moment, his breath hot on her face and his chest heaving as he processed her words. But she didn't stand down or step aside. Instead, she stood her ground and held his gaze. He might have taught her a lot, but she could teach him some things, too.

Like why it was so important to keep those you love close.

After a few tense moments, he stepped back and relaxed his shoulders. "You better defeat this monster, Astor, because afterwards I have some more choice words for you."

Oh, of that she was certain.

She laughed. "I'll be waiting."

Jax stomped off to the porch.

Nova turned to Mehta. "I'm glad you came."

"I'm sorry it took so long." He cast his gaze toward the ground and shuffled his feet. "I didn't understand what I had heard at first. Once I figured it out, I was worried I was too late."

Nova reached out and rested a hand on his arm. "You're right on time."

He smiled at her, then turned his gaze to Fynn. "I think I owe you an apology, Voss. I wasn't exactly...welcoming to you when we met. I have a complicated past with elves, and—"

Fynn stuck out his hand. "I have a complicated past with witches. Let's put that behind us and move on."

Mehta's mouth dropped open, then curved into a grin. "You're on." He took Fynn's hand and shook it.

"Oh, Mehta!" Raelyn sauntered in from the dining room, carrying a carafe of coffee. "I was wondering whose voices I was hearing. And why Jax was so angry. Welcome!" She poured coffee into the empty mug she had in her other hand and held it out to him.

Nova watched the mug pass into his hands, inhaling a whiff of her favorite aroma. Or perhaps now her second favorite aroma, behind cedar and salt air. She may have already had one cup, but she would need more—at least two more—before she was ready to fight the deocre.

Raelyn tutted as if reading Nova's mind. "Guests first, Nova. I've got another whole pot brewing specially for you."

Nova eyed her sister carefully. Considering Esta's abrupt departure and their conversation last night, she was unusually chipper, even for someone who made a habit of being excessively happy. She turned back to Mehta. "Jax can explain everything on the way to the village. Thank you for coming. Really." She flashed him a smile, then pulled Raelyn by the arm through the dining room and into the kitchen.

Fynn didn't follow them, but then, she hadn't expected him to. He knew better. It was one of the things she loved about him.

Once the swinging door shut behind them, Raelyn ripped her arm free of Nova's grasp and set down the carafe. "What was that about?"

"Fynn told me Esta left, but you're out there serving coffee like it's any normal day."

Raelyn sighed and leaned back against the counter. "We ended up parting on amicable enough terms." Nova raised an eyebrow. "She understands my hesitations and didn't want to push me. She actually offered to stay, but I told her it would be better if she left. That I would come find her when—if—I'm ready. But I also told her not to wait for me because I have no idea how long it's going to take to get the shit in my brain figured out."

Nova swept her sister into a hug. Her heart swelled with not only pride, but also admiration.

"Whatever you need, I'm here for you." She inhaled deeply and squeezed Raelyn tighter. "And I'm proud of you."

"Yeah, yeah, I know." Raelyn pushed her gently away. "Now let me finish your personal pot of coffee." She turned back to the press that was steeping and curled her hands around the outside, watching it glow faintly purple, not dissimilar to how the whiskey bottle had glowed in the laboratory.

"I was thinking," Nova said, stepping up next to Raelyn. "Maybe you could teach me how to do your special coffee trick. It is my last morning with magic, after all."

Though part of her was excited to be free of the burden that magic had become, another part, nearly equal in size, was dreading the outcome of today's battle. It hadn't taken long for magic to become part of her. To become something she used instinctually. But soon, it would be ripped away again.

Breathe, breathe.

"Oh, no, sis, you're not guilting me into that one." Raelyn pressed the coffee filter down, then grabbed a mug from the shelf. "What good am I to you if you can make your own coffee?" She filled the mug, then turned to Nova with a grin and handed it to her. "Besides, I'm not convinced you're going to lose your magic."

Nova sipped the piping hot coffee. She appreciated Raelyn's never-ending optimism, but honestly...this was not the time for false hope. "What else could my donation be?"

"No idea." Raelyn shrugged. "But I just have a feeling it's not as simple as we all think."

"We'll see. But also—" she grabbed Raelyn's hand with her free one "—you're worth way more to me than the coffee you make. Even if it is excellent."

Raelyn laughed. "Oh, I know. But I'm still not giving up my best-kept secret." She poured herself a mug, clinked it with Nova's, and said, "To defeating the darkness and saving the world."

51

NOVA

HALF AN HOUR BEFORE noon, the entire group was gathered in the living room, listening to Mother review the plan one last time.

"Jax and Mehta will be stationed in town, guarding the temple and as much of the town as possible from harm." She turned to the two male wielders. "If you can get as many of the citizens into the temple as possible, that would be helpful. Use the priestesses to help you and come up with some excuse to get them there."

"A storm's brewing," Mehta offered.

Mother's eyes twinkled. "Excellent. I'm glad you've joined the team." She turned back to her notes, which were spread across the coffee table. "Benedict, Daro, and Nova will be in the arena, knives ready to perform the blood donation as soon as the deocre arrives. Remember, it's possible that it's corporeal by now, so we don't know exactly what it will look like. But I think we'll still know when we see it."

Nova nodded and rubbed the sweat pooling in her hands onto the skirts of her dress. It had been so easy to feel confident earlier today, but now, with the reality of the situation setting in, the end of her magic within grasp, she couldn't stop the fear from brewing within her. It was fueling her magic, making it dance and sing and swirl in her blood, but luckily containing it was easy.

She could do it without even trying.

"I...I really don't know," Benedict said. He was standing in the corner of the room, wringing his hands and trembling. "This isn't—"

"No backing out now, coward." Jax stomped across the room in three large strides until he stood in front of the man, his gaze boring down on Benedict. "You *will* participate."

Benedict looked at him for a moment, then his eyes turned glassy, and he nodded. Jax remained where he was for another moment before he strode back to his spot next to Mehta with a huff.

Persuasion. Nova hadn't yet seen it in action, but now...that was a powerful and dangerous tool. In the wrong hands... She shook her head, looking back at her mother. Jax had control over it. He only used it when necessary for the greater good.

Mother looked back and forth between Jax and Benedict, her brow furrowed. Did she know about Jax's power? It was probably better kept a secret.

"And then?" Nova prompted.

Mother nodded slowly and continued, "Fynn, Raelyn, and I will be right behind you, ready to amplify you as soon as the blood donation is made." Her gaze shifted to Raelyn. "And then leave the arena immediately. Come back to the cottage, where Kael will be standing guard. Understood?"

Raelyn rolled her eyes. "Yes, Mother. Get out of danger as quickly as possible."

"I still don't like the idea of you being out there alone," Fynn said. His finger found Nova's chin and pulled it gently so she faced him. "I want to be there, even if I can't do anything."

"So do I," Kael agreed.

Nova shook her head. There was nothing she wanted more than for everyone else to be far, *far* away from her and the deocre when she attacked. With no experience wielding this particular spell, she couldn't be sure she wouldn't accidentally hurt them. "No, I need you out of harm's way." Her eyes shifted to Kael. "Both of you. If I can't be sure of your safety..."

"Understood," Kael said, though his face said otherwise.

Fynn wasn't as easily swayed. His finger moved from her chin to her bottom lip, tracing it. The same pain she'd seen in his eyes this morning flashed in them now. "I understand. But it goes against everything I am to leave you there alone."

Nova took his hand in hers and pulled it from her face. "I know." Because what else *could* she say?

"Nova?" her mother asked, drawing her attention away from Fynn. "You know the spell, right?"

Nova swallowed. "Yes." She'd gone over it extensively with Mother yesterday. It was complex, yet simple. Beautiful, yet terrifying.

"You're ready." It wasn't a question, but a statement, one that Nova knew in her heart was true.

She was ready. She could do this.

She *had* to do this. To save Astria, to save her family. To have any hope of saving Kael, Jax, and Fynn from Mistfell.

A gust of wind slammed into the house, rattling the windows and causing Raelyn to jump.

"Looks like a storm is actually brewing," Kael said. He was standing in his favorite spot by the sliding doors, looking out over the beach and the ocean.

"Excellent," Mehta said, stepping forward. He turned to Jax. "Let's go warn the town."

He retreated from the room, Jax following closely behind without even a wave back. He'd been shaken by Mehta's appearance but had settled enough to explain the situation—deocre, Kael, and all—to him shortly afterward. To Mehta's credit, he believed the entire story without hesitation, jumping in only at the end to ask what he could do to help.

Nova stood and followed them out. "Jax!" she called after her friend.

He and Mehta stopped and turned to look at her.

"Thanks for helping with the town. We dragged you into this back in Aerdmure without really giving you a chance to say no. I just want you to know I appreciate everything you've done for me, for us. For Astria."

She was rambling, but she couldn't shake the need to get her gratitude out. To make sure he wasn't still upset with her for bringing Mehta into this.

To her disbelief, he smiled and pulled her into a hug. "You forget, I'm in this just as much as you are, Nova." He pulled away, leaving a hand on her shoulder. "Justice for my mother and all."

"Right." She crossed her arms. "I promise we'll get your name cleared after this, too. We'll find a way."

His hand fell to his side, but the smile remained. "I'm not worried about it. I know we will."

"We gotta go," Mehta said from behind him, motioning to the door.

Jax looked at his former partner, then back at Nova. "Go smash that deocre, Nova. You were born to do this."

He turned and followed Mehta out of the house, leaving Nova alone with her thoughts. Was she born for this? The goddesses had very twisted ways of managing fate. Of foreseeing what was to come. Had they known that Luc would use dark magic, regardless of whether he became a wielder?

She shook her head. It wasn't worth debating the intentions of the goddesses now. They had a plan, and she needed to focus on the next steps ahead of her. Get through today. Then figure out the *next* next steps.

Drawing in a deep breath to steady her magic and her heart, she turned back to the living room and reclaimed her spot on the couch next to Fynn.

"All good, Al?" he whispered into her hair.

She looked at him and nodded.

"It's time," Kael said from his spot next to the glass door.

Outside, just beyond the porch, the waves were picking up in intensity, the wind now treacherously strong. And the clouds rolling in...they were pitch-black and approaching quickly. In a matter of moments, they would be cast in darkness.

Nova's heart hammered so fiercely she could hear the echo of it in her ears. Fynn must have heard it, too, because he squeezed her hand. This was it. The moment that would change the course of their lives forever.

It all came down to her.

"Breathe. Breathe." Fynn's voice floated into her ears over the roar of blood rushing into her head.

She closed her eyes and inhaled deeply. She could do this. She would do this.

Nova stood and smoothed the skirts of her dress, tucking her hair behind her ears. She'd opted to leave it down today, but with the winds whipping around outside, Canta knew how long that would last.

"Let's go."

52

NOVA

Nova held out her hand, willing a small flame of light to appear in her palm.

The darkness the deocre brought to Adenaport had completely engulfed the arena so that it looked more like midnight than noon. The sun was completely shrouded, but some light from the cottage trickled through. Enough so that, from where she stood in the arena, she could see the porch and the outline of Kael standing watch. Though she couldn't make out his face, it was for the best; she was certain she'd find worry etched there.

In front of her was nothing but inky black.

"Good idea," Daro said, nodding at her palm. It didn't do much, but at least they could see a few feet in front of them now.

Daro palmed one of his daggers, passing it to her free hand. Then he held one out to Benedict. "Don't do anything stupid with this."

Benedict nodded but didn't say a word. His body was trembling even more than usual, but he was here. That was all that mattered now.

"Wait until I give the signal before you cut," Daro said, his hand now holding a third dagger.

"I know what I have to do," Benedict said. His voice was shaky and weak, nearly carried away by the wind.

Daro nodded at him, then turned to Nova. "And you?"

Her eyes stayed trained on the blackness in front of them. She wasn't normally afraid of the dark, but this...this dark was different. Her skin prickled with goosebumps. She managed to reply, "I'm ready."

The furious wind swept her hair around her face, her skirts billowing around her ankles in the gale. Fynn, Raelyn, and her mother were a few paces behind her, close enough to get to her when the time was right but not so close as to interfere with this first part.

For now, it was just Nova, Daro, and Benedict. Three descendants of the goddesses. Astria's last stand against this horrific dark magic.

Nova's magic tapped against her skin, sensing that she was building it up for this moment and letting her know it was ready. *She* was ready. Her eyes clenched shut briefly as she committed the sensation to memory. What it felt like to have magic flowing through her veins before it was ripped from her in the impending sacrifice.

Despite living nearly her entire life without it, she would miss it. She would miss how it swirled within her. Would miss how she could control it, force it to do her will. How it was a thing of beauty, of strength, of—

Power.

No. She pressed her eyes shut tighter. That line of thinking was exactly what had gotten them here, what had led Luc down the path of treachery and darkness.

Power was not the determination of worth.

Rather, it was how one used that power that showed one's character. To suppress or to uplift. To harm or to heal. To scorn or to love. And she wouldn't let power control her like it nearly had when the intruders came. Never again. She was stronger than that.

Benedict whimpered, forcing Nova's attention back to the present. Her eyes sprang open, her gaze resting on... No, it couldn't be.

Emerging from the darkness on the other side of the makeshift arena was Luc Astor, sauntering toward them with a devilish smirk on his face.

Except...it wasn't Luc at all. This version of Luc was younger, all signs of age washed away, and bigger, both in height and in stature. His chestnut hair was pristinely styled, unaffected by the wind, and the black tunic and trousers he wore had not a speck of dust, dirt, or sand on them.

"It's corporeal," Nova heard her mother gasp from behind her.

It was certainly easier to fight a corporeal being than a spirit demon, but the fact that he looked like Luc...

Nova shuddered. Memories from the lab came rushing back over her. How she'd hesitated to attack the man who had raised her, the man who had betrayed her on so many levels, rather than striking an early blow.

How she couldn't kill him. She hadn't had it in her.

And now, even though she was infinitely aware this was not, in fact, Luc Astor, she was going to need to destroy him just the same.

A lump formed in her throat, and sparks flared from her fingertips.

Breathe, breathe, she could almost hear Fynn whisper.

"Looks like I've got quite the welcoming party," Deocre-Luc said as he approached. His voice was silky and booming, piercing through the wind like a knife.

Daro unsheathed his longsword, still holding the small dagger in one hand. It was instinct, probably, that made him do it.

A blade stood no chance against the deocre.

Somehow, Nova found the will to say, "Hello, demon."

The deocre tutted. "Come now, let's not resort to name-calling. It's just me. Your father." He continued to close the gap between them.

"You have never been my father," she said through clenched teeth. Her fist clamped tightly on her dagger.

He was standing close enough now that he reached out and traced a single finger down her cheek. Her body shook, a betrayal of her fear. "No. I suppose I haven't."

Benedict continued to tremble next to her, his eyes glued to Luc, while Daro, on her other side, had his sword pointed at Luc's chest. Except the tip left no mark, no sign of a wound at all, against the deocre's flesh. Nova watched in horror as it slipped in and out of Luc's body, which sealed itself completely around it.

At least that was confirmed. Blades were no good.

A growl escaping his lips, Daro tossed his sword to the side. It landed in the sand with a soft *thunk*. He raised a fist to punch the deocre, but, knowing that was just as futile, Nova moved faster.

She summoned all her power and *pushed*, forcing Deocre-Luc backward. He didn't stumble like he had in the labs, though. Instead, he flew gracefully through the air, landed on two feet, and widened his grin. His laugh echoed on the wind, sending a chill down her spine, but at least he was far enough away now that they could perform the blood donation.

"Now!" Daro screamed. In perfect unison, he and Nova ran the daggers over their palms until tiny droplets of blood formed and began to fall into the sand. Nova's heart leaped: Step one was almost done! She turned to Benedict to collect his donation and found him still standing there, shaking uncontrollably, his palms intact.

"Benedict!" she hissed at him. Luc was starting to walk closer. If he got close enough and realized what they were doing...

And then Fynn was there, his knife to Benedict's throat. "Let me show you a different kind of persuasion," he said in the man's ear.

"Fynn," Nova said, laying a hand on his arm, "let him go."

Fynn dropped his blade and stepped back, his hands raised. But it had worked. Benedict shakily raised the dagger to his palm and sliced, a wince accompanying his gasp.

"Don't mistake my hesitation for reluctance," Benedict said, moving closer to join his palm with Daro and Nova's. "Terra came to me last night, to let me know my sacrifice."

Nova, who a moment ago had been rolling her eyes at his excuses, all while the deocre prowled closer, snapped back to attention. Terra had approached him? Why hadn't Canta spoken to her?

She turned to Daro. "Did Dalia—"

He shook his head, then returned his gaze to Benedict, prompting him to continue.

"My life has not been my own for a long time." Benedict's voice wavered, nearly inaudible over the roar of the wind and the waves. "I've made many mistakes, but there is one thing I can still do to right all my wrongs." He paused and drew in a deep breath. "My sacrifice will be my life. And though it's a fair exchange, I fear I don't have the courage to do this."

The revelation hit Nova like one of the wild waves from the surf crashing into her, nearly knocking her off her feet. For a moment, she completely forgot about the deocre, even as he continued to draw dangerously closer with death in his eyes. She forgot about the mission to destroy the monster and save the country.

All she could see was a terrified, small man, who, in order to make amends to his goddess for his errors, had to face death with bravery. With valor. Had to self-sacrifice in a way that many could not.

He said it was fair, but...was it?

Jax hadn't needed to persuade him to stay. He would have stayed on his own. He had to, or this sacrifice wouldn't work. But he'd required the boost. The extra bit of validation that he was *needed*.

"Benedict, I—"

He held up his bleeding palm. "Let's just do this. And then kill that fucker, ok?"

Nova met his gaze, holding it for a moment but seeing nothing but resolution behind his eyes. She nodded and grasped his hand.

"What are you doing?" Deocre-Luc asked, his voice harried with panic. His gaze darted between the three of them, then his eyes widened, as if the realization of who stood before him had finally sunk in.

The exact moment he started to move toward them with more vigor, Daro forced his hand into Nova's, and the ground shook as a blinding light swallowed them all.

53

NOVA

NOVA LOST HER GRIP on Daro and Benedict, but she could already tell it didn't matter.

When her eyes finally adjusted to the sudden arrival of the light, she found that she was now alone in the arena, the deocre her only company. But he'd been knocked off his feet. He stood back up and brushed the sand off his clothes, turning his attention to Nova.

This was it. Her moment. Her time to shine.

She burrowed down into her power, summoning as much of it as she could, and braced herself for Luc's attack.

"You...found all three?" he asked, clasping his hands behind his back. It made Nova uneasy, not being able to see his hands. "Clever. I admit I did not foresee that. Dalia's line in particular was hard to trace. I thought it had died out a century ago."

She clenched her fists. Any second now, Fynn, Raelyn, and her mother would be here to amplify. She just needed to keep him distracted until then. "And here it turns out her line had been hiding under your nose this whole time."

Though the afternoon sun had returned, the wind still whipped around the arena. Nova hoped Jax and Mehta had gotten the townspeople to shelter and that their protection spell was holding.

Sun glinted into her eyes, and she had to put up a hand to shield her face from the light. The split second cost her; Luc attacked, sending a bolt of lightning toward her.

Nova threw herself to the right and into the sand, but not in time. The bolt hit her ankle, sending ripples of pain coursing through her body. But she would *not* scream. She would not appear weak.

Her ankle throbbed, but she could heal it. It would take precious drops of the magic she'd been saving up, but if she couldn't stand, she couldn't fight.

Fynn was by her side a breath later. "Al, are you ok?" His voice was breathy, his brows pressed together as his eyes scanned her body.

"Ah, the elf," the deocre snarled, his upper lip curling. "I believe we have unfinished business..."

Luc disappeared, then reappeared as a wisp of smoke, barreling toward Fynn. Nova threw up a shield, the same defense she'd been working on since the earliest days of her training in Aerdmure, rendering her and Fynn invisible.

The smoke collided with an invisible wall. It swirled around them, trying to find a way in but unable to. Her ward was too strong for the eddying smoke to break through.

Nova winced as pain seared her ankle. Recalling all that Jax had taught her about healing, she placed a hand on her ankle, releasing a tendril of magic. As it found its way to the wound, she pulled it taut, and warmth replaced the pain. She moved her hand away, exhaling in relief that the pain was gone.

"Beautiful spell work, Al," Fynn said, his hand tracing slow circles on her back.

She looked up at him. "Daro and Benedict?"

"Daro is fine," Fynn said, helping her to stand. "He's with Kael now. Benedict..." His voice trailed off, but that was enough.

His donation had been accepted.

"Can you hold on while I run us over to your sister?" he asked, lacing his fingers with hers. Already, she could feel her power growing at his touch. She inhaled deeply and nodded, allowing him to scoop her up and run.

The ward followed them, but the deocre didn't, unable to see where they had gone. When Fynn set her down a dozen or so yards away, she turned back to find the smoke had disappeared, and Luc was standing in its place.

"Nova!" he screamed. "You cannot hide from me!"

"Watch me," she said under her breath.

But she wouldn't be able to hold both the shield and the spell to destroy the deocre at the same time. It wouldn't be long until she was exposed again. She just hoped it was long enough for Fynn, Raelyn, and her mother to get to safety first.

Luc darted around the arena, throwing spell after spell to try to find Nova, but never getting anywhere near where they were huddled.

Fynn's hand was still clasped in hers. Her mother grabbed her other one, whispering, "I'm so proud of you," while Raelyn placed a hand on her back.

The power surging through her—it was unlike anything she'd ever experienced. All three of them, at the same time. It was easy to see how she could get drunk on this. How she could be overcome.

But if this was the last day she had magic, if this was the last day she'd get to feel this way, she'd be damned if she let it overtake her.

She was in control.

Magic continued to accumulate. She closed her eyes, letting the wind whip through her hair, letting her ears fill with the sound of the waves, drowning out Luc's manic bellows entirely. It no longer felt like she was casting a shield. The shield simply *existed*.

Raelyn shrieked, and Nova's eyes flew open.

Luc stood in front of her, nearly toe-to-toe with her.

"There you are." He bared his teeth as he slashed through her shield with a single claw of his hand. But then his eyes caught on something over Nova's shoulder. No, not something—someone. His top lip curled in a snarl. "Raella."

Before Nova could react, Luc snatched Mother's arm, transformed both of them into smoke, and flew across the arena. They rematerialized far enough away that Nova could only make out their indistinct forms. Their voices didn't pierce through the fierce winds.

"Fynn, get Rae!" Nova screamed. "Then meet me over there."

Thank Canta he didn't protest her command, even if Raelyn did. Fynn scooped her up, ignoring her cries for her mother, her fists pounding on his chest as he ran her back toward the cottage.

Drawing in a sharp inhale, Nova set off at a run across the sand, her feet sinking too far for her to make quick progress. Pain shot up her ankle, but she sent a surge of magic down to suppress it. Not too much—not enough to deplete her stores. Just enough to cut through the sharpness.

But she needn't have bothered. A moment later, she was horizontal, held tightly in Fynn's arms as they made their way to Luc and Mother.

"Rae?" she asked.

"Safe," he replied, not taking his eyes off their destination.

Luc's voice was finally discernible as his and Mother's figures came into full view. "All this time, you betrayed me."

Mother fought to wrench herself free of the invisible restraints binding her hands behind her back. "You betrayed your family and your country first. The Blackmores were our friends, Luc!"

Fynn set Nova down in the sand a few feet behind Luc, who hadn't yet acknowledged their presence. "Can you attack him from here?" he whispered.

She shook her head. "Not without knowing if it will hurt Mother, too. Take her and get her—"

A scream pierced her ears. Brushing strands of hair out of her face, Nova saw her mother tumble to the ground, her shoulder jutting at an awkward angle. Bile rose in Nova's throat.

He'd hurt Raelyn. Now he'd hurt his wife, too. There was nothing he wouldn't do to hold onto his power.

"Luc!" she bellowed, her fists clenched. Magic sparked at her fingertips, desperate to be exploited.

The deocre turned to face her, the corners of his dark eyes crinkling with his vile grin. Out of the corner of her eye, Nova saw a Fynn-shaped blur dash past her. Another blink, and Raella's shape joined the blur as he carried her to the safety of the house.

Hopefully Kael could heal her there.

Luc's gaze chased Fynn, clearly conflicted over whether to follow him or stay to attack Nova. His subsequent bellow was loud enough to shake the world. "I will kill you, elf! Just like your father!"

The magic under Nova's skin was becoming more and more difficult to contain. She needed to make her move. Fast. "The only one dying here tonight is you, monster!"

She lifted a hand, ready to cast the spell, but Luc waved his own hand, sending her flying back onto her ass in the sand.

"No need for name-calling, daughter." His eyes flicked for a moment toward the cottage, and Nova's heart lurched. If he turned back into smoke, he'd get there before she could... "Ah. Lovely. Look who's coming back to save you...again."

Nova got to her feet and glanced in the direction Luc indicated. Fynn was making his way back across the sand. *No, no, no, stay away!* She didn't want him anywhere near this.

"Turn around, Fynn!" she yelled at him. The wind carried her voice in the opposite direction, but his elf ears would hear her. Sure enough, he stopped, but the look on his face was pained, sending a dagger right through her heart.

She hated that she was forcing him to relive his past traumas. Hated that there was no way for him to help while she was in danger.

But she had to do this alone.

"Good girl," Luc hissed. He stepped in front of her, close enough that she should have been able to feel his breath—if he'd been breathing. "Now it's just you and me."

Before she could gather the power within her to cast the spell to destroy him, he flung his hands outward, sending magic barreling into her. Pain racked her body, her throat letting out a shrill scream as she went rigid, unable to move, unable to fight the agony tearing through her body.

Fynn's voice made its way into her ears, but the words were indiscernible. *They had better stay that way.* She could endure this if it meant he stayed away. If it meant he would be safe.

As quickly as it started, the pain evaporated. Nova fell onto her knees in the sand, her chest heaving, her muscles weak, desperately trying to bring her awareness back to her magic. Did she still have the magic that had been amplified? Had the spell zapped it out of her?

No. It was still there. As the pain receded from her limbs, she could feel it still pushing against her skin, ready for its turn.

"What'd you think of that?" Deocre-Luc asked. She lifted her gaze to find him hovering a few feet away, his arms crossed over his chest. "There's plenty more where that came from. I'm just getting started."

He approached her and knelt so his face was inches from hers. "You don't think I'm letting any of you out of here alive, do you?"

Nova stared the monster down, feigning weakness when, in reality, she was poised to strike. It was now or never. "You don't get to be the one who decides our fates."

With that, she channeled her deepest power and unleashed the spell that would destroy the deocre. Magic flew out of her, pulsing through her arms and out through her hands. Her body shook violently at the sheer amount of power that coursed through her.

The deocre screamed, flying backwards from the force of the blast. But he found his footing and stood again, now a few yards away. Light—beautiful, shimmering light—blasted from Nova into the deocre, but it wasn't enough. Luc was pushing his way through the wall of light, slowly but surely, to get to her.

Sweat beaded on Nova's brow, her hair sticking to it as it whipped in the wind. It wasn't enough. The amplification hadn't been enough. She wasn't going to be able to stop this. Her stomach twisted in knots, but she held onto the spell. She kept giving it everything she had while her mind spun, searching for another option.

Fynn knelt beside her a moment later, his hand pressing against the exposed skin of her back. But there was nothing. No surge of power from his touch. She'd taken all she could from him, and probably from Raelyn and her mother, too.

"You've got this," he whispered in her ear, though the tiny voices in her brain—the ones she had learned to suppress over the last few months—telling her she didn't were growing louder. The deocre was coming closer, fighting its way through the light like it was trudging through quicksand.

"It's..." She drew in a sharp breath. "It's not enough." Her arms were already exhausted, threatening to drop, to break the connection and end the spell. What would happen then? If she'd amplified as much as she could, there was no way to try again.

Daro and Benedict had already sacrificed. Benedict was *gone*. There wouldn't be another chance to fight.

Fynn shifted at her side. Nova stole a glance and saw he'd unsheathed his dagger. "No, Fynn—"

Fynn stood and threw the dagger. His aim was true, and had the deocre been *real*, it would have pierced his heart. Instead, it sailed through Luc, who roared with laughter and sent a wave of shadow toward Fynn.

"No!" Nova cried, reacting instinctually, finding the magic within her to throw a shield around Fynn. But with so much of her focus on the other spell, it was weak. A small portion of the demon's attack trickled through, hitting Fynn square in the chest. He collapsed to the sand. "Fynn!"

He was breathing, that much she could see, but it wasn't until he lifted his head that Nova breathed a sigh of relief and returned her focus to Luc, who was still fighting against her spell to reach them.

Fynn's voice was raspy when he spoke. "I'm ok, Al." He crawled over to her until he was kneeling next to her in the sand. "Just had the wind knocked out of me."

"Stupid." It was all she could manage to get out. He didn't reply.

The momentary shield had cost her precious drops of magic. *Damn Fynn and his protective instinct!* There was no way she could end this now. No way she had enough left...

"You are enough," Fynn whispered in her ear, as if he'd read her mind. He gathered her hair in his hands, keeping it from lashing her face.

Luc was only a few paces away now. In another moment or two, he'd be on top of her. He'd go for Fynn again. She was running out of options. She was out of time. Out of strength.

But then another voice spoke on her other side. "You are magnificent, Allie."

Kael. Her father.

She broke away from watching Luc's progression to meet Kael's eyes, the deep emerald of them still a precise mirror of her own. His shaggy hair was blown back from his face in the wind, so she could read his expression perfectly.

Pride. Love. Hope.

That's what he saw in her.

And that's what she'd always wanted in a father.

They weren't out of options after all.

"Father," she breathed. A bead of sweat—or maybe a tear—dripped down her face, but she didn't care. A new hope blossomed within her.

Kael's eyes brimmed with tears. "I'm here."

He reached out a hand tentatively, hovering it over her back. When she nodded to him, he placed it just under her shoulder blade, exactly where Fynn's had been a moment ago.

And the light blazed brighter.

The force of the connection her magic made with Kael's nearly sent her backward into the sand, but Fynn grabbed her arm and helped her get to her feet. Kael kept his hand steady as he rose with her. Though her legs were shaky, she stood, holding on to the spell with all she could muster.

Love was her amplifier. And she had nothing but love for the man who never got to raise her.

It was definitely tears that streamed down her face as she savored every moment of their connection—the only time she would ever feel it. Just like the way her magic reacted differently to Raelyn, her mother, and Fynn, it pulsed entirely anew from Kael's love. Like the lightest caress over her skin, it moved through her body to her core, where the rest of her power was anchored. It mixed with what remained of the rest, giving Nova the strength to do what she needed.

She stumbled again under the pulse of the increased power emanating from her fingertips, but Fynn's grip held her firmly upright. Luc's voice rang through the air, laced with pain and anger, but Nova didn't stop. She didn't yield. Kael's hand still on her back, she held the spell long enough to watch the deocre evaporate into nothingness, long enough to watch the light overtake the darkness that remained in his place, long enough to feel the tremors in the ground beneath her, to hear the roar of the wind and the waves around her, to feel the burn of the blinding light in front of her. All four elements, come together to devastate the darkest evil.

She held the spell long enough for the remnants of darkness to explode into a million tiny pieces that floated away in the wind. And only then did she allow the exhaustion of her body, the depletion of her magic, to overtake her.

54

FYNN

"HOW IS SHE?"

Fynn turned from where he was sitting on the bed he shared with Nova to look at the doorway. Kael was standing there, holding a folded piece of paper in his hands, his shoulders hunched slightly like he was nervous to intrude.

Fynn looked back at Nova, still unconscious on the bed next to him. After she'd done it—*she'd fucking done it*—and collapsed on the beach, he'd brought her back here. Kael and Raella had given her a once-over, deducing that she was physically fine, but magically... They couldn't tell yet what the sacrifice she'd had to make had been, but it had clearly taken its toll on her.

The enormous amount of power she'd wielded had taken its toll on her, too.

That had been hours ago, and Fynn hadn't left her side for a moment. He'd used a warm cloth Raelyn brought to wipe her clean of the sweat and sand that clung to her body, then Raelyn had helped him change her into something more comfortable. Before they laid her back down, he'd brushed and braided her hair. Jax had even come in to check on both of them, insisting on giving Fynn some healing energy that he really hadn't needed.

And not once had her eyes flickered open. Not once had she shown any signs of life other than her breath.

What if the sacrifice had been her soul? The very essence of her being? What if he'd lost her forever?

He laced his fingers through hers, thankful they were still warm. Why had he let her fight the deocre? Why hadn't he fought harder against it? If he could go back in time...

Breathe, breathe. The words whispered through his head in *her* voice.

"No change," he finally replied, a single tear falling down his cheek. He'd been so hopeful about her condition when they'd first come back. Of course it was expected she'd be exhausted. She'd just exerted more magic than any witch ever had. But it was nearing midnight now, and nothing had changed.

Kael approached and stood next to the bed, looking down at his daughter. "She will. She's got the fight in her. And the will to come back." Fynn could sense Kael's gaze on him, but he couldn't meet it. It was too similar to hers. "Something to come back for."

Fynn could only hope that was true. But even if it was, they'd only gotten through the first hurdle. They still had to deal with clearing his, Jax's, and Blackmore's names.

And figuring out how to explain to all of Astria what the hell had been going on over the weeks since Luc's death.

Silvana had been clear when she spoke to the group in Aerdmure: *Tell no one. Keep the circle small.*

The truth was not an option. They could not tell the world about the deocre.

Fynn let out a sharp exhale. "I hope, if she does come back, we can make the world right again. Make it all worth it."

"When." Kael's voice was firm. He placed the folded paper on the small table next to the bed. "*When* she comes back."

Easy for you to say. Kael didn't know what it felt like to lose the woman he cared for more than the world.

Fynn straightened. Except, he did. He'd lost Wynna. Had watched her burn alive in front of him. *Wow, you're such an asshole, Fynn Voss.*

He nodded to the note, desperate to change the subject. "What's that?"

Kael looked down at the note, scratching the side of his neck. "A way to make it all worth it."

Cryptic. But Fynn was too exhausted to ask him to explain. Instead, he just nodded.

"Will you make sure she gets that once she wakes up?"

"Won't you be able to do that yourself?" Fynn's hip was starting to ache, so he shifted his weight, not letting his hand drop from Nova's.

Kael walked toward the window above the side table and gazed out over the dunes. "I have an idea for how to end this. For how to make sure her sacrifice was worth it. So that when she does wake up, she doesn't have to fight anymore."

"Really?" Fynn's heart started to race. Why hadn't Kael mentioned this before? There were probably things they could all do to help! "What's your idea?"

But Kael was too engrossed in the view outside to answer. He continued to stare and stare, his hands clasped behind his back. After what seemed like an eternity, he turned from the window. "I need to check on one thing in the village first. Then I will explain." He smiled weakly at Fynn, resting a hand on his shoulder. "If she wakes while I'm gone..." His voice caught, and he stopped, pursing his lips. With heavy-lidded eyes, he looked at Nova again, then gave Fynn's shoulder a squeeze. "Thank you, Fynn," he whispered, leaving the room.

Kael's behavior was odd. Fynn should have asked more questions. Should have asked what he should do when Nova woke if Kael hadn't returned. Should have insisted Kael tell him more. Should have demanded to know where Kael was going at this time of night to get the confirmation he sought.

But it was late, and he was tired. Kael had promised they'd talk when he returned, which surely wouldn't take too long. By breakfast, they'd be formulating their plan.

Fynn curled up next to Nova on the bed, no longer able to hold his body upright. The steady beat of her heart and warmth of her breath soothed him as he drifted off to sleep.

A hand pressed forcefully into his chest. "Goddess, Fynn, wake up!"

Fynn's eyes jolted open to find Nova lying next to him, facing him, blessedly *awake*. The room was still cloaked in darkness, but he could see the twinkle in her eyes, could hear the smile on her lips as she said, "You really do sleep like the dead!"

She was ok. She was alive.

He choked back a sob as he wrapped his arms around her, pulling her close. She tucked her head into his chest, and he pressed his lips to her hair. "You're alive."

"Of course I'm alive." She pulled away from him, enough to look into his eyes. "You're ok, too?"

Fynn pressed his fingers into his chest, which was slightly sore and bruised, but he'd suffered much worse. *Losing her* would have been much worse. "I'm fine." Nova raised an eyebrow at him. "I promise. Jax checked me out."

That seemed to appease her. "How long have I been out?"

He had no idea what time it was now, but the house was still quiet. "Maybe twelve hours or so?"

"Explains why I feel so awake right now." She reached up and brushed away a lock of hair that had fallen onto his cheek. "You were worried, weren't you?"

He hated admitting it, but there was no way he could lie. She could probably read the truth all over his face. "Horribly."

Nova sighed. "I'm here. I'm not going anywhere." Her hand found his, and she pulled it to her chest, placing it over her heart. "I'm still here."

But as soon as the words were out, she stiffened, her eyes flaring wide.

"What's wrong?" Fynn squeezed her hand tighter, searching her shadowed face for a hint of what had startled her.

"My donation," she muttered. Without his elven hearing, he wouldn't have even heard it.

She propped herself up on her elbows and looked toward the lamp next to her bed. With a snap of her fingers, the lamp lit, Fynn shielding his eyes from the sudden glare. He blinked, then found Nova filling the water in the glass Raelyn had left beside her bed. Another moment and a flower sprouted in the glass, though it disappeared as quickly as it had appeared a moment later. Before he could say anything, a light breeze blew through the room, just enough to blow out the lamp.

Fynn shivered. Fire, Water, Earth, Air. She still had all four elements. So what had her donation been?

"You've still got magic!" His heart leaped with joy for her, that she had been able to keep the powers that she had come to love so much. She didn't *need* them. No, she was who she was even without them. But if she could use them to do some good in the world...

His thoughts stopped dead in their tracks when her eyes, hollowed and sad, met his. She reached for his hand again, a whimper escaping her lips at his touch.

"The amplification is gone. I can't *feel* you." Her voice was laced with such sorrow that Fynn's heart threatened to shatter, but he held himself together. For her. "My magic has reacted to your touch since the very first time in the library. I didn't realize how attached to it I had become. How reassuring I had found the way I could feel your love through that connection. But now there's...nothing."

A tear trickled down her cheek. Fynn brushed it away, leaving his hand on her cheek, his thumb hovering over the scar near her eye. "You don't need your magic to confirm I love you. I'll tell you I love you every second of every day of every lifetime. It might not be the same, but I hope it will be enough." It had to be enough. His heart was hers to break, and if it wasn't enough...if she left...

She smiled weakly, and his heart started to strengthen again. "*You* are enough, Fynn. I just...I was expecting all of my magic to be gone, and now that some of it remained but *that* was ripped from me...it seems unfair. I'd rather it have been the other way around. If all I had was the way your touch made me feel—"

"Oh, I'm fairly certain my touch can still make you feel things." His hand slid down her cheek, over her shoulder, down, down, down...

Before he could get past her waist, she batted him away with a laugh. "Point taken." She lay down again, this time facing away from him, pressing her back against his chest. "Let's try to rest. Or at least you should," she whispered into the dark.

Fynn wrapped his arms around her, holding her close.

He would never let go.

55

NOVA

B ASED ON THE STEADY rise and fall of Fynn's breath and the way he didn't even flinch when she extricated herself from his grasp, Nova was certain Fynn was still deep asleep. Sleep that he so clearly needed, given yesterday's events and how mentally and emotionally exhausted he must have been.

Darkness still poured in through the window, though less so than when she'd last awoken. Sunrise must have been near. She'd heard footsteps—Raelyn's; she'd recognize that gait anywhere—in the hall just a moment ago, so she forced herself out of bed to go find her sister.

And hopefully get her to make a big batch of coffee.

Nova eased the bedroom door open, slipped through, then closed it as quietly as she could behind her. Why she was being so stealthy, she had no idea. Fynn could clearly sleep through anything.

The stairs creaked lightly underfoot as she padded down them, making straight for the kitchen. Wafts of chicory and nuttiness floated her way, the smell alone nearly enough to kickstart her body. She crossed the threshold into the kitchen, and, sure enough, there was Raelyn, hovering over the coffee press and readying a mug.

"Hope there's enough for two," Nova said.

Raelyn jumped, the mug slipping from her hand and shattering against the stone floor. "Nova! You're...awake!" She moved toward Nova, stepping carefully over the broken shards.

Nova sank into her sister's embrace, her hands finding their way to Raelyn's back. But, just like with Fynn, there was no reaction to Raelyn's touch. No jolt of peace, no waves of comfort. It was an ordinary hug.

No. What she and Raelyn shared was anything but ordinary.

Raelyn pulled away but kept her hands on Nova's arms. "You look unharmed. How do you feel?"

"Unharmed." It was the easiest answer. "Mother?"

"Just a dislocated shoulder. Kael had her fixed up quick."

Nova breathed a sigh of relief. "I still have my magic."

Raelyn straightened and clapped once, a grin sweeping across her face. "Oh, that's wonderful!"

"Watch." Nova gestured for Raelyn to step aside, then repaired the mug with a wave of her hand.

Raelyn stooped to pick it up. "First cup's for you, then. Nova, I'm just so thrilled." She approached the counter with the mug and started to pour, but stopped, the press lifted in midair. "But then what—"

"My amplification." Nova blinked back tears that had started to form. How ridiculous to be so upset over losing something she didn't know she had until a few weeks ago. Her whole life, she'd been fine without it, but now...

Although, if she truly reflected, she hadn't really been without it. That power had shown up in other ways. The times she'd nearly broken the suppression spell as a child had been under Raelyn's touch. Who knew when else it had manifested and in what ways? But it had always been there. Had always been a part of her.

"Oh, well, that's not so bad, is it?" Raelyn bit her lip, realizing she'd said the wrong thing. "I mean, it's awful. I can't imagine how empty you must feel." She turned back to pouring the coffee and handed the mug over.

Nova could only smile as she wrapped her palms around the warm mug. "No, you're right. It's not that bad." She took a small sip of the still-piping hot brew. "It'll just take some getting used to."

"Of course." Raelyn poured herself a mug, then leaned back against the counter. "But hey, you did it, Nova. You destroyed the deocre. You got rid of the dark magic. You saved the country. You saved *us*."

No matter how many times she heard that, Nova didn't think it would truly set in. How could it? She'd barely started to understand her powers before she used them to their fullest in a way that she would never do again. And it wasn't even like they could tell the world about it, not like she could even celebrate the win with anyone outside of this cottage. Not even Cassie and Bea, her best friends, could know the truth...

The truth. There was still more of the truth to expose. "I took care of the first part. Now we have to take care of the second part."

"You took care of the hardest part." Raelyn shrugged. "Now that the governors are truly out of Fa—*Luc's* thrall, it should be easy to convince them of Kael's innocence."

She spoke so confidently, like she could see the path forward with perfect clarity, but Nova's heart still clenched. Benedict was gone, and without his testimony about what had truly happened with the research and the lab, there were no more direct witnesses, aside from Mother, who hadn't even truly been a part of the whole charade. Nova doubted the governors would take the word of the four witches and three elves who knew the story because they'd been told by Kael himself. The governors would surely be convinced they were all manipulated, under his spell, and couldn't be trusted. Or, worse, needed to be saved somehow...

They were going to need to carefully formulate a plan, consider all the potential setbacks, and gauge how much the governors remembered of Luc's regime. If they came with an awareness that they'd been manipulated themselves, maybe there was a chance they could understand Luc's dark past. But if not...

Nova shuddered. The path ahead was not going to be easy. But they still needed to work fast if they wanted to clear not only Kael's name, but Fynn's and Jax's, too.

She drank more of her coffee as she extricated herself from her thoughts. "I'm not sure it will be that easy, Rae. I hope you're right, but a big part of me worries it will take more than that."

"Tell me what worries you."

Another sip to clear her throat. "That the governors won't understand that they've been bewitched. That they'll come out of the spell but have been in it for so long that they can't tell right from wrong anymore. That we don't have a good witness for the governors to believe Kael's story—aside from Mother, but she wasn't there, she wasn't directly involved; she only heard about what happened from Luc after the fact and then from Kael recently, so how believable is her testimony?"

"She formed a covert operation to try to stop Luc. Surely that, along with the testimony of the Defiance, will be enough—"

But Nova shook her head. "We can't tell them that. We can't bring the deocre into this."

"The Defiance wasn't just fighting the deocre, though!" Raelyn straightened abruptly, sending a wave of coffee from her mug to the floor with a splash.

"I know." Nova sighed. "They were also trying to prevent Luc from getting to all the governors. But they failed. And if the governors don't want to admit, or can't admit, that they were bewitched, the testimony of the Defiance is worthless."

Raelyn was silent for a moment, her mug hovering near her lips but not taking a sip as Nova's words sank in. Her eyes closed as she drew a deep breath. "They are a prideful bunch, those governors. You're probably right. Even if they recognize they'd been under a spell, they wouldn't admit it."

Nova nodded, then finished her coffee and set the mug on the counter.

"Bastards," Raelyn spat. "We'll find another way. This is a smart group. Together we can find a way. Once everyone else wakes up, we'll start to plan."

No rest for the weary, Nova thought. Her gaze drifted out the window across the room, where the sky was lightening into pinks and baby blues as the sun began its ascent.

The dawn of a new day. A new start. And, hopefully, soon, a new life. The last five months, since word of Kael's escape had reached them here, had been overwhelming. Exhausting. Exhilarating. But they were one step closer to the finish line. There was only one last hurdle to overcome before they could go back to Arkwood and their normal lives.

And though she wasn't entirely sure what normal was anymore, she had to keep the faith that it was coming.

"I'm going to get some fresh air. Watch the sunrise," Nova said. Raelyn nodded, but didn't follow her to the deck, which was just as well because she wanted to be alone for a moment. There had been so few opportunities to be alone recently, something Nova generally craved.

She slid the door closed behind her, the cool air biting her skin and triggering goosebumps. She wrapped her arms around herself, wishing she'd grabbed a sweater or shawl. The caw of a seagull in the distance snagged her attention, and she turned her gaze down the beach in search of the bird. Instead, she found herself staring at a woman.

Not just any woman. One she recognized from the temple in Aerdmure, from the statue that mere weeks ago had brought Nova to her knees.

Canta stood a little ways down the beach. Except...no. *Stood* was not the correct word. She...*hovered*? The spirit of the goddess was floating over the dune just beyond the stairs of the deck, watching Nova with a smile. Almost completely transparent, Canta's hair flowed around her despite the stillness of the air while her skirts swirled around her ankles. But her eyes...they were dark as midnight, a stark contrast to the rest of her silvery body.

"Ah, daughter." The goddess's voice was deep, echoing across the open expanse of the beach like a ripple. "Glad to see my summons to bring you outside worked."

Nova, dumbfounded, continued to stare. Her hand had flown to her heart when she realized who this spirit being was. Words utterly failed her.

"I wanted to speak to you, alone." Canta floated ever so slightly closer.

"Why?" Nova managed to croak. Why on earth did her ancestor goddess want to speak with her? The goosebumps on her arms prickled in earnest again.

When Canta reached the deck where Nova stood, she stopped. The goddess reached out a hand to touch Nova's cheek, her caress no more than a warm whisper of breath. "To tell you how proud I am of you. You've faced hardships I would never have wished on anyone, especially one of mine, but you've come out stronger. Bolder. Wiser."

Nova didn't respond, her heart wavering between anger at this goddess for allowing those hardships to occur and pride in herself for having them acknowledged. She continued to stare into Canta's dark, bottomless eyes.

"And, I suppose," the goddess continued when she realized Nova was not going to speak, "to let you know there is more to come. But what is coming must come. It is the best way. And you will be happy again."

Nova's mouth dropped open before she could stop herself, but she shook her head and somehow found the means to shout, "No, stop with the puzzles. *What* is coming?"

If a spirit or a ghost or whatever this apparition was could shuffle her feet, that's what it looked like Canta did. "I wish I could say more. I need you to trust me. What is coming must come." Canta started to fade. "Remember this…"

"No, don't you go anywhere—" Nova lunged for the goddess, but she had vanished like a puff of smoke blown away in the sea breeze.

Sea breeze. The scent reminded her of Fynn, and the thought that he might be worried if he woke up and she wasn't there next to him. She should sneak back upstairs and into bed to wake him. See what he made of this message.

Because she was furious. Absolutely furious that, after all this time, Canta would deign to show up *now*. That she would deliver a message in puzzle form and then leave again. After all Nova had done in Canta's name. After all she had done to save Astria…

"Damn it!" Nova stomped her feet and slammed her fist into the rail of the deck like a petulant child. The wood gave way, snapping not from her force but from the uncontained magic swirling within her.

She righted herself, clenched her fists, and forced herself to breathe through it. After a few meditative inhales and exhales, her body cooled, her magic settling down within her. A wave of her hand repaired the rail.

With one last deep breath, one last longing stare out over the ocean, she turned to head back inside and face what was to come.

56

Nova

No one else had emerged from their rooms yet, and Raelyn seemed to have disappeared back upstairs. When Nova tiptoed back up to her room, she found Fynn exactly where she had left him: sound asleep. He'd stolen her pillow, cradling it to his chest like he'd done with her before she'd gotten up, a small, sweet gesture that warmed her heart.

How had she gotten so lucky to have found him?

Carefully, she extricated the pillow from his grasp and snuggled up against him in its place. She could smell that cedar and sea-breeze scent she loved, relishing the way it soothed her.

She'd once told a student, Addy, that there were other forms of magic: science and math. Now, Nova thought, scents—and particularly their ability to trigger memories and sensations—should be added to that list.

"Al?" His voice was raspy from sleep as he blinked open his eyes.

Nova tilted her head back so she could see him properly. "Morning." She leaned forward to kiss him gently.

He pulled her closer, his fingers grazing lightly up her arm until they reached her chin, which he tilted up so he could deepen the kiss. Nova wrapped an arm around his torso, trailing her fingers up and down his back.

Fynn pulled away first. "Good morning." He smiled, his eyes moving over her entire body, inspecting. "How do you feel?"

"Physically, better than I could hope. Mentally?" She relayed the strange conversation she'd had with Canta on the deck moments ago.

Fynn's reaction was...underwhelming. But, then again, his eyes were still barely open, so maybe he was simply that tired.

"Odd. Was this before or after you had coffee?" he asked, rubbing the sleep from his eyes.

Nova slapped his arm and laughed. "After, thank you very much. And even if I hadn't been caffeinated, it doesn't mean I would have hallucinated."

"Is there any more of that coffee, or did you run us dry?"

"There's more." She sat up, pulling his hand so he would sit up too. "Come on, let's go get some. I'm overdue for my second cup anyway."

It took another few minutes for her to get Fynn to actually start moving back downstairs, and by the time they arrived in the kitchen, the rest of their motley crew was already congregated. Raelyn was serving coffee from the large carafe, shoving full mugs into Nova and Fynn's hands as they entered the dining room. Their mother, Jax, and Mehta were sitting at the small table, full plates of bread, cheese, and salami in front of them. Daro was loading up a plate at the buffet. Everyone looked joyous, though there was a tension in the air hinting that the events of the prior day sat heavily on their minds.

"Nova!" Mother stood quickly, dropping her napkin in the chair and running over to embrace her. "Oh, darling girl, I'm so glad you're all right!" She stepped back, performing the same visual inspection that Fynn had done, gaze roaming Nova's body.

Nova smiled as she brushed her mother's hands away. "And you? Everyone else is all right?" She surveyed the group, finding not a scratch among them. "Jax, Mehta, how did it go in town?"

"Nothing worse than a hurricane." Jax held his mug up in salute. "The priestesses helped us get most of the townspeople into the temple just as the darkness was truly setting in, and we safely rode it out together. I doubt anyone suspected a thing."

Mehta chuckled. "Two wielders running through Adenaport, yelling about a horrific pop-up storm. Nope, nothing weird about that at all." He looked at Nova and winked. "Great job doing the hard work."

Fynn pulled her close, planting a kiss on her temple while she laughed—genuinely laughed—at Mehta's response. Despite Canta's visit, despite everything that had happened yesterday, relief washed over her. They'd all made it out alive. Astria was safe.

Daro set his plate down at the table's last open seat before stepping toward Nova. A quick glance at his hand confirmed the lack of scar from their donation, the same as she'd noticed on her own palm earlier. No lasting physical markers of the job done.

He stuck his hand out to Nova. "Well done, Astor."

She took it and shook. "Couldn't have done it without you. Never thought I'd say this after how we met, but thank you."

Daro chuckled as he took his seat and began his breakfast.

"What about..." Nova started, wanting to confirm Benedict was truly gone but not wanting to say his name. He'd always be a traitor and would never have earned her respect, but he did at least deserve recognition for the part he played.

"Gone," her mother said, and the tension Nova hadn't realized she'd been holding in her shoulders released. She sipped her coffee as her mother continued, "I've never seen anything like it. He just...disappeared in the same moment the light from your donations appeared."

"Like dust in the wind," Raelyn added, waving her hand in the air. "You know, he may have royally screwed everyone here over at various points in his life, but at least—"

The front door crashed open. Nova snapped her head around to see who was entering the house, but found herself tucked behind Fynn, who had unsheathed his sword. Standing, Daro positioned himself in front of the table, his hand moving to his sword's hilt as well.

The footsteps echoed loudly off the floorboards as the intruder made their way through the foyer. But that gait—it was familiar somehow. Nova recognized it.

Her memory clicked into place the moment she saw Mr. Larson burst into the dining room.

Fynn and Daro, having never met Mr. Larson, held their stances, but Mother stood and put a hand over her heart.

"Oh, Mr. Larson!" She stepped toward him. "You gave us such a fright."

"Apologies, ma'am." Mr. Larson's brow was damp with sweat, his chest heaving as he caught his breath. "But I wanted to be...the one to tell you. I assumed...news hadn't yet reached here." He spoke slowly, struggling to get the words out between his breaths.

"News?" Nova said, stepping around Fynn, who relaxed but didn't sheathe his sword yet. "What news?" Had word somehow reached town about the governors? Had they realized what had happened to them that quickly, and already started to make changes?

Mr. Larson wiped his brow. "They caught him. Or, rather, he turned himself in. Just a few hours ago in town. Seems he was tired of being on the run and knew his time was up."

Nova's heart began to pound, the echo of it filling her ears. She put a hand on Fynn's arm to steady herself, certain that if Mr. Larson continued, if he said anything more, she would collapse.

"Who? Who turned himself in?" she asked, her voice no more than a whisper.

He looked at her, his eyes beaming with joy as he spoke, unaware of the impact his words would have on his audience.

"Blackmore. They've got Kael Blackmore."

57

Fynn

THANK THE GODDESSES THAT Nova's hand was on Fynn's arm. The moment this strange man had flown into the house like a loose cannon, Fynn had sensed that something was off.

Then he confirmed Kael had been captured, and all hell had broken loose.

Nova's hand nearly slipped off Fynn's arm as she folded toward the ground, but Fynn was faster. He grabbed her arm and pulled her close, supporting her weight with one arm while attempting to sheathe his sword with the other.

Raelyn dropped the carafe she had been holding, which clattered to the ground and shattered, the last of the coffee spilling everywhere.

Jax and Mehta had stood so quickly, their chairs toppled over, one of them hitting Daro in the back of the leg. The elf let out a groan at the impact.

Raella was the only one who had kept her cool, grabbing this Mr. Larson by the arm and pulling him toward the front door. Hopefully to see him off.

One should never kill the messenger, but right now, Fynn sure wanted to hurt that man for the pain he had unknowingly caused.

"Al? Al? Look at me." He tried to get Nova to stand on her own and face him, but she was hysterical, hammering her fists into his chest, tears streaming down her cheeks, just as frantic as she had been when Raelyn had been taken to the lab. Sparks began to fly from her fingertips, little zaps penetrating his skin. It didn't hurt, but if she couldn't get control of herself soon, they'd have a bigger mess to clean up.

He removed his grip on her arm. She collapsed to her knees, and he followed her to the floor, taking her face in his hands.

"Al, look at me."

When those emerald-green eyes finally met his, the rest of the world disappeared. Only the two of them remained in that dining room. Fynn couldn't have cared less what the rest of their friends were doing right now, as long as he could keep Nova safe.

"Breathe," he said, inhaling deeply. She copied him. "Breathe."

They stayed like that for a moment, her body starting to still, her shoulders visibly relaxing. Then she reached up and placed a hand over his against her cheek.

"Good," Fynn whispered, brushing a kiss against her forehead.

"Nothing about this is good, Fynn." Her voice sounded more broken than he had ever heard it. "How could he do that? How could he have turned himself in without even telling me first?"

Fynn's heart stopped. The note. Last night, before he had collapsed into sleep, Blackmore had given him a note. As far as Fynn knew, it was still up on the bedside table where he'd left it. Fynn had been so exhausted last night and so elated to see Nova alive this morning that he'd completely forgotten about it.

"I think," Fynn said, trying to control his voice, "he may have tried. Wait right here. Don't move."

He waited for her to nod her agreement, then dashed upstairs, grabbed the note, and rushed back down. He'd moved so quickly, Nova hadn't even had time to stand.

The note was heavy in his hand as he held it out to her. "Let's go somewhere private to read this."

Nova took the note slowly, holding it with both hands like it was a fragile heirloom. She didn't take her eyes off the paper as Fynn guided her out of the dining room.

58

NOVA

THE AIR OFF THE sea blew gently against Nova's face, but she ignored it. Just like she ignored the roar of the waves and the warm caress of the sun on her face. Fynn guided her to one of the chairs on the back deck and sat her down. He was speaking, but all she could hear was a buzzing in her ears as she stared at the note in her hands.

Kael had left this for her. It probably explained why he'd turned himself in. Why he hadn't talked to her before he left.

But reading it would only confirm that it was real. That what Mr. Larson said was true.

She wasn't sure her heart could take that.

They were supposed to find a way to work this out together. A way for everyone to win. For Kael to be exonerated. For Jax and Fynn to be let off the hook for Luc's death.

For her to go on and live her life with a real family.

"Nova."

Fynn's voice was soft, barely audible over the roar of the ocean. She shook the intrusive thoughts from her head and looked over at him.

"Read it." He held out his hand. She intertwined her fingers with his, using her free hand to unfold the note, and began to read:

Alinova,

I must first say how tremendously proud I am of you. I spent decades in Mistfell wondering what you would have done with your life, how you would have turned out, had you lived. Those dreams do not hold a candle to the real thing.

I had hoped you'd be kind. In truth, you are more than kind. You are empathetic and compassionate. You put others before yourself and aren't afraid to step in to protect those who need you.

I had hoped you'd be smart. You're not only smart, you're clever. You get that from your mother, though I take some of the credit for your brains.

I had hoped you'd have siblings to play with, learn from, and bond with. You not only have the most amazing bond with Raelyn that I've ever seen between sisters, but you've built an entirely new family around the two of you.

I had hoped you'd one day find love, and you sure did. He's a keeper, Alinova. Don't let him go. He's good for you, and you're just as good for him. Don't blame him for not stopping me from leaving. My mind was made up days ago.

But, in all honesty, I don't deserve to be proud of you. I had very little hand in any of what makes you <u>you</u> (although, it's quite obvious you inherited my eyes!). You became who you are in spite of your circumstances. In spite of the fact that neither myself nor your mother had any involvement.

And that means all of the pride should live in you.

Be proud of who you are. Be proud of who you've become.
Be proud of what you will do.
It was for that reason that the best role I can play in your
life now is to allow you to continue down that path. To
give you the chance to continue to grow and blossom in
the family and the life you've cultivated. You don't need
me. But you do need Fynn. You do need Raelyn. Yes, you
even need Jax.
And I can give that to you. By turning myself in, by
confessing that I was responsible for Luc's death, for the
attack in Arkwood, and for yesterday's "storm", I can
set the rest of you free. Free to start a new life, wherever
and however you choose to do it, without the burden of
lies and secrecy and the fears of being found out.
My part here is done. My role in this world is fulfilled.
In truth, it probably was long ago.
But I'm so glad I had the last few weeks with you, to
know you, to learn you, and to love you.
All my love and your mother's too,
Your father

By the time she read the last line, tears streamed down Nova's face. She wanted to rip up the letter, throw it into the wind, and pretend she'd never read it, pretend this had never happened.

But in her heart, she knew he was right, and that's what hurt the most. By turning himself in and taking the blame for everything, they *could* all be free, could go back to normal. They could just...continue to live their lives.

Not that she was sure what her life was anymore. At least now she would have the chance to explore it.

Nova handed the letter to Fynn, who took it without a word. He squeezed her hand harder as he read, his violet eyes brimming with tears and his shoulders starting to shake.

When he finished, he pulled her into his lap. She tucked her knees up to her chin, letting her forehead rest atop them but leaning her body into Fynn's. His arms wrapped around her, and she allowed herself a moment to cry.

"Nova?"

She peeked open an eye, peering past the strands of black hair that had fallen over her face, some sticking to the fresh tear tracks on her cheeks, to see Raelyn stepping out on the deck. As her sister pulled the door shut behind her, Nova straightened her knees and brushed away the hair. Her eyes were probably red and puffy, but there wasn't much she could do about that. Fynn began to rub circles on her back.

Raelyn sat in the chair Nova had occupied moments ago. "Mr. Larson said the governors are all on their way here to commute Kael's sentence and oversee the..." Her voice trailed off, her eyes breaking contact. But Nova understood.

Kael was going to die today.

Raelyn cleared her throat and continued. "Mother thinks she may be able to speak to the governors, to try to get them to see reason—"

But Nova shook her head. "No."

"No?" Raelyn tilted her head to one side.

"No. It won't work. We can't interfere." Canta had told her as much this morning. As much as she hated to believe *this* was what the goddess had been referring to, in her heart she was certain it was. Nova quickly relayed the brief conversation to Raelyn. Fynn's hand stilled on her back, sliding down to grip her waist as she spoke. Raelyn, on the other hand...

"I refuse to believe that's what she meant." Her brown curls bounced as she shook her head. "Hell, I almost refuse to believe you even saw the real Canta."

"You think I'm making it up?"

"No, I'm saying maybe you didn't understand what she was say-ing—"

"I understood perfectly." Nova clenched her hands into fists. Why did her sister have to make this harder? "There is nothing we can do. This is the will of the goddesses. I wouldn't be surprised if Canta planted the idea with Kael herself."

Raelyn stood, shaking her head. "Why are you giving up so easily? Why don't you want to fight for his life?"

"I do, Rae, I do. But *he* doesn't want me to." Nova threw the note at Raelyn and watched as her sister picked it up and read it. Raelyn's hand flew to her mouth as her eyes scanned further down the page. "See? He's doing it *for* me. For us, actually."

Raelyn's brown eyes met hers once she finished scanning the letter. "Nova Astor. You are not a coward. You are going to march down to town with Mother and I right now to make this right. To save him."

A glimmer of hope sparked in Nova's heart. Was there actually a chance they could? Did they have one last trick up their sleeve to make this right? Nothing came to her mind except the truth, but maybe they could get the governors to understand. Maybe her mother still had some level of influence.

It was small, but it just might work.

"We'd have to leave right now," Raelyn said, handing the note back to Nova. "The...well, we only have about half an hour."

Nova looked at Fynn, seeking his assent. He nodded and squeezed her hand.

So, she let that glimmer of hope grow into an ember and stood.

59

Nova

Nova summoned a wind at their backs to push them as they ran into town. The carriage wouldn't have been ready in time and there were only two horses, so she, Fynn, Raelyn, and their mother had taken off for the city on foot. Though Fynn could have run her there faster, all three Astor women needed to be there for their argument to be effective, and, though strong, he wasn't capable of carrying all three.

Besides, the wind she conjured made them almost as fast.

They made it into Adenaport's main square in less than ten minutes to find a crowd gathering right in front of Terra's temple. Given that the town was populated almost entirely by humans, Nova wasn't surprised to find they made up the vast majority of the crowd, though a few witches and elves were scattered among them. Everyone was facing the steps leading up to the temple, where a smaller group was standing. At the top of the stairs stood a few of the temple's priestesses, clad in Terra's preferred green robes. And just a few steps below them was—

Kael.

He was held in alloy shackles, bound by both hands and feet and surrounded on three sides by Astria's guards. He looked thus far unharmed, and his face was a mask of resolve. *Of course it was.* He wouldn't have walked himself into the lion's den and then shown any signs of fear. That's not who he was.

To the right of him, Nova recognized the remaining eight governors. One of the elven governors, Mina Ather, currently the longest-serving governor, stepped forward and lifted a hand to quiet the crowd.

They were too late. There would be no way to pull the governors aside now.

Nova's heart clenched like someone had taken it in their fist and squeezed. Her knees threatened to collapse, but Fynn, always present, always steady, reached out to support her.

"Citizens of Adenaport!" Mina spoke, her voice amplified by a spell one of the witch governors must have performed. "We have gathered here at your doorstep because, after five months of eluding authorities, we have apprehended the escaped criminal, Kael Blackmore. Fortunately, we apprehended him before he could cause any direct damage to your beautiful town, but the hurt he has caused to our countrymen has been immense. After today, your town and your country will be safe once more."

A cheer rose from the crowd, but nausea roiled through Nova's stomach. She pursed her lips into a thin line. Out of the corner of her eye, she saw her mother starting to push her way through the crowd toward the temple. Raelyn grabbed Nova's hand and pulled her along after their mother. She lost Fynn, but her focus remained on Raelyn and their mother just up ahead. They had only minutes.

They wove in between townsfolk, who were still cheering on Kael's arrest, all utterly rapt by Mina's words as she continued.

"This man has confessed to not only murdering one of our governors—may Luc Astor's soul find Canta in peace—"

Fuck that, Nova couldn't help thinking, shoving a stocky human woman to the side.

"—but also for causing devastation on a large scale in Arkwood's northern neighborhood, killing elves along the way." Mina paused, allowing the crowd to roar again, this time a chorus of boos.

Raelyn pulled Nova through a particularly tight spot, but Nova stumbled over the foot of a man near her. She twisted, so her hip hit the ground first, but Raelyn's vise-like grip on her wrist kept her from falling too hard. Still, she'd probably bruise tomorrow.

But at least I'll be alive *tomorrow.*

It was more than she could say for her father right now.

With Raelyn's help, she hoisted herself upright and continued through the crowd. They were only about halfway to the temple, the crowd getting rowdier and denser as they neared.

"This man," Mina bellowed, "has been sentenced to death by the unanimous decision of all remaining governors."

The guard to Kael's left took a step forward, his hand moving to his longsword.

No, no, no. This could not be happening. They weren't going to make it.

Nova looked up, searching for her mother, but could no longer see where Raella Astor had gone. Raelyn turned to meet Nova's gaze, her brown eyes wide with panic. The realization must have hit her at the same time it hit Nova.

"Nova, I'm sorry." Raelyn stopped and gripped Nova's shoulders, trying to block her view. "Look at me, Nova. Don't look up there."

The hiss of a sword unsheathing somehow echoed across the plaza, despite the roar of the crowd. Nova watched as the guard grabbed Kael roughly by the arms and dragged him down until he was just below

Mina, shoving him at her feet. He hung his head, as if he were *trying* to make his own execution easier by exposing his neck.

This isn't happening. This isn't real. Stand up, Father, STAND UP.

"Nova! Nova, look at me."

But Nova couldn't tear her eyes away. Couldn't stop watching as Mina nodded to the guard. He hoisted his sword in the air, like it was no more than a twig fallen from a tree. Tears filled Nova's eyes. Her entire body shook. And still, she watched as the sword fell, slicing through Kael's neck like it was butter.

The crowd roared joyously, drowning out the wail that burst forth from Nova's throat. She collapsed into Raelyn, who held her tight, whispering something incomprehensible into Nova's ear.

But it didn't matter what she said. Nothing could bring back the dead. No spell, no twist of fate from a goddess. Nothing.

Kael was gone.

60

FYNN

FYNN WAS FAIRLY CERTAIN that Nova had no recollection of how she'd made it back to the cottage that afternoon. If he was being honest, he hoped she had very little recollection of the entire day.

He'd watched his own father die right in front of him a matter of weeks ago, but that had been in private, with no one else around. It wasn't like they'd had a great relationship anyway; they'd been estranged since his mother had died.

Still, Persy had been his father, and it hadn't been an easy experience.

It paled in comparison to what Nova had gone through today.

He watched her through the window as she and Raelyn lay in the sand, watching the late afternoon clouds float by. Despite the events of the day, the weather was preternaturally calm.

When he'd finally found Nova and Raelyn in the crowd earlier, they were both crouched on the ground, Raelyn essentially shielding Nova from the rest of the world. The noise he heard coming from Nova...until his dying breath, he hoped he never heard that sound again. It wasn't until he'd squatted beside the two of them—a tough feat with how dense the crowd had been—and started whispering in her ear for her to breathe that she slowly took back control. Of her body, her magic, and her emotions.

They'd completely lost Raella, but he wanted to get Nova out of there as quickly as possible.

"I'll take her home," he'd told Raelyn. "You find your mother."

Raelyn nodded, and not a second later, he'd scooped Nova up and walked through the crowd until it thinned enough that he could run the rest of the way home.

She'd been silent since they arrived, curled up against his chest on the couch. Jax had tried to offer help, had tried speaking to her, but all it had earned him was a blast of wind that pushed him out of the room. He must have conveyed the message to Daro and Mehta, because neither attempted to enter the living room after that.

"Al?" he'd started a few times, but it had just led to her sobs starting all over again, her fingernails clawing at his chest, so instead they sat together for nearly two hours until Raelyn and Raella finally made it home.

"Come, Nova," Raelyn had said, her voice full of compassion. At first, Nova hadn't moved, but once Fynn gave her the tiniest push, she forced herself to stand the rest of the way and followed her sister out onto the beach.

Fynn wasn't sure what they were talking about, but if there was anyone he trusted to take care of Nova right now, it was Raelyn. He'd been doing a piss-poor job of soothing her anyway.

"I spoke with the governors."

Raella's voice startled Fynn from his circumspection. He turned and saw her standing in the doorway, wringing her hands. Her cheeks were flushed, and her hair was in disarray—at least compared to how he was used to seeing her. In the late afternoon light, she looked older, more tired, the dim light casting her face in shadow.

Fynn didn't say anything, just waited for her to continue.

"It appears Luc's spell work was more thorough than we expected. They aren't spellbound anymore, of that much I am certain, but they also remember the last few years perfectly. And they swear they were acting of their own volition." She stepped into the room and rested a hand on the back of the couch.

"Then how can you tell they are no longer under some sort of spell?"

Raella sighed. "I know these governors intimately. I've been watching, learning, and studying them since each was elected. If you know where to look, there are subtle changes that you would notice when someone you know well is no longer acting of their own free will. And, just the same, you would notice when that free will returns."

Fynn nodded, impressed. Raella's reputation had clearly been carefully crafted and maintained over the years so as not to attract unwanted attention or to arouse suspicion. But it meant that the world saw her as a vain social climber and not as the clever strategist she actually was.

"Oh, don't look at me like that, Fynn," she said, waving a hand and smiling. "I know what you're thinking. I don't need your pity."

He took a step closer, his mind racing, seeking recovery. "I'm not—"

"Yes. You are. And it's ok." Her gaze drifted out the window to the beach, where her daughters were rising from the sand. "Anything I've sacrificed has been worth it for their safety. And now..." She sighed again. "Now they are safe. We can all start anew."

Raella walked over and joined him by the glass sliding door.

"I don't think this will be as easy as 'starting anew,'" Fynn said, looking down at Raella. "At least not for Nova."

She met his stare. "Don't misunderstand me. I would never expect any of us, least of all Nova, to be able to erase completely what we've been through. To move on as if it had never happened. I just mean that we've all been living our lives on a certain trajectory, based on what we knew or what we were led to believe. But now..."

Fynn nodded in understanding. *The truth will set you free.* That was the easiest way to sum it up. None of them were meant to forget or dismiss Luc or Kael's actions. Instead, they needed to take what they'd learned and live in a way that made them happy.

He and Nova hadn't yet discussed what that would look like for them. Would they go back to Arkwood? Live elsewhere?

As his thoughts drifted to the capital city, he remembered Fox, Elodie, and the rest of the Defiance. "What of your Defiance?"

"Ah, yes." Raella smiled. "I'd already sent a coded message via raven to share the news about the deocre yesterday. I expect they are back in Arkwood, celebrating and trying to figure out what to do with their lives. We certainly don't need a Defiance anymore."

"I'd like to see them again when we get back. I don't think I ever properly thanked them for sheltering me." And he meant it. Even Fox deserved his gratitude.

Raella nodded. "I owe them mountains of thanks as well. I'll make sure we arrange something."

Through the window, he saw Raelyn and Nova approaching the door, hand in hand. Fynn didn't miss the slight upturn of Nova's mouth and sent a silent blessing to all three goddesses for that smile.

Raella squeezed his arm. "Happy to have you as part of this family, Fynn." With a final smile, she turned and left the room.

With a squeak, the sliding door opened, and the two sisters stepped through. "We can call it Earthy Grounds," Nova said, pulling the door shut behind her.

Raelyn grimaced, which made Nova laugh. "We'll work on the name," Raelyn said. She looked over at Fynn and winked. "Just dreaming about that coffee shop we're going to open now that we're giving up teaching."

Nova nodded. "Half of the proceeds will go towards my new organization to promote equality among the races, including wielders." Her eyes were still puffy and red, but her cheeks were dry.

Fynn breathed a sigh of relief. "Whatever you want, Al, I'll stand beside you." And he meant it. There was no doubt in his mind that she could take such an organization far, that she could use it to make a difference in the world and counteract all the cruelty that Luc had put into place.

Nova's small smile became a wider grin as she shuffled over to him and wrapped her arms around him. He sighed, breathing in her lavender scent and pulling her close. "I'm not going to insult you by asking if you're ok, Al, because after what you've been through, I know it's not an easy road to being ok. But there are no words to express how much joy it brings me to see you smiling."

She tilted her head up to meet his gaze, her lips so close that it was hard for him to resist kissing her. Her green eyes sparkled, attempting to veil the sorrow he could still see peeking through them as she said, "I'm a long way from ok today, Fynn, but if there's one thing I know with one hundred percent certainty, it's that with you," she turned to look at her sister, "and Rae by my side," her eyes met his again, "one day, I will be."

The restraint in him snapped as he leaned down to kiss her, his hands sliding up her back and into her hair. He heard Raelyn slip out of the room with a giggle, but he didn't look up. This woman was his and his alone, and he was never letting her go. Just like he'd told her the first time: until all the stars in the sky turned to dust and all the oceans ran dry, he would love her. Even if she couldn't feel it anymore—even if that same love didn't amplify her anymore—it wasn't diminished.

It never would be.

Epilogue

Nova

Nova closed the door to the café behind her, locking it with a quick wave of her hand. The outside air was crisp, biting at her skin and forcing her to pull her shawl a little tighter around her neck to fight off the sting.

Winter had arrived.

She glanced up at the wooden sign that hung over the shop. The metal chain holding it in place creaked slightly as it swayed in the breeze, but the name of the café was visible: Earthy Grounds.

The four-year anniversary of their grand opening was approaching. Raelyn had been busy planning a huge party, which Nova had been happy to let her do. Going into business with Raelyn had been easier than she'd expected, but, technically, Nova now had two businesses to run, so when it came to Earthy Grounds, she let Raelyn take the lead.

Besides, it had been just a few weeks ago that they'd held a smaller, more intimate gathering that Nova had insisted on planning herself.

The faint smell of the last brew of the day still lingered in the air. Nova breathed it in and smiled, then started the short walk home.

So much had changed these last five years. So much good had happened. But there was still so much loss that hung in the air, too.

The memorial she'd held in Kael's honor a few weeks ago had been the first time since he had been killed that she'd made it through the anniversary without shedding a tear. Not that she hadn't been sad; a piece of her heart was still missing. It had vanished the day he died. But grief was a mysterious thing. It could strike like a tidal wave when you least expected it, dragging you down into its depths, making you think you'd drown in it. Just as quickly, it could recede again, letting you come up for air and leaving you with the good memories, the newfound strength, the resilience to carry on.

It never truly disappeared. You simply learned to live with it. To live through it.

The apartment she and Fynn had moved into four years ago was a few blocks from the coffee shop, situated in the northern neighborhoods of Arkwood, near where the deocre had attacked. Fynn had wanted to help with the rebuilding of the area, and by the time the neighborhood was back on its feet, they'd both spent enough time there to fall in love with it.

So, they'd found a house and settled in.

As Nova walked the darkening streets back home, she reflected on how much had changed since she and Raelyn had quit teaching to open a coffee shop and establish a foundation. That first year had been...rough. They'd actually moved back into the penthouse with their mother, helping her sort through all the memories and belongings that had been kept there in the decades since she and Luc bought it.

To the outside world, they appeared to be a family in mourning. And in some regards, they were. But they weren't mourning Luc. Well...that wasn't entirely true, either. Despite all he had done, despite what had happened since his death, it was impossible not to miss the man who raised them. Nova had seen the toll it had taken on her mother as well. Though she'd spent the better part of twenty-four years actively fighting against her husband, he had still been her husband. At one point, she had loved him. At one point, she probably hoped she could save him.

Now, she never would.

The three Astor women had stuck together as much as possible, eventually emptying the penthouse so that Mother could retire to the cottage.

Nova smiled, remembering when they had visited her there last summer. Mother had been so...*happy*. So carefree. So herself in a way that Nova had never known her to be. Adenaport suited her.

Fynn had been around that first year, too. He'd helped with rebuilding and reconnected with his sister, Aury, who was an absolute delight. Nova needed to remember to send her a note to see if she could join them at the new year celebration they were planning.

Aury had helped Fynn clear out the Voss house, the one that both Persy and Maura had died in. Neither sibling wanted to keep it, so they'd sold it and split the profit.

Something cold hit Nova's nose. She refocused her attention on the world around her and discovered that snow flurries had started to fall. "Oh!" she gasped, picking up her pace, eager to get home quickly to share the news.

But when she arrived, she found that Fynn wasn't alone. Another man, one she had come to know quite well in the last five years, was pulling on his overcoat in the doorway as she barged in.

"Fox, hi!" she said, shifting over to the side so she could close the door and sneak by him. "I didn't realize you were coming over today."

Fox smiled at her. When they'd first met, there had been a certain...awkwardness in the air between them, mostly due to his past with Fynn. But one stern talking-to from her mother and a few years of cordial relations, and they'd relaxed into more of a friendship. He even got along with Fynn now.

Sure enough, Fynn poked his head around the corner from the living room when he heard them speaking. "There's my wife." He swept her into a hug and planted a kiss on her forehead.

Sometimes she missed the way her magic would swirl inside her at his touch. But most days now, it was a forgotten memory. It had been replaced by all the wonderful things they had done, the life they had built and the memories they had accumulated since she'd sacrificed her amplification.

"And I'm just leaving," Fox said, securing the last button on his coat. He met Nova's gaze. "I was in the neighborhood, figured I'd drop in to say hi and deliver my new year's RSVP in person."

Nova started to unwind her shawl. "You're coming?"

"Wouldn't miss it." He smiled, then his eyes lit up at something. "By the way, we found something in one of the annals we rebuilt this week. Another descendant."

Nova's heart quickened. Her hands, still holding her scarf, stilled. "Oh?"

Fox nodded. "Turns out there's another branch of Terra's line that is still very much alive. Which is good news. Just in case."

Fynn's hand caught Nova's elbow as she breathed a sigh of relief. "Just in case," her husband echoed.

"Let's hope it's not the case that we need to enlighten them." Fox dipped his chin, waved, and opened the door to step out onto the street.

How about that? Benedict had a long-lost cousin.

Fynn peered through the doorway as Fox closed it behind him. "It's snowing?"

"Yes!" Nova undid the buttons on her coat and shrugged it off. "Winnie's first snow! Where is she?"

"In her chair."

All thoughts of descendants, deocres, and Benedict forgotten, Nova raced around the corner, through the living room, and into the kitchen, where she found the tiny dark-haired girl, her six-month-old daughter, sitting in a chair Raelyn had magicked from wood. Winnie was mashing some kind of gooey food with her hand, but she looked up when Nova entered the room, flashing her big green eyes, and squealed, a toothless grin spreading across her face.

"Winnie!" Nova grabbed a towel off the counter and wiped her daughter's hands. "It's snowing, my love! Would you like to come see?"

She scooped up her daughter and carried her toward the living room window, where there was a better view of the street. The snow was falling from the sky in earnest now. It was just starting to accumulate on the sidewalks and the cobblestone street out front.

Nova held Winnie up to the window so she could see. Fynn came up behind them and pressed a hand lightly to the small of her back. He used his other to point out the window, but Winnie quickly snatched his finger and wrapped her tiny fingers around it.

She may look just like me, Nova thought, *but she's a daddy's girl through and through.*

Motherhood was something Nova had always dreamed about. But when Winnie was born, it exceeded her wildest dreams. The tiny little being she and Fynn had created, with tufts of dark hair, eyes like emeralds, and slightly pointed ears, had latched onto her heart instantly, and from that moment on, Nova would do anything for her daughter.

It was why Nova had finally started her foundation, Wynna's Warriors, named for her daughter *and* her mother. As a half-elf, half-witch, it was unclear what type of power or lifespan Baby Wynna might have. But it also *didn't matter*. A life was still a life. Everyone deserved their shot, regardless of their power or race. And Wynna's Warriors made that their mission.

Nova had big plans for the foundation, but it had only been launched officially two months ago. It would all come in time.

"Isn't it beautiful, Winnie?" Nova whispered to her daughter as they watched more snowflakes hit the pavement.

Winnie cooed.

Fynn's hand slipped into the hair that was falling loosely down Nova's back. "It sure is," he whispered in reply.

Nova looked up to find his eyes on her. It had been five and a half years since she met him, but he'd barely aged a day. He still wore his hair pulled back in a loose bun, still kept daggers and his longsword sharpened and nearby. But he claimed his warrior days were over. He had forgone his most recent Academy renewal, despite Nova's protestations—secretly, she had just wanted to go with him to see what it was all about—and instead, using Aury's connections, had decided to pursue a government strategy role.

Nova had no idea what exactly it was he did—something very secretive—but he loved it. And that was all that mattered to her.

A dark figure ran past their window, barely visible in the glow of the streetlamps, but Nova would recognize those curls anywhere. Sure enough, a moment later, she heard a knock on their door, followed by the creak of it opening.

Raelyn never waited for them to answer.

"I was not expecting it to *snow*!" Raelyn's voice echoed through the first floor. "I would've dressed more appropriately."

Nova laughed, pulling Baby Wynna away from the window to go greet her sister. "If only we knew a good aero who could predict weather patterns." She found Raelyn unwinding her scarf, then starting to pull off her boots. Her sister was wearing a light jacket over an ankle-length dress that was certainly not warm enough for the weather.

"Right? How have we not befriended one yet—oh, there's my darling little niece!" She reached out to take Wynna from Nova, and the baby went willingly. She was besotted with her aunt. Wynna giggled as Raelyn tickled her belly. "How's my favorite baby?"

Nova waved her out of the cramped entryway. "Come on in, Rae. Want a cup of cocoa to warm up a bit?"

"Just a quick one." She followed Nova into the kitchen, where Fynn was already starting to add milk to the kettle. "Hey, Fynn."

"Hi there, Rae." He passed the kettle to Nova to heat and turned to face Raelyn. "What are you dressed up for?"

Nova scrunched her brow, turning back to Raelyn to take in her presence again. Now that they were in the light of the kitchen, rather than the shadows of the entryway, it was easier to see that the dress was indeed one of her nicer ones, cinched at the waist and with a square neckline that showed off just enough of her chest to entice. On her cheeks and lips, she had dabbed a bit of rouge. On her eyes, a line of kohl.

Nova nearly dropped the kettle she was magically heating. Raelyn was dressed for a *date*.

"You're meeting someone, aren't you?" she asked, her mouth gaping.

Raelyn sat on one of the stools that lined the small island in the kitchen, plopping Wynna on her lap. "Don't make a big deal out of this."

"But Rae," Nova started working her magic to warm the kettle, "this is a big deal. You haven't gone out with anyone since…"

She let her voice trail off, but the name left unspoken hung in the air like a fog.

Esta.

And it was true. Since Esta had left the cottage right before the deocre was vanquished, Raelyn hadn't even considered dating anyone, even when Nova had offered to allow her to bring a guest to the small wedding she and Fynn had held. Even when Nova had gotten pregnant and Raelyn went on and on about how much she'd like to be a mother one day, too.

Nova hadn't pushed it, but she had tried to ask her about Esta every once and a while. Usually, she got shut down very quickly.

Fynn got out three mugs and scooped cocoa powder into each.

"I haven't felt like I was ready. You know that." Raelyn kept her eyes trained on the hot milk that Nova poured into each mug.

"But now," Nova set the kettle down on the stove, "you do." She pulled out a spoon to stir the cocoa, passing Raelyn the first cup.

Wynna tried to grab the hot drink, but Raelyn was faster. She pushed the mug out of the baby's reach. "I realized after Kael's memorial that I finally figured it out."

"Figured what out?" Fynn asked, grabbing his own mug of cocoa and taking a sip.

"Myself." She paused to sip her cocoa, leaning to the side so it was out of Winnie's grasp before continuing, "I know who I am now."

Nova smiled, putting her hands around her mug to warm them. Raelyn had struggled, probably more than anyone else, when they'd gotten back to the city. If someone were to compare their losses from that year side by side, it wouldn't have made any sense to an outsider why Raelyn took it all the hardest. But Nova knew Raelyn as well as she knew herself. Raelyn didn't do anything halfway. Her emotions were all-consuming: the highs grand enough to infect those around her with joy and the lows severe enough to wreak magical havoc in nature.

The grief she had suffered at losing Luc, realizing what Luc had become, then losing Esta and Kael...it had been more than her heart had ever had to cope with.

Comparing grief was a futile, unfair exercise.

"And who are you now?" she prodded.

"Arkwood's premier coffee maker," Raelyn said with a grin. "The world's greatest aunt and sister. A damn good business owner, which I know none of us saw coming."

Fynn and Nova laughed. It was true: Raelyn had ended up with a business acumen that surprised them all. She'd turned Earthy Grounds into a wildly successful business, and not only because of her prowess with the coffee bean itself.

"A part of me misses teaching, I realized," Raelyn continued. "I was starting to think of ways to integrate stories or tutoring or *something* at the shop."

"That's a great idea," Nova said, meaning it. She missed teaching, too, but her work with Wynna's Warriors kept her engaged with the youth of Astria to fill that void.

Raelyn took a deep breath, taking one of Baby Wynna's hands in hers. "But I also know I'm someone who doesn't want to be alone. So I've spent the last few weeks since the memorial tracking down Esta."

This time, Nova did, in fact, drop her mug. It shattered into pieces at her feet, the warm cocoa soaking through her socks. She could have cleaned it up with a wave of her hand—her magic so in control now—but she was too in shock to do so.

Thank the goddesses Fynn kept his wits about him. "And you found her."

Raelyn nodded. "I'm meeting her for dinner tonight."

Nova wanted to squeal, she wanted to sing from the rooftop, she wanted to squeeze her sister, but she kept what was left of her cool. "Rae, that's fantastic news."

"We'll see." Raelyn's tone was demure, but there was a smile tugging at the corners of her mouth, a sparkle in her eye that hadn't been there a moment ago.

"Will you let her know she's welcome over for new year's?" Ok, so Nova could only keep her cool *so* much. She probably should have waited to mention that until she heard how the date had gone, but her mouth moved faster than her brain.

To her relief, Raelyn laughed. "I'll invite her. Who all is coming so far?"

"All the usual people." Nova ticked them off with her finger. "Cassie. Bea. Elodie. Daro. Fox just let us know he's in. Jax and Mehta are coming in from Aerdmure—"

"Oh, thank Canta, it's been ages since I've seen them!" Raelyn pulled a curl that Wynna had grabbed out of the baby's hand. "I owe Mehta a drink from that bet I lost last time he was here. Wonder if he still remembers..."

"Without a doubt," Fynn said, chuckling. "You gonna clean that up, Al, or should I get the broom and mop?"

Nova looked over at him, then followed his gaze down to her feet, where the mug and the mess remained. "Oh. Right." She waved a hand, and the mess disappeared. Another wave and the mug repaired and flew to the counter. But she'd have to make herself a new batch of cocoa if she still wanted it...

Wynna clapped. She was always impressed by Nova's magic, though she hadn't yet shown any displays of it herself. If she had magic, it would come in time. And if she didn't, it certainly didn't change a damn thing.

Raelyn laughed, hugging Wynna close. "Well, I'll let you get back to your evening." She finished off her cocoa. "I just needed to tell someone what I was doing. I couldn't keep it a secret anymore. My nerves were going to explode."

Nova padded over to her sister, scooping up the baby with one arm and wrapping the other around Raelyn. "Happy for you, sis."

"Don't be happy unless it goes well. Esta could very well hate me after all this time."

"I doubt it." Fynn winked at her, grabbing her mug and placing it in the sink.

Nova shuffled Raelyn out the door, insisting her sister take one of her own warmer coats and bidding her good luck as she closed the door behind her. Then she returned to the kitchen, Wynna still on her hip, to find Fynn standing there, gazing into space, his eyes slightly watery.

"You ok?"

He blinked, then looked at her. "Better than ok." He ran one hand down his cheek, then pushed off the counter and walked over to her. "I'm still not sure how I ended up this lucky."

"Ah, feeling sentimental now that Esta might be coming back in the picture, are we?" Nova teased, setting Wynna down in her chair and handing her a wooden cup to play with.

"It just brought back memories. Good and bad." He took another step closer to her, cupping her face between his hands. His thumb traced the barely visible scar on her cheek.

A shiver raced down her spine, a different kind of magic at play under his touch than had been five years ago.

"I love this life we've built. I love our family, the friends we call family. I love our house. I love the new world you're working on shaping. But most of all, Al, I fucking love you."

She turned her head to kiss his palm, then turned back to meet his gaze. "Until all the stars in the sky turn to dust and all the oceans run dry, I will love you."

A devilish grin spread across his face as he leaned in and kissed her.

Thank you for following along with Nova and Fynn's story! If you want more from Astria, make you sure check out *The Rebel's Rose,* an arranged marriage prequel novella set 500 years before the events of *The Witches of Astria* duology. It's available for free to my newsletter subscribers or on Amazon.

Acknowledgments

Another book done and my first series complete. How absolutely freaking WILD. I'm proud of this book in a completely different way than I was of its predecessor. I've learned so much since writing *The Wielder's Discovery*, new and better skills in the craft that I was able to implement into *The Wielder's Sacrifice*, making it not only more fun to write, but richer, deeper, and far more fulfilling. And I didn't do it alone. There are so many people to thank for that.

First and foremost my family. My husband, who is always one of the first to read my books and even though romantasy isn't his jam, he pretends it is for a few days. My mom, dad, brother, and in-laws, all of whom continually support me, ask me about my writing, recommend my book to their book clubs, shout about my books to the rest of the family, and are just generally there for me, no matter what.

I'm also forever in debt to my critique partner, Emily. Without your support, advice, reactions, and guidance both in writing and in life, I would not be the writer I am today. Thank you for asking to be my CP! I gained not only a writing buddy but a lifelong friend.

And of course, my editor, Kelly, who's guidance and feedback on this story brought me to the proudest happy tears I've ever cried. And Erin – I'm so glad I found you because the final version of this story is so polished under your careful eye!

I have so many other author friends I want to thank for supporting me and guiding me in my publishing journey. My AuthorsConnect buddies, especially Audrey, Mads, the Haleys, and AC. My TFAL comrades, especially Tri, Jill, Tay, and all of those who did writing sprints with me (too many to name!).

My Street Team has been an invaluable resource for me as well. The hype, the love, the motivation, the laughs, you all are there for all of it and I'm so grateful you found your way to me and love my stories as much as I do! As Cloi put it, thanks for putting up with my chaos and crap :)

TWS had a number of early readers as well. Thank you to Casey, Jess, Tay, and Kayla for all of your feedback and for taking a chance on an early (messy) draft. Maybe when you read it you'll see tweaks made that were based on your feedback!

I'd be remiss if I didn't shout out my awesome Kickstarter backers, who helped make the TWD audiobook a reality, especially Grau, Ed Szoc, Bubby, Sherri, the Reeves Family, Ashlee, Kayla Cheyenne, Jenn Pruski, Mark, Sarah Hodgin, Brandy Cannon, Shea Bennett, and Carrie.

I also wanted to shout out a few of my IRL besties, who have supported me in my writing and beyond: my Pelobuddies, Boom Club, Group, #friendsweekend, and Xaddy's Girls. I love and adore all of you more than words could ever say!

And lastly, you, reader, thank you for reading my debut duology. There is more fun to come and I hope you'll stick around to see what's next. If you made it this far, I have high hopes you will be.

xoxo

Leave a Review!

One of the best ways to support an indie author, like me, is to leave us reviews. I would be so grateful for just one more moment of your time to leave a review on your favorite platform or two. *The Wielder's Sacrifice* is available to review on Goodreads, Storygraph, Amazon, and, of course, social media.

ALSO BY

The Witches of Astria

The Wielder's Discovery

The Wielder's Sacrifice

The Rebel's Rose, A Novella of Astria

About the Author

When not dreaming up new fantasy worlds or teaching her toddlers how to recognize her favorite bookish characters, Meredith can be found curled up with a book or planning adventures with her husband. Though a chemical engineer by day, she's been writing stories for as long as she can remember, most notably finishing her first novel (which will never be published) at the age of 12. After growing up in Virginia, she now lives outside of Philadelphia. Find her on Instagram @meredithkasianauthor to learn more about upcoming releases and to join her newsletter!